LORD AND LADY SPY

SHANA GALEN

sourcebooks
casablanca

Published by Sourcebooks Casablanca, an imprint of Sourcebooks, Inc.
P.O. Box 4410, Naperville, Illinois 60567-4410
(630) 961-3900
FAX: (630) 961-2168
www.sourcebooks.com

Printed and bound in Canada
TR 10 9 8 7 6 5 4 3 2 1

For mothers, especially those who know the pain of loss.

One

THE SPY CALLED SAINT HUNKERED DOWN IN THE bottom of the wardrobe she'd occupied for the last four hours and attempted to stifle a yawn.

She didn't need to crack the door to know the activities in the bed across the room were still very much in progress. She could hear the courtesan urging her "horse" onward, the woman's demands punctuated by the man's loud neighs.

Saint sighed, shifting so her muscles remained limber. She'd given up being embarrassed about three and a quarter hours ago and now wondered how much longer the game could persist.

Where was Lucien Ducos? If Bonaparte's advisor didn't make an appearance tonight, Saint was going to have a lot of explaining to do. Despite being ordered to track Ducos to France, she'd elected to remain right here.

Something told her Bonaparte's advisor would visit his mistress one last time before leaving. It was a feeling—her intuition speaking to her. And Saint always listened to her intuition.

It had led her to this wardrobe, where she'd been treated to The Sassy Upstairs Maid, The Very Bad Boy, and now Horse and Rider. Ducos had better turn up soon—before someone decided to play Hide and Seek and discovered the wardrobe held more than clothes.

The horse's neighs grew louder, and Saint covered her ears. How much longer? She was definitely leaving as soon as the horse… was stabled.

She sighed. Oh, who was she fooling? Of course she wouldn't leave. She'd stay as long as necessary to secure Ducos.

That was her mission.

Failure was not an option.

The horse neighed frantically, and Saint dropped her head in her hands and tried to remember why she was putting up with this. Bonaparte had escaped after his defeat at Waterloo. England—nay, Europe—would not be safe until he was apprehended and dealt with. All sources pointed to Ducos as the man who knew where Bonaparte was hidden.

Her mission was to find Ducos and make him talk.

And she'd do her duty. She'd tracked him here, discovered the name of his courtesan, and set the perfect trap. So where was the Frenchman?

Suddenly the slaps and neighs were interrupted by three loud bangs on the front door. The courtesan's house was small, the outer door located down a short flight of steps near the bedroom. In the abrupt silence, Saint could hear the housekeeper's shoes clicking through the vestibule.

"What are you doing?" the horse asked the courtesan in one of the seven languages Saint knew well. "You can't stop now."

"One moment," the woman answered, her voice tense.

Saint's nose itched, and she sat forward, careful to remain absolutely silent. She heard a man's voice, the housekeeper's negative answer, and the man's voice again. She could tell, despite the housekeeper's refusal of entrance, the intruder had entered.

Inside the bedroom, the courtesan scrambled to dismount as the intruder spoke again.

In French.

Saint allowed herself a smile—the first in weeks. It was Ducos. It had to be. She heard his footsteps on the stairs and extracted her pistol from beneath her mantle, shifting the dagger to her other hand.

The footsteps drew closer, and the courtesan's whispers grew more frantic. "You must hide. If he catches me with you—"

"Ha! You think I am afraid of some little French clerk? His time is over."

Little French clerk? Ducos was over six feet tall and known for violent outbursts.

"Please," the courtesan all but begged. "Please, hide."

If the stallion had an ounce of sense, he'd listen.

The courtesan continued, "Hide in the wardrobe. I will get rid of him."

Saint's eyes widened. *No! Not the wardrobe. Damn!*

She scrambled to arrange a dressing gown so it concealed her, but she knew the furnishing would never fit them both. The wardrobe shook as the stallion stumbled against it.

Footsteps thumped on the landing, and a tap rattled the bedroom door. "*Ma chérie*? Are you in there?"

"Who is it?" the courtesan called innocently. Then she hissed, "Never mind, there's no time. Get under the bed."

Saint exhaled and closed her eyes in relief.

"*Ma petite chou*? Open the door, *chérie*."

"I'm coming." There was the sound of clothing rustling, and then the woman's footfalls as she crossed the room and opened the door.

Saint squinted through the keyhole in the wardrobe. Lucien Ducos, wearing a black greatcoat with a *chapeau bras* tucked under his arm, stepped into the room. Wasting no time, he pulled the courtesan into his arms and kissed her.

Saint held her breath. Now was the time to take action—burst out of the wardrobe, pistol in one hand and dagger in the other. In a matter of moments, she could disable Ducos, tie up the courtesan and her lover, and begin her interrogation.

Heart drumming, Saint extended two fingers and pushed gingerly on the wardrobe's door.

It didn't move.

She pushed again, this time using her whole palm.

Nothing.

Damn! The ridiculous stallion must have turned the key when he knocked against it. She was locked in here—and Ducos was out there.

This could *not* be happening. She had not spent four hours cramped in a wardrobe only to be thwarted by a flimsy lock and insignificant key. She considered and discarded several ideas, and then the perfect solution flashed into her mind. She shifted her weight, curled her fingers around her pistol, and—

Before she could pull the trigger, the silence in the room was broken by the dissonant sound of glass breaking followed by an eardrum-shattering crash. Saint froze as pandemonium erupted in the room.

The courtesan screamed, Ducos swore, and Saint heard the crack of a gunshot. The lead ball blasted through the door of the wardrobe and smashed into the wood just above her head.

She slammed her head and shoulders down hard and swore. Her instincts were to panic, to escape, but her training took over. *Keep a level head. Assess the situation.*

Her ears were ringing, the sound like a bell clanging against her brain. Shaking her head, she strained to hear what was going on. The sounds were muffled—a low voice telling Ducos to put his hands behind his back. She plugged and unplugged her ears, trying to clear the awful ringing. Ducos was arguing, and there was a thump and the sound of struggle.

Saint knelt and peered through the bullet hole. A man in a gray cape and tricorn hat that hid his face was wrestling with Ducos, who was trying to regain his footing after being knocked on the bed. The courtesan stood off to one side, holding her robe closed with trembling fingers. Finally the man in the cape managed to pin Ducos's arms. The man freed a set of hand shackles from inside his cloak and clapped them on Ducos.

Saint gaped. There was only one reason the man would have shackles with him—he was after Ducos, too. She jabbed at the wardrobe again. *Damn it!*

The man jerked Ducos off the bed and pushed him toward the door. Saint couldn't see his face, but she saw him nod to the courtesan as he took his leave.

Saint bristled. The intruder was *not* absconding with her man. She sat back and kicked the wardrobe door hard.

Once.

Twice.

The wood cracked and splintered on the third kick. She pushed the broken door aside, and the courtesan, in the process of helping the horse out from under the bed, looked up, startled. "Who the hell are you?"

Saint arrowed for the open door. "Maid. Cleaning the wardrobe." Ignoring the woman's curses, she closed the bedroom door behind her. The gray-caped man was gone, but he couldn't be more than ten seconds ahead of her.

Readying her pistol, she charged down the steps. Upon seeing her, the housekeeper screamed and put a hand to her throat. Saint dodged the woman and leapt for the door. She threw it wide, rushed onto the stoop, and stared at the empty street before her.

She looked right, then left, then right again. *No!*

Frantic now, she ran down the walk, hopped the small gate, and chose a direction. Running at a light jog, she scanned the houses and buildings. She had excellent vision, even at night, but she saw no one. She slowed, peered harder.

Nothing.

"Damn it!"

"Such language. Tsk-tsk," someone said in English. She spun around, lowering her pistol when she recognized the face. "Agent Blue. I should have known. What in bl——?" She cleared her throat. "What is going on?"

Blue, so called because of his startling azure eyes, frowned. "As fond as I am of standing about on street corners discussing covert operations, I believe my carriage would be more apropos." He unfurled his fingers, indicating a coach waiting at the corner. Then he crooked one finger and beckoned her to follow.

When they were inside, she settled back on the squabs and closed her eyes. Her mind was racing, thoughts and questions piling one on top of another. How had she lost the man in the gray cloak? Should she have gone right instead of left? No, her instincts had been correct, but——

She opened her eyes and stared at Blue. Her nose itched… something was wrong.

Blue's expression offered no answers. He had a face easily forgotten. It was nondescript, except for those amazing blue eyes. And even that worked to his advantage. People remembered the eyes and little else.

Blue had known she was after Ducos. He had given her the orders to apprehend Bonaparte's advisor— orders straight from the top echelons of the Barbican group. Who else knew she was here? And who but an agent of the Barbican group could act with such efficiency, such calm in the midst of chaos, as the man in the gray cloak had shown?

"That man in the gray cloak," she said, finally piecing the events of the evening together. "He was one of ours."

It was a calculated guess. Her ears had been ringing so loudly she hadn't been able to detect anything about the man's voice or accent, let alone his affiliation.

Blue inclined his head, proving her supposition correct.

"Is that... all you noticed?" Blue asked smoothly.

Saint narrowed her eyes. There *had* been something else. Something familiar about the gray-cloaked man. The way he moved perhaps. Or the way he stood.

She shook her head. She'd been peering through a bullet hole and had seen no more than mere snatches of the intruder.

"Ducos was my target," she said. "If I was pulled from the mission, why wasn't I notified?"

Blue gave her a dubious look. "You disobeyed a direct order to leave for France."

"Because I knew Ducos would stay here."

"You took a guess, and while I will admit your instincts are unsurpassed, they are no excuse for disobeying orders."

"My orders were to apprehend Ducos."

"Your orders were to follow the plan—and your part of the plan was to leave for France."

"Plans," she scoffed. "A good agent thinks on her feet."

"A good agent does as she's told."

She rolled her eyes. "Who was he?" Saint asked, returning to her original subject. "The man in the gray cloak? Ducos was mine, and I want—"

Blue shook his head. "It doesn't matter."

"It doesn't matter? I've been tracking Ducos for weeks."

"And now we have him. Ironically, we don't need him anymore."

"But of course we need him! Ducos might be the

key to finding Bonaparte. He…" Saint stared at Blue, comprehension dawning. "You have him—Bonaparte."

"Yes. Bonaparte surrendered two days ago. He's on a ship, bound for exile."

Saint blinked. It was good news. And yet…

Blue was watching her, his expression one she'd never seen before. "I've been sent to tell you the King appreciates your services, but they're no longer needed."

Saint started. "What do you mean?"

Blue gave her an impatient look. "You know what I mean. It's the same for most of us agents. The war is over."

"But there are other conflicts—other missions. I could—"

Blue shook his head, and Saint suppressed an exasperated scream. No point in venting her anger on Blue. He was only the messenger, and the group's message was final.

She was no longer needed.

She sighed, resigned for the moment. "So that's it. Thank you and good-bye." She tried to imagine her life without missions and targets and felt her stomach roil uneasily. She'd been an agent, in one capacity or another, practically all her life. Without her work, what did she have?

Nothing but failure—empty dreams, an empty house, an empty cradle. And now—now she was being summarily dismissed, back to that barren life. To be reminded, daily, of her domestic failures.

"It's a shock, I know," Blue said, "but look on the bright side. You can go home to your—who are you going home to?"

Under normal circumstances, such a personal question would never have been asked, much less answered, but she was out of a job. Her life's work ripped out from under her. Saint didn't see the point of concealment anymore. "I have a husband."

"Ah, well, go home to him. No doubt he misses you terribly."

Saint raised a brow. "No doubt."

No doubt he never even noticed she was gone. Their wedding had been nothing more than a union between two noble families, their marriage a failure from the start. And five years later, Adrian was a stranger to her. And she to him—a necessary circumstance in her line of work. There was a palpable distance between them. She knew, because she had fostered and nurtured it.

It kept her safe.

And lonely.

She shook off her self-pity. Loneliness wasn't important. It quickly dispersed when she embarked on another mission. And surely the Foreign Office would find something consequential for her to do.

Wouldn't it?

She glanced at Blue, noted that unfamiliar expression again. Except now she placed it: pity.

Saint stared out the window at the lights of the alien city, at the residents' energetic hustle and bustle, at her glorious career for the Foreign Office fading away.

Two

"What do you mean, you no longer require my services?" Adrian Galloway, Lord Smythe, rose from his chair and planted his hands on Lord Melbourne's desk. "I just delivered Lucien Ducos to you. I risked my hide for this office—again."

"And we appreciate your services."

With a flick of his wrist, Adrian dismissed the meaningless sentiments. He leaned closer, so his gaze was level with the secretary's. "Do you know how much I'm worth to the French?" His voice was little more than a tense whisper. "Do you know what the bounty on my head will be after they learn I took Ducos?"

"That is precisely what I am attempting to explain," Melbourne said, appearing unfazed by Adrian's glower. "The French are no longer our enemies. We have Bonaparte."

Adrian stepped back, his eyes never leaving those of the older man. Melbourne was in his early fifties and still retained his athletic build. Adrian had heard Melbourne was the premiere spy of his day. Now the man served as secretary for the elite Barbican group, a subset of England's Foreign Office.

Less than a handful of Englishmen knew of the existence of the Barbican. Its own members usually worked alone, and Adrian knew of only one other agent—an operative named Blue, who had done a job with him in Brussels last year. Adrian's sole contact with Barbican came through Melbourne. The older man had been a good friend and mentor—at times more like a father than a superior.

And now Melbourne was dismissing him, cutting Adrian out of the only family he'd ever really known. The sting of it burned, felt more like a personal betrayal than a professional decision. He had to put the personal aside.

Adrian let out a long breath and, gripping the arms of the chair behind him, took a seat. "Fine. We have Bonaparte. I'll take another assignment. Surely the French are not the only threat to English sovereignty. What about the bloody Americans?"

Melbourne steepled his fingers and pursed his lips, and Adrian wanted to fly across the polished cherry desk and erase Melbourne's cool demeanor. How could the man sit there so calmly and annihilate Adrian's life?

"As Agent Wolf, you have been a great asset to your country and this organization. God knows no other operative has your gift for strategy. When your country needed you, you answered the call. But I think it time you explored other avenues of interest."

Adrian clenched his jaw. "I see."

"Your king and your country are eternally grateful for your services. If you had not already been granted a knighthood for your bravery and sacrifice, we would bestow one on you—secretly, of course. But, as it stands, we have no choice but to retire you."

"I'm thirty-five," Adrian said, his voice a cold whisper. "That's a bit young for retirement."

"Yes. Well…" Melbourne cleared his throat, and Adrian tapped his fingers impatiently. He knew exactly what his friend was telling him. He had known this day would come eventually. But that didn't mean he would go without a fight. That didn't mean he would make this easy or painless for Melbourne.

Melbourne straightened. "What about parliament? You hold a seat in the House of Lords."

"Parliament?" Adrian's his lip curled. "It's a gaggle of self-important idiots who, rather than take any action, stand about listening to themselves speak."

"What about a hobby then? Gardening?"

Adrian gave him a pained expression.

"Golf?"

Adrian sighed. Loudly.

"Poetry?"

Adrian flashed him a warning glance, and Melbourne shrugged. "Listen, Adrian, I know how much the Barbican group has meant to you. I know why you need it."

Adrian's chest tightened, but he didn't speak. Didn't move.

"But you've done your duty—more than your duty. Whatever demons you're still fighting, let them go. Your father—"

"Don't." It was the one word Adrian could manage without choking. Even so, his voice was strangled, the word garbled. "Don't," he said again.

"Fine." Melbourne rose. "But like it or not, you'll hear my advice—stop being a martyr, and start living your own life. As Wolf, you invented a thousand identities for yourself, but I don't think you know the first thing about Adrian Galloway. Who are you, Adrian?"

Adrian opened his mouth, but Melbourne hurried on. "Other than a spy for the Barbican group."

Adrian closed his mouth again.

"And what about that pretty wife of yours?" Melbourne rounded his desk and moved toward the door behind Adrian. "In the last year, you've been away more than you've been home. Now might be a good time to start a family. A couple of hale and hearty boys running about the house would be good for you—both of you. You'll soon see there's more to life than missions." Melbourne opened the door, and the empty hallway beyond yawned at Adrian.

He rose. "About Bonaparte—"

"Go home to your wife," Melbourne continued before taking Adrian's shoulder and guiding him through the door.

No fool, Adrian knew this battle—though not the war—was over.

The door closed with an echoing thud, and Adrian stood in the deserted hall and stared at the stone walls. This wasn't the end. He wouldn't give in that easily. He couldn't—no matter what Melbourne said. There was so much still left to do, to prove. In the meantime...

Adrian sighed.

His wife. Even the thought of Sophia caused a flicker of pain. A couple of hale and hearty boys, Melbourne had said. They had tried that.

He'd married Sophia because he was the eldest son, and he was expected to marry and produce heirs. She was from a good family, and his mother and step-father had encouraged—very well, practically insisted on—the match. Adrian hadn't argued.

He knew his duty and figured he could have done worse. He had better things to do than waste time at balls and soirees flirting with females. Things like saving his country.

Sophia wasn't the kind of woman to demand attention or interfere with his work. Even when he was courting her, she never asked intrusive questions and never complained at his long absences.

More importantly, she never mentioned his father.

He was already working for the Foreign Office, taking the most dangerous assignments in order to prove himself to Melbourne and the leaders of the Barbican group.

Then, just a day after the lavish wedding, he'd been asked to lead a very dangerous mission. His success would mean an invitation to join the Barbican group—work he considered far more important than any wife or marriage.

At precisely the time Adrian would have spent hours in seclusion with his wife, coming to know her intimately—perhaps even falling in love with her— he'd been in France, doing surveillance from a cold, austere garret.

When he'd come home, his town house had felt

little different. But two months into his marriage, he'd been inducted into the Barbican group.

He'd tried to be a good husband when he was home, and for a time they'd been happy.

Expectant.

But mostly there had been pain and disappointment. He'd never expected his marriage would be a love match. Loyalty, honor, sacrifice for king and country—those meant more to him than any woman.

And, unlike his father, he would never allow himself to forget it.

But he had allowed his marriage to unravel. At this point, he couldn't say where Sophia was or what she was doing. He couldn't even remember what she looked like.

No. That wasn't true.

He remembered all too well.

Adrian began to walk, frowning as he stepped out of the nondescript building housing the secretary's office and into the bright summer sunshine on Pall Mall.

Perhaps Melbourne was right. Perhaps he could use this holiday—he refused to think of it as a retirement—to repair his fractured union. They might even try for a child again.

Adrian made his way down Piccadilly then turned onto Berkeley Street, nodding to a gentleman from his club. Adrian needed something to distract him for a week or so, until he could find a way to convince Melbourne he was still indispensable. Adrian didn't even think he'd need to convince Melbourne. The leader of the Barbican group would come to him, no doubt.

Until then he would spend time with Sophia and

concentrate on beginning the family he'd always wanted. But how to broach the topic of children with Sophia? She'd closed the subject and her bedroom door to him a year ago—or was it two? He shook his head. It had been some time since he'd shared her bed.

Quite some time.

It wasn't that he didn't want her. Despite her huge glasses, severe hairstyle, and high-necked gowns, he knew she was a lush, tempting woman. She might try to hide her beauty, but he knew her with her wild chestnut curls tossed over a pillow, her red lips parted, her dark eyes drowsy with pleasure.

His body tensed as the images, each one more wanton than the last, flooded him. Need, like a fire, licked at him. Perhaps this was why he avoided his wife.

Adrian had thought of acquiring a mistress, but infidelity always seemed a sordid business to him. His father had taught him that and taught him well.

Adrian turned onto Charles Street, and after passing The Running Footman tavern, his elegant town house came into view. The sight robbed him of most of his resolve.

Perhaps the subject of children was too bold a start. It might be better to begin with the basics.

A simple conversation, for example. They might discuss the weather or the… price of corn. The idea wasn't promising, but it was a step up from their usual *good morning*, *excuse me*, and *good night*.

He approached the town house door and took a deep breath. One day he would understand how he could enter a room full of armed men intent upon killing him and not even perspire, while the thought of ten words with his wife made him all but break out in hives.

Adrian gritted his teeth and opened the door.

⌘

Sophia Galloway caught the lamp just as the small table tumbled over. Unfortunately, she was not quick enough to grasp the Sèvres porcelain plate, and it crashed to the wooden floor, splintering into a hundred pieces.

Norbert, the devil child who'd knocked the table over, erupted into loud screams at the noise, and his mother, who'd been stuffing her face with tea cakes and scones, scowled at Sophia.

"Good lord, Sophia. What are you thinking, putting those dangerous objects in a child's path?" Cordelia scooped the howling Norbert into her ample arms and patted him absently on the back. "Norbert could have been hurt. There now, sweetheart. Would you like a cake?"

The chubby-cheeked toddler's tears disappeared in an instant, and he reached eagerly for the sweets.

"Had I known you were coming," Sophia said, placing the lamp on the drawing-room mantel and righting the table, "I would have moved the items." And everything else of value.

She adjusted the glasses slipping off her nose and caught sight of Eddie, her sister-in-law's other demon child, peeking out from under the heavy draperies. Before he could stick a piece of broken porcelain in his mouth, she grabbed him.

Sophia yanked the shard out of his hand, and then

he, too, exploded into wails of displeasure. "Sophia!" Cordelia screeched around a mouthful of crumpet, and it was all Sophia could do not to pull the dagger she had hidden in her boot and fling it into her sister-in-law's chest.

But that would only make the children cry louder and probably wake Edward, her husband's snoring half brother. And so, instead of dispatching Cordelia, as she would have liked, Sophia smoothed her skirts and took a stiff-necked seat in her favorite chair, a Sheraton upholstered in cream satin.

And to think a week ago she'd been Saint: England's most resourceful, most skilled, most elusive spy. How quickly she'd been reduced to... this.

Wallace, her butler, stepped unobtrusively into the room, and Sophia made a motion toward the shattered Sèvres piece. He nodded. "I'll send the maid—again, my lady."

Cordelia had finally quieted both of her children, and now she leveled her gaze on Sophia. "This house is entirely too dangerous," Cordelia pronounced. "Who puts a table in such a precarious location?"

Tempted as she was to respond with her true feelings, Sophia resisted the urge. Adrian's family knew her as his meek and docile wife. It was a ruse that had served her well while working for the Barbican group. Who would suspect a mouse like her to live a double life as a secret agent? She had only to keep the pretense going. Surely the Barbican group would have need of her again, and this ridiculous ruse would once again be useful.

"You're right, Cordelia," Sophia answered, though

she thought it perfectly reasonable to place a lamp table between a couch and chair, where a lamp might actually be needed. "Perhaps you have some ideas on how I might rearrange the furnishings in this room."

Cordelia puffed up like a bird looking to mate and launched into a litany of helpful suggestions.

Sophia pasted a smile on her face and glanced surreptitiously at the clock on the mantel. Adrian's family had been here exactly twenty-three minutes. How long was she expected to put up with them?

Not that she had anything better to do now that her career as an operative was at an end. In truth, since she'd arrived home from her failed attempt to apprehend Lucien Ducos, she had done nothing but pace, her mind turning over every possible way she might regain her position. Or any operative position.

She glanced at Norbert and Eddie. Devil children that they were, her heart constricted. She must make the Foreign Office take her back. But how?

The past few days she'd tried every distraction she knew. Usually reading helped, but Adrian's library contained mostly sermons and biblical treatises. What she'd really wanted was a volume on weaponry. She was a master with a dagger, relatively good with a rapier, but her aim with a pistol might be improved…

Sophia clenched her hands into fists. *No thinking of pistols!* It would drive her mad.

"And those draperies," Cordelia was saying. Sophia nodded absently, attempting to ignore Eddie, who stuck his tongue out at her.

To clear her mind of pistols, Sophia had also tried taking an active part in a few of the charitable organizations in which she was supposedly enormously involved. But while the women were kind to her—she was a viscountess, after all—they seemed far more interested in gossip than helping war widows and orphans.

And so she'd ended up staring out her bedroom window for hours on end. The view was depressing, as the garden had been sadly neglected these past years. Perhaps she could try her hand at botany. She'd always been interested in the components of poisons...

Damn! She had to stop thinking about poisons and pistols! Perhaps if she treated this as a temporary assignment, it would be more bearable.

She took a deep breath. She was Sophia Galloway, Lady Smythe, a peeress, a lady of the *ton*.

She glanced at her sister-in-law, whose life revolved around fashion, nannies, and, of course, tea cakes. Perhaps it wasn't such a bad life. Perhaps she could figure out a way to lace tea cakes with a tasteless poison...

"What are you smiling about, Sophia?" Cordelia asked, her small eyes narrowing with suspicion. "Do my suggestions amuse you?"

Sophia blinked and composed her features. "No, not at all. In fact, I was imagining this room with all of the changes you've recommended. The final effect will certainly be charming."

"Do you really think so?" Cordelia's brows lifted. "I thought you would object to sealing the fireplace."

Sophia almost coughed. "Sealing the—? Ah, no, splendid idea. Why is that necessary again?"

"To protect your children, Sophia." Cordelia spoke as though Sophia were a child, even though, at twenty-eight, Sophia had six years on Cordelia. "Surely you and Lord Smythe would not want your little son or daughter to fall into the fire."

Sophia stiffened. She should have expected this. She should have prepared a response. Now she was left speechless, mortifying tears welling in her eyes. She blinked them back, her eyes stinging.

"Sophia?" Cordelia was studying her. "Is there something wrong? Or—something you want to tell me?" She clapped her hands together. "Oh, I knew it! You're expecting."

"No!" Sophia shook her head emphatically, but it was too late. Cordelia was out of her seat, engulfing Sophia in her arms. Sophia tried to speak, but the sound of voices below interrupted them.

"Ah, there's the new papa now," Cordelia gushed.

For once, her husband's timing was perfect. Sophia needed out of this room before the tears started in earnest. She rose, intending to make certain Wallace showed his lordship into the drawing room. If Adrian so much as thought about avoiding his brother's family and retreating to his library, Sophia would strangle him.

"Lord Smythe!" Sophia called down the stairs, knowing it was exceedingly gauche to do so and not caring a whit. "My lord, come up to the drawing room. We have visitors."

She could almost hear his hesitation and could picture the frown on his handsome face. But true to his predictable nature, Adrian started up the stairs. His boots clomped on the marble, and Sophia waited until he came into view.

He glanced up at her, his gray eyes full of his displeasure. "Good afternoon, Lady Smythe."

"Good afternoon, my lord."

He reached the landing and raised a brow. "And who are these guests?"

"Your brother and his family. Isn't it wonderful?"

His expression said the visit was anything but. Still, he continued climbing the steps. To her chagrin, Sophia found herself taking a step back as Adrian came closer. He'd always been a handsome man. Exceedingly handsome. So handsome, in fact, that when they'd first met, he'd all but taken her breath away.

And that was precisely why she shouldn't have married him. She'd always known she had to marry. No innocent miss could ever hope to secure a place in the Barbican group. But from the first, she'd known Adrian was the wrong man. She had a duty to her country to keep who she was and what she did a secret. She had vowed never to allow anyone to get close to her, to know her, to suspect what she really was.

Adrian made her want to break that vow. Adrian, with his muscled body and his skilled touch. At times, it took all she possessed to stay away from him.

For so many reasons, life was easier if she avoided him and his bed. Not that he wanted her in his bed. And she could hardly blame him. She'd turned him out of her bedroom, shut the door in his face. He thought he was not welcome. Heaven help her if he ever realized the truth.

And now here he was—her husband—that prime

specimen of male magnificence. His short, dark blond hair framed a square face of hard edges and flat planes. He had a slash of eyebrows over those mesmerizing gray eyes, and his Roman nose cut his stark features in two. His lips were full, even when tightened in displeasure, and his jaw was strong and angular. Though he was only an inch or two taller than average, his broad shoulders and wide chest gave him an imposing presence. He looked larger than he was, especially when one noted the way his chest tapered into a slim waist, lean hips, and long legs.

Her pulse sped, and she took a shaky breath.

He reached the top step so that Sophia felt as though he truly did tower over her. She teetered on the line between short and medium height, so she squared her shoulders in an attempt to appear taller. Glancing up at her husband, she waited—almost hoped—to see some flicker of interest in his eyes.

Were his hands clammy at the sight of her? Did his chest feel tight? Did he imagine their bodies naked and entwined?

She stared at his broad chest, traced the stubble on his jaw with her gaze, and met his gray eyes. In them she saw nothing.

Thank God. If he ever looked at her with more than passing interest, her resolve would surely falter. She couldn't allow that to happen. She couldn't drop her guard, not even for an instant. She couldn't go through that pain again. She couldn't face the hollow nursery, echoing with the keening rock of the empty cradle. The cradle Adrian had made, lovingly and with his own hands. The cradle they had both knelt beside, fingers and gazes linked, long ago when they still touched, still had dreams of happiness.

"My brother is here," Adrian said now, stating the obvious.

Sophia nodded. "As are Mrs. Hayes and the two boys. I am certain they are anxious to see you, my lord."

"I suppose I can spare a moment."

Sophia smiled tightly. He was going to spare more than a moment. In two minutes, she was going to recall an important meeting and rush away. Let Adrian amuse the demon children and listen to Cordelia's decorating schemes.

She turned to follow him into the drawing room, but he paused before entering, turning back to her. "I need to talk with you later. We should have a... conversation."

Sophia raised a brow at the uncharacteristic expression on her husband's face. "Very well, my lord," she said slowly. Adrian was never one for mystery. Still, she dared not allow him to pique her interest. He had probably misplaced his copy of the *Times* again and wondered if she had taken it.

Adrian stepped into the drawing room and was immediately assaulted by Cordelia. "Lord Smythe, I have just heard the good news."

"Oh?"

Behind him, Sophia grimaced. There was no way to escape this now.

"What good news?"

Sophia heard Edward Hayes snuffle and wake. "What? What?"

She could not see the state of the room. Adrian's

broad back blocked her from view, and she was more than glad to hide. She did not want to see her husband's face just now.

"Oh, Mr. Hayes!" Cordelia screeched. "Didn't you hear? Lady Smythe is in a delicate condition."

Adrian's body tensed immediately, and she realized too late the conclusion to which he'd jumped. Cordelia was speaking again. "Oh, but Lord Smythe, didn't you know? You look surprised."

Sophia imagined he was indeed surprised. He turned to her, gray eyes hot like molten steel. "Sophia, is this… happy news true?"

All eyes were on her—even the glowing red eyes of the demon children. But it was Adrian's eyes that stopped the denial on her lips. For the first time in—she could not think how long—she saw his eyes darken with interest. It was probably anger, but he was looking at her as more than an object at the moment. And in that moment, she wanted desperately to tell him it was true. There would be a baby—a darling, sweet, soft baby. She wanted him to keep looking at her that way. She wanted the closeness they had shared—so briefly—back again. She wanted something—someone—to share with him.

But it wasn't true, and she didn't have to humiliate herself in front of Cordelia and tell him so. If he had any ounce of intelligence, he would know it wasn't true, and he wouldn't have put her in this position.

Forcing a smile, she announced, "I do believe I have just remembered a pressing engagement. I am so sorry, but I must be off. Good day!"

She walked out of the drawing room and didn't look back.

Three

ADRIAN SAT AT HIS POLISHED DESK IN HIS SMALL, spartan library and attempted to concentrate on the newspaper. He should be reading the article before him, advocating changes in a commerce law. There was a parliamentary session this afternoon, addressing that very issue, but if Adrian's lack of concentration now was any indicator of what was to come, he'd be wasting his time at Whitehall.

Perhaps part of the problem was the incessant pounding outside his window, where his once quiet, undemanding wife claimed to be gardening. How was he supposed to concentrate on commerce law when his wife was carrying another man's child?

Sophia had been unfaithful to him.

Rage like he'd rarely known welled up inside him. Rage and anger at his own stupidity. What had he thought would happen? He was never here. Of course Sophia—young, attractive, intelligent—would find another man to warm her bed at night.

This was his own damn fault.

If he even believed it. He'd been furious last

night, unable to sleep or even lie down most of the night. But this morning, he'd had moments of lucidity. Sophia had never actually confirmed she was pregnant. She'd given no response to Cordelia's pointed questions. He knew how delicate the subject of pregnancy was to Sophia. Should he be surprised that rather than deny the pregnancy—something she'd had to do countless times—she chose to escape and say nothing?

There was only one way to know for certain.

Ask her.

And wasn't that what he'd wanted to do all along— broach the subject of their marriage and trying once again for children? He wanted children. He wanted to be the father he had never had.

The pounding in the garden seemed to increase, and Adrian thought that perhaps the conversation could wait a little longer.

He looked at the article on his desk again then sighed. Perhaps the problem wasn't Sophia at all. Perhaps he just didn't care about the nuances of commerce law. Perhaps he didn't care for the life of a viscount—estates, tenants, rents, the House of Lords…

Adrian had always lived a simple life. He served his country; he protected its sovereignty; he atoned…

That was where life grew complicated.

His father's treason. Even after all these years, anger lanced through him, still raw and blistering and festering with shame.

He should forgive his father. The man was long dead, and God knew he'd paid for his crimes. Melbourne was right. Adrian should forget his father, step out from his shadow. After all, he'd barely known the man.

But the more Adrian contemplated having his own family, the more his father's legacy haunted him. Adrian swore he would be different. His children would be proud to call him father, proud of what he'd accomplished.

If he ever had children. A new pain, this one a dull throb, replaced the anger.

The sharp, staccato pounding continued, and Adrian pushed out of his chair, rose, and stomped to the window. What the hell was the woman doing out there? Gardening was supposed to be a peaceful, quiet activity—tilling the soil, dropping in seeds, pulling weeds. Why did it sound like she had taken shovel to stone? And why did he care? The banality of life at home was driving him mad. He wanted to throw open the French doors, stride to Melbourne's office, and force the secretary to reinstall him.

Adrian massaged the bridge of his nose. Even as a child, he'd hated being told *no*—a selfish trait everyone said he shared with his treacherous father.

Stop it, he told himself. He was nothing like his father. James Galloway had been a criminal, and he'd been tried and hanged for his treason. Adrian was knighted for his service to England.

He closed his eyes and leaned his head against the window. But was it enough? Had he done enough to wipe the taint from the family name?

Can you ever do enough? a dark voice whispered.

"Yes," Adrian muttered to himself. But he hadn't yet. He could do more, would do more, and if Melbourne thought he could stop him—

He heard a tap on the door. "Enter."

A footman did so, carrying a silver tray. Even from across the room, Adrian recognized Melbourne's handwriting on the card in the center. Adrian stiffened as the familiar rush of anticipation coursed through him.

☙

Adrian was angry, and it didn't take a spy to figure that out. For the past day, he'd stomped around the town house like an irate dragon. This morning he'd snapped at one of the maids for dusting too loudly. Before long, Sophia wouldn't just be imagining smoke furling from his nostrils.

He'd even deigned to notice her. He was usually benignly neglectful toward her on the infrequent occasions they dined together, but at breakfast this morning, he'd scowled at her.

How she wished she could scowl right back, tell him he was being ridiculous if he believed she was pregnant. She would never betray him. How could he even believe that of her? If he thought that little of her, he deserved to stew. Besides, he wasn't the only one in an infernal mood, and at least she had a valid reason for her ill temper. Yesterday afternoon, she'd tried to gain an interview with Lord Melbourne, secretary of the Barbican group, and her request had been denied. She was no closer to reinstatement than before. Her patience, never her best trait, was wearing thin.

Thank God she had this garden as an escape. This hot, overgrown, dirty garden. She'd been out here for

several hours and had accomplished almost nothing.
The only task she seemed capable of was tapping her
metal spade against a large rock protruding from what
should have been her flower bed.

Clank. Clank. Clank.

The sound was oddly soothing—perhaps because
it drowned out the loop of desperate pleas racing
through her head.

"What on earth is that infernal noise?" A voice rose
from the other side of the gate, and Sophia jumped
in recognition.

With a furtive peek at the house behind her, she
rose. "What are you doing here?"

"Saving you, as usual," Agent Blue said, crossing
one ankle over the other and leaning one shoulder
against the gate. "And not a moment too soon." He
gave Sophia a quick perusal. "I've seen you look better
after a knife fight. Good God, Saint, where did you get
those *enormous* glasses?"

At the sound of her code name, Sophia glanced
back at the house again. Adrian was probably asleep
in his library chair, but she didn't want to take any
chances. She placed a finger over her lips and opened
the gate. After walking through, she closed it silently
and pulled Blue to the side of the stone wall. They
could still be seen by neighbors and passersby, but they
were obscured from the household's view.

"How did you find me?" she asked, still whispering.

Blue cocked a brow. "I'm a spy, remember?"

Actually, that fact was rather difficult to digest at
the moment. She had never met with Blue when
they weren't on assignment, and his appearance now

was a bit unsettling. And not only because she hadn't expected to find him in her garden. He looked... the kindest word Sophia could think to describe him was *eccentric*.

Sophia never thought much about whether the other members of the Barbican group disguised themselves when they were off-assignment. She used disguise because that had always been her custom. She'd joined the group after working domestically for the Foreign Office. That is, she had investigated suspicious persons and allegations of treason and spying in London.

As a gentleman's daughter, the daughter of a man who had himself been secretly part of the Foreign Office, Sophia had unprecedented access to the world of the upper classes—a world where power reigned and corruption was a constant threat.

How much easier to remain anonymous and unnoticed by the *ton* if she dressed plainly and played the meek mouse? In fact, so few people took notice of her, she became a master at her profession. And she had been rewarded for her skills. The day she had been invited to join the ranks of the Barbican had been the happiest of her life.

But, for whatever reason, Blue apparently also found disguising himself in London a necessary evil. And his attire today was certainly evil. He wore orange pantaloons, a green silk waistcoat, and a purple tailcoat. His stockings and cravat were white, and his brown hair was curled and tousled within an inch of its life. For once, she didn't notice his blue eyes.

"Why are you dressed like this?" she asked.

Once again, he looked her up and down. "I might ask you the same thing. Is that gown made out of sackcloth?" He reached forward to finger the material, and she slapped his hand away. For some inexplicable reason, she was embarrassed.

"Why are you here?"

"Finally. Thank God you haven't been asked to do many interrogations. It takes you a moment to get to the point, doesn't it?"

Sophia raised her brows. "Only when I'm over-whelmed by so many varied and clashing colors." She flicked a finger at his clothing, but Blue only struck a dashing pose.

"Like it?"

"No."

He huffed. "Well, if I had known you were going to be this cold, I would not have called. Perhaps you don't want to be saved."

"Saved?" Sophia stepped back and peered through the garden gate to ensure she hadn't been missed. "Saved from what? Or whom?"

Blue indicated the house and gardens behind her with a sweep of one lace-bedecked sleeve. "Saved from this life of drudgery. But if you prefer to stay home, work in the dirt, and let the rest of us have all the adventure, so be it." He turned and began to walk away, but Sophia gripped his horrid tailcoat and tugged him back.

He immediately shrugged off her hand. "Careful, madam! You'll wrinkle it."

"I'll do more than that if you don't explain what you mean. Is another assignment available? Does the group need me to come back?" She pushed her unnecessary glasses onto the bridge of her nose.

Blue gave her a hesitant look. "Not exactly. This is more of a private matter."

"I don't understand."

He reached into his grape-colored tailcoat and withdrew a slim card. "Come to this location tonight at midnight, and all will be explained."

Sophia eyed the card and snorted. "You cannot be serious. As though I would traipse about in the middle of the night without a very good reason."

Blue took her hand and pressed the card into it. "Whether you come or not is entirely your decision, but be aware that you are not the only one in contention for the position. If you are late or do not make an appearance, you lose."

With a nod and a bow, he turned and began to walk away. Sophia watched him for a moment and then called, "Lose what?"

Without looking back, he raised a hand and waved.

∽≪≫∽

"I did not ask you here to call you back into service," Melbourne said as he opened his office door to admit Adrian. Immediately, the surge of pleasure Adrian had been riding since receiving the summons this afternoon vanished.

He stepped into the office and scowled. "I see." He made a show of taking out his pocket watch and studying the face. Nine o'clock in the evening. "I don't have time for social calls."

Ignoring him, Melbourne lifted two brandy

snifters from his desk drawer and filled each from a decanter he unearthed as well. He offered one to Adrian. "Brandy?"

Adrian accepted it, sipped the liquid, and crossed his arms. The older man took a seat and proceeded to savor the amber liquid. Adrian felt a heave of impatience as he watched the other man's languid, unhurried movements. In contrast, Adrian's heart beat quickly, and every muscle was taut, but he controlled his expression, controlled his breathing. He might seethe with irritation, but Melbourne would never know.

"Care to sit down, old chap?"

"I'll stand."

"Suit yourself."

Adrian closed his mouth, exerting considerable effort to refrain from asking the purpose of Melbourne's urgent summons. He could be as patient as the devil, if need be.

"You must be wondering why I called you here," Melbourne said before finishing the last of his brandy.

Adrian lifted one shoulder slightly. "I'm used to coming when called. It's one of many things about the group I won't miss."

"And yet, two days ago, you were at loose ends. I was left with the distinct impression you rather wanted to remain part of the group."

Hell, yes, he'd wanted to remain part of the group. He *needed* the Barbican group. Melbourne knew it, but Adrian would eat the snifter before admitting how much he wanted his position back. Let Melbourne think domesticity suited him perfectly. Let Melbourne worry about losing his best agent for a change. "I've found other amusements."

"I see." Melbourne poured another two fingers of brandy for himself. He raised the decanter toward Adrian. Much as he wanted another glass, Adrian shook his head and watched Melbourne relish another swallow.

"Then I suppose you would not be interested in a new venture recently come before me," Melbourne said. "You are, after all, a free man now."

Adrian swallowed and waited five long heartbeats. "What new venture?"

"Nothing to do with our group," Melbourne replied with a wave of his half-empty glass. "Not directly, at any rate. This is a private matter, but it requires the involvement of someone in whose loyalty we are absolutely secure."

Adrian shifted slightly and clenched his hidden fists to keep from blurting out a barrage of questions. Finally, he settled on, "Who is we?"

Instead of answering, Melbourne sipped his brandy and searched another drawer, unearthing a small white card, which he held out to Adrian. Printed in neat black script was an address and *midnight*.

Adrian's eyes met his superior's. "A midnight rendezvous? What is this? A love affair?"

"Hardly. It is a matter of extreme consequence, but as I said before, you are free from my command. What you do with the information on that card is entirely your decision."

"So I'm at perfect liberty to go home and to bed."

"If that is what you wish."

The two men locked gazes for several seconds.

"But you won't."

Adrian pocketed the card and turned to the door. "Good night, sir."

Four

By the stroke of midnight, Sophia had swept through the rendezvous building to familiarize herself with the layout, and now she crept down the slick back staircase, wincing as a step creaked under her. She paused, listened. Somewhere in the distance was the drip and splat of water. She supposed the decrepit building on London's East End must have a leak or ten somewhere, but that didn't explain why the staircase felt so slimy. There was more than water underfoot.

She tested the next step then moved gingerly downward, inwardly cursing her black mantle. She was suffocating in the heavy garment, the perspiration making its way down her back in tepid rivulets.

Why did these rendezvous always have to be in dank, smelly hovels? Why could one never receive a summons to meet in a bright, airy drawing room? And why was midnight always the appointed time? It was practically cliché, not to mention it made things dreadfully difficult.

When Sophia had slipped out tonight, she had to escape not only the notice of the staff but also her husband. Adrian usually spent evenings at his club, but tonight he'd stayed home. When she'd crept past his bedroom door, his light burned, and she could hear him moving about.

The soft plop of a footstep in water made Sophia catch her breath and flatten her back against the wall beside the stairs. She looked up at the origin of the sound and then down at the darkness before her.

She wasn't alone.

Her own boot was still wet from trudging through that puddle at the top of the stairs. When she'd searched the ground floor of the building and found it empty, she'd decided to try the lower level. Obviously, someone else had the same idea. It could be Blue behind her, but until she was certain, she was taking no chances.

Sophia didn't hear the interloper again, but that didn't mean he—or she—wasn't there. Balancing caution and speed, Sophia took the last few steps and descended into the musty gloom of the lower level. She felt along the base of the damp, moldy stairs until she found an opening underneath which to crouch.

A cobweb brushed across her face, but she ignored it and focused on unsheathing the dagger strapped to her thigh. She was lowering her skirts and mantle again when she heard the step squeak—the same step she had made creak a moment ago.

The intruder was close.

She adjusted her weight so she was balanced on the balls of her feet then loosened the grip on the dagger so she held it firmly but could still manipulate it. Like she, the person on the stairs had paused when the board whined, but now he—his step had been heavier than hers, and Sophia was fairly certain it was a man—was moving forward again.

She had to give him credit. She could not hear him moving—he was as silent as the fog—but she could feel the subtle disturbance in the air as he continued his descent.

Sophia counted the steps in her head. Four.

Three.

Two.

She leapt nimbly from her hiding place and thrust her hand out at the dark shape before her, intending to disable him. Once she was in control and knew with whom she was dealing, she could decide how best to proceed. She'd aimed for his throat but had to adjust when he was taller than she expected, and her hand hit him in the chest.

Before she could wrap her fingers about his windpipe and force him back against the wall, he had his own hand around her wrist and was squeezing painfully.

Sophia did not cry out, and it only increased her concern when, despite her surprise attack, her assailant made no sound. She knew he had not heard her. She had taken him completely by surprise.

And yet, he was reacting with calm and skill that came only from years of training.

Blue?

No. This man was taller and heavier than Blue. He was certainly far more muscled and powerful than she. Not that she considered this a problem. It was merely an observation.

Blocking the pain of his punishing hold on her

wrist, Sophia brought her other hand up and slashed with her dagger. She cut him across the forearm and heard him hiss. His hold on her wrist loosened, and she jerked free.

She knew she had some space behind her, and she moved away, giving herself room to maneuver. The farther she pulled back, the more she was shrouded from the meager light near the stairwell. She could use the darkness to her advantage only so long as the man, who she now knew must be a trained operative like herself, was unsure of her location. The lower level was almost without light, and she could barely make out the indistinct shapes of boxes and crates behind her. She stepped carefully to avoid disturbing anything and giving away her position.

She had been taught to strike first and ask questions later. Whoever this man was, she considered him a threat.

The threat moved forward. Whether by chance or skill, he came directly for her. Sophia shifted to the side, trying to clear his path. Without the benefit of surprise, a direct attack favored the larger, stronger participant. If she wanted the upper hand, she would have to ambush him.

But the man had eyes as keen as hers.

As soon as she shifted out of his path, he shifted to follow. He couldn't possibly have seen her movements. Even with her acute vision, she was practically guessing at his location. Could he hear her?

Suddenly, he lunged, and she ducked, narrowly avoiding capture. But she came up fighting. Dagger in hand, she slashed at him, catching his cloak and, unfortunately, nothing else. He reached for her weapon, caught her wrist, and there was a brief struggle. He tried to shake the dagger free of her grip, but she would not release it. Instead, she kicked, connecting with what she thought must be his knee.

With an "oof"—the first sound he had made—he stepped back.

He did not release her hand.

Sophia tamped down a surge of frustration and tried a new tactic. She pivoted, presenting him with her back and driving her elbow hard into his middle. Little surprise, that part of him was as firm and unyielding as the rest. But she was not through yet. She shoved into him, as close as a lover, then arched her neck and slammed the back of her head into his chin.

The blow reverberated through him, and he staggered back.

Unfortunately, he took her with him.

They stumbled blindly for a moment. Sophia's heavy mantle caught on something, but he managed to right himself.

The counterattack was swift and sure. He propelled her forward, throwing her off-balance then whipping her around. Again, he shook her wrist, trying to loosen her fingers from the dagger. Although her nerves screamed for release from the pain, she would not comply. She slammed against the wall behind her, ducking before he could grasp her throat with his free hand. Instead, she struck out first, catching him hard on the jaw. She heard the pop as his head snapped back and then grunted when the retaliatory blow came: a hard jab to her abdomen.

For a moment, she could not breathe. Small dots

of light danced before her eyes, and then with a roar, she launched herself off the wall and collided with his body.

He lost his grip on her wrist, and she fell awkwardly, losing possession of her dagger in the process. The clink of the metal on the hard floor startled them both, and as one, they began to grope for the weapon.

They were on the floor, her legs tangled with his as their hands patted the cold dirt beneath them. Sophia felt a jolt as his hand brushed over hers, and her reaction was to kick out at him, increasing the distance between them. It was then that she realized how close to the stairwell they'd fallen. Three or four steps, and she could be on the stairs and away. For the first time in her career, she was not certain she would win a battle. And why did it matter? There was no Lucien Ducos to take prisoner. No Napoleon Bonaparte to defeat. Exactly what was she fighting for?

She shoved at the man again just as she heard the dagger scrape against the ground. He had it, and now was her chance. While he closed his hands about the weapon, she freed her legs from him and dove for the stairs.

She had gained the first one and would have gone farther had her skirts not tangled about her ankles. Damn! She knew she should not have worn this gown. It was her own vanity, her own desire to please whoever had arranged this meeting, which had caused her to be impractical.

And now she would pay for it. Her slight delay gave her attacker the perfect opportunity, and she felt his hand close on her ankle.

"Oh, no, you don't," he murmured.

"Oh, yes, I do," she growled, lowering her voice to disguise it. Sophia kicked back and felt her ankle collide with his jaw. Thank God she had worn her half boots and not some silly satin slippers. And yet the man seemed almost unfazed by the blow. He pulled back on her ankle, hard, and she went down. Kicking free, she gained the stairs once again, but this time his hand snagged her waist, and he pulled her off her feet and back into the darkness of the lower level.

"Let go!" she barked, kicking and clawing fiercely. Sophia much preferred a disciplined, structured attack, but she was not averse to an unruly approach. Only this time, neither seemed to work.

He had her, and he had her firmly. They stumbled back, and as he struggled to maintain control, his hand brushed over her breast. He must have felt it, too, because he jerked and then clamped his hand hard about her flesh.

"Bloody hell. I knew it!" he exclaimed. They fell into a wall, the reverberation from the impact jarring both of them. But not jarring him enough to release her.

Even muffled by the pounding in her head and the blood rushing through her veins, his voice sounded familiar. If she could just place it...

"Knew what?" she asked, ramming her elbow into his gut. A whoosh of air escaped his lungs, and he squeezed her breast hard in retaliation. "Knew you were being beaten by a woman?" The words came out between gasps as she fought to suck in air.

"I am hardly being beaten, madam. If I so chose, you would be on the floor, unconscious."

She gave a bitter laugh. "You are most welcome to try."

He pushed her free, and she did fall, but at the last moment, she tucked her legs and rolled into a crouching position. Without waiting for him to recover, she shot forward, ramming her head into his gut. She'd hit him there repeatedly now, and she knew he must feel the pain.

But he grabbed her shoulders and thrust her back, spinning her about and, once again, imprisoning her about the waist. But this time, his arm had come around her, confining her limbs so she could not use elbows or hands.

She kicked back, but he danced out of her reach. She could hear his own gasps for breath, and then his mouth was beside her ear. "Who are you?"

"I might ask you"—she fought to take another breath—"the same question. Let go." She was positive now that she knew the man. The spy from Calais? The double agent from Lisbon? If she could just grab a moment to think...

"Stop fighting." His breath was warm, and it tickled the sensitive skin of her ear. She felt her body heat in response and shook her head to clear her mind.

What was wrong with her? This man held her prisoner, would probably kill her, given half a chance, and she was becoming aroused? No wonder the Barbican group no longer had need of her. She was going soft.

"You are not going to win." His velvet voice rumbled through her, and his breath skated over her neck. She shivered. There was something about his voice. It was doing something to her, having this erotic effect on her.

"I've never lost." She managed to wiggle her hand

into the slit at the side of her skirt. The pockets tied underneath held her last hope.

"Famous last words."

"Yours." And with that, she freed the small pistol and pressed the muzzle into his thigh.

He stiffened.

"Now, let me go. Slowly."

She'd expected immediate compliance, but for some reason, the man hesitated. She dug the muzzle harder into his flesh. "Let go."

But he was still, listening. "Wait a moment." His voice was far away, distracted.

Damn. He'd recognized her voice. That was the last thing she needed. She tried to distract him with another nudge from the pistol, but he shook his head. "Who are you?"

"Someone with whom you should not trifle."

"Sophia?" The word was strained and almost high-pitched, and before she could stop herself, she jerked, giving all away. "My God." His hands suddenly flew from her, releasing her as though she'd just told him she had the pox. "It *is* you."

Sophia landed on her feet, stumbled, then whirled to face him. There was a scratching sound, and the acrid smell of smoke assaulted her nostrils. A lone match flared, and she was staring into Adrian's face.

Shock, like the blow of a blacksmith's hammer, slammed into her. She felt as though her head had been cleaved in two, and she could make no sense of the apparition before her.

"Adrian?" she managed before the flame went out. "But how—?"

The sound of footsteps above them jerked her back into the danger of the situation. She went absolutely still, noting Adrian did the same. As one, they slid toward the shelter of the staircase. Sophia ducked down, bumping shoulders with Adrian as he did the same.

"Get out of my way," she hissed.

"You're in my way."

The footsteps began again. "Shh," they said in unison.

Sophia bristled. Who was he to shush her? And what was he doing here? Adrian's idea of excitement was walking home from his club in a drizzle. She had to be imagining this… or was it some kind of test? Had whoever arranged this meeting brought Adrian here to evaluate her loyalty? Or perhaps to expose her…

"Are you down there?" a man's voice called from the top of the staircase. The warm glow of lantern light flickered above and cascaded over them.

"Who the hell are you?" Adrian called, careful, she noted, not to reveal himself.

"Why, Lord Smythe, come upstairs and see for yourself. You, too, Lady Smythe."

Sophia snapped a look at Adrian, but he appeared as confused as she.

"No need to worry," the man said. "I know all about you and the Barbican group."

Sophia was still staring at Adrian, and it was then that she saw it.

He was wearing the gray cloak. The same gray cloak the operative who had stolen Ducos out from under her had been wearing.

Her eyes must have widened, because Adrian's

expression went from bewildered to alarmed. "What is it?"

"You," she spat. She reached forward and grasped a handful of the offending cloak. "It was you. I do not believe this. It's impossible."

And it was. Adrian? *He* had been the agent to apprehend Ducos?

Adrian looked at the wadded material of the cloak in her hand, looked at her face. "What are you talking about?"

"Lucien Ducos."

His face showed no reaction to the name. "I don't follow."

It was a blatant lie, and yet his voice betrayed nothing. He was good. Damn! He was good.

"You stole him from me," Sophia spat. "You're the bastard who walked in and stole Ducos from under my nose."

His gray eyes widened. "You're the other spy? You're the agent who couldn't catch him?"

Her jaw dropped indignantly. "*Couldn't*—I had him, you fool. That was my trap you stepped into. Days of preparation, and you ruined everything."

Adrian shrugged—arrogant, cocksure. It was a new look, a novel attitude for him. She hated it and was drawn to it at the same time. This man was *not* her husband.

"I guess we know who the better agent is," he drawled.

"Better at pilfering, perhaps. But who won the confrontation down here?" She gestured to the lower level. "I had you right where I wanted you."

He glanced at the pistol she still held and snorted. "With that toy? I was hardly concerned."

Sophia's eyes narrowed, and she raised the weapon. "This toy, as you call it, will put a nice hole in your belly."

"If you can even fire it straight." He crossed his arms over his chest.

She inhaled sharply, partly because of the insult and partly because it was truer than he could have guessed. Handling pistols was not her forte. But even she could not miss at this close range. She cocked the hammer. "Shall we test that theory?"

They locked eyes.

The man at the top of the stairs cleared his throat. Neither Sophia nor Adrian looked away.

"If you two want to kill each other, fine with me. But if you are interested in this assignment, I suggest you make your way upstairs. I will not be kept waiting."

He withdrew, taking the lantern with him, and the lower level was once again pitched into darkness. Neither Sophia nor Adrian moved. There was silence, except for the drip of the water.

Plop, plop, plo—

"I'm going up," Adrian announced. "If you want to shoot me, now is your chance."

And Sophia was just tempted enough by the conceited tone in his voice to do it too. Instead, she eased her hand off the pistol's hammer and lowered the weapon. "This isn't over."

"Not by a long shot," he agreed.

They rammed shoulders as both attempted to take the stairs.

"Excuse me," he said, trying to shoulder past her.

She shoved him back then stepped nimbly out of his way. "Go right ahead, my lord. I've always said, 'ladies first.'"

Five

"LADIES FIRST." ADRIAN GAVE HIS WIFE A POTENT scowl before starting up the stairs. "You're terribly amusing, madam. I don't know why I never noticed before."

"Perhaps because you have no sense of humor."

"Perhaps because—"

"My lord and lady," the gentleman at the top of the stairs interrupted, "I am waiting."

From behind him, Adrian heard Sophia hiss in a breath. He reached back, assuming she'd fallen through one of the steps or slipped on a wet patch, but she pushed his hand aside. "I do not need your assistance. I only…" She paused and motioned him closer. They had almost reached the ground-floor landing, and Adrian assumed she wanted to keep their exchange private. "I—my nose itches."

She was whispering, and Adrian had to put his ear next to her mouth to catch her words. It had been a long time since he'd been this near to his wife, and he couldn't help but notice the sweet scent of oranges. It was a scent he'd always associated with her, and yet he'd forgotten until this minute that the smell of citrus clung to her. It was in her skin, her hair, her lips…

He had a mental picture of how she'd looked a moment before, when the lantern had illuminated them both. She'd looked wild and sensual—her glossy brown hair falling in unruly curls down her back and her creamy white skin tinged with a rosy blush. Her chocolate brown eyes had—well, actually they had shot daggers at him—and she'd looked full of life.

Life and sensuality.

He couldn't remember the last time he'd seen her look like that, and it aroused him.

And then he saw she still held the dagger in her hand. It looked sharp and deadly and… comfortable there.

And just like that, the arousal faded and the hard truth that she was an operative, like he, crashed into him. This was not some beauty who needed rescuing, or the mousy, docile wife he knew. This was a trained agent. Earlier, she might have killed him—well, caused him some minor injury, anyway—and who knew what assignments she had completed for the Crown. Abduction? Murder?

Seduction?

He clenched his fists and glowered at her. "Your nose itches. Is that supposed to mean something to me?"

"It means something to me. I should trust my instincts."

"And what are your instincts telling you?"

"The man upstairs is Lord Liverpool."

Adrian almost snorted. "The prime minister? Here in the East End?"

She nodded. "Doubt me if you want, but hurry. The prime minister is waiting."

To humor her, he turned and climbed the remaining steps. The prime minister. He didn't believe for a moment Lord Liverpool was standing about in a ramshackle building in London's East—

He stepped onto the landing, and the man with the lantern turned to face him.

"Lord Liverpool," Adrian said, belatedly executing a stiff bow. "My apologies for making you wait, my lord."

"Do not allow it to happen again. Lady Smythe." Liverpool came forward to take her hand and sweep her past Adrian. She smiled up at the prime minister, and for the first time in his married life, Adrian felt a surge of jealousy.

He hadn't known Sophia and Liverpool were acquaintances. And now he wondered what else she'd kept hidden.

Her looks, for one.

This new Sophia was a beauty. The hasty vision of her from below was now made clearer as she stepped into the glow of the prime minister's lantern. He remembered her looking beautiful before, but after months and months of seeing only her drab dress and mousy appearance, he'd almost forgotten how fetching she truly was. Adrian couldn't believe taking her hair down and removing her spectacles could enact such a change. But as she gazed into the prime minister's face, a mixture of anticipation and mischief in her eyes, Adrian saw the true alteration.

She held herself straight. She looked poised and confident. Bloody radiant. There was nothing mousy or shy or sweet about this woman. She swept past him with languid predatory moves, right past him and… practically into Liverpool's arms.

Adrian reached out and deftly plucked her back again. This confident, sensual woman was not the wife he knew. And, as if to prove it, she didn't submit to his touch.

"My lord!" She shook his hand off her waist and spun to scowl at him. "I beg your pardon."

Adrian glowered. "Oh, I'm supposed to stand here idly while you flirt and simper?"

"Flirt and—for your information—"

"Oh, God forbid, you're starting again." Liverpool shook his head and turned, holding the lantern high enough to reveal three surprisingly sturdy chairs in the corner of the dilapidated room.

Immediately, Adrian's gaze fixed on a man dressed in black and standing in the shadows. Undoubtedly, he was Liverpool's assistant and had brought the chairs.

"Just now seeing him, are you?" Sophia said, with a hint of smugness in her voice. "Not very observant, but then that shouldn't surprise me." She moved to join Liverpool at the chairs. "You spend all your time at that club of yours."

"About as much time as you spend at your charitable societies, I imagine," he drawled, and her eyes widened with the realization that he spent no more time at his club than she did at her charities. They were liars—both of them. He gave her a tight smile and moved to stand before the open chair.

Liverpool lifted his tails and took a seat, motioning for Adrian and Sophia to follow. "If you two are through arguing?"

"My apologies, your lordship," Adrian said, watching Sophia remove her mantle. "This has been something of a sh…"

He was aware his voice had trailed off and that his mouth was hanging open, but he was simply too stunned to do anything but stare. What the bloody hell was his wife wearing? And why hadn't she ever worn anything like that for him?

The low-cut red silk clung to her every curve, and what it didn't cling to, it molded and revealed—the arch of her neck, the slope of her shoulders, the swell of her breasts, and the flare of her hips. Realistically, Adrian knew her gown was no more revealing than those other women of the *ton* wore. Indeed, it was a good bit less revealing than what most wore. And yet, he'd never seen her dress in anything other than ill-fitting, high-necked dowdy creations, and the astonishment of seeing her dressed so fashionably, so attractively, shot heat through his veins.

She took the seat beside him, carefully arranging her skirts as she did so, and Adrian's eyes narrowed. Where exactly was she going this night? After meeting with Liverpool, did she intend to rendezvous with her lover? How many other nights had she slipped out of the house, unbeknownst to him, to meet with other men? He remembered Cordelia's congratulations. *Was* Sophia with child? Another man's child?

Adrian would kill him. He'd kill *her*.

He clenched his fists on the arms of the chair and glared at his wife. She gave him a perplexed glance and then turned her attention to the prime minister. "I think what Lord Smythe is attempting to express is that we did not expect to see one another tonight."

"Yes." Liverpool nodded at his assistant, dismissing the man. "It is a testament to your considerable skills that neither of you ever revealed yourself to the other. Good God, but my wife probably knows more about me than I do. Nosy woman."

Adrian noted he said the last fondly. But it was no compliment to Adrian's marriage that he and Sophia were taken completely by surprise tonight.

"In any case, I have it on good authority that you, Lord Smythe, and you, Lady Smythe, are two of the best agents we have. And I have need of an operative with superior skills."

Adrian unclenched his hands and leaned forward, now all business. "I think I should tell you, my lord, I mentored under Lord Melbourne and am recently retired from the Barbican group. Whatever it is you need, I am your man."

"Perhaps his lordship does not need a man," Sophia drawled from beside him. Adrian gave her a sideways glance and saw, despite her apparent nonchalance, her jaw was clenched. "I, too, am recently retired from the Barbican group."

Adrian started. That was impossible. She couldn't be a member of the Barbican group. She couldn't—

He frowned. She couldn't be involved in this affair tonight, either, and yet there she was, seated beside him.

"And I think, your lordship," she continued, "if you look at my record, you will see I am your agent. I will see whatever you need is done."

"Ah, yes," Adrian said, leaning back and giving her

a bored look. "The same way you saw to the capture and questioning of Lucien Ducos?"

She narrowed her large, lovely eyes at him. Without the spectacles, they dominated her face. "Exactly the same way. Except this time, you won't be stepping in at the last minute to claim all the glory and benefit from my weeks of hard work."

Adrian shot forward. "You think I did not work that case? All of the intelligence I gathered was my own, madam. And I never wanted your glory. If glory is what you desire, you are welcome to it."

"By Jove." Liverpool shook his head. "Is this what you two are like at home? No wonder you risk your lives abroad."

Sophia began to speak, but Liverpool held up a hand.

"Not another word. The next person who interrupts me goes home."

Adrian clamped his mouth shut and noted Sophia sat back and pursed her lips. He didn't know what this mission entailed, but whatever it was, he wanted it. It might be his entrée back into the Barbican group. If not, he wasn't going to lose an assignment: not to another member of the Barbican group, not to a woman, and most especially not to his wife.

She shouldn't even be here. She should be in Mayfair, tending his hearth and home. There was no way in hell he'd allow her to go gallivanting about on a dangerous mission.

That was a man's job. His job.

"What I need," Liverpool was saying now, "is an investigator. Someone who is discreet yet thorough. Someone who can keep a secret." He looked at

Adrian and then Sophia. "A few weeks ago, my half brother was murdered."

The prime minister waited for a response, but neither Adrian nor Sophia so much as blinked. She was definitely a professional, Adrian grudgingly conceded again. Whatever she was thinking or feeling, she didn't reveal it.

"As you may know, my brother is George Jenkinson, the product of my father's union with his second wife." The prime minister stood and began to pace. "My brother is not involved in politics and had no known enemies. On the night of the murder, I was summoned from bed at approximately four in the morning and called to the Jenkinson household. Jenkinson's valet, Callows, had discovered my brother's body. We estimate that George had been dead about an hour when Callows found him."

Adrian found himself nodding. Liverpool was calm and lucid. Though the death of his brother must be a difficult topic to discuss, the prime minister did it with clarity and brevity.

"I do not have to tell you murder is almost always grim and shocking, but this was far beyond shocking. This was—" He stumbled slightly. Adrian saw him clench his hands into tight fists. Liverpool was intent on keeping hold of his emotions.

The prime minister swallowed loudly. "The way my brother was killed. T-the state of his body was"—he shuddered and turned away—"gruesome. I want to know why he was killed thus and by whom." Liverpool turned back, his features once again a mask of composure. They might have been discussing the weather.

There was a long moment of silence as Liverpool paused, possibly to allow the information to sink in. Sophia raised a tentative finger.

"Yes, Lady Smythe. You may speak now."

"My lord, I am dreadfully sorry for your loss. I had heard something about this affair, but I thought the matter had been turned over to Bow Street."

Adrian saw where she was going and had to agree. As much as he wanted a new assignment, this was not what he had been trained for. "We are spies, my lord, not murder investigators."

"This is not to imply that solving your brother's murder is not important and necessary, but..." She glanced at Adrian, silently asking for help.

It was a strange feeling, to share the same side as Sophia. Until tonight, he'd never considered her an enemy, but she hadn't been an ally, either. Now it appeared they actually agreed on something: this was not a case for a member of the Barbican group. It was... amateur.

But he wasn't giving up entirely. "My lord, perhaps there is an international matter in which I"—Sophia glared at him; he ignored her—"could assist you?"

The prime minister crossed his arms.

"A dangerous double agent?" Adrian suggested. "A code to be cracked?"

The prime minister sighed and looked at the ceiling.

"An arms smuggler? An..." Adrian trailed off.

Liverpool looked back at him. "I am aware you are probably overqualified for this task. Bow Street thought it would be an easy case as well, and they have yet to solve it. I am also aware both of you were highly regarded operatives for the Barbican group, but might I also point out that you are both *out of work* operatives."

Adrian winced. Liverpool had a point there.

"I had hoped you might take this case purely as a favor to me." The prime minister glanced at Sophia, and Adrian wondered again at their relationship. "But I am prepared to offer compensation."

Sophia looked up from the hands she'd clenched in her lap. "We don't want your money."

Adrian nodded agreement.

"I wouldn't dream of offering it," Liverpool said icily. "But what about reinstatement into your precious Barbican group?"

"I thought the group was being disbanded," Adrian said.

"Severely reduced in number but not disbanded."

Adrian clenched his fists. Melbourne hadn't mentioned this small fact to him. And no wonder, as it would have been even more of a blow to Adrian's ego. It wasn't that his country didn't need the Barbican group—the country didn't need Agent Wolf.

"We retained a few agents," the prime minister continued, "but now there has been an... unexpected opening."

Adrian could almost feel the excitement radiating from his wife, and his own was bubbling up as well. "Are you saying if we solve this case, we shall be reinstated into the Barbican group?"

"No." The prime minister shook his head. "There is only one position open in the group, and I have need of only one investigator. There is no *we*."

Adrian leaned back. "I see. Then you called us here tonight with the intention of choosing one of us for the position. Very good, my lord. Though it is out of my usual line of work, I will be happy to accept."

Beside him, Sophia made a sound of protest. "Of all the arrogant, egotistical men I have met—and I assure you, Lord Smythe, there have been many—you have, by far, the most swollen head."

Lord Liverpool raised a brow, and Adrian stared at his wife. Where the devil had this little hellion come from? She'd never so much as raised her voice to him before.

"I do not have a swollen head," he said, attempting to remain calm. "I am merely stating the obvious. You are a woman and should therefore have no part in this investigation. We are dealing with a murder, and that is a subject not fit for female discussion."

Sophia sputtered indignantly, and Liverpool said, "So, Lord Smythe, you believe because you are a man you should automatically be given the assignment."

"Of course. You cannot possibly think to choose a woman over a man for this assignment or reinstatement into the Barbican group."

Liverpool looked thoughtful. "And yet, I asked Lady Smythe here tonight. She comes very highly recommended, and by your own Lord Melbourne, as well as other agents."

"That may be," Adrian said, rising to his feet, "but this is a job for a man. Lady Smythe should go home and focus on what is important—my home."

Sophia jumped to her feet. "What home? We

barely live there and certainly take great pains to avoid one another on the rare occasion when we are both in residence. We don't have any children and never will."

"Now wait a moment—"

But Sophia would not be deterred. "And might I remind you, sir, the year is 1815, not 1515. Women have rights. I am in every way your equal, and in this instance, I am your superior. My training and skills are unsurpassed, my exemplary service for the Barbican group undisputed. No one has my instincts and intuition."

Adrian stepped closer to her. "Instincts and intuition? Those are not skills." He was towering over her, purposely attempting to make her back down.

She didn't. She put her hands on her hips and glared up at him. He ignored her defiance. "You are my wife, and I will not have you involved in this work. You are to go home and wait for me there. Leave immediately."

But instead of acquiescing, she laughed, throwing her hands up as though he were an exasperating child. "I'm not going anywhere except to begin my investigation of this case."

"Not if I begin it before you."

"You two are worse than the bloody Parliament!" Liverpool roared, stepping between them. "I have half a mind to choose someone else entirely and send both of you home."

Adrian glared at Sophia. If he lost this assignment, there would be hell to pay.

"But I am not going to do that."

Adrian practically sighed with relief.

"And I have made my decision."

Adrian's head shot up, and he straightened. Now she'd see where her place was.

Liverpool gave both of them slow, stern looks. "Before I announce my decision, I want to make it clear I do not have time to arbitrate domestic disputes, so there will be no argument. My decision is final. Is that understood?"

Adrian glanced at Sophia. She was looking right back at him. And when Liverpool cleared his throat, he saw her nod grudgingly. Adrian did the same.

"Good," the prime minister gripped his hands behind his back. "You are obviously both talented operatives who deserve a position in the Barbican group. I can choose only one of you, but that does not mean the decision has to be made today."

Adrian frowned. "But—"

Liverpool raised a hand. "To that end, a little competition never hurt anyone." He looked at the two of them and seemed to reconsider. "Well, it never has in the past. I believe, in this case, competition could be beneficial. Therefore, I am assigning both of you to my brother's case. The operative who solves the murder of my brother first will be reinstated into the Barbican group. The other operative receives nothing. That is my decision. Do you understand it?"

"Yes, sir," Sophia answered with a huge smile.

Adrian shook his head, tried to clear it. Liverpool couldn't be serious. He couldn't actually expect Adrian to share this assignment with a woman.

"Lord Smythe?" Liverpool asked. "Am I understood?"

Adrian gritted his teeth and ground out, "Yes, my lord."

"Good." The prime minister gathered his hat from where it had fallen in his haste to rise. "Then I shall expect my first briefing at Lord Dewhurst's ball. Good night, and do not fail me."

Adrian watched as the man disappeared into the darkness. A moment later, the assistant returned to collect the chairs and the lantern.

And then Adrian was thrust into the shadows. Beside him, his wife, his competition, pulled on her mantle and sighed. "I declined the invitation to Dewhurst's ball."

"You'll have to call on Lady Dewhurst. Say it was a misunderstanding."

"The invitation was addressed to both of us. You should call on Lord Dewhurst and accept."

He shook his head. "Don't be ridiculous. Everyone knows wives handle correspondence and invitations. You—"

"*I* am thoroughly exasperated."

He could see the outline of her hand as it cut through the gloom.

"How are we to work together to solve a murder," she continued, "when we can't even settle a benign domestic issue? This is never going to work."

"Of course it's not going to work. I propose—"

"I'm leaving."

"You're not going out alone at this time of night in this part of town."

"Watch me." She strode out of the room, and he heard the door creak closed behind her. He had just enough pride to stay where he was. He wasn't going to chase after her.

But he had another idea.

Six

SOPHIA STEPPED INTO THE LIBRARY AND SILENTLY closed the French doors behind her. She latched and secured them, though she knew it was scant protection against intruders. She found the lock easy enough to pick.

She waited a moment for her eyes to adjust to the darkness in the room. The town house was silent but for the occasional creak and settling. She could hear the tall case clock in the library's corner ticking quietly, and it soothed her as much as the room's smell of leather and musk.

She realized it smelled like Adrian.

It was after two in the morning, and as easy as it would be to assume no one in the house stirred, she knew that was a mistake. Adrian could be here. Waiting for her.

She'd left him in the dilapidated building in the East End and found her own way home. He hadn't been happy when she'd walked away in the middle of their tiff, but he hadn't come after her, either.

Not that he would have caught her.

But if she had been caught, would that have been so bad?

Yes, she told herself as she stomped through the library. *Yes*.

This turn of events, this revelation of her true identity, was a horrible mistake. It was going to change everything. She could already see Adrian was going to behave as a typical man and try to keep her from her work. She expected no less from him or from any man.

But his attitude would make this investigation difficult. And it would make life difficult. She had the feeling Adrian would not be so easy to avoid from now on.

She cracked the inner library door, scanned the adjoining music room and, seeing it was clear, stole past the pianoforte and the music stands housing her much-neglected sheet music. She walked silently, used to secretly climbing the dark staircase in the wee hours, knowing which floorboards creaked and which nooks servants might use for late-night rendezvous.

When she reached the second floor, she paused outside her bedroom door and glanced down the hallway. Adrian's bedroom was on the opposite side, two doors down.

She remembered being relieved when, after they married, Adrian had not insisted she take the room adjoining his. Having her room across the hall gave her much more freedom of movement on nights like tonight. Now she saw it gave Adrian equal freedom.

She was tempted to listen at his door to determine if he'd arrived home yet, but she decided against it.

She'd had enough confrontations with her husband tonight. Safer and more practical to slip into her own room, lock the door, and make plans for beginning her investigation tomorrow.

It wasn't that she didn't trust herself, she thought as she slipped the key to her bedroom from her pocket and put it in the keyhole. Nothing would occur if she was standing outside Adrian's room and he happened to open the door.

Shirtless.

Hair tousled.

The same smoky look in his eyes he'd given her earlier tonight when she'd removed her mantle.

She opened her bedroom door and checked that the trap she left had not been sprung. It was still full of ink, so she disabled it, closed the door, and leaned her forehead against the hard wood frame. She felt almost breathless remembering Adrian's gaze on her. He'd acted as though she were stripping bare, when, in reality, underneath the mantle she wore her gown, her shift, her petticoats, and her stockings.

She hadn't been the least bit indecent. And yet, she couldn't remember Adrian ever looking at her like that, even when she had been indecent before him.

She hadn't known he had heat like that in him. She hadn't known it would cause something akin to a volcanic eruption in her. Her belly was still full of tremors and flutters. Now they tickled their way down, settling into a low throbbing ache between her legs.

She almost groaned aloud before she managed to push the desire away. He was another spy. A competitor. This attraction for him was nothing more than weakness and, like any weakness that might interfere with an assignment, it had to be dismantled and destroyed.

Now she need have but one thought—to change from these damp, filthy clothes and into something clean and warm. She stepped back from the door and reached for the tie of her mantle. She yanked on the cord once, and then her hands stilled. With effort, she kept them from shaking.

She wasn't alone.

She didn't know how she knew; it was a whisper of her intuition in her ear. Anyone else would have shaken it off as paranoia, but all of Sophia's senses snapped to attention.

Her eyes darted to the trap by the door—a simple string and pulley a child could rig.

"Simple but effective," a man's voice said from behind her.

Sophia whirled and watched Adrian rise from where he'd been reclining on her bed. The moonlight filtering through her curtains illuminated his face, which, to her annoyance, was free of ink. "Obviously not effective enough, my lord." Another glance at the trap confirmed the ink that should have sprayed all over any intruder was still intact and untouched.

Damn it!

Adrian spread his hands. He had already changed into a clean shirt and breeches. How had he made it back so quickly? "It's a bit amateurish. Easy to circumnavigate."

"Apparently." Her hands were still at her throat, and she realized now they were clutching her mantle close to her skin. She did not think it wise to remove the outer garment with Adrian in her bedroom, so near to her bed, but she could see he was watching her—his eyes alert for any sign of weakness. If she continued to clutch the mantle to her throat, he was going to find what he sought.

She forced her stiff fingers to tug the mantle's cords again then allowed the garment to slip from her shoulders. She would have turned away from him, but she didn't trust him enough. As the heavy garment slid off, revealing her evening gown, she realized how seductive the gesture probably appeared.

She hadn't meant it to be so, but Adrian's eyes grew dark. "It's been a long time since I've been in this room," he said, voice low and husky. Her throat went dry, and she tried to ignore the blood pounding through her veins. Suddenly, she was too warm, scorched by Adrian's hot gaze.

"A long time," she agreed, fumbling with the mantle. "Um, eleven months, two weeks, and four days." She dropped the mantle. "Or something like that," she added, knowing it was too late, knowing she had given herself away.

Adrian tensed then moved closer. "I had no idea you were counting."

She shook her head, angry at herself and angry at him. She supposed he was laughing at her now, imagining her to be some pathetic, needy woman. In the months since their last encounter, he had probably bedded every barmaid from London to Rome, while she had been faithful to him.

The more fool she, to honor marriage vows that were little more than lies.

"I'm good with numbers," she said flippantly. "I remember dates and times whether I want to or not."

She bent to retrieve her mantle, and he moved closer. She could feel the heat of his body and her own body tingled in response to Adrian's nearness. She rose slowly, taking the time to breathe deeply. "If you don't mind, I think I'll go to bed now, my lord."

"Oh, really?" He raised a brow.

She gave him a tight smile. "Alone."

"Ah. That might have to wait. I have several matters I'd like to discuss with you, not the least of which is your running off tonight and—"

She raised a hand to silence him. "I don't want to discuss that or anything else tonight." She moved past him on the pretense of shaking out her mantle. In truth, she needed space so she could catch her breath and form a coherent thought. She tossed the mantle over a mahogany armchair upholstered in pale lavender and ivory silk. Wonderful. Now the chair's upholstery would need to be cleaned, as well. She sighed. Taking a moment to glance about the room, she tried to see it as he might: the lilac walls, the lavender coverlet and curtains, the silver knobs and accents. The violets in a pretty pot on the windowsill—at least she'd succeeded in growing something.

"I-I don't want to argue with you," she said, keeping her face averted. "I don't want to fight anymore."

It was true. She was weary in body and spirit. She didn't think she was up to yet another battle of words and will.

She felt Adrian's solid presence behind her, his heat tickling her back. "Then let's not fight."

His fingers traced a lazy path down the back of her neck, and she couldn't stop a delicious shiver from zinging through her body. Lord, but his hands were so warm. She hadn't realized she was cold until he'd touched her. Then again, his touch had always been a revelation to her.

She was a confident, happy, independent woman. She had more money than she needed, servants to cater to her, and she was one of the best operatives in England.

But whenever Adrian touched her, her cloak of lies was ripped away. She was lonely; she was cold; she was desperate for affection—no, desperate for Adrian's affection.

Much as she denied it, even to herself, her husband was a glaring chink in her armor. When Adrian touched her, she forgot how much her work mattered to her. She forgot she was supposed to be happy and independent. She forgot everything but the need to turn into him, to embrace him and give herself to him.

Of course, she'd never allowed herself to do it. To give herself to him would make her vulnerable—very well, more vulnerable than she already was to him. King and country demanded she keep her identity secret, even from those closest to her.

Her own heart demanded it as well. She couldn't afford to forget Henry. Her poor brother had paid the price for his imprudence. Even now, years after his murder, a lump rose in her throat when she thought of him. She'd needed his advice countless times over the years, needed his friendship. Instead, she'd struggled through the darkest times alone.

She looked at Adrian. Even in their most intimate moments, her secrets and walls kept her isolated from him. But keeping Adrian at a distance during their infrequent episodes of lovemaking had been a struggle that hadn't diminished even after years of marriage.

And now, now she stood here, after a night when one of her deepest secrets had been laid bare to him, and tried to think why she should keep fighting him.

His touch was light and feathery—playful—but she knew from experience it could also be intense and demanding. She knew from experience she liked it intense and demanding.

His fingers breezed along her neck, caressing her chin and moving down her collarbone. She couldn't stop her eyelids from fluttering closed. Her head wanted to loll back, to find respite against his broad shoulder, but she resisted the impulse.

She knew she should also tell him to stop touching her, to stop the inevitable path of his fingers down her bodice, but her lips were paralyzed. Her body was paralyzed by his fingertips—those tender, teasing, slightly roughened fingertips.

She shuddered.

"Do you want this?" His voice rasped in her ear like a cat's tongue against silky fur. "Do you want me?"

She wanted to say no, to deny all she was feeling, but her body seemed disconnected from her mind. No, that wasn't quite true. Her flesh was *blatantly* disregarding her brain's better judgment.

Adrian's fingers dipped into her bodice to brush lightly over the swells of her breasts. She felt her flesh heat in response, and her legs wobbled.

"Tell me you want me, Sophia."

Her name. It sounded like a foreign language on his tongue. She couldn't remember the last time she'd heard him use it in that seductive tone.

"Tell me," he whispered, his hand cupping her breast. His touch was becoming more persuasive, more compelling. She knew she wouldn't be able to resist much longer.

"I-I can't," she said, voice strained and urgent. Voice mirroring what her body was experiencing.

"Three words," he said. His breath tickled her neck, sending new shivers of pleasure rippling through her. "Three words, and you can have what you want."

Before she could concede or protest, the hand that had been on her back went to work. He loosened several fastenings at the back of her dress so it slipped down her shoulders. The bodice gaped, and he pushed it down. The room was dark, lit only by moonlight and the banked fire, and still the thin material of her chemise and stays seemed scant protection against the power of his gaze.

She couldn't even see him, and yet she could feel his eyes on her. She heard his soft intake of breath as he freed one breast from the confines of her stays. His finger brushed over her nipple, and Sophia couldn't suppress a tiny moan.

That was all it took. Whatever control Adrian had been exercising seemed to shatter. Roughly, he spun her around in his arms. She barely had time to find her balance before his lips were on hers. His tongue invaded her mouth while his hands plundered her body.

And she loved it. She reveled in it.

She wanted more.

His hands had freed both her breasts now, and her nipples were so hard they throbbed. She felt his thumb brush over one, and she gasped into his mouth. His response was to pull her close, cradling his erection against her belly.

He was hard. Rock hard, and he wanted her to know.

She moved her hips, giving him the response he wanted. His reaction was a low growl. He pulled away, and when he looked down at her, his eyes were liquid silver in the darkness. His face was a plane of light and shadow, and a wicked smile played on his lips.

She opened her mouth, tried to speak, to say no. Her mind was still screaming at her to tell him no, to stop this plunge into madness. Instead, she stepped back slightly and arched her back, offering herself to him.

Lord, what was she thinking? Why was she behaving so recklessly? She should be pushing him away. But when his hands circled her waist and he lowered his mouth to her breasts, all she could do was whimper with pleasure.

His tongue stroked her, slicked over her sensitive skin, teasing her nipples until they ached with pleasure. He attended to one and then the other, his skillful fingers—he'd always had such skillful fingers—ministering to that ache. And just when she knew she couldn't take any more, his lips brought her to new heights. He took one nipple into his mouth and sucked.

Sophia cried out at the pleasure slamming through her. She had known it would be like this. Had known when she finally surrendered to him there would be no going back.

And still her mind screamed warnings. She knew where this could lead. She knew the heartbreak of that empty cradle. Sophia tried to heed the warnings, but the feel of Adrian's lips on her was too much. She couldn't think, couldn't speak, could only experience.

And then he claimed her mouth again, and she tasted on his lips the orange-scented soap she used. "I want you," he said between kisses. "And I know you want me, too."

She shook her head, her mind making a last bid for restraint. "I don't. We can't."

"Yes, we can, Sophia," Adrian said. "We should."

"No, we sh—" she began, but she was having trouble concentrating. His lips were nuzzling her neck, and she couldn't seem to form the words she wanted.

"I'm your husband," he murmured, his hands pulling her close so she could feel that glorious erection against her belly again. "Trust me. Obey me. Kiss—"

But it was too late. Sophia's spine went rigid, and she pushed back.

Away from him.

With a quick yank, she covered herself, holding the silk material of her gown over her breasts.

"What the hell—?"

"Get out," she spat. "Get out now."

He stared at her, appearing perplexed. Ha! She should have guessed he'd be an excellent actor.

"Sophia." He reached for her, but she stepped out of his grasp. "What's wrong? I only wanted—"

"To control me? To bend me to your will? To take my place in the Barbican group?"

Now his expression hardened. "I don't know what you mean."

"Oh, I'm sure you don't." She backed up again, wanting to put as much space between them as possible. As though physical space would diminish the pain lancing through her at his betrayal. "'I'm your husband,'" she mimicked him. "'Obey me.' Next you'll be telling me to stay home while you steal my position in the Barbican group, just like you stole Ducos."

A muscle in his jaw ticked. "I didn't steal Ducos from you, and I wasn't going to tell you to stay home."

She raised a brow.

"All right." He spread his arms. "I wasn't going to tell you that right now. I honestly wasn't thinking of anything other than…"

"Getting me into bed?"

He was silent.

"And then what? Lure me into some warm cocoon of lovemaking, and when you'd done your best to make me think I was half in love with you, you'd wheedle a promise from me to stay away from the case?"

She saw a quick flicker of something flit across his face—something akin to anger—and then it was gone. "That's what you think of me?" His voice was even, no note of accusation, but she felt it all the same.

Was it possible she'd been wrong about his intentions? He hadn't planned to use their lovemaking against her?

She shook her head, shook her doubt off. It didn't matter. She should never have trusted him anyway. It seemed that was a mistake she was doomed to repeat, even though she knew the consequences: trust someone, and they inevitably betrayed you. Look at what had happened to Henry! She clenched her fists, fighting the pain.

Adrian was no different. In fact, he had more reason to betray her than most. He wanted that position in the Barbican group as much as she.

And yet, he was her husband. She wished she could trust him, wished she could believe there had been no strategy behind his seduction.

And if she believed that, then she deserved to be betrayed by him.

It was time she saw him as the threat he was. Her feelings for him made her vulnerable, which meant she had to keep him at bay. If he ever realized the depth of her desire for him, there was no question he would use it to his advantage. He could end her career and destroy her heart in one swift blow.

"What I think of you is of no consequence," Sophia finally replied. "We're competitors. I think it best we associate as little as possible." She turned away from him and adjusted her clothing again. She couldn't fasten and secure the various layers and undergarments without the aid of her maid, but she managed to cover herself securely. Then she lit the candles on her dresser and, ignoring Adrian, began to sort through her brushes as though preparing for her nightly toilette.

After a moment, she glanced over her shoulder, the

look on her face intentionally impatient. "Was there something else?"

He'd crossed his arms over his chest, and the glint in his eyes could only be described as fierce. Her heart stuttered when she saw that look, but she kept her expression scornful.

"I'm not a servant to be dismissed, Sophia."

"Please don't refer to me so intimately."

"Oh, I'm going to do more than that." He took a step closer, into the light of the candles, and she took a shaky breath. Yes, he was good and angry now. She could see that. But better he was angry than aroused. Anger she could deal with.

"You want things to go back to the way they were? Me on one side of the house, you on the other?"

"Splendid proposal, my lord. I recommend we institute it immediately."

"Why so eager to draw the battle lines, Sophia?" He moved closer.

"I told you not to—"

"What are you afraid of?" He was so close now she could have kissed him with very little effort.

She turned her head away. "Don't flatter yourself. You don't frighten me."

"Good, because while you may want to keep me at arm's length, I subscribe to a different theory—keep your friends close, and your enemies closer."

"I see." She was having trouble breathing again. The way he was looking at her was not at all congruous with his tone. His eyes were burning into her, all but daring her to resist touching him again. "I see," she said again, hating the breathlessness in her voice.

"I doubt it, but you will. I'm going to keep you close, Sophia." He reached out and stroked a lock of her loose hair. Wrapping it around his finger, he tugged gently, pulling her a whisper from his lips. "So close you'll think we're the same person. We'll eat together, sleep together, breathe together. You're mine. Again. Always."

Seven

ADRIAN WATCHED SOPHIA'S DARK EYES GO DARKER yet. He could tell his nearness affected her. She wanted him. Badly.

Gently she lifted one arm and cupped the back of his neck. A simple gesture, and yet, he could feel himself growing hard all over again. Another kiss, another one of those urgent moans from her lips, and he would be unable to stop himself from laying her down on that bed and plunging into her.

She leaned close, her cheek against his, her lips touching his ear. "Get. Out. Now."

Not exactly the words he'd been longing to hear. She pushed away from him, which wasn't exactly the response he'd been yearning for, either.

"You don't like my proposal?" he said, talking to her back as she moved away from him. "Abandon this case. Then I won't have to worry about you."

She spun to face him. "*Worry* about me?" She closed her eyes in what appeared to be disgust. "The only thing you need worry about is that position in the Barbican group, because I'm not giving it up."

Damn it. Why the hell did she have to be so unreasonable? And why did she have to be so damn tempting? Even now, when he needed all his faculties to argue with her, he couldn't stop thinking how to get her into bed.

He gripped the back of her small desk chair, a delicate three-legged armchair with claw feet. If he sat in it, he'd probably flatten it. "Sophia, listen to logic."

She raised a brow—never a good sign from a woman.

"No, never mind logic. Listen to your husband. I don't want you involved in this case. In any cases from now on. It's not safe. Had I known you were involved before, I would have put an end to it."

"Oh, really? You think you have that authority?"

"I *am* your husband."

"And I married you only because I couldn't move up in the ranks otherwise. I was an operative before you knew me. I worked for the Foreign Office long before I met you."

He stared at her. He didn't believe it. Her father would never have permitted it.

"My father not only allowed it—that's what you were thinking, was it not?—he encouraged me."

"But how—?"

"You've heard of the Black Baron?"

He narrowed his eyes at her. "Of course. It makes for a good story. A myth, nothing more."

"No. My father was the Black Baron."

Adrian almost snorted, but something in her eyes made him swallow the sound. Peter Carlisle, Baron Carlisle, was the Black Baron? He shook his head. "I don't believe it."

"Why? Because he doesn't look the part?"

Adrian didn't like to admit it, but that was a large component of his reasoning. Sophia's father was a small, thin, unassuming man. He wore spectacles and disappeared into his library whenever company called. Soft-spoken, the baron avoided confrontation of any kind. Peter Carlisle was the furthest thing from a spy that Adrian could imagine. "It's not possible," Adrian said finally.

"Just like it's not possible that I was in London's East End tonight. That I beat you in combat—"

"You didn't beat me."

"Ask yourself how I know Lord Liverpool so well. Ask yourself how I became involved in the Barbican group."

Damn it! Everything she said made sense, and he was acting like an amateur who judged on appearance alone. But if what she said was true, she'd been raised by one of the best spies England had to offer. Was spying a family business for her? Exactly how long had she been an operative?

"Since I was twelve," she answered.

He scowled at her. "Stop doing that. Stop reading my mind."

She gave a dainty shrug. "I can't help it. It's one of my many talents."

"If I didn't want you to know what I was thinking, you wouldn't."

She didn't argue.

How could she? After all, for five years now, she'd known nothing of his life as Agent Wolf.

And he'd known nothing of her life as Agent…?

What was her code name? Did Melbourne know of her? Adrian knew there were some agents whose identities were secret, even from the secretary.

Adrian suddenly felt bone-weary. Pushing the chair aside, he made his way to her bed and sat, head in his hands. The spot behind his eyes throbbed. All this new information, all of these revelations were too much.

"You may retire to your own room at any time," Sophia said, voice full of ice.

Adrian ignored her. He'd leave when he was good and ready, and that wasn't going to be before he'd accomplished at least one of his objectives: end her career or get her naked and into bed with him.

An image of his hands cupping her ripe breasts flashed in his mind, and his mouth went dry. He clenched his hands.

Pull yourself together, Adrian.

First things first: make her forget about pursuing this position in the Barbican group.

He looked up at her, tried not to notice how swollen her lips were from his earlier kisses, tried not to notice the flush on her cheeks or the way her hair fell over one shoulder in chestnut curls made fiery by light from the hearth. She looked back at him, and he wished he hadn't noticed the stubbornness in those chocolate eyes. This was not going to be easy.

Perhaps if he convinced her to work with him…

He glanced down again to hide a smile. Yes, if he convinced her to work *with* him, then he could give her some safe, time-consuming work, and he could take the dangerous part. He'd solve the case before she even had a chance to realize what happened.

And if that didn't work—well, there was always Plan B.

Adrian groaned inwardly. He really hoped he didn't have to use Plan B. He glanced up at her. "You want me to leave?"

She raised a brow in that cheeky way he was beginning to like.

"Then say you won't pursue Liverpool's investigation."

She sighed. "You're wasting your time."

He pretended to acquiesce. "Fine. Then say you'll work with me."

She stared at him, openmouthed, and Adrian knew he'd surprised her. Good. He'd have to keep her guessing at his every move.

She was shaking her head. "That won't work. There's only one position in the group."

"So we work together on the initial investigation and part ways when it comes to the actual apprehension. Best man—er, operative—wins."

"I prefer to work alone."

So did he. "Rubbish. What is it people always say? Two heads are better than one?"

Adrian stood and moved closer to her, a tactic designed to rattle her. It had the added benefit of putting him in close enough proximity to catch her citrus scent. God, he hoped she agreed soon, so he could move on to his second objective. Her bed looked extremely inviting.

"Not when one of the heads is yours. I don't like arrogant men."

"And I don't like stubborn women, but I think we could help each other."

She let out a bark of laughter. "And how exactly can you help me, Lord Smythe?"

"You're forgetting I was the man who snatched Ducos from under your nose. Obviously I have some talent."

He could tell by the way she narrowed her eyes he'd snagged her interest. The Ducos affair still bothered her.

Good, he could use that to his advantage. "Aren't you wondering how I knew where to find Ducos when everyone else, including the top echelons of the Barbican, was certain he'd returned to France?"

"*I* didn't think he'd returned to France."

Adrian inclined his head. "See, already we think alike."

She couldn't stop a smile then. He knew he was being a bit audacious, but he could also tell she liked it.

"Very well. If we think so much alike, if we're the perfect team—as you want me to believe—then tell me how you knew where to find Ducos that night."

"Good question." And it was, but his answer might reveal more than he wanted. On the other hand, caution hadn't worked for him thus far. Perhaps he ought to try disclosure. He leaned one shoulder against the wall, effectively cornering her. She didn't move away, but Adrian felt her tense at his nearness.

"Simple answer," he said. "I put myself in Ducos's boots. I read every letter from his hand we'd intercepted. I talked extensively with those who had come into contact with him. I made a detailed chart of every sighting we'd had of him for the past six weeks, and I logged each on a map. Then I compiled all the evidence, and the conclusion was obvious."

"Was it?"

"Yes. Ducos had no reason to return to France. He'd planted the rumor because he knew we were getting close to him, and he wanted to throw us off the scent. It almost worked."

She nodded, evidently impressed by his thorough, detailed analysis. "So, basically, you were lucky."

Adrian gaped at her. "Lucky?"

"Yes. You don't really believe in all that mapping and charting, do you? You had a feeling, and you followed it."

"A feeling." He clenched one fist and then relaxed it. "Is that how you knew Ducos hadn't left for Paris? A *feeling*?" Now who was the lucky one, eh?

"No, I knew Ducos hadn't left for Paris the same way I knew Turnbull was hiding in Amsterdam." She must have seen his eyes widen at the name of the infamous double agent, because she added, "Yes, it was I who captured him, and I didn't need a map or a chart. I used a spy's true weapon—instinct."

Adrian barked out a laugh. "So basically, *you* were lucky. *You* had a *feeling*."

She gave him a long, disapproving look. "I didn't have a feeling. I used instinct."

"What's the difference?"

"Instinct is a skill, sharpened and honed. Instinct is what tells you to ask an informer one more question. It's what tells you to duck during a fight to avoid a blow. It's what led me to Ducos."

"Preparation is what tells an agent the questions to ask an informer, practice tells him to duck, and luck is what led you to Ducos." He leaned in close to speak the last few words, close enough to see the sprinkle of freckles on her nose. They were light, almost invisible on her otherwise porcelain complexion.

"Are you saying you never think on your feet?"

He shrugged. "Rarely necessary. I always have a plan."

"But what do you do, sir, when you encounter a situation for which you have no plan?"

He frowned. "Never happens. I have a plan for every contingency."

She shook her head. "Impossible."

"Not impossible. Effective. It worked with Ducos, and it will work to capture Jenkinson's killer."

"That I would like to see."

Adrian knew an opportunity when it arose. "Be my guest, but I must say you are not an ideal partner. I need someone who can strategize and plan. Someone with an analytical mind. That's obviously not you." And yet he intended to keep her busy—and out of danger—analyzing maps and letters and anything else he could get his hands on that related to Jenkinson. She might not catch Jenkinson's assailant, but he'd teach her something about strategy and analysis.

She'd probably end up thanking him.

"Capturing Jenkinson's killer will require intuition and quick thinking. I need a partner who is flexible and dependable. That, sir, is obviously not you."

"Would you like me to prove you wrong?"

"I can think of no better amusement than to watch you try."

"Good, then it's settled. We meet first thing in the morning to discuss strategy."

She shook her head. "We meet first thing in the morning and see where our intuition leads us."

He gave her a tight smile then reached out and wrapped one of her curls around his finger. "In the meantime, there are other matters I'd like to settle."

She raised a brow. "And what might those be?"

He leaned in to kiss her, but she stepped back. He followed, and she moved just out of his reach again. He frowned. "I'm not in the mood for games."

"And I'm not playing a game, my lord. I asked you to leave."

He scowled, anger churning inside him. He knew she wanted him, damn it. Why was she refusing? Was he so repulsive? Did she feel nothing for him? "I'm not leaving."

"Fine." She scooped up her mantle. "Then I will." She made to sweep past him, but he caught her arm.

He felt her stiffen and instantly released her. Good God. Even his touch repulsed her. "I'll go. You've made it clear my advances are distasteful." He turned, walked to the door.

"Adrian."

He stopped, hand on the handle. She never used his name. Never.

"Your advances… you aren't distasteful. I just—I can't do it all again." Her voice wavered, the first sign of emotion she'd shown.

He looked at her. She was staring at him, fists clenched.

"Do it all again? What does that mean?" He'd never even known her before. Tonight felt like a new beginning.

She frowned at him, the gesture indicating he should have known what she referred to. "The pregnancies," she said, her voice wavering. "The losses. I can't go through that again."

He wanted to go to her, then. He wanted to hold her, kiss her, cradle her. He wanted, more than anything, to take away the pain he saw in her eyes. He hadn't been able to do it at the time. He'd felt inept and incompetent. He'd taken assignments instead of staying with her, grieving with her. He'd thought she'd do better without him near. But he could see now she'd been more hurt by the losses than she had let him, perhaps anyone, see.

"Sophia, I—" But what could he say? He didn't know what to say. *It won't happen again?* But how could he know that? It had happened three times. And then she'd shut her door to him.

And tonight he hadn't been thinking about the consequences of their lovemaking. He just wanted her. She was his wife. He was entitled to want her. But now he saw it wasn't so simple, not for either of them.

He thought of Cordelia's congratulations. "Then I take it you're not...?"

"No." She closed her eyes. "Cordelia is a fool."

"Yes." He moved closer to her, but the look in her eyes warned him not to try and touch her. "I know the past was... painful." God, he sounded like an idiot. How did one have a conversation like this? He was no good at it. Still, he must stumble forward. "But we don't know what the future holds. Things might be different next time." He wanted to be a father, the kind of father he'd never had. "I'd like a child."

"And you think I don't? You think I didn't want those children with every fiber of my being? You think I didn't take every conceivable precaution when I suspected there was even the slightest possibility I could be with child?" Her voice rose, and tears sparkled on her lashes, but she shook her head, swiped at her eyes, and swallowed. "Perhaps we're not meant to be parents. Lord knows we're no good at being husband and wife. How much worse would we be at raising children?"

He sighed. Should he agree? Argue? Remain silent?

He wanted to say he thought she'd be a wonderful mother. She was so patient. She could sit through an entire opera and appear interested. And she was thoughtful. Somehow she knew all the servants' birthdays and remembered when he'd be home for dinner and had Cook prepare his favorite meals. She took care of everything and everyone. She'd dote on a child. But would she want to hear such words? Thankfully, she spoke again.

"In any case, we're both tired. This isn't a discussion we need have tonight."

"I'll leave you, then." Or should he offer to stay? What if she didn't want to be alone? But if he offered, would she assume he was trying to bed her again? He was a capable, intelligent man. Give him a spy to track or a missive to decode, and he went to work without hesitation. But right now, right here, he felt flustered and useless.

She nodded. "Good night."

"Good night." She opened the door for him, and he walked through it. But when he turned to say something—he knew not what—*something*, God help him—she'd closed the door. He stood and stared at the dark wood paneling and wondered where he'd gone wrong.

Again.

Eight

SOPHIA STOOD ACROSS FROM THE HONORABLE, NOW the deceased, George Jenkinson's town house and watched the flurry of activity. Apparently, a mere three weeks after her husband's murder, Mrs. Jenkinson was at home to callers. A steady stream of ladies went in and out of the modest dwelling. Mr. Jenkinson had been half brother to the prime minister and the second son of an earl, which meant the Jenkinsons had a large social circle. They were not members of the *ton*'s upper echelons, but Sophia recognized many of the ladies who called as wives of the wealthy and titled.

She was not acquainted with the Jenkinsons, but she'd come to call, nonetheless. And she'd come alone. Adrian might prefer plans and strategies, but she was one for action. As the closest person to the victim, Mrs. Jenkinson was the logical place to begin. So when Sophia's butler, Wallace, had come to inform her Lord Smythe awaited her in the dining room, she'd merely nodded, gone downstairs, and slipped out the kitchen door. Cook didn't even blink.

She didn't sneak away—and wasn't *sneak* too strong

a word?—because she was afraid to face Adrian. It wasn't because she was embarrassed at the way she'd behaved the night before. She'd revealed far too much, let him see a part of her she didn't allow anyone to see. No, that wasn't it. She'd avoided him because she wanted reinstatement into the Barbican group. Sitting around, planning, making maps and charts wouldn't get her position back. Let Adrian waste his time strategizing. In the meantime, she would solve the murder.

She started across the street then gaped at the man approaching the door at the same time as she. He was dressed in a beaver hat, tailcoat, simply tied cravat, waistcoat, trousers, and polished black boots ending at the knee. He made quite the handsome picture—a picture she didn't want to see. Sophia hurried and intercepted him before he could start up the steps. "What are *you* doing here?"

Adrian looked down at the hand on the sleeve of his gray morning coat, and she quickly removed it.

"I might ask you the same question, madam. We had an appointment this morning."

Sophia pursed her lips. "I thought I would be of more use to the investigation if I called on Mrs. Jenkinson. That would leave you free to plan our next move."

He cocked a brow. "Or you thought you'd solve the murder before me and take my place in the Barbican group."

It was *her* place, but she didn't want to begin that argument again. "Whatever my motivations and whatever your plans, we have both come to the same conclusion. Mrs. Jenkinson needs to be interrogated—er, questioned. You can't be the one to do so."

"Why not? I *questioned* Lucien Ducos."

Sophia resisted the urge to smack him with her reticule and, instead, smiled sweetly. "Yes, but Mrs. Jenkinson is not a criminal, and, as far as I know, you have never been introduced to Mrs. Jenkinson."

He seemed undeterred. "I'll tell her Lord Liverpool sent me."

She blinked. "You can't do that."

"Why not?"

"Do you want her to know we're investigating this murder? What if she killed him? We'll get more out of her if she isn't on guard."

Adrian frowned at her. She was used to that frown. "You think Mrs. Jenkinson killed—?"

"Stop." Sophia held up a hand. "Women are just as capable as men of murder. You can't dismiss her simply because of her gender."

"Very well, point taken. But I don't see why it matters if she knows I'm looking into the case. This isn't a mission for the Foreign Office. I'm not acting as Agent Wolf."

"Agent Wolf?" Sophia felt her jaw drop. "*You're* Agent Wolf?"

"You've heard of me?"

Oh, yes, she'd heard of him. And she'd been so impressed with what she'd heard, she'd actually wanted to meet him. Once, perhaps twice—but only when she was very bored, sitting in a carriage, waiting hours for an informant or some other monotonous task—she'd even fantasized about what would happen when she did meet him. She'd tell him she was Agent Saint, and he'd take her hand, kiss it, look into her eyes, and say, "I know all about you. You're the best agent we have."

And she'd argue he was the best. And he'd say she was undeniably the most beautiful. And oh, her cheeks flamed in embarrassment at how ridiculous it all seemed now she was standing in front of Agent Wolf, and it had been Adrian all the time!

Adrian, who did not tell her she was the best agent the Barbican group had to offer. Adrian, who told her to stay home so she wouldn't stub her toe.

"I heard something about you," she muttered.

"Who were you?" he asked.

Oh, no. She wasn't about to tell him. What if he'd never heard of Saint? What if all he'd heard was how she muddled that affair in Paris? One mistake. She'd made just one in her entire career, and she never forgot it. No matter that her record since then was flawless. No matter Paris had been one of her first missions for the Barbican group. She still remembered Paris. She wasn't about to take the chance Adrian— Agent *Wolf*—knew about Paris.

She shook her head. "Let's focus on the task at hand. One of us needs to question Mrs. Jenkinson. I think it should be me. She and I are both members of the Benevolent Society for the Aid and Prosperity of Orphans."

"The what?"

"We have a common interest."

Adrian raised a brow. "Have you ever attended a

meeting of the Benevolent… Orphan Aid…?" He waved a hand. "Have you ever even been to a meeting?"

"Of course I've been to meetings." She looked away.

"Of the Benevolent Orphans?"

"It's the Benevolent Society for the Aid and Prosperity of Orphans, and no." She scowled at him. "I haven't attended one of their meetings. I was too busy saving England from certain French domination. But I do care about orphans. I do want them to prosper."

"I see."

She closed her eyes briefly. "We're wasting time."

"Agreed."

"Fine." She would show him how questioning a suspect was really done. "Let's both question Mrs. Jenkinson."

"Agreed." He took her arm. "Your dress."

Sophia blinked. "My dress?" She looked down at the pale blue-and-white-striped day dress. It was simple with an edge of white lace along the round neck and knotted tabs attached to the puff sleeves. Underneath the short sleeves, a gauzy white material extended to her wrists, where it flared. The pleated bodice had decorative buttons, giving the dress an exquisitely feminine look. She felt rather pretty and somewhat silly in such a dainty dress, but she was making calls this morning, not hiding in bushes or scaling gates.

She'd thought about wearing one of her ill-fitting ugly dresses, but what was the point? She was no longer part of the Barbican group. Adrian knew she was a spy. Who was she disguising herself for? Her days of anonymity and domestic surveillance ended when she married Adrian and joined the Barbican group. She'd maintained her mousy persona only for Adrian's benefit.

She'd pulled out a hideous brown frock this morning then stashed it away in favor of this one. She might look about seventeen, but better young than dowdy. Today she wanted to look like a woman. She wanted to look like Sophia Galloway, Viscountess Smythe. Maybe if she dressed like her, she'd know who she was.

"What of the dress?" she asked cautiously. Did she look like she was trying too hard?

"It fits, and it's fashionable," Adrian drawled.

She glanced at him, raised a brow as they started up the Jenkinson's walk. "What do you know of women's fashion?"

"Very little, thank God." His bicep tensed under her fingers. "I know what I like."

Sophia blinked, all but speechless. Adrian was not a man who gave many compliments. "Thank you," she said simply.

Adrian knocked on the town house door, and the butler answered promptly. He took both their cards and promised to return momentarily.

Sophia studied the vestibule. It was small and dark, not entirely welcoming. Did the killer enter through the vestibule that night? The stairs were just ahead. He or she could have stolen through the door, passed through the dark vestibule, and gone up the stairs without much risk of detection.

That's how she would have acted.

But how would he or she know which room

was Jenkinson's? He couldn't very well go about trying them all. Not without arousing suspicion, and Liverpool had made it clear no one had any idea who the killer might be.

If the killer had managed to enter the house and find Jenkinson without alerting Jenkinson's wife or any of the servants, that meant either the killer had been in the house before or knew the layout. Or perhaps the killer lived in the house.

The wife? The valet? Another servant? "What about the valet?" Sophia said aloud.

"The valet?" Adrian said, appearing to study the vestibule as well. She wondered what Agent Wolf saw in the cramped, gloomy room. Something she didn't? "I'll question him."

She sighed. Would everything be a struggle with him? "If you think I'm going to sit back and allow you to wrest control of this investigation from me, then—" She closed her mouth when she heard the butler's step.

"We'll discuss it later," Adrian said, gray eyes hard as steel.

"No we won't," she muttered.

"Mrs. Jenkinson is at home and will see you in the drawing room. If you'll follow me, Lord and Lady Smythe." He started up the stairs, and Sophia followed with Adrian behind her.

The drawing room, Sophia noted. Not the parlor, where the butler had sought Mrs. Jenkinson and where she had probably been entertaining her other guests. No, the drawing room was for formal callers. Which she supposed they were, being as she didn't know Lady Jenkinson from the Queen.

Well, actually, she had met the Queen…

"Lord and Lady Smythe," the butler intoned after throwing the drawing-room doors open.

Sophia stepped inside a room somewhat less gloomy than the vestibule and stared as a woman in the middle stages of pregnancy rose to greet her.

Sophia felt her heart stutter, and a great lump rose in her throat. She opened her mouth, but no words came. Nothing but a horrible groaning sound.

Quite suddenly, she felt Adrian's hand on her back. His touch was warm, steadying. He pulled her close and said, "Mrs. Jenkinson, how good to finally meet you at last. My wife tells me so much of your charitable works with the orphans."

He drew her forward, and somehow Sophia forced her legs to move closer and closer to the pregnant woman before her. She couldn't breathe, couldn't look at anything but the woman's pregnant belly, and she wanted nothing more than escape. She would have preferred to stand before a firing squad rather than remain one moment more in this woman's presence. Her brain screamed, her hands shook, and her heart pounded. Only by concentrating on the feel of Adrian's hand at her back did she remain upright.

"The orphans?" Mrs. Jenkinson looked confused, but she indicated a settee. Adrian sat and pulled Sophia down beside him.

"You and Sophia are both members of the Benevolent Society for the Aid and Prosperity of Orphans. Correct?" He looked at Sophia, playing the doting husband. "Did I make a muddle of the name again, dear?"

"Ah—" She cleared her throat. "No. That's it. Darling," she added the endearment too late. And how did he suddenly rattle off the name perfectly? She was going to have to pay closer attention to him. She kept forgetting he was Agent Wolf.

She kept forgetting everything—except Mrs. Jenkinson's condition. After the last loss, Sophia had been so careful to avoid pregnant women. Now Mrs. Jenkinson absently rubbed a hand over her belly, and Sophia felt her heart constrict. Could Mrs. Jenkinson see how Sophia longed to feel her own belly swell with child? Could Adrian see her heart breaking? She couldn't take this anymore. She had to get away.

She tried to rise, but Adrian gripped her hand and yanked her down.

"Oh, of course," Mrs. Jenkinson said. "I'm afraid I haven't attended many meetings lately. I've been in mourning."

Mourning. Of course. Her husband was dead, murdered. *Focus on the mission.*

But Adrian stepped in before Sophia's foggy mind cleared completely.

"We were saddened to hear of the death of Mr. Jenkinson. We came to offer our condolences."

"Oh, I see." The look on Mrs. Jenkinson's face clearly indicated she didn't see. "Thank you."

"It seems an awful business," Sophia said before Jenkinson's wife could turn the conversation or Adrian could snatch it out from under her again. "Were you at home that night?"

"I—ah—" The hesitation spoke volumes.

For the first time, Sophia noted Mrs. Jenkinson's

face. She should have done so upon entering the room, but she'd been too distracted by the woman's pregnancy. Now she quickly took in the whole picture. Mrs. Jenkinson was in her early thirties. She was pretty, her features refined and set by age and a little of life's experience. She'd lost the wide-eyed innocence and sweetness of youth, and it had been replaced by a calm serenity. Or perhaps that was the effect of the pregnancy. But Sophia wasn't going to think about that.

Mrs. Jenkinson had brown hair, styled simply but attractively, wide-set brown eyes framed by arched brows, and a thin but pleasant mouth. Her cheeks were rosy, but Sophia did not think she used cosmetic enhancements. Her dress was unremarkable. She wore black crepe and no jewelry or other adornment. Mrs. Jenkinson looked like the perfect grieving widow.

But she had not been home the night her husband was murdered. Her hesitation and the look of pure guilt that crossed her features said that much.

"I'm afraid I really don't want to talk about that night," the widow finally managed. "You understand."

"We do," Adrian said, voice sympathetic. "Are you close to your brother-in-law? Lord Liverpool?"

"Robert? Why?"

"We are friends of the prime minister, and he mentioned Bow Street had not yet solved your husband's murder. He asked if I—we—might look into the matter."

Sophia pursed her lips in annoyance. Now he'd only confused the poor woman.

"You?" Mrs. Jenkinson looked from him to Sophia. "Why would Robert ask you to assist?"

Adrian waved a hand. "We have experience with investigation. I take it you were not at home that night. Where were you?"

Sophia watched the widow's face, watched as she debated trusting the strangers sitting before her. Sophia knew what she had to do, hesitated, then clenched her jaw and rose. Mrs. Jenkinson sat on a chaise longue across from them, and Sophia indicated the empty space beside her. "May I?"

"Certainly, Lady Smythe."

"Please, call me Sophia." Sophia sat and tried very hard not to look at the woman's belly. "And may I call you…?"

"Millie. Yes, of course."

"Millie." Sophia took her hand. "I know this is difficult to talk about, but I assure you whatever you tell us will be kept in the strictest confidence. Lord Smythe and I have no interest in your private affairs. We only want to help." She took a chance. "Who were you with that night?"

Millie looked down, studied her hands. "I suppose it's not that much of a secret. George knew. I wouldn't say he approved, but he knew."

"Knew what?" Adrian asked.

Millie looked at Sophia. "Knew I had a lover. Knew the child wasn't his."

It took all she had within her to hold her hand steady, but Sophia managed it. She had a thousand questions, and one glance at Adrian told her he had more than he knew what to do with as well. Sophia had not done many interrogations, but the one rule she did know was to allow the suspect being interviewed to speak as much as possible. Sophia cleared her throat. "Perhaps you should explain, Millie."

Millie looked down at her skirts, smoothed the material with her free hand. Sophia squeezed her other hand reassuringly. Without looking up, Millie said, "George and I have been married ten years. It's been a happy marriage. We liked each other. George could make me laugh."

Sophia met Adrian's eyes. She couldn't remember a time he'd made her laugh. Adrian didn't look away, and Sophia was the one to break contact when Millie spoke again.

"We were happy," she repeated.

"And yet you took a lover," Adrian said softly.

Sophia wondered if he already knew the reason and, like her, needed to hear Millie Jenkinson say it—for form's sake.

"Yes. You see, George and I couldn't have children. We tried for years. Last year I turned thirty. I knew I didn't have much time left, so I took matters into my own hands. I took a lover. Not because I didn't love George. Because I needed a baby to love, too."

"Were you certain Mr. Jenkinson was the reason for your…?" Sophia stumbled, swallowed, and pushed forward. "Infertility?"

Millie shook her head. "I took a chance. As you see"—she indicated her swollen belly—"I was correct."

"And your husband knew the baby was not his?" Adrian asked.

Millie nodded. "But he was going to give the child his name. He wanted to raise him as his own."

Sophia took a breath. "Millie, your husband was murdered three weeks ago. You obviously knew you were pregnant at that time. If you had what you desired, why were you with your lover that night?"

Millie's hand jumped in hers, and the widow covered her eyes. "I didn't mean it to happen. That wasn't what I wanted."

Sophia saw Adrian stiffen, knew the dark conclusion he had reached—the widow hadn't meant to kill her husband. Sophia held up a hand to stall Adrian. He frowned at her but held his next remark.

Sophia leaned close to Millie. "You fell in love with him. Your lover."

Millie nodded, the action that of a repentant child. "And that's why I was with him that night. I should have been here. Perhaps I could have done something, helped George…"

"No." Sophia shook her head. "There was nothing you could have done, Millie. If you'd been here, you might be dead, too."

Millie's head jerked up. "You think I don't know that? And at times I wonder if that would have been better. I feel so guilty for… for everything." She rubbed her belly absently. "I don't understand who could have done this horrible thing. I don't know who would have wanted to hurt George."

Adrian leaned forward. "So he had no enemies, no one who wanted to hurt him? No one who'd threatened him recently?"

Millie shook her head. "No—"

"Take some time. Think about it."

"But I have thought about it. I've thought of little else! Honestly, Lord Smythe, I don't know who could have done this horrible thing."

"Is there anything you can tell us, Mrs. Jenkinson? Anything about the last days or weeks of Mr. Jenkinson's life?"

"What kinds of things?"

"Anything unusual," Sophia said. "Anything that made you pause or that didn't feel right. I believe in trusting your intuition." She ignored the roll of Adrian's eyes. "Did you have any feelings of something amiss?"

"No. Not at all…" She paused.

Adrian leaned forward. "What is it?"

"I wouldn't say this was unusual, but George spent quite a lot of time in his library. Often I would think he was alone, but I would pass by and hear him speaking in hushed tones."

"Do you know with whom he was speaking?" Adrian asked.

"I assumed his business partner, Mr. Hardwicke."

"What type of business was your husband in?"

Sophia could have told Adrian it was a wasted question.

"I don't know," Millie said predictably. "I never thought to ask."

"Is there any reason for you to think your husband was speaking to someone other than Mr. Hardwicke?" Sophia asked.

"I suppose it could have been a foreigner."

Sophia nodded, though the comment made little

sense. "Why do you say that? Did your husband know many foreigners?"

"No, but in the weeks before he died, two different men came to call. Both were foreign."

"What nationality?" Adrian wanted to know.

Millie gave him a blank stare. "Ah, German? Or possibly French. Perhaps American?"

Adrian blew out a sigh.

"You've been very helpful, Millie," Sophia said. "I assume you didn't reveal any of this to Bow Street."

She shook her head. "They didn't ask."

"We're going to need the name of your lover, Millie," Sophia said. "We'll need to talk to him."

"Randall? He had no part in this. As I said, I was with him the entire night."

Sophia patted her hand. "But he might be able to shed some light, and certainly we can't investigate a murder without interviewing everyone with any kind of motive."

"But Randall had no motive! He—"

"He's the father of your child." Adrian stood. "A child legally belonging to your husband. That makes him a suspect."

"But—"

"It's all right, Millie," Sophia reassured her. "We only want to talk to him. I'm sure he had no part in Mr. Jenkinson's murder."

Millie took a deep breath. "Very well. Randall Linden. He lives on King Street in St. James."

Sophia squeezed her hand. "Thank you. One last thing. I'd like to speak with the valet."

Adrian threw her a scowl, but Sophia ignored it.

She was going to allow him to be present. Since the valet could not be pregnant, she wouldn't balk and would be far more effective from the outset.

"That's impossible," Millie said.

"Why?" Adrian put his hands on his hips.

"I gave Callows leave. Naturally, he was distraught after finding the body. He needed some time away."

"Where is he?" Adrian asked.

Millie shrugged. "I didn't think to ask where he was going."

"Did you ask when he'd be back?" Adrian's tone was sarcastic, and Millie looked a bit abashed.

"Yes. He should return by the end of the week, but I don't know why. Without George, I don't have a position for him."

"When Callows returns," Adrian instructed, "contact us immediately. I want to speak with him. Before we go, we need to speak with the other servants present that night."

"All right. I'll arrange it."

"You have our card?" Sophia stood, and Millie followed, her movements awkward until she'd gained her feet.

"Yes. Oh! I didn't offer any refreshment. Would you like tea?"

Sophia smiled. "No, thank you. You look tired. Perhaps you should rest."

Millie nodded. "Yes, I will. Lady Smythe?"

Sophia looked back from across the drawing room. "Thank you."

Nine

ADRIAN TOOK THEM HOME. THEY'D SPENT THREE hours interviewing the Jenkinson servants to no avail. The staff didn't know any more than Millie Jenkinson. Adrian wanted to go directly to speak with Randall Linden, but Sophia was shaken and tired and needed time to regain her bearings. He didn't give this as his reasoning—she would have fought him tooth and claw. But when he casually suggested they return home, she didn't argue.

That was telling in itself.

If she'd been on top of her game, she would have wanted to speak to Linden immediately. She would have pressed the servants harder. Instead, he caught her staring into space several times during the interviews.

Sophia was good at her job. Even shaken by Millie Jenkinson's pregnancy, Sophia had done what she needed to do—put the woman at ease, questioned her, and received answers that furthered the investigation. He wondered if he would have done as well without her.

He didn't know how she had traveled to the

Jenkinson residence, but they took his coach—he supposed it was hers as well—back to their town house. Sophia was quiet and thoughtful on the short trip, but finally as they turned onto Charles Street, she said, "I cannot believe she allowed the valet to leave Town."

She sounded as frustrated as he felt.

"No wonder Bow Street has made little progress." The coach slowed to a stop, and she allowed their footman to assist her down the steps. Strange to see her accept all the little courtesies now that he knew she had absolutely no need for them. The footman was a tall, well-built fellow, but Adrian would put his brass on Sophia any day.

He followed her up the walk. "She should have been advised to keep all the suspects available," Adrian said, nodding to Wallace, who opened the door for them. "Lord Liverpool did not do his job."

"To say the least."

"My lord. My lady." The butler nodded at the two of them as though he saw nothing amiss in the couple returning together from a midday outing. Adrian thought he could count on one hand the times he and Sophia had gone anywhere together. "A package arrived for you while you were out."

"Oh, good. It's probably the file from Lord Liverpool," Sophia said. "Is it in my parlor?"

Adrian cleared his throat. "I'm sure Wallace has put *my* package in the library."

Sophia looked as though she had a retort ready, but instead of voicing it, she turned to Wallace. "Well?"

The butler looked unperturbed. "The package was addressed to both of you. I left it in the drawing room."

"Ah, neutral territory," Adrian murmured.

Sophia ignored him and started up the stairs. Adrian handed Wallace his greatcoat and took a moment to admire his wife's backside. Her fashionable blue day dress suited her. Strange to see her dressed so well. No high-necked sack that hung on her as though she were a scarecrow. No large glasses concealing her face and eyes. Apparently, she'd put away her disguises. Adrian heartily approved—even if this new Sophia was distracting.

When she was out of sight, Adrian turned to Wallace. "Put any additional deliveries in my library."

The butler raised his brows but did not comment. Fists clenched, Adrian started up the stairs. At one time he'd been Agent Wolf and the most powerful men in the world snapped to do his bidding. Now he could hardly command his own butler.

Or his wife.

He stepped into the drawing room. Sophia already had the package open and was thumbing through the contents.

Adrian strode forward and plucked it out of her fingers. "I believe that was addressed to both of us."

She raised her brows. "Yes, and I'm certain just now you were telling Wallace he did right to put it here."

Adrian squinted at her. Had she overheard, or was he that predictable?

"It's a file on the Jenkinson murder." Sophia indicated the documents he held. "Lord Liverpool must have thought we might find them useful."

"He should have given these to us last night." Adrian glanced at a document listing Jenkinson's financials. "It might have saved us time."

"Let's peruse them on the table over there." She pointed to a table large enough to seat two.

"I'd rather use my library."

Sophia snapped the file out of his hand. "And I like the ambiance in here." She pulled a Sheraton chair to the table and sat. "Ring for tea, would you?"

"I—" Adrian was about to protest when he realized he was actually quite hungry. So he bit his tongue and rang. Yanking another chair to the table, he sat. He held out his hand for the file, but Sophia handed him only one document—the one she'd just finished reading.

"Apparently Bow Street knew of our friend Millie's affair. They have Mr. Linden's address here." She glanced through the remainder of the file, and it took all Adrian possessed not to rip it from her hands. "It does not appear as though they questioned him." She glanced up at Adrian. "We probably should have gone directly."

"Yes, I thought of that."

"Then why… oh. Yes, I see." She looked down, and he saw a hint of color on her cheeks. "You needn't coddle me. I'm fine."

He raised a brow then looked back down at the document in his hand.

"What does that look mean?" Sophia asked, her tone rising.

He knew that tone. When a woman—when your wife—spoke in that tone, a sensible husband made a hasty retreat. Adrian didn't move. "It means you were shaken. Millie Jenkinson shook you."

"And your point?" Her color was higher now.

Anger, not embarrassment, he surmised. "I did my job," she continued. "I asked her questions, received the answers we needed."

"Would you have been able to do so had I not been there?"

She leaned forward and glared at him. He was definitely not being sensible. He was practically goading her. He didn't know if it was because Sophia looked so fetching when her cheeks were pink with emotion or because he had wanted to provoke this exact conversation.

"Would you have received any information *at all* had I not been present?" she said. "Your interview tactics leave something to be desired."

"*My* interview tactics? I think you mean your own, madam."

She bounced to her feet. "*You* think to criticize me? Are you daft? Were you even present in Millie Jenkinson's drawing room this morning?" She stalked toward him and pointed a finger at his forehead. "*I* calmed the woman. *I* reassured her. *I* helped her to remember the information about the foreigners."

"A lot of good that will do us. She can't tell the difference between an American and a German accent! And the Americans speak English!"

"That's debatable and beside the point." She bent so they were at eye level. From this angle, he had an unimpeded view of the rounded tops of her breasts as they pushed against the little lace decorating the round neck of her gown. He liked that lace. Was it meant to indicate innocence or to tempt him?

"You and I are the spies," she continued. "We're

good at gathering intelligence. It's up to us to determine from whence George Jenkinson's mysterious visitor hails."

"Of course it is."

She blinked, momentarily confused by his agreement. Good. He'd thrown her off.

The housekeeper opened the drawing-room door and rolled the tea cart to the dining table. Sophia returned to her seat and lifted a document. Adrian did the same. Both he and Sophia quietly studied the papers before them while the housekeeper set up the service. After what seemed an eternity of silence, the woman said, "Will there be anything else, my lord?"

"No, that's all. Thank you."

She bobbed and retreated. When the door closed behind the housekeeper, Sophia said, "We were agreeing."

"Yes. I don't even remember now what we were arguing about."

"I'll tell you what we're arguing about. You said—"

He put his hands on her waist, lifted her out of the chair, and pulled her into his lap.

"What are you doing?"

He grinned. "What does it look like?"

"I'm trying to have a discussion."

"You want to have an argument, and I would rather kiss you."

She tried to stand, but he held her firmly. "I don't think this is a good idea."

"Why not? I'm your husband. Kissing me is always a good idea."

She shook her head. "I'm angry with you right now.

You tried to coddle me. You"—she looked away, searching for the words—"you *made allowances* for me."

"Good God, say it isn't true!"

She tried to push away, but he cupped her cheeks and turned her face so he could see her eyes. "Sophia, Mrs. Jenkinson's pregnancy upset you. You and I both know it, and we both know why. You needed support, and fortunately, I was there."

"I could have handled myself if you hadn't been."

He shrugged. "But why should you? There's no need for you to traipse about London, looking for a killer and upsetting yourself. I'd rather you stay home—"

"You really are afraid I'm going to beat you."

"Not at all." He had no worries whatsoever—even if she was a far better spy than he'd expected. "I don't like competing with my wife."

"Because you're afraid you'll lose."

He shook his head and tried to ignore the feel of her soft bottom on his thighs.

"And you should be afraid. I doubt Mr. Linden or Mr. Hardwicke will be in a delicate condition, and that means I won't need you to bolster me. And, even though you'll never admit it, you needed me with Millie Jenkinson this morning. Someone had to hold her hand. Someone had to calm her nerves. Only another woman could do that."

Bloody hell. She was right. But he didn't care at the moment. She smelled like sweet oranges, and he wanted to lean closer and inhale more deeply. "I would have ferreted out the information without you," he said, pulling her nearer.

She arched back slightly. "Not as well as you did *with* me."

"Are you proposing we continue to work as a team?"

"No, and don't think I don't realize you suggested that last night only because you wanted to keep me under your thumb."

"That wasn't why I suggested it."

She was still arching back, trying to avoid close contact. But that only thrust her breasts closer to his lips. He'd been tempted enough. Time to act.

"Then why did you suggest it?"

"Because I wanted to keep doing this." He cupped the back of her neck, pulled her to him, and kissed her.

She fought him, of course. He hadn't expected anything else, which was why he kept the kiss light and teasing. He tasted her lips, nibbled one then the other while his hand kneaded the tense muscles of her neck. Slowly, he felt the tension drain out of her, felt her give in to his ministrations.

"You see," he whispered, "I'm not so bad."

"Yes, you are. You're taking advantage of me."

He chuckled. "I don't think that's possible. Bloody hell, you're tense."

She moved her neck, and he dug his fingers in more deeply. She groaned, and he felt himself harden. She must have felt it too, because she glanced down at him, her dark gaze meeting his. "I think this is the first time you've ever kissed me in the daylight."

It was true. They'd always behaved as strangers in the daylight. "I'll have to make a habit of it. I like seeing your reaction." He liked the way her eyes unfocused, the way her cheeks pinkened, the way her mouth seemed to bloom with color and sensuality.

"Why?"

He frowned.

She shook her head. "Why are you doing this now? Why are you suddenly interested in me?"

"There's nothing sudden. I've never stopped being interested in you." He could only wish he had. It would have made the long months without her more bearable. "You're the one who closed the bedroom door on me."

"Yes, but you weren't exactly knocking it down before that."

He sighed, not wanting to discuss this now. She'd been in pain, physical and emotional, after the loss of the last baby. Was he supposed to demand conjugal rights, when every time he passed her door he could hear her weeping? He'd left her alone, but that didn't mean he desired her any less.

"I never stopped wanting you," he repeated and ran his hand under her skirt, feeling the silky skin of her calf.

She shivered. She couldn't control that, he noted. She reacted to him. She wanted him. He could break through that firm control, even for a moment, and see the truth.

"It's because of the gowns and the hair," she said, her breathing hitching as his hand made lazy circles on her knee. "I'm not wearing those ugly glasses."

He smiled. "It helps." His hand went to her thigh. How was it possible her skin was so soft? "But I've seen you without anything on. You think an ugly gown and glasses could erase that image?"

"No, but I wasn't wearing the disguise for—Adrian!"

His hand had delved between her thighs and was inching toward her warm feminine heat. He raised a brow. "Something distracting you?"

She narrowed her eyes. "Hardly. I think you're the one who is distracted—oh! I mean, we should get back to work. We have this file…" Her voice trailed off as he stroked her. She was so warm. He ached to turn her so she straddled him, free himself, and plunge into her. Instead, he dipped one finger into her, and she gasped.

"You were saying something about the file?" he said, voice blasé.

"Was I?" She arched her hips and wriggled against his hand. "I mean, I think we should concentrate—"

He cut her off, sealing his mouth to hers in a searing kiss. Her arms came around him, and Adrian had had enough foreplay. Heedless of the file and its contents, he put his hands on her waist and lifted her, depositing her on top of the table. Standing now, he bent to kiss her again, but she put a hand between them.

Bloody hell. He should have never stopped touching her. He'd given her a second to think, and when Sophia started thinking, it was always disastrous. "In another moment, we're going to ruin these papers," she said, her eyes once again focused.

"A slight wrinkle won't do any harm." He bent again, determined to distract her, and up came the restraining hand. He frowned.

"You need to see the financial reports. Jenkinson was deeply in debt."

Despite his aroused state, she'd managed to snag his attention. "How do you know that?"

"I told you, there are financial reports."

He squinted at her. "Which you perused one time."

She shrugged. "I'm good with numbers."

Not quite willing to give up on the seduction, he rested his hands on her thighs. "Who are you?"

"Sophia Galloway. Your wife."

He didn't blink. "You know what I'm asking."

"I'm sure you haven't heard of me."

"Try me."

"Saint," she said, looking down at his hands. "Agent Saint."

He squeezed her thigh. "Agent Saint is a man."

"No. I'm Agent Saint."

He withdrew his hands, and careful not to disturb the file, she jumped her feet. "But Agent Saint…" He raked a hand through his hair, paced. He'd heard of Agent Saint. The man had done good work. Adrian had actually hoped to have the opportunity to work with the operative one day. Yes, there had been that fiasco in Paris, but that was ancient history.

He looked at Sophia. She stood quietly, hands folded before her, wide brown eyes watching him. How the bloody hell could *she* be Saint?

"You're thinking about Paris, aren't you?" she said, her cheeks flaming and her chin notching up. "I can explain Paris. It was my first assignment, and someone gave me bad information—"

"Oh, good God! That couldn't have been you."

She arched a brow at him. "Why not?"

"You couldn't have been more than twenty-three! We were newly married."

"And?"

And he hadn't even been part of the Barbican group yet. He'd heard about the Paris incident after he'd been inducted. He'd also heard how Agent Saint had used his—*her*—wits to salvage the whole operation. He stared at her, anger and something else—admiration?—rising inside him. "I wasn't even part of the Barbican group yet."

"I know. Agent Wolf came on after I joined. If it's any consolation, I was allowed to join only after we married. Lord Melbourne didn't find it seemly for an unmarried miss to work as a spy."

"So you married me for the entrée it afforded you into the Barbican group."

She sat in the cream Sheraton chair she'd pulled to the table where the Jenkinson file still lay, now in some disarray. "It's as good a reason as any. Why did you marry me?"

He felt himself begin to squirm and tamped the feeling down. "I needed a wife and an heir. You weren't as silly as the other girls. You didn't pepper me with questions about my whereabouts or cling. I thought we would get on well." And she'd never mentioned his father.

She sighed. "Obviously, we're both hopeless romantics."

He grinned at her.

"Well," she said, clearing her throat. "I suggest we return to the task of studying this file. Jenkinson's financial distress certainly gives someone—perhaps Hardwicke, as he was owed the bulk of the money—a motive for murder." She picked up the file and began to sift through the pages.

In that moment, he wanted her more than he ever had. She was Agent Saint. She was Sophia. She was his wife. *His.*

She tucked a chestnut curl behind her ear and glanced up at him. "What is it?"

He stepped toward her. "I think the file can wait."

"Earlier you said Liverpool should have sent it straight away."

"Earlier I didn't know you were Agent Saint."

"Oh, well, in that case, I order you to study this file."

He'd been about to take another step toward her, to lift her out of the chair and into his arms again, but now he stopped. "You order me?"

"That's right. As I've been a member of the Barbican group longer than you, I'm your superior. That gives me the right to give orders."

He stared at her. She was right, of course. That was how the group worked, but he'd be dammed if he was going to take orders from a woman—from his wife!

"And if I refuse your orders?"

She opened her mouth, closed it again.

"That's right. Neither of us are part of the Barbican group anymore. Those rules don't apply."

She shrugged, looked back at the file. "Fine. I don't care for rules much anyway. But if you think you're going to distract me with kisses and caresses, think again. Work comes first."

"Is that so?"

She flipped a document over, studied the back. "Mmm-hmm."

"So right now any advance I made would have no effect on you."

She lifted another document, set the first aside. "Right. No effect," she said absently.

Well, he couldn't walk away from a challenge like that, could he? He closed the distance between them, grabbed her arms, and yanked her out of the chair. The page she held fluttered to the floor, but before she could sputter out protests, he closed his mouth over hers.

Immediately, he was flooded with the flavor and the scent of oranges. Did she eat them for breakfast? Did she bathe in them? No matter, he drank it in, slanted his mouth over hers, taking and taking, delving into her, tasting and teasing. His hands were as busy as his lips. His first task was to free her hair, feel it tumble heavily over his hands. He felt the weight of it, the thickness, the silky tresses brush his skin, and fisted his hand in it. He yanked her head back, giving him access to her neck, and plundered the sensitive skin there.

Sophia grabbed hold of him, not to push him away, he noted, but to hold on. He risked a glance at her, saw her eyes were closed, her head thrown back. He definitely wouldn't classify this reaction as *no effect*.

He wanted to continue his seduction, but he'd made his point. And there was the small matter of his pride. He wanted her to come to him. He wanted her to want him, even if it was only a fraction of what he felt for her.

Abruptly, he released her.

She stumbled but caught the table with one hand, steadying herself. "Wh-what was that?"

"That was the lack of effect I have on you." He

started for the door. "Leave the file in my library when you're done reading it."

"You're not going to read it with me?" she asked. Was it his imagination, or did he hear a faint note of pleading in her tone?

"No. I have other business to attend to." And he strode out the door.

Ten

SOPHIA TOOK HER TIME STUDYING THE CONTENTS OF the file Liverpool sent. It wasn't easy when half her mind was on her husband, where he'd gone, what he was doing. What he might be doing to her, with her, if he were here…

She found she alternated between worrying he was angry at finding out she was Saint and worrying he was pursuing some avenue of the case she hadn't yet considered.

But she was a professional. She could put personal matters aside and concentrate on work. She did so as she perused the file. Then she sat back, closed her eyes, and cleared her mind.

Millie Jenkinson had been a great deal of help. She'd mentioned her husband meeting foreigners and conducting secret meetings. Millie also had a lover and was pregnant with said lover's child. But the child was legally George Jenkinson's. Was that a reason to kill? Sophia didn't know, but she would keep that fact and Randall Linden in mind for the present.

Further, Millie was in love with Linden. Love was

a motive as old as the ages. Linden was Millie's alibi, and undoubtedly she would be his. Sophia thought it unlikely Millie was a murderess, but she hadn't become Agent Saint by accepting the obvious. Still, her instincts protested against pregnant, tearful Millie Jenkinson as a murderess.

Then there were Jenkinson's financial problems. He owed a great deal to his business associate, Hardwicke. That didn't give Hardwicke a motive for murder. If Hardwicke killed Jenkinson, how would he claim the money he was owed? And how did the secret meetings and foreigners fit in with Jenkinson's debt? Or did they?

Liverpool had been visibly upset about the state of his half brother's body. Sophia had thought to question the valet, Callows, about that, but as he was out of town, she might need to pay a visit to Liverpool for particulars. She wished one of the other servants had heard something or seen something. The fact that they didn't served only to reinforce her initial reaction. When she'd stood in the Jenkinsons' vestibule, she'd been thinking the murderer had to either know his or her way around the house or must be someone whose presence would not raise suspicion.

Hardwicke's presence wouldn't raise suspicion during the day, but in the middle of the night...

She sat forward, clasped her hands. "Millie Jenkinson." She raised one finger. "Spoke to her. Has an alibi." She raised another finger. "Randall Linden. Also has an alibi. Need to speak to him." She raised a third finger. "Callows is away from Town. Most annoying and vexing. I want to speak to him." She stood, paced. "Hardwicke is owed money by Jenkinson. Business associate. That makes him a suspect, but the motive is weak."

She continued to pace, annoyed with herself for thinking so much. She was turning into Adrian. It was already afternoon. She only had time to visit either Hardwicke or Linden.

"Hardwicke or Linden? Hardwicke"—she scratched her nose—"or Linden?"

Sophia halted and tapped her nose. "Hardwicke."

She wore her spencer. The weather was warm and the garment unnecessary, but she couldn't afford to appear unfashionable to a businessman like Hardwicke. She checked the address in Liverpool's file and saw Hardwicke's offices were in a less than ideal area of Town. Perhaps the spencer didn't matter after all.

But her nose itched again, and she decided looking fashionable would play well with a businessman, no matter how destitute. With that thought in mind, she stopped in her room to restore her coiffure and trade the cap she'd worn to Millie Jenkinson's for an O'Neill hat decorated with feathers. A French hat would have been *au courant*—everything French was in style now—but Sophia liked the brim of the O'Neill better. It was less feminine, less fussy than round rims and satin ties under the chin.

On her way downstairs, she thought of Adrian again. Now that he knew her true identity, she no longer had to sneak out of the house in unfashionable clothing or heavy mantles. She could wear what she liked, be herself—whoever that was. Well, she knew one thing about herself. She liked O'Neill hats.

Would he call at Hardwicke's offices? She wouldn't bet against it. Perhaps his plan all along had been to distract her with the file while he met with Hardwicke. Or perhaps she gave him too much credit. Could she give Agent Wolf *too much* credit?

At one time, she would have thought Adrian would be at his club. Now she knew better. She wondered if he even belonged to a club. If so, she wondered which.

That would be easy enough to discover. She was a spy, after all.

Wallace met her at the bottom of the staircase and beamed his approval at her choice of wardrobe. "Would you like the carriage, my lady?"

So Adrian hadn't taken it. Wherever he'd gone, he'd gone on foot. Or horseback. She might have asked, but she preferred to avoid revealing to the servants how little she knew of Adrian's plans and whereabouts.

"Yes, the carriage would be lovely, Wallace."

"Will madam be home for dinner?"

"Ah…" She squinted for a moment, tried to remember the day and her plans. A pit formed in her stomach, and she sighed. "No, Wallace. His lordship and I will be dining away."

"Very good, my lady."

She wanted to tell him that no, it was not very good, but instead she stood in the vestibule and waited for the carriage to be brought around. Edward and Cordelia were hosting a dinner party tonight. Sophia would have liked to send a note saying plans had changed and she could not attend, but the consequences of such an action might be worse than the actual party. Cordelia would come to call here, to demand an explanation, and then Sophia wouldn't be able to get rid of her. At least at the dinner party she could leave early, claiming a headache.

She settled into the carriage and rubbed the bridge of her nose. She did have a headache. She rolled her neck, thinking unwillingly of Adrian's skilled fingers earlier. He would certainly be able to knead away her pain. He'd be able to do a great deal more than that...

In the past twenty-four hours, he'd touched her more often and more intimately than she'd been touched in months. She could still feel the press of his hand on her thigh. Her body ached, remembering his touch between her legs. She wanted that touch again.

It would be an easy matter to seduce him. She wouldn't even have to seduce him. If she looked at him too long, he would probably rip her clothes off.

And then what?

She didn't want another doomed pregnancy. Unlike Millie Jenkinson, Sophia had given up. Still, there were other ways to find pleasure. Would Adrian accept that compromise? And did she want him to?

She had not thought overly much about what he did for amusement after she shut him out of her bedroom. In her mind, Adrian preferred reading to living, preferred his library to the city streets. Agent Wolf was another matter entirely. Would Agent Wolf suffer eleven months without a woman?

She didn't think so. And so the issue became, should she question his faithfulness? Those types of discussions would only bring them closer. Did she want to be closer to him, or did she prefer to return to her safe, lonely existence?

She peered out the window and saw Hardwicke's ramshackle building come into view. Several dangerous-looking men loitered on the street, eyeing the well-appointed carriage with curiosity. She wasn't worried about them. She could handle herself with thugs. What she couldn't handle were the emotional entanglements of her marriage.

But she would put that aside for now. The Barbican group was calling.

❧

Adrian sighed when Sophia stepped into the public room of Hardwicke's offices. He supposed he'd been overly optimistic to assume Liverpool's file would have occupied her most of the day. That was exactly the kind of work he'd wanted to use to keep her busy, but apparently she wasn't content to work at home. No surprise.

He supposed he was going to have to implement Plan B. Meeting her outside Millie Jenkinson's Mayfair residence was one thing. Meeting her here, practically on the outskirts of Seven Dials, was quite another.

She spotted him immediately and gave him a weary look. "Don't you have a club where you can while away the hours?"

"Don't you have an orphan-society meeting?"

She glanced about the room, her gaze lingering on the closed door across from them. "Have you spoken with him yet?"

"I just arrived. His clerk tells me he's with a client."

Sophia raised her brows. "And you didn't barge in to disrupt the meeting?"

"Like you"—he noted she'd donned a fashionable hat and had her hair styled again—"I thought professional behavior might have more sway."

"I see." With a dubious glance at a dilapidated chair upholstered in hideous orange, she sat beside him. "I sent the carriage home. I didn't like the look of the men across the street, didn't think Jackson would be safe."

Adrian gaped at her. She was so small, so pretty with her gloves and her hat and her striped blue dress and gauzy sleeves. "You didn't think our coachman would be safe? What about yourself, madam?"

"I can handle myself."

Bloody hell. She probably could.

She was studying the offices, much as he had upon arrival. Her brown eyes were sharp, missed nothing. No doubt she noted the worn carpets, the shabby furnishings, the poor construction. "Why would Jenkinson associate himself with a man like Hardwicke?" she asked. "Surely he could find better business partners."

"I would think Liverpool might give him something of a hand up," Adrian agreed.

"Yes, but the Jenkinson home was nice—not the home of a wealthy man, but nicely appointed."

Adrian agreed with her assessment. It was strange to sit here with Sophia and discuss what he considered work. He'd never had a partner, never had anyone to agree or disagree with his thoughts and impressions. When he'd thought of Sophia, which was probably not as much as he ought, he thought of her safe at home, busy with her societies and ladies' charities. He never considered that while he was in

Amsterdam, she might be in Morocco, doing much the same work as he.

Or had she? Adrian wondered. He knew so little about Agent Saint. He understood why now. No doubt Melbourne and the Barbican group didn't want it common knowledge one of their top operatives was a woman. Her gender made her that much more valuable. No one suspected a woman of being a spy—at least he never had.

Sophia started to say something else, but Hardwicke's thin wooden door opened, and the scrawny red-haired clerk stepped into the opening. "Lord Smythe, Mr. Hardwicke will see you now." His eyebrows went up, and the freckles stood out on his pale skin when he noticed Sophia, who had risen with Adrian. "May I help you, madam?"

She smiled. "Lady Smythe. Also here to see Mr. Hardwicke." She glided to the door ahead of Adrian, who clenched his fists rather than grab her wrist and force her to sit back down. He'd had this entire interview planned, and now he knew she and her *intuition* were going to make a muddle of his well-laid plans.

Adrian followed Sophia into Hardwicke's office. The man stood behind a desk that might once have been a fine oak piece. Now it was scratched and worn and messy with scattered files and papers.

"Mr. Hardwicke," Sophia said, extending her white-gloved hand.

Adrian watched as Hardwicke's eyes opened wide and the round gentleman hurried around his desk to take her fingers and kiss them. Adrian shook his head. She did have a way about her. No denying that.

"Ah, Lady Smythe," Hardwicke stammered. "What an unexpected pleasure. Lord Smythe." Hardwicke gave a quick bow.

"I'm sorry we don't have an appointment," Sophia was saying. She moved about the office in the way women do, picking up knickknacks and touching papers and the contents of the desk absently. Adrian seated himself in one of Hardwicke's chairs and watched her work. He could see how being female benefited her. He would have had to find a way to get Hardwicke out of the office or come back later to peruse the man's things. Sophia could do so without so much as raising an eyebrow. Adrian admired the way she worked, even as he cursed inwardly that she'd have knowledge before he would. He'd have to ask her to share. He hated having to ask for anything.

"Please take a seat, Lady Smythe," Hardwicke said. "May I offer you refreshment?"

Sophia seated herself with a flourish and waved away Hardwicke's offer. "I'm afraid you're going to think this very strange, Mr. Hardwicke, but we've come with some questions for you. They pertain to your business associate Mr. Jenkinson."

"Oh?" Hardwicke paused in the act of sitting, his expression turning from curious to wary. Interesting, Adrian thought. But he had to stop Sophia before she made a mistake.

"Darling," he said, putting his hand on her arm so she knew he was not just speaking for Hardwicke's benefit. "Allow me to ask the questions." From his pocket he pulled a sheet of vellum on which he'd jotted down the most effective questions and the order in which they should be asked. He didn't need the sheet; he'd committed it to memory. But he wanted to show Sophia he had a plan.

She didn't look quite as impressed as he'd expected. "You have a list?" she asked, her voice light. But he could hear the tone of annoyance underneath.

"I'm prepared."

Her brows shot up. "And I'm not? You don't need a list for an interrogation"—she glanced at Hardwicke apologetically—"not that this is an interrogation. You need only ask questions that follow the natural progression of the, er, discussion. My lord," she added belatedly and in a tone that was somewhat less than submissive.

"Nevertheless, I'll ask the questions."

"Fine."

But he could tell she didn't mean it. He could tell this was not the last he'd hear from her.

Hardwicke was looking from one to the other with interest. "If you two need to discuss this alone…"

"That won't be necessary," Adrian said. "I'm here to inquire about your relationship with your late business partner, George Jenkinson."

"I see." Hardwicke steepled his fingers. He was a round man, middling height and losing his mud brown hair. His head was shiny where it peeked through the long strands he'd combed over to conceal his loss. He had unfashionably bushy sideburns and longish, unruly hair. Eyes were brown, Adrian decided. Nothing remarkable about the man—except his business partner had been murdered. "Isn't that Bow Street's task?" Hardwicke asked. "They already came with their questions."

"Lord Liverpool asked us to make additional inquiries," Sophia said, jumping in where she was most definitely not wanted.

"Why?" Hardwicke narrowed his eyes.

"We're close friends with the prime minister."

Adrian could have told her that while an answer like that might mollify Mrs. Jenkinson, it would not appease a man like Hardwicke.

"What does friendship have to do with finding a murderer?"

Sophia opened her mouth to say God only knew what, and Adrian interrupted, "I have some experience at this sort of thing. Now, if you don't mind, Mr. Hardwicke, I'll ask the questions."

The man's mouth thinned, and he sat back in his chair, arms crossed over his considerable girth.

"Where were you on the night of Mr. Jenkinson's murder?"

"At home."

"Do you have any witnesses who might corroborate your alibi?"

"Alibi?" Hardwicke sat forward, slammed his palms on the desk, making the piece shake precariously. "I've done nothing wrong. I don't need witnesses, and my whereabouts on the night of the murder are not an alibi." He stood. "What the hell is this? Excuse my language, madam. I think you'd better leave."

Adrian rose. "I think you'd better answer my questions."

"I'm a businessman, not a criminal. If you proceed to threaten me, I'll call the constable."

"Go ahead. I'd like him to hear what you have to say."

Hardwicke blinked, not expecting his bluff to be called. "B-but—"

Adrian sat, crossed his arms over his chest. "Go ahead. Send your clerk. I'll wait."

When the man made no move to call for the clerk, Adrian glanced around the office and tapped his fingers. "What kind of business do you do here, Mr. Hardwicke? I sincerely hope it's all aboveboard. Wouldn't want to call the constable in if you have anything to hide."

"Why, you bast—" Hardwicke glanced at Sophia. "Begging your pardon, madam."

"Mr. Hardwicke, if you'd allow me to speak a moment," she said, "perhaps we might come to a better understanding."

Adrian glared at her, silently urging her to close her mouth. He had Hardwicke right where he wanted the man. Why was Sophia interfering?

But Sophia, though she must have felt his stare—the shop girl across the street could feel his stare—steadfastly continued. "We don't think you've done anything wrong, do we, Lord Smythe?"

Adrian glared at her harder.

"Well, we don't." She leaned forward, her eyes beseeching and full of compassion. How did she manage that? "But Lord Liverpool is such a dear friend, and he is most distraught by the loss of his only brother. You understand?"

Damn him. Hardwicke was nodding and looking sympathetic. "I do. I feel the same way. It's been most upsetting."

"Of course it has." She leaned forward, patted

Hardwicke's hand. "You must be beside yourself with grief."

Hardwicke was nodding more vigorously now. Adrian wanted to reach out and smack the man. Who cared about his grief? His partner was dead. If Hardwicke was really concerned, he'd help the investigation.

"And we're both so sorry for your loss." She indicated Adrian.

Hardwicke gave Adrian a dubious glance.

"But in the interest of finding the real murderer," Sophia said, as though implying Hardwicke could not possibly be a suspect. Adrian gritted his teeth. Her methods were not his, but they were not completely without merit. "Might you answer a few questions? Might you tell us where you were the night of Mr. Jenkinson's murder?"

"Certainly. As I told your husband, I was at home."

"A man like you," Sophia said, sitting forward and toying a little with the plume in her hat, "must have a manservant or two. Were they at home that evening?"

Adrian was torn between watching Sophia stroke the feathery plume—he'd never seen her act so coyly—and admiring the way she flattered Hardwicke without making it seem like flattery. A manservant was more expensive than a maidservant. Judging by the state of the offices, Hardwicke couldn't afford either.

"I have a housekeeper," Hardwicke said. Adrian was surprised to hear it and thought the scullery maid Hardwicke paid to straighten and clean twice a week might be surprised at her elevation in status, as well. And Adrian was willing to wager Sophia didn't know that much about Hardwicke. But Adrian had not been idle this afternoon. He'd done his research.

"And was she working that evening?" Sophia asked.

"No. As I told your husband, I have no witnesses. But I don't need them. I didn't kill George Jenkinson."

"Then who did?" Adrian asked.

Hardwicke shook his head. "Damned if I know. Pardon the language, madam."

"Hardwicke owed you money," Adrian said, returning to the list of questions he'd formed. "How much?"

Hardwicke narrowed his eyes. "A considerable sum. You think I killed him for money?"

"It wouldn't be the first time greed played a part in murder."

"It wasn't like that," Hardwicke said, speaking to Sophia. "George and I were friends. Several years ago we invested in a shipping venture. The ship sank, and we owed our creditors a considerable sum. I paid what was due and told George he could repay the debt when he had the blunt."

"That was very kind of you—" Sophia began.

"Yes, kind," Adrian grumbled. "Why were you so… kind?"

"I told you. George and I were friends."

"With a considerable sum standing between the two of you, a friendship might sour."

"But George was paying me back," Hardwicke said. "He'd already repaid me six thousand pounds."

Adrian glanced at Sophia. She met his gaze. Her face was neutral, no sign of triumph in her eyes. She hadn't known about the repayment.

Bloody hell. There went Hardwicke's motive. Why would he kill a man in the midst of repaying his debts? Unless Hardwicke wanted the business all for himself…

"I wonder if you have any ideas as to where Mr. Jenkinson acquired the funds to repay you," Sophia said, looking only half-interested.

"I have no idea."

If that was true, Adrian would eat that feather Sophia persisted in stroking.

"When I called on Millie Jenkinson recently—Millie and I are both members of the Benevolent Society for the Aid and Prosperity of Orphans—she mentioned her husband had recently made the acquaintance of several foreigners. Do you think that might have something to do with the repayment?" Sophia blinked, looking completely innocent, as though the idea just occurred to her. But Adrian was no longer so much a fool to believe that.

Adrian had considered that Jenkinson's meetings with foreign men might have something to do with acquiring money to pay his debts, but he had several questions planned to lead Hardwicke to that topic. He frowned at Sophia. Where was she going with this?

"I wasn't aware you were acquainted with Mrs. Jenkinson," Hardwicke said, melting a little more and smiling at Sophia. Adrian gripped his chair in frustration. This was an interrogation, not a social call. Hardwicke didn't need to like them to answer their questions.

In fact, Adrian preferred Hardwicke stopped conversing with Sophia altogether.

"The plight of orphans is, naturally, something that concerns both of us."

Adrian sighed. Heavily. Why were they talking about orphans?

"And now she'll have her own little one," Sophia said with a smile.

"Yes." Hardwicke frowned, and Adrian leaned forward. So, Hardwicke knew about Millie Jenkinson's infidelity. Had Jenkinson shared that with him, or was it common knowledge? And damn him if he hadn't thought to pursue that avenue of questioning.

Still, Sophia's haphazard approach annoyed him. Could they not exhaust one line of questioning before beginning a new? What had happened to structure? Order? His plan?

"So distressing that the expectant father will never meet his son or daughter, especially considering he'd recently come into some money."

"I wouldn't say that…"

"But, Mr. Hardwicke, you said yourself Mr. Jenkinson was repaying the debt owed you." Sophia blinked again, appearing without guile.

Hardwicke looked at Adrian, and Adrian raised his brows. He didn't know how he'd lost control of this interrogation, but he knew better than to try and regain it now.

"I don't like to speculate," Hardwicke began slowly. Adrian's pulse jumped, but he kept his face carefully blank. Sophia continued stroking her plume and blinking.

Hardwicke stood, paced his small office. "I think it was the French."

"Oh!" Sophia put a hand over her heart.

"No need to worry, dear lady," Hardwicke assured her. "Bonaparte is safely exiled, and for my part, none too soon—"

"About the French," Adrian interrupted before Hardwicke started giving unwanted opinions on Bonaparte. "You think they're in some way responsible for Jenkinson's death?"

"As I said, I don't like to speculate, but those foreigners Mrs. Jenkinson mentioned were French. I didn't like that, George associating with frog-eaters." He looked at Sophia, and she nodded her support. "I met one once. I was leaving George's, and one was coming in. I warned George against doing business with them, but he ignored my warnings."

"Warnings?" Adrian asked.

"He said he knew what he was doing. And then a few weeks later, he began repaying the money he owed. It doesn't take a spy to put two and two together."

"No, it doesn't take a spy," Adrian said, leaning back in his chair.

"And do you think the Frenchman had anything to do with Mr. Jenkinson's death?" Sophia asked.

"Who else would have killed him?"

Adrian could think of a host of others with more reason and motive than some mysterious—possibly imaginary—Frenchman. He wasn't yet willing to fully discount Hardwicke as a suspect.

"Well, thank you for your time," Sophia was saying. She rose.

Adrian shook his head. "We're not done here."

"Oh, my lord, I'm so sorry. I know we haven't

addressed all of the questions on your paper, but we really can't afford to be late."

"Allow me to escort you out." Hardwicke took Sophia's elbow.

What the bloody hell was going on? Sophia was leaving, Hardwicke was escorting her out, and Adrian hadn't even begun to ask all the questions he wanted. And now she was talking about being late for something. *This* was why he preferred to work alone. He stomped after Sophia and Hardwicke. "Lady Smythe."

She turned and smiled at him. "We must hurry if we don't want to keep Cordelia and your brother waiting." She turned to Hardwicke. "Lord Smythe's brother is hosting a dinner party tonight. I'm afraid I need a few moments in my dressing room so I can look presentable."

"Oh, my dear lady," Hardwicke said, "I'm sure you would look well dressed in nothing."

Adrian halted, and Hardwicke gave him a hasty glance, the rotund man's face turning purple. "I-I... what I meant was..."

"I know what you meant." Sophia patted Hardwicke's arm, and Adrian stepped between the two, took her hand, and placed it on his sleeve.

"Yes, we know exactly what you meant." He leaned close to Hardwicke. "I'm going to check on these Frenchmen. If anything you've said doesn't fit, I'll be back."

He strolled out of the office, pulling Sophia in his wake. It was time he put an end to Sophia's "assistance." Time he made sure she understood who was really in charge.

Eleven

SOPHIA STALKED AFTER ADRIAN. "WILL YOU BE threatening and intimidating every suspect we encounter?" she asked as they stepped into the twilight of early evening. "Or only those who give us valuable information?"

Adrian cut her a glance and began a brisk walk. It was no hardship for her to keep up with him, but she slowed anyway, not liking having her pace set for her.

"Hurry up. Hardwicke's information isn't valuable. He told us little to nothing."

"He corroborated Millie's statements about the foreigners."

Adrian glanced at her then back at the deserted street ahead. "*After* you told him what Mrs. Jenkinson said. He didn't mention it of his own accord."

Sophia frowned. He had a point there. Hardwicke could have taken her statements and used them to fabricate information to point suspicion elsewhere. She should have been vaguer when mentioning Millie's statements. "You're right," she murmured. "That was my mistake."

Adrian skidded to a stop. He turned to her. "What did you say?"

She sighed. "I can admit when I'm wrong."

He began walking again. Quickly. "This is the first you've done so."

"That's because this is the first time I've been wrong about this case." But Hardwicke's comments about meeting a Frenchman outside the Jenkinson residence fit with her initial theory. The murderer was someone who had been in the house and knew its layout. She blinked, coming out of her musings, and saw Adrian several steps ahead of her. "Why on earth are you walking so quickly?"

He looked over his shoulder. "Because I don't want them to catch up to us."

Sophia knew to whom he referred—the three men who'd been loitering on the street when she'd arrived. She glanced over her shoulder. The three thugs were gaining on them. She'd been so lost in thought, she hadn't been paying attention and hadn't noted—until Adrian pointed it out—they were being followed.

So that was two mistakes in one day. She couldn't afford a third. In Paris, it had been the third mistake that cost her.

She reached into her reticule and withdrew a small, slim dagger. "You take the one on the left." She nodded to a dark-haired youth in a faded blue coat. "I'll take the blond and the short one." The three were probably after money. She didn't think this would take long.

"I don't think so." Adrian was pulling her arm. "If we hurry—"

"If we hurry, we'll enter that alley even quicker. That's what they want. We stand a better chance on this street where we can maneuver." All of her instincts told her to stand and fight.

"Bloody hell."

She didn't know if he swore because she was right or because the men were too close for escape now.

"You're not taking two of them," he said, pulling a knife from his boot. "I'll take Blue Coat and Blondie. You take Shorty."

Now was not the time to argue. She'd dispatch Shorty easily and then help Adrian with the others. As one, they turned to face their attackers.

"Hey, little lady," Blue Coat called in a singsong voice. "What are you doing so far from home?"

Sophia offered a smile. "I was hoping to meet the three of you." She held up her dagger, pricked her thumb with it negligently. "It's been ever so long since I've had to clean the blood off this little blade." She looked at Adrian.

"Two days, at least," he drawled.

She gave him a genuine smile. He *did* have a sense of humor!

Shorty held up his fist. "I got something for you, gov."

"Oh, that's no good," Sophia said. The men were closing in now. She could see their strategy. They thought to surround her and Adrian. "We already divvied you up. You, Shorty, are mine."

Shorty laughed with surprise. "You hear that, Will? She said I get to have her first." And he lunged for her with one dirty hand. Sophia flicked her wrist and slashed his hand, opening a line of bright red.

"Bitch!" Shorty screamed, cradling his hand. "She cut me!"

His companions jumped to his aid, but Adrian stepped in front of her, pinning her back to a wall. Frustrated, Sophia tried to scoot around Adrian, while he aimed one kick at Blue Coat and punched Blondie in the chin. "Grab him and hold him," Blondie yelled in a hoarse voice.

Shorty grabbed one arm, and Adrian wrestled to keep the other free from Blue Coat. He was losing ground, though, because he was trying to shield her.

"I don't need your protection," she said, attempting to duck under his arm. "Move out of the way so I can hit my target."

But Adrian ignored her, swiping at Blue Coat with his knife while blocking her attempts to engage Shorty. "Run, Sophia. I can handle this."

Ridiculous man. But he didn't give up ground. She dodged right, and he blocked her. She screamed in frustration just as Blondie landed a blow to Adrian's jaw. "*You* run, my lord. *I* can handle this."

Didn't he remember their meeting in the East End? She'd more than held her own. But he still didn't trust her abilities. She'd have to prove to him, again, she could handle a fight.

Finally she saw an opening, skirted past Adrian, and stepped in front of Shorty. In surprise, he released Adrian's arm. She hoped Adrian could hold the other two at bay and used her dagger to force Shorty into retreat. Now she was far enough from Adrian to keep him from interfering and to give herself room to fight. Having been stuck once, Shorty was eyeing the dagger warily.

"Why don't you put that down, missy? Try to behave like a lady." He lunged at her, and she easily sidestepped.

"Because I'm not a lady, and if you don't run on home now, you're going to see exactly how unladylike I am."

She heard a muffled yelp behind her and the sound of a body slamming into the ground. Shorty gaped at whatever he saw, and she took her opportunity. She swiped her leg at his feet, throwing him off balance, then used the side of her hand to smack him across the nose. Blood, watery and plentiful as the Thames, gushed out. Instinctively, he put his hand to his face, and she moved in, slipping behind him. She wrapped an arm around his neck and slid her dagger under his chin.

Immediately, he stopped squirming.

"That's right. Don't move," she murmured near his ear. He smelled like he hadn't bathed in days, but she couldn't afford ladylike sensibilities right now. She could play the delicate lady tonight—at Cordelia's dinner party.

Damn! The dinner party. They were surely going to be late now. She glanced at Adrian, able to see his progress from her new vantage point. He was doing well. Blondie was on the ground, and Blue Coat was taking a beating. She could dispatch Shorty and assist Adrian, but she knew from experience operatives liked to finish what they'd started. Besides, she liked watching him work. As long as he hurried…

"Lord Smythe!" she called.

He glanced at her before turning to deflect a punch aimed for his eye. "Madam, I'm a little busy right now."

"I can see that. Do you mind hurrying a bit? We're going to be late for the dinner party. *Un*fashionably late."

He ducked to avoid Blue Coat's fist as Blondie stumbled to his feet and charged. He hit Adrian in the middle of the chest, propelling Adrian back against the wall with an "oof."

He recovered quickly, his boot landing in Blondie's abdomen, sending the man sprawling again. The move bought him a moment before Blue Coat charged. Adrian ducked under Blue Coat's arm and sidled behind him. Sophia, with her knife still at Shorty's throat, nodded her approval. He was good. Perhaps she could have run home. She might have had a chance at being ready on time…

"As much as I hate to inconvenience my sister-in-law…" Adrian panted, shoving Blue Coat against the wall of the building adjoining Hardwicke's offices, grabbing Blue Coat's hair and smashing his face into the brick. "I'm occupied at the moment."

"Would you like my help?" she offered sweetly, digging her dagger in and drawing blood when Shorty tried to elbow her. Damn. The blood from his broken nose had seeped onto the sleeve of her spencer. It was ruined now.

"No."

Adrian made to smash Blue Coat's face into the wall again, but Blondie jumped on him.

"Oh, for heaven's sake," Sophia moaned to no one in particular. "This is going to take all evening."

She shoved Shorty against the brick wall, dug her knee into his back, and with a tug, pulled his shirtsleeves over his hands. She tied them off, yanking Shorty's hands tightly behind his back and knotting the material. Then she pushed him onto the ground and put her heel on the back of his neck.

"Don't kill me," he begged. "I was only hoping for a few shillings to buy something to eat."

She snorted. "You were going to rape me, kill him, rob us, and buy gin. Not very nice." She ground her foot.

"Sorry!" he croaked.

She shook her head. They always were. "Listen, Shorty," she said, "if you so much as lift your face out of the dirt, I'll have to come back and slash your throat. Understood?"

He whimpered.

"You know I will do it." She applied more pressure with her foot then jumped away, picked up her skirts, and joined Adrian's fight. She pulled Blondie off his back, and when he looked over his shoulder in surprise, she punched him in the nose.

Holding back her wince—it had been some time since she'd punched a man and had forgotten how much it hurt her hand—she kicked him between the legs and watched him crumple to the mud-packed street.

There. A quick and effective move. Adrian should have done it earlier, but men rarely resorted to damaging another man's nether regions. She supposed it was out of sympathy. Unfortunately for Blondie, she was fresh out of sympathy. Who was going to sympathize with her when Cordelia complained all evening about how late she was? Not Blondie there.

She wiped her hands on her skirts, noting the pale

pink material had blood spatters on it. They were worse than usual, and she wondered if her maid could get them out. Normally, Sophia tried to keep bloodshed to a minimum.

She glanced impatiently at Adrian and smiled as he finally sent Blue Coat tumbling to the ground. The man rolled into a ball on his side. Adrian stepped forward, prepared to give the man another kick for good measure, but she put a hand on his arm. "We're late, remember?"

He blinked at her as if just remembering where he was and who she was. He glanced about him, saw Blondie clutching his balls and Shorty facedown in the dirt. He stared at the man and then at her.

"I told you I could take care of myself."

He bent and caught his breath. "Thank you."

"You don't have to treat—what? What did you say?" She bent and looked into his gray eyes. He scowled at her. "Did you *thank* me?"

"Am I going to regret doing so?"

"No." She stood straight again, shook her head. Adrian had thanked her. *Agent Wolf* had *thanked* her. She looked about the dirty street, the decrepit buildings, the sniveling men, and thought this was the best day of her life.

Adrian, still bent, was looking at her. "Why are you smiling?"

She leaned over, took his face between her hands, and kissed his lips. "Thank *you*." Blondie tried to grab her ankle, and she shoved him back down with her foot. "Now, we really must go. Can you hail a hackney?"

❧

Despite Sophia's masterful management of the jarvey, their staff, their coachman, and Adrian himself, they were an hour late. The dinner party was to have begun at nine, and when they breezed in at five past ten, Cordelia's look could have produced snow in August. "Lord and Lady Smythe," she said icily, "we were about to sit down without you." She wore a light blue dinner dress heavy with what Adrian thought were called flounces. She had matching blue ostrich feathers in her dull brown hair, which was arranged with a profusion of ringlets about her face.

"How rude of us to make you wait," Sophia said before Adrian could reply. Cordelia stared at her, as Sophia rarely spoke if she did not have to. "It's my fault completely." She shrugged off her mantle—the same one she had declined to relinquish to the butler just moments ago—and handed it to the servant now. "I simply couldn't decide which gown to wear."

Cordelia gaped. Edward, Adrian's brother, gaped. Every man in the room gaped. And Adrian turned to look at his wife and saw why.

Sophia wore a gown like those he'd seen in Paris recently. It was startlingly blue, simple but elegant. Nary a flounce to be seen. But true to the current Parisian fashion, it was cut very low in front and behind—very low. She'd had the mantle over her hair to conceal the gleaming pearls set in the thick chestnut waves. It wasn't in ringlets on the side of her face, as was the current fashion, but swept up in a sophisti-cated coil, threaded with more pearls.

"Why, Sophia, you look… different," Cordelia managed.

That was not precisely how Adrian would have described her. He would have said she looked ravishing.

And half-naked.

He wanted to throw his coat over her. Even more, he wanted to touch her—her face, her hair—find the true Sophia in there. Something told him *this* was she. This was the woman he had married, the woman who had been hiding under the disguise of large spectacles and tentlike gowns. He wondered when he would become accustomed to seeing her like this… in all her splendor.

And nakedness. He tightened his fingers at his sides to keep from hiking the gown up and over the swells of her breasts. Or dragging her off so he could yank it down…

"I see your condition agrees with you." Cordelia stood.

Though Sophia undoubtedly knew exactly what his brother's wife referred to, she gave her a puzzled look. "What condition?"

Cordelia looked at him, and Adrian merely blinked.

"Why, your pregnancy, of course," Cordelia said, looking about the room. Several of the ladies in attendance raised their fans. Women did not usually speak so bluntly. Everything was couched in terms like "delicate state." Obviously, Cordelia was out of sorts.

Sophia waved her hand jauntily. "I'm not pregnant," she said breezily. "Did you want to go in to dinner? I'm sure your cook is wringing her hands."

Adrian closed his eyes, knowing Sophia had just usurped Cordelia's duty as a hostess.

"Y-yes. Of course," Cordelia stammered.

And just like that, Adrian found himself leading Sophia into the Hayes's dining room. He cut her a sidelong glance. Her chin was high, her smile bright, but the hard press of her fingers on his arm told him Cordelia had wounded her. He knew, now, how much Sophia wanted to be pregnant. Did Cordelia know as well? Was that her way of sniping at his wife? He'd always known the two women were not the best of friends, but he never thought much of it. He'd seen their interactions as little more than womanish squabbles, but now he felt Sophia's pain at Cordelia's thoughtlessness. And he felt a stab as well. Unlike his brother—blessed with two healthy sons—Adrian had no children to carry on his shoulders or bounce on his knee.

Adrian glanced at Edward—pudgy, balding, and pale—who took his place at the head of the table. Adrian had no ill feelings toward his brother. He didn't care one way or another about Edward, though Adrian knew their mother tended to favor Edward. Adrian could hardly blame her, though, when Adrian resembled his traitorous father so completely. Even at the age of eight, Adrian had known his mother's marriage to his stepfather represented a desperate attempt at a new start. Edward was the tangible proof of that.

Adrian took the seat offered him and looked around the table. Besides the host and hostess and he and Sophia, there were three other couples. It was unfashionable for a husband and wife to sit beside one another, so he was between two women and across from the other. Sophia was similarly situated. Adrian tried not to notice how the men on either side of Sophia smiled at their good fortune.

Surely they would bore her in a matter of moments. Seated across the table from him, in her formal gown and gloves, Sophia looked the perfect viscountess. But he had seen her only a few hours ago easily dispatch two dangerous men. It was *that* Sophia—the woman with blood on her gown and a dagger in her hand—he wanted to get alone.

The first course, a white soup, was served, and Adrian tried to focus on something other than his wife. "Have you heard from Mother, Edward?"

Edward sipped his soup and nodded. "They are still in the Lake District. She says London in the summer is unbearable and plans to stay away as long as possible."

This was news to Adrian. He rarely saw his mother and had not known she was out of the city. In fact, he'd expected to see her and his stepfather here tonight. Apparently he knew more about operatives in Munich than the whereabouts of his own family.

Well, part of his family.

He glanced at Sophia. Her gaze had been on him, but it slid away quickly.

For once, he knew exactly where she was.

But it pained him that he'd grown so distant from his mother and had no relationship with her. He had always thought a career as an operative with the Barbican group was more important than anything else. But now he saw how isolated he'd become— from his mother, his brother, his wife…

"Oh, the Lake Country sounds just wonderful this time of year," the woman beside Adrian gushed. The oversized feather in her hat poked him in the eye. "Have you ever been, my lord?" She touched his sleeve and smiled.

"No." He looked down at her hand, and she quickly removed it. Across the table, Sophia smiled and tilted her head as a gentleman wearing a blue coat and a spill of lace down his chest enthralled her with a tale. The man's hair looked like a rag upon his head, but Adrian surmised it was supposed to look fashionably tousled. He looked down at his own dark blue coat, simple cravat, and buff breeches. He thought of his boring, untousled hair.

Surely Sophia wasn't interested in a fop like the man beside her. But then he'd never through she cared much for fashion, and she was undoubtedly the most fashionable woman in the room tonight. So perhaps he didn't know her at all.

What the bloody hell was wrong with him tonight? He felt as though his world had been turned on its side. He was a bad husband, a bad brother, and, he supposed, a bad son.

He'd been a good spy, and at one time that had made up for the rest. But he wasn't a spy anymore. Yes, he could win his place in the Barbican group back—he *would* win it back—but would that be enough anymore?

Dinner dragged on for several hours, with partridge, cheeses, trifle, and more. Adrian ate mechanically, not tasting his food and making little conversation. The meal was torture. Worse than the time he'd had two toenails pulled out by two French agents who hoped to get information out of him. They hadn't. But seated across from Sophia, able to see her, hear her, and not touch her was just about enough to break him.

Finally the meal ended, as expected, with port and cigars. Adrian escaped the dining room as quickly as possible. The ladies were in the drawing room, playing cards, but when Adrian peeked in, he didn't see Sophia.

No doubt she wasn't missed by Cordelia.

Sophia wouldn't have left without him, but she'd probably slipped away to avoid Cordelia. Where might she seek respite? Nowhere any of the members of the dining party might find her. She'd spent much time in their garden at home of late, so he headed for his brother's garden.

The garden was small but lush. The fragrance of roses and some other flower he could not determine— perhaps dahlias—crept over him. And the faintest hint of orange… The moon was full in the sky, the evening warm but breezy. He made his way along the path, noting some of the flowers had been trampled, no doubt by his young nephews.

In the center of the flowers and shrubs, Sophia sat on a bench, head bent as she rolled her neck from side to side. When he saw her, the tension in his neck drained away. He knew she heard him approach, but she didn't move as he stepped behind her and put his hands on the long column of her neck. He began kneading her tight muscles, and she hissed in a breath. "Relax," he said.

Her shoulders slumped, but she was still on edge. "What happened to port and cigars?" she asked.

He smiled. "I had some earlier at my club. Spent all day there."

"Hmm. Sounds like an uneventful afternoon."

"What happened to whist?"

"I play it all the time. Ah, yes. There." She sighed with pleasure when his fingers dug in. "I wanted a moment alone."

"And I'm interrupting your solitude."

She hesitated. "I don't mind."

He continued to massage her. He'd thought it would be amusing to play the old game with her, now that they both knew it was a lie, but he found it less than entertaining. "Is this how it's to be? We pretend even when we're alone?" He sat beside her.

"How do you want it to be?" She gazed at him.

He shook his head. "I bloody well knew you were going to ask me that."

She smiled. "You were far too hard on Hardwicke this afternoon, Agent Wolf."

He grinned at her. So she didn't want to play games either. "And you were too soft," he said, remembering the meeting with Jenkinson's associate.

"You don't have to scare people to get the answers you want."

"And you don't have to flirt with them, either."

"I wasn't—"

Adrian held up a hand. "I don't want to fight with you. I don't want to talk about Jenkinson." He wanted to know the woman he'd married. He wanted to be a decent husband, host a dinner party, discuss the day's plans over breakfast—even if those plans included fighting off thugs or questioning suspects. Unable to express all of this, he said, "I want us to be husband and wife."

A line appeared between her brows. "How do we do that?"

"Hell if I know."

She laughed, leaned back, and looked up at the stars. "I don't know who I am with you," she said after a long silence. "I don't know if I'm Lady Smythe or Agent Saint."

"Why not Sophia Galloway?"

"I don't know who she is anymore." She looked from the sky and met his gaze. "Maybe I never did. I've been pretending to be someone else for so long, I don't know who I really am."

"Yes." Adrian thought of the meeting with Melbourne. "When I was retired from the Barbican group, Lord Melbourne told me that as Agent Wolf, I'd invented a thousand identities for myself. Then he said, *who are you, Adrian?* I still have no idea how to answer him."

"We're spies," she said simply. He could feel the warmth of her body now they'd been sitting beside one another for several moments. He could smell her citrus scent above that of the flowers. "We're whoever they tell us to be."

That was true enough. He thought of all the disguises he'd worn, all the identities he'd invented for himself. Sophia had done the same. "What's the most outlandish part you ever played?" he asked, the impulse to know something more about her taking over.

"A pirate," she said without hesitation. "I had a peg leg and an eye patch, believe it or not."

He stared at her. "I don't."

"Well, the man I was trying to get information

from did. He not only told me what I needed to know for the operation, he told me where to find buried treasure. One of these days, I may even go dig it up."

Her laugh was infectious, and Adrian found himself smiling.

"How did you manage the peg leg?"

"Good balance." She stood, pulled her leg under her dress, and hopped on one foot. "I had the peg attached to my knee and wore a long, wide frock coat. I hopped around like this." She demonstrated, managing to remain surprisingly fleet-footed. "And I talked like this—*argh, matey!*"

Adrian shook his head. "That's horrible."

She plopped down beside him. He tried not to watch the neckline of her dress, but he feared—hoped?—her breasts might spill out with the next sudden movement. "Your turn."

He raised his eyes. "Hmm?"

She shook her head. "I probably didn't even need the pirate costume." She put a finger under his chin to keep his eyes on her face. "If I'd just walked in with a low neckline, I could have distracted the man into revealing the information I needed."

He frowned, his gut tightening. Jealousy, hot and venomous, surged through him. He knew his next question would anger her, and he was going to ask anyway. "Was that ever one of your assignments?"

She rose, plucked at a pink rose on a nearby bush. "Distracting a man into revealing information? Of course. I wouldn't have been a very good operative if I hadn't used every means at my disposal."

She was being evasive, which only made the jealousy burn hotter. "*Every* means?"

She turned, and even in the dim light of the moon, he could see her eyes flash. "Just say what you mean, Adrian. Have I ever seduced a man as part of a mission? Is that what you want to know?"

He tightened his hands on the bench, feeling the cold, hard stone under his rigid fingers. "Yes."

"Yes, I've seduced my share, but—"

"Never mind." He was on his feet before she could finish. "I don't want to hear this after all."

He made to move toward the house, but she caught his arm. "If you'd let me finish, you pig-headed man, I was going to say I never bedded any of them. Flirt? Yes. Lower my lashes coyly? Yes. Promise all manner of perverse pleasure? Yes. But I never followed through. I've never betrayed you. I've never betrayed our marriage vows."

He wanted to believe her, but she was trained to lie.

"Why would I lie to you?" she asked. "I've lied to you for years, and our marriage is falling apart. I don't want to lie anymore. I want one person in my life with whom I can be myself. One person with whom I can be honest."

He let out the breath he didn't know he'd been holding. This was no facade. He could look in her eyes and see the truth of her words. Sophia *had* been faithful to him. This beautiful creature standing before him, this woman whose beauty and vibrancy he'd taken for granted, had been only with him.

She was his wife. *His*.

He reached for her, but she sidestepped. "What about you?"

"Me?"

She looked down, kicked at a withered purple flower—hell if he knew the name of it—fallen on the walk. "I don't expect you to tell me you've been faithful. I know that's too much to expect, but be honest with *me*. Do you have a mistress? Have there been many other women?"

What the bloody hell was she talking about? Mistress? But then could he blame her for reaching that conclusion when he'd thought the same of her?

"Don't look at me like that. I'm no innocent miss, and I think we're well past pretending we follow the rules of society and don't discuss such unseemly topics. Be honest with me, Adrian."

It was the use of his name that had his heart clenching. He saw the hurt in her eyes, the expectation of what she thought he would say. "I've been faithful to you."

She frowned, and he understood her doubt. Like she, he was a trained liar. He took her hands, looked directly into her eyes. "I don't have a mistress and never have had. There haven't been any other women. Only you since we married."

She gaped at him. "But surely you've had opportunity."

"And because I'm a man I can't resist?" He was not his father.

"But I—I haven't been much of a wife to you this last year. I assumed you would go elsewhere."

She really didn't know him at all. Tonight that would change. "I did go elsewhere—Madrid, Lisbon, Berlin. I worked, and yes, I met beautiful women. But I always knew I was your husband. I do not take vows lightly."

He could see by the bewildered look on her face she didn't know what to say, what to think. "Thank you," she finally stuttered. "This is more than I expected."

"Because you don't know me. You don't know…" He paused, tempted to shield this part of him. But then they'd go on as before, and she'd never know him. "You don't know what my father did." He stalked past her and shrugged out of his coat. It was cooling off, and he could see Sophia's skin covered in goose flesh. "Here, put this on. That dress is too flimsy." He draped the coat over her bare shoulders. "Seductive as hell, but flimsy."

"I think that was a compliment." She sat on the bench they'd abandoned. Her hand went to her neck, a gesture he now knew indicated she was conflicted. Finally, she said, "You're mistaken, Adrian. I do know about your father. I know all about him. I know we never talked about him. I could tell the subject pained you."

Of course she would have known all about his father. She was a spy. Her father had been a spy—he'd been the bloody Black Baron. Hell, Sophia probably knew more about his father than he did.

"What does your father have to do with this?"

He cut his eyes to her. What did his father have to do with this? Was she blind? He had everything to do with this. She held up a protective hand. "We don't have to talk about him if you don't want to."

"He didn't just betray his country," Adrian said, pacing in front of the bench. Hearing the words, making himself utter them made him cold and angry. A man with less control might hit a wall or rip out one of the rosebushes. Instead, he said calmly, "He betrayed my mother. I heard them arguing once when I was about three. She was crying, asking him not to go to one of his mistresses. He laughed at her."

Adrian could still remember the hard pit of sickly fear in his belly as he'd peeked through the cracked door of his father's bedroom. He hated to see his mother cry. Her face was blotchy and uncharacteristically unattractive. Adrian wanted to hug her, comfort her as she so often comforted him.

But his father's face was hard and—Adrian hadn't known the word then, but he did now—impassive. Her tears meant nothing to him. He had merely straightened his cravat in the mirror and made to leave.

Adrian had jumped back, prepared to hide before his father caught him eavesdropping, but his mother went to his father and put her hand on his arm. "Please, James. I need you. Your son needs you. That woman doesn't need you."

He took her hand and removed it from his sleeve. "But I need her. Good night."

Adrian would have hit his father then if he hadn't been so afraid of him. Instead, he'd ducked behind a statue in the corridor until his father was away. Then he'd sat outside the bedroom and listened to his mother weep.

Adrian looked at Sophia, wondering how many times he'd made her cry. Was he no better than his father, after all? "I vowed that night I would never be like him. When I make a vow—to my country, to my King, or to my wife—I keep it."

"I didn't know about your father's mistresses. I'm sorry. And of course you keep your vows. I always just assumed... I never thought... but it was my mistaken assumption. You're very loyal. The most loyal man I know—even before I knew you were Agent Wolf. You're nothing like your father."

He felt some of his anger fade. These were words he'd wanted to hear. "I'm far from perfect."

She reached up and took his hand. "Neither of us have been model spouses. We can still change that."

Adrian squeezed her hand, wishing he felt her optimism. "Can we? One of us is going to win that position in the Barbican group. The other will lose it. How will you feel if I'm reinstated and you're not? I know how I would feel, sitting at home while you're in Geneva, hunting down some assassin or chasing a traitor in Cádiz." He released her hand.

She rose, tucked a tendril of hair behind her ear. "I see now. You think you need this position to prove you're not him, you're not your father."

"I proved that long ago." But did he believe that?

"You had to work hard to attain your position, as hard as I, a woman, did, I'm sure. Melbourne would have watched you closely. Ridiculous, but people still assume like father, like son."

"I can hardly blame them. My father's treachery is legendary."

"No worse than Benedict Arnold or any of the other traitors to the Americans."

He started to argue, but she cut him off. "James Galloway wasn't an operative for the Crown. He was a general who forgot what side he was fighting for. The American conflict was complicated. Who was a loyalist, who a rebel?"

"He knew what side he was fighting for."

Sophia may have known the stories about his father, but she knew nothing of the man.

Adrian continued, "He gave the Americans information that cost lives. British lives. His confusion—as you put it—resulted in the death of several hundred British soldiers."

"I don't condone his actions, but I can understand how it might have happened. Still, he was punished—as he should have been."

Adrian might have said his father was made an example of. He was publicly hanged, drawn, and quartered as crowds cheered. Adrian's mother had not wanted him to attend, but her brother had insisted. They had to show their loyalty was to Britain, not James Galloway. Adrian would never forget the sight of his father sliced open, his bloody bowels being pulled out of his body as he screamed.

He'd been five when his life had changed, when his mother and the rest of Great Britain learned of James Galloway's treason. Adrian's father had never expected to get caught. He thought he'd covered himself well, but as Adrian knew from years as an operative, there are no secrets. Someone always sees, always knows. His job as a spy was to find that someone.

In his father's case, the someone who had witnessed James Galloway's treason found him and tried to blackmail the viscount. Galloway wouldn't pay with money and ended up paying with his life, his honor, his son's honor.

"I know how he paid," Adrian said. "I was there."

Sophia's head jerked up, and she grabbed his arm.

"No, Adrian, you couldn't have been more than five or six."

"Five."

Her face was white. "Why? Why were you made to attend?"

"My uncle demanded we show solidarity and loyalty to England. We cheered with the crowds."

She put a hand on his face, ran it through his hair in a distinctly motherly gesture. "I'm sorry. I'm so sorry. No one ever told me you were at the execution."

"Why would they? You weren't even born yet." He took her hand, kissed her palm. She was beautiful, standing there in the moonlight with flowers surrounding her. "I don't want to speak of it anymore. It doesn't change anything."

"No, it doesn't, but—"

"I don't want your pity, Sophia." He parted the collar of the coat he'd given her, stroked her collarbone. "I've seen worse since then. I've done worse."

"And I haven't?" Her eyebrows arched, her curiosity obviously piqued. "What have you done?"

"What haven't I done?" He smiled. "More than you, I guarantee."

Twelve

Oh, so he wanted to play that game, Sophia thought. Well, she could play as well. "Knife fight?" she asked, beginning small.

He raised a brow, indicating the question was beneath him.

She smiled, liking the challenge. "Sword fight?"

"Of course. *You've* been in a sword fight?"

"Rapier and cutlass."

He looked down at the hand he still held. "Such small, delicate fingers." He kissed them, one by one, and even though she wore gloves and couldn't feel his lips, she shivered. "I can see these fingers wrapped around the hilt of a sword. I can almost picture you in your pirate garb, wielding a cutlass." He winked. "Perhaps the next time we're alone, you might help me solidify the image."

She laughed. She was *not* dressing up as a pirate for him. But the thought of being alone with him...

"What about pistols?" he asked.

She shrugged. "I've shot a man."

"Killed him?"

Her smile faded. "Yes, when I had to. I don't enjoy killing."

"I don't either. I do it if necessary."

"Yes." She understood completely. She leaned toward him, raised her eyebrows. "Ever been shot?"

"Madam, please."

"Really?" Her voice rose in mock disbelief. "That many times?"

"At least three. One shot grazed my temple. Don't you remember that ball we attended at Carlton House? I had to wear a bandage, and I told everyone it was the cure for a headache."

"I knew that was ridiculous. But then I was actually hoping it might work, so I could try it myself. I had a horrible headache that night, as I'd had a vase smashed over my head the day before while in pursuit of a French operative."

"Ming or Meissen?"

"Nothing so valuable or easily shattered. It was thick, heavy peasant stock, and my head ached for days." She touched her forehead, remembering the pain. "Where else have you been shot?"

"Back and shoulder." He loosened his cravat and unfastened his shirt.

Now this was interesting. She'd been wanting a glimpse of him without his shirt, wanting to see if his chest was as muscled as she remembered. Unfortunately, his shirt didn't unbutton enough for her to see much more than his throat. He pulled the material aside.

"Here's the scar."

She peered closely, traced the skin of his shoulder

with her finger. It was thick but smooth. "Hmm. I never noticed it before. The surgeon did good work."

"Surgeon? I sewed that myself."

"I did this one." She pulled down her glove and showed him a scar on her forearm. "Dagger wound."

"You sewed that?" He stared at the small, even line on her skin. With one finger, he traced it, mimicking her earlier exploration. "It looks clean."

"I'm good with a needle and thread. But I always allow the surgeon to sew up my bullet wounds."

"*Wounds*? Plural?"

"I've been shot four times."

He frowned. "Now you're just bragging."

"Do you recall the time we were at the opera about two months after we married? I went to the ladies' retiring room and was gone about an hour. When I returned, I had blood on my gown. I told you it was jam."

"Did I believe that?"

"You didn't question it."

"And what really happened?"

"An agent from Milan with orders to assassinate me showed up and shot me in the leg. I was in excruciating pain for the rest of Haydn's *La vera costanza*."

"Oh, I remember why I didn't question the jam. I'd just returned from Strasbourg where I'd had some sort of chemical thrown on my face. It burned my eyes, and I couldn't see a thing for a fortnight."

"Chemical? I wonder if it's similar to the burn I sustained." She turned and shrugged his coat off then slid the sleeve of her gown down so it gaped a bit in the back. "Can you see that red mark? That's a chemical burn as well."

She felt his hand on her back. "Hmm. Yes." She liked the warmth of his hand on her skin. She felt like a naughty child telling secrets. And at the same time, she was so relieved to finally have someone to confide in. She hadn't realized how lonely she'd been. Oh, she and Blue had compared stories once or twice, but the feeling wasn't the same as when sharing them with a lover, a confidant.

Was that what Adrian was—would be? Her lover and her confidant? He was already her husband. Could they be more than strangers sharing a house? Could she welcome him back into her bed?

Adrian removed his hand from her skin, and she felt the cold seep in again. "Do you know what's worse?" he asked.

She glanced at him over her shoulder. "What?"

"Snake bite."

"Snake bite?"

But he was already sitting on the bench, pulling his boot off. A moment later, he had his calf bare and pointed to a mark. Sophia had to lean close to see it. Indeed, it did look like two puncture marks. "What kind of snake?"

"Cobra. It happened in Egypt."

She touched the bite. He'd beaten her. She'd never been bitten by a snake. "You were fortunate to receive the antidote."

"No antidote. I had to suck out the venom. My leg swelled for a week."

She sat beside him. "I can't best you. I've never been bitten by a snake."

He shrugged. "I've been shot only three times.

Show me the scar on your leg. The wound you sustained during Haydn."

Sophia raised her brow. "Why, Lord Smythe, could this be a ploy to catch a glimpse of my leg?"

He gave her a wounded look, which didn't fool her for a moment. "I showed you mine."

"Very true." Her left leg was the one bearing the scar, and as it was closest to him, she bent and lifted the hem of her skirt. She could have done it quickly, matter-of-factly, but she didn't. She watched him watch the silk slide up past her ankle, her calf, her knee. She heard his slight intake of breath when he saw the white garters.

The wound was high on her thigh and toward the inside. She slid the hem higher, knowing much higher would reveal everything to him.

"There," she said and pointed at the wound. It was several years old but still had a reddish tinge. The skin was slightly irregular where the surgeon had sewed it closed after removing the ball.

Adrian peered at it, and she felt his breath tickle her flesh. She let out a small moan, but if he heard, he didn't react. "You're fortunate the ball didn't damage any major vessels."

"Yes," was all she could manage.

"The sewing is superb. Your work?" He looked up into her face.

She shook her head. "Surgeon for the Barbican group."

"Farrar?" He was looking at the wound again, his breath tickling her. She gripped the material in her hands as though it was the edge of a cliff and she were falling. How could his breath on her skin feel so good? And wouldn't he find her utterly ridiculous if she were to ask him to simply breathe all over her? But at the moment, she could think of little she'd like better.

"Yes, Farrar was the surgeon." Her voice sounded slow and thick as cream.

"Good man. I've seen him at work. May I?" He glanced up at her again, held his hand up. He wasn't wearing gloves.

Dear Lord, he wanted to touch her. If she was this aroused from his breath, what might happen if she allowed his hands on her?

But before she could do the sensible thing—throw the dress down to cover herself and tell him they should return inside—she said, "Of course." She didn't even recognize her voice.

Oh, but she recognized his touch. His touch was, as she remembered it, light and sure. His fingers had calluses. She'd never understood why before. How did one obtain calluses when one spent all day in the library or at the club? Now she knew where those calluses came from. She wanted to kiss them, wanted to kiss every part of him, because it was all new to her.

"Does it still pain you?" he asked, running his fingers over the wound then placing his warm hand on her chilled thigh.

"Yes. I mean, no."

He glanced up at her, and she saw the smile on his lips. He was playing with her.

She tossed the silk down and began to rise. "I think we'd better return inside. We shall be missed."

He pressed her back on the bench with his hand. His touch was light, not forceful, and yet she found herself unable to rise. "We won't be missed. Cordelia is probably relieved you aren't stealing her share of the attention."

Sophia couldn't argue with that logic. "But Edward—"

"My brother has a cigar, port, and a few moments without his wife and children. He's not thinking about me." The hand on her thigh moved lower, and she felt him trace the garter holding her stocking in place.

"Very well, but the other guests might wonder to where we've disappeared."

"We're married. No one is worried about your virtue." His hand dipped into her stocking, and one finger tickled the back of her knee. It was an extremely sensitive spot, and he obviously remembered she'd liked to be touched there, kissed there. But surely he wouldn't attempt that in the garden.

"I'm worried about my virtue," she breathed.

"You should be." His mouth met hers, and the feel of his lips on hers was like putting on her favorite chemise or stays and realizing someone had made adjustments so that what once fit comfortably was now perfectly contoured for her body alone. She knew his mouth. She'd kissed it earlier today, and yet she didn't remember his lips being this tantalizing. She didn't remember the way he gave so freely and then took from her so effortlessly. She didn't remember the shock of his tongue meeting hers and all of her nerves jumping into awareness. She didn't remember the sound of his groaning... no, wait—that was she.

He surfaced, and she realized his warm hand was

now on her bare hip. "I don't think you really want to go inside."

"Don't I?" She allowed her fingers to explore—just for a moment—the open vee of his shirt. His skin was so bronze. How did he manage that?

"No." He dipped his mouth to her chin and kissed a light path to her ear. "You want to stay out here with me," he whispered.

"I don't think that's the sensible thing to do."

"You're not sensible." He took her earlobe between his teeth, and she dug her nails into his shoulder. The skin under her hands flexed, but he didn't protest.

"I'm perfectly sensible." She angled her neck so he could kiss the spot—yes, there—just under her ear. How good of him to remember she liked that.

"You've been shot four times," he murmured against her skin. "A sensible person would have quit after the first time."

She reached down and pulled his shirt from his waistband. She needed to see his chest. She might need to touch it, taste it. "Most spies are poor marksmen. I wasn't in any danger."

"Oh, yes, you were." His hand was in her hair. She knew he was freeing it, and she really should protest. Everyone would know what they were doing out here if she returned to the dinner party with her hair loose. But she liked the feel of his hands in her hair, and it was so heavy, it was giving her a headache. "That's why you didn't quit. You like danger."

"Is that why you've been an operative for so long?"

He had to pause before answering, because she pulled the shirt over his head. Oh, my. Yes, she was certainly glad the moon was full tonight. He was as magnificent as she remembered. "I like danger. I like taking risks. I'm going to take one now."

She put her hand on his chest, traced the muscles. "Are you?"

"Mmm-hmm." He tugged at the bosom of her gown, revealing more of her breasts. The material was flimsy and the stays she wore underneath little better. She would be half-undressed in mere moments. "I'm going to make love to you here, in the garden."

She pretended to be shocked. "But, my lord, what if someone comes looking for us?"

"It's a risk." He tugged her bodice again, freeing her breasts. Oh, she felt deliciously sinful now, sitting on the garden bench with the cool night air on her skin.

"Do you think," she said as she traced his muscles down to his hard stomach above his waistband, "everyone would be appalled if they saw us right now, in this state of *déshabillé*?"

"Moderately." He cupped her breasts, ran his thumbs over her nipples. She was playing a dangerous game now, she knew. She did not intend to allow him to have her, not fully. Even in her state of arousal, she hadn't forgotten her fears. But she wanted to see how far they could go. The very real possibility of discovery made her want him all the more.

"Only moderately?" she teased. "And is there something we might do to truly appall them?"

"Yes." His voice was rough as he bent his mouth and took one of her nipples inside it. She arched her back, feeling his tongue lap at her, feeling his mouth suck at her, feeling her legs go weak and a slow burn begin low in her belly.

She groaned and then quickly stifled the sound. She did not want to be discovered. She did not want this to end. How had she survived eleven months, two weeks, and five days—or was it six now?—without Adrian's touch, without his hands on her body, his mouth on her skin?

His hands moved lower, and somehow he loosened the gown and slid it down to her hips. Her stays were loosened next, and she was glad, because they were biting into her skin. He'd always been able to undress her quickly.

He bent her back, laying her down on the bench. The stone was cool against her skin, a delicious contrast to his hot mouth on her neck, her breast, her belly. Her skirts were shoved up, and his hands were on her hips, her buttocks, her thighs. His mouth met hers again, and she murmured, "You're wearing too many clothes."

He laughed against her lips. "I'm not taking my boots off."

"Oh, yes. Bare feet would be scandalous." She unfastened his waistband and allowed his erection to spring free. She shoved the material over his hips and slid her hands over his skin. He tensed at her touch, but he didn't stop kissing her. And then as she stroked his erection—there was that groan in the back of his throat; she loved that sound—he opened her legs and slid his fingers along the tender flesh inside.

Now she was the one who was groaning.

"I want to be inside you," he murmured as she stroked the length of him. He was so hard. Hard for her.

"Use your fingers," she whispered, opening for him.

He slid his finger into her, and she arched her back. He knew exactly how to touch her. He hadn't forgotten what she liked—the pressure, the long strokes, the teasing. He spread her legs farther and tossed her skirts over her belly so she was bared to him. She liked seeing his eyes darken as he watched her writhe at his touch.

He jumped in her hand, and their gazes met. Now was the moment. She had to allow this to go farther or stop it altogether. Or might he allow a compromise?

"I want to be inside you," he said again.

"No." Though her thoughts swam, she was firm. Her voice wasn't breathy or quavering. She didn't falter. "I can't."

She saw him swallow, saw him struggle for what to say, what to do next. "Do you want me to stop?" he said finally.

She shook her head and made to sit up. He stepped back, but she took hold of his hips. "Let me show you what I want. Then perhaps, if you're a good student, you can reciprocate."

She pulled him to her and heard his gasp of surprise. They had never done this. She had never put her mouth on him like this. He—the perfect gentleman—had never asked it of her, and she— disguised as the drab little mouse—had not wanted to seem too adventurous. But now he knew she was Agent Saint. She didn't need to hold back.

She took him into her mouth, stroked him with

her tongue, her lips. She let his reaction guide her, learning quickly how to touch him to please him. Within moments, he was gripping her shoulders. "Sophia, I'm going to…"

She gripped his hips, pulled him close, and felt his climax. She'd never realized how powerful it was before, how consuming for him.

A few moments later, he sat beside her and pulled her against him. "You didn't have to do that."

She shrugged. "Curiosity has always been my downfall."

"Downfall? Hardly, madam. Bloody hell, your shoulders are ice." He rubbed her arms up and down.

"I am rather cold." She gazed into his eyes. "Do you think you could warm me?"

He bent, kissed her lips gently. "Don't let it be said I'm not a good student." He tossed his coat on the bench, and kissing her again, laid her on top of it. She was glad now for the garment's warmth, glad as his body covered hers, as his mouth traced a trail of kisses from her neck to her belly. "You're so beautiful," he murmured against her ribs. "Our first night together, I couldn't believe how lucky I was. Under all those drab gowns, you were hiding a body like this."

She didn't know what to say in return. When she'd met him, she'd thought him the most handsome man she'd ever known. She couldn't believe he would want to marry a mouse like her. True, she wasn't as hopeless as she made herself appear, but she took no great pains with her appearance. She hadn't cared what she looked like then. It was only after years of learning to play one part after another that she found she could appear beautiful when necessary. She learned she was beautiful.

But Adrian had thought so their first night together, and she didn't have words for how much that meant to her. She'd been so young, so inexperienced, and so overwhelmed by him. She'd wanted to do everything right, and she feared she was a disappointment to him. He hadn't even stayed with her a full day.

"A mission!" she said now.

He looked up at her. "What?"

"That's why you left after our first night together. You had a mission."

He kissed her belly again, and she struggled not to arch into his lips.

"Surveillance in France. It was the mission that proved my worth to the Barbican group. Why are you thinking of that now?" His fingers played over her skin, dipped under her skirts, and stroked her thigh.

"I… no reason." She could hardly concentrate with his fingers stroking her leg like that.

"Tell me." He stopped touching her for a moment. "I want to know."

She shook her head. "It seems foolish now. It was so long ago. You don't have to stop."

He laughed. "I'm not going to stop, but I don't want secrets between us anymore."

He bent and kissed her again, and somehow it was easier for her to speak to his dark blond hair. "I thought you left because you were… unhappy with me."

His head jerked up. "What do you mean?"

She struggled to sit, but he levered himself over her, keeping her down. "I told you, it's foolish. I was so young. I was a little infatuated with you, and when you left, I thought…"

"You didn't please me."

She looked away, focused on the spiky purple delphinium growing beside the bench. His hands cupped her face tenderly and drew her gaze back to his. "You never said anything," he murmured.

"What should I have said?"

He kissed her eyes, then her cheeks. "You're right. I should have said something—not about the mission—but something to reassure you. I didn't think."

"Of course you didn't. It's the nature of the job. I know when I have a mission, it's all I can think of as well."

"But you were a new bride. I should have taken that into consideration."

She reached up, pushed the lock of hair fallen over his forehead back. "We can't apologize for every wrong we've done one another," she said. "It would take months, perhaps years. And these are old wounds. I hardly feel them anymore." Not anymore. Not tonight. "I don't feel them at all when I'm with you like this."

"Sophia." His mouth was on hers again, and she drank in the taste of him. Agent Wolf was kissing her. Agent Wolf was making love to her. *Adrian* was making love to her. But as much as she was enjoying it, she feared the night was growing late.

"We really should go inside. Someone will be looking for us shortly."

"I hope they don't find us like this." He tossed her skirts over her legs and belly and dipped between her legs.

"Adrian..." She really should stop him. They had been missing too long. But then his mouth was on the inside of her thigh, and she couldn't seem to make her mouth work. "Adrian," she whispered as his tongue touched her, swirled against her center. Her body went into shock. She was hot and cold, shivering and burning all at the same time. She couldn't seem to still her hips or stop her thighs from falling wantonly apart.

Half of her mind was on the path, her eyes focused on the agapanthus near the walkway. She knew someone would come down that walkway any moment—Cordelia or Edward or one of the guests. But Adrian seemed in no hurry at all. He teased her until she was moaning and fisting her hands in the silk of her dress, and then he pulled away, leaving her gasping for more.

"Adrian!" she scolded him. She wanted him to hurry, and she wanted him to continue forever. Why had she not insisted they return home? He could do this all night if they were in bed together.

"Patience," he murmured. "A good agent has patience." He slid a finger into her, and she moaned.

"A good agent accomplishes his mission," she sputtered as his mouth touched her again. How did he know just what to do to bring her the most exquisite pleasure? How did he know exactly how to stoke her, how to use his tongue on her like that? They'd never done this before, and clearly she had been missing out. Adrian had always been a good lover, but this—this was beyond... she couldn't think of words anymore. She could only feel. She cried out, not caring that the sound carried through the gardens and probably into the house.

A long time later, she opened her eyes. Adrian was smiling down at her. "Did I accomplish my mission?"

She reached for him—

"Lord Smythe? Are you out here?"

Sophia froze. "Cordelia!" She darted her eyes to the agapanthus, but Cordelia hadn't reached it yet. "Hide!" she hissed, throwing her skirts down and pulling her bodice up. Oh, her underclothes were all askew. She would need a good quarter hour and a maid to put herself to rights.

"You hide," he said. "I can handle this."

She looked up from her skirts to see Adrian already had his shirt back on and was shrugging into his coat. His cravat was loose, but that was a small thing. At that moment, Sophia envied the male species exceedingly.

"Lord Smythe?" Cordelia called again. The agapanthus moved, and Sophia dove behind a rosebush, stifling a curse when her hair caught and pulled painfully on the thorns. She tried valiantly to restore her gown without rustling the hydrangea or the lilies. At least the garden smelled good. She'd been forced to hide in far worse circumstances—the Paris sewers came to mind, and she was thankful for the sweet roses, even with their thorns.

"I'm right here, Cordelia," Adrian was saying.

"Oh, Lord Smythe. I—is everything all right?"

Sophia raised her eyebrows. Was that a note of interest in Cordelia's voice? Adrian was standing with his cravat loose, his hair tousled, and his shirt unfastened about the neck. And yet, Cordelia didn't sound as though she thought it strange he was disheveled. She sounded as though she thought he looked good enough to eat.

"Perfectly fine. I was looking for Lady Smythe. Have you seen her?"

"No."

Now there was the tone of voice Sophia expected from Cordelia. Sophia managed to right her petticoat and began the arduous task of arranging her stays.

"Ah." Adrian moved away from the bench and the rosebush concealing Sophia. "Perhaps we should look for her inside. The hour grows late."

"It does. Edward is already asleep, and most of the guests have left."

Sophia scowled and yanked her dress over her bosom. Now she had to do something about her hair.

"How rude of me. I've been out here enjoying your garden."

"If I'd known you were alone, I would have come and kept you company."

Sophia almost burst into laughter. Did Cordelia really think she was enticing Adrian? If she thought he was the kind of man who would betray his brother with the man's own wife, Cordelia didn't know Adrian at all. But of course she didn't. Sophia hadn't known him herself. She smiled. He'd always been faithful to her.

She stuck the last pin in her hair and, hiking her skirts, crouched down to move farther away from the bench. She wanted it to seem as though she was entering from another part of the garden. She knew her clothing still looked somewhat awry, but she'd had to change clothes quickly on so many occasions that she could gauge whether or not her appearance would pass. She smoothed her hair and stood straight.

"That's quite all right. I enjoy my solitude," Adrian was saying.

"Lord Smythe, there you are."

The smile on Cordelia's face faded as Sophia skirted the lavender and sweet pea and came into view. "Oh, Cordelia, you are here, too. Darling…" She reached for him, and he took her hand. "Are you ready for home?"

"Yes. Home and bed." He winked at her, and Cordelia inhaled quickly. Sophia had to hold back a laugh. And all this time, she'd assumed Cordelia didn't like her because she was the viscountess. But the other woman was jealous of her marriage to Adrian. Sophia had never seen it before. She'd never seen Adrian before.

Cordelia led them through the garden, her eyebrows winging up when she caught a glimpse of Sophia in the glow of the chandelier. But Sophia only smiled and took the mantle the butler offered. "Good night, Cordelia," she said. "Thank you for a wonderful evening."

"We should have our own dinner party," Adrian said.

"Oh, yes! Do!" Cordelia answered, eyes shining with expectation.

Sophia looked at Adrian and tried to imagine Agent Wolf and Agent Saint hosting a dinner party—worrying over seating arrangements, place cards, and stationery for invitations, and hoping they weren't called away midmeal to stop a Belgian assassin. Adrian must have guessed her thoughts, because he began to laugh. She followed. Cordelia frowned at them and shook her head as they made their exit.

A few moments later, Sophia was seated across from Adrian in the Smythe carriage. Adrian closed the curtains and moved beside her. "Now, where were we?"

Thirteen

THE NEXT MORNING, ADRIAN SAT AT THE DINING TABLE
with the *Times* in one hand and a cup of black coffee
in the other. He did not drink tea. He'd learned to
prefer coffee in Morocco. The sideboard was buckling
from the amount of food Cook had produced so he
might break his fast this morning, and he had already
finished a plate of eggs, ham, and black pudding, and
he was thinking of making another pass to try the
scones and clotted cream.

"Are you going to eat all day or help me catch a killer?"

Adrian glanced up and raised a brow at Sophia, who
was standing, arms crossed, in the dining-room doorway.

"And good morning to you, Lady Smythe. Coffee?
Tea?"

"I'm not hungry. Should I go on without you?"

He was hungry. One look at her, and he was
famished. Had it been only two hours since he'd left
her warm bed? It felt like years. He wanted to drag
her back.

He studied her in her prim walking dress of
burnished red. With her chestnut hair and chocolate

eyes, the color suited her. She wore the same hat she'd
worn to Hardwicke's office—remade with a plume
matching her dress—and looked, he thought, quite
businesslike. Perhaps that was what appealed to him.
He knew the soft, warm flesh that lay underneath that
prim, high-necked gown.

She slapped her gloves into her palm and raised her
brows. "Am I to expect an answer, or shall I just stand
here while you ogle me?"

"There's much to ogle." He grinned. "You look
beautiful."

Nothing in her expression changed, so he could not
tell the effect, if any, of his words.

"Sit down. Have breakfast with me." Bloody hell.
Could he stop being so polite?

"I'd prefer to start for Mr. Linden's residence. The
hour grows late."

Adrian sipped his coffee, wondering at this impatience in her. Was it the Jenkinson case, or had he
done something to provoke her? Or was it something
else entirely? He felt the awkwardness between them.
It was one thing to reveal oneself fully in the dark
but quite another to drop all pretense in the light of
morning. Sophia, unsure of her new standing, was
standoffish. He was all politeness. They'd slipped back
into their usual roles.

"It is barely ten," Adrian pointed out with a glance
at his pocket watch. "A bachelor like Linden will not
even be out of bed yet. And even if he were, I see
no reason to rush to speak with him. I know Randall
Linden. He didn't murder George Jenkinson. He's far
too indolent to go to the trouble."

"Very well." Sophia pulled her gloves on. "I will go alone then." She turned, and for a moment, he stared at her back.

"Bloody hell." He had long ago abandoned Plan B with her. He was contemplating devising a Plan C, but he rather thought he'd be doing well at the moment just to keep step with her. He was up and after her in a matter of seconds, catching her as Wallace opened the door.

"What is bothering you this morning?"

"Nothing. I simply want to do the job Lord Liverpool assigned me."

If it was nothing, he would eat his cravat. He thought back to the night before. Somehow Sophia had managed to evade him in the carriage and then again when they arrived home. He considered it a small—very small—victory that he'd been able to coax her into allowing him to share her bed. But she had managed to keep him from making love to her as he wished—making love to her fully.

He'd tried to persuade her, gently, but she'd put him off... and then done things to him with her mouth and hands that made him almost forget the idea of being inside her. Almost.

He'd fallen asleep more than sated, and yet even as he'd held her in his arms, he felt there was still something between them, something still separating them.

He felt it even more keenly this morning.

Adrian glanced at Wallace. "Have Jackson bring the coach around."

Sophia shook her head. "I prefer to walk. The weather is lovely this morning."

Adrian clenched his fists. First she was in a hurry to go, and now she preferred to walk. "Very well." He gestured to a footman. "Fetch my walking stick."

"You needn't come with me," Sophia said again. "When I return, I'll be happy to share what I've learned."

"I'm coming. But first I need to retrieve something from my study. Stand there and do not move."

She frowned at him, and he could see her planning her escape already.

"If you leave without me, madam," Adrian growled, now impatient and out-of-sorts himself, "I will find you, and the consequences will be most unpleasant." Without another word, he stomped to his library, retrieved his Manton pistol, and on his way back to the vestibule, took his walking stick from the footman.

Sophia was still standing there, looking somewhat perturbed. But she had waited. Small victories.

"Wallace." He nodded to the butler who opened the door. "Madam." He offered his arm, and she took it. They descended the steps of the town house together, looking every bit the fashionable *ton* couple out for a stroll. Except he had a pistol, and his walking stick concealed a knife. He didn't know what weapons Sophia had with her. Several, he imagined.

"What did you need from your library?" she asked when they were on the walk, heading toward St. James Street near where Linden rented a flat. The St. James area was a strictly male preserve, housing the clubs and gaming hells the young bucks preferred. It was bad *ton* for a lady such as Sophia to be seen on St. James, but Adrian did not think Sophia would care.

And as it was daylight and he accompanied her, he did not think anyone who saw her would comment.

Not that he cared what other men thought of his wife.

"I wanted my pistol," he said, finally answering her question.

She glanced at him, raised her brows. "Do you anticipate trouble?"

"No. I like to be prepared."

They walked along Charles Street in silence for a few moments, nodding to those of their acquaintance—almost exclusively ladies—out paying morning calls. Adrian took in their fashionable gowns and hats, their flirtatious smiles and lowered eyelids, and felt nothing. Curious that he didn't feel even a remote interest. This required further analysis. He thought for a moment and surmised the reasons for his indifference were twofold. First, Sophia was far more beautiful than any of these women. Second, she was far more exciting. He wouldn't be a man if he didn't note the beauty of other women, but his deductions led him to conclude he had the woman he wanted beside him.

If only he could be certain she wanted him.

For some reason, that was a question he was hesitant to ask. He wasn't certain how to bring back the intimacy of the night before.

"What weapons did you bring?" he asked. "Besides your biting wit and poisonous tongue."

He caught the ghost of a smile on her lips before she said, "A dagger and a small pistol, in addition to my natural attributes, which you so eloquently described."

"Ah. Do you expect trouble?"

She gave him a sidelong glance. "Always."

They continued in silence for a few more moments, turning onto Berkeley Street. Adrian still felt awkward. Sophia didn't want to discuss what had happened between them the night before, but now he did. He couldn't allow her to shut him out again.

"Last night…" Adrian began.

"I don't think we should discuss it," Sophia said before the words were even out of his mouth. "We need to focus on the mission."

"I'm able to do both."

She pressed her lips together, tacitly admitting his victory. No matter how much she wanted to avoid the topic of their night together, he knew she wasn't going to say she couldn't focus on more than one thing at a time.

"Mr. Linden is a friend of yours," Sophia said, obviously trying to avoid his chosen topic. Very well. He'd allow the evasion and plan another method of attack.

"Not a friend, but I knew him at school and see him at my club on occasion," he answered.

"So you do have a club."

"He's not our murderer. He has faults aplenty, but he didn't kill Jenkinson."

"Because he's too lazy."

They were nearing Piccadilly, which was quite congested. Men and women of every class hustled past one another on their morning excursions. Merchants plied their wares—flowers, muffins, oysters, warm meat pies, the smell of which made Adrian's stomach growl. Carts and carriages raced past, adding to the noisy tumult. And the smell was a mixture of manure, roses, unwashed bodies, and the meat pies his stomach hadn't quite forgotten.

Instinctively, Adrian pulled Sophia closer, and then gritted his teeth when she gave him an indulgent smile. She may not need his bloody protection, but that didn't mean he wasn't going to provide it. She was still his wife, even if she was a trained agent.

"Linden is far more interested in drinking, gambling, and seducing women than in murder. He runs with the Byron set," Adrian told her, resuming his analysis of Linden.

"Lord Byron? The poet?" Was that a hint of interest in her tone?

"Yes. I don't claim Linden is as dissolute as Byron, but he's not far behind. Mrs. Jenkinson chose the father of her child poorly."

Byron had recently separated from his wife, and allegations of perverse practices were whispered behind every fan. He was indeed "dangerous to know," as Caroline Lamb had claimed, and any association with him was grounds for exile from the most fashionable circles.

"Byron isn't as bad as everyone claims," Sophia said, nodding to Lady Something—Adrian couldn't remember her name, though he knew he should.

"Don't tell me you know Byron."

"I've met him on occasion."

"Of course you have." He was the most depraved man in England, and Sophia was probably exchanging letters with him. "But Byron isn't our concern.

Linden is, and once you meet him, I dare say you'll agree with my assessment."

"I'm sure you're right."

"Good. Now that we've addressed that issue, what happened last night?"

She stumbled slightly then quickly recovered. She smiled at him. "Did you want the names for the acts or a summary of the liaison?"

"You know what I mean. What happened when we returned home?"

She blinked as though thinking. "We retired to my bedchamber—"

"No. I had to practically demand entrance. You tried to shut me out again."

She scowled at him. "I did not. I was tired."

"You proved quite energetic once I was in your bed."

"Are you complaining?"

"No." Hell, no, he was definitely not complaining about that. "But I get the feeling you only…" He eyed a passing matron. "You did what we did only to distract me from my true objective."

"And what was that?" she asked, all innocence.

She was no innocent. He leaned down and whispered in her ear. "I wanted to be inside you." He heard her breath catch and continued. "I wanted to feel you close around me, feel you tighten when you—"

"Adrian."

He smiled. Her voice sounded slightly breathless. "You asked." He drew her aside so that her back was against that of a bookshop. The merchant selling apples in the cart beside them gave them a curious look and then continued shouting, "Apples! Fine, ripe apples!"

"You want me, Sophia. Admit it."

She glanced at the apple cart. "I think I showed you last night. I didn't do anything I didn't want to, my lord. I—"

"My name is Adrian."

"I know."

"Use it." He braced both hands on either side of her, not caring who saw them or how many eyebrows they raised. He doubted Sophia cared overmuch, either. "I like how my name sounds coming from your lips." He put his gloved finger on her ruby lips, parted them slightly. "I'd like to hear you scream it when I'm inside you."

"Pardon, gov."

Adrian glared at the apple merchant.

"Beggin' yer pardon, yer lordship, but I'm tryin' to sell me apples here. Yer scaring away my business."

Adrian reached into his pocket and found a pound note. "Here." He handed it to the merchant, whose dirty hand snatched it even as his eyes went wide. "Go stand over there for a minute."

"I will, And for that, I'll make sure ye get a bit o' privacy." He planted himself in front of Sophia and Adrian and began saying, "Move along now. Nothing to see here. Apple?"

Adrian rolled his eyes and looked back at Sophia, who was smiling. "You were saying?"

"I want to be inside you."

"This isn't the time or the place."

"And apparently your very private bedroom under our own roof isn't the time or place, either. Why?"

She looked down. For the first time since he'd

learned she was a spy, she looked embarrassed. "I told you before. I—I can't."

The quaver in her voice, the way she avoided his eyes, the way she obviously enjoyed lovemaking but refused to complete the act. Suddenly, it all made sense. "You're afraid you might conceive again."

"I—" She looked down. Adrian could have sworn he saw the shimmer of tears on her lashes, but an instant later they were gone. "Yes."

Her words shocked him. He wanted to take her in his arms, hold her, comfort her, but even with the apple seller shielding them, that was too bold an action. He settled for putting his hands on her shoulders. The Sophia he was coming to know wasn't afraid of anything. To hear her sound so fragile roused his protective instincts and quelled his annoyance at being told no by her. He hated being told no, but this was no longer about him. If denying him was what Sophia needed, then he could put his own desires aside. He was not so much a bastard as to think only of himself.

She looked up at him, her brown eyes dry. "I can't lose another one, Adrian. I won't survive it."

"You would." He squeezed her shoulders. "You're strong, and you have me—really have me—now. We'll get through it."

She was shaking her head.

"Sophia, what if you didn't lose the child?"

She glanced up at him, and he saw the flicker of hope in her eyes.

"Sophia, I want a child. I want something that's part of both of us. I want the family I never had."

She shook her head. "I can't give that to you. I'm sorry. I know I've failed you, failed as a wife."

"No—"

"Lady Smythe?"

Adrian turned at the sound of the woman's voice and saw Mrs. Jenkinson. He shut his eyes briefly in frustration. "That's all right," he said before the apple seller could shoo her away. "Go back to your cart."

Sophia stepped forward, all traces of sadness gone. "Mrs. Jenkinson. How are you?"

"Fine, thank you." And she did look well in a loose black bombazine gown that almost disguised her condition, and a frilly little cap on her dark hair. "Are you unwell, my lady?"

"Lady Smythe felt dizzy. She needed a moment's rest," Adrian answered.

"Lord Smythe was worried for nothing. I'm perfectly fine."

"I'm glad I found you. It saves me the trouble of sending a note. My valet, Callows, will return the day after tomorrow. Did you still wish to speak with him?"

Finally. Adrian wanted to shout with victory. Now they would make progress on this case, and none too soon, as they were to meet with the prime minister at Lord Dewhurst's ball tomorrow night.

"Yes," Sophia was saying. "May we call on you when he returns and speak with him?"

"Of course. Do you mind if I ask if you've made any discoveries?"

Sophia glanced at Adrian, and he said, "We've spoken with Mr. Hardwicke and are on our way to

speak with Mr. Linden now." That was as much as he
was prepared to reveal to her.

"Oh. I doubt Randall is awake this early."

Adrian gave Sophia a sidelong look, which she ignored.

"Oh, well, you can't worry too much about the
niceties when you're investigating a murder."

"Is that what you're doing?" The woman's eyes
were huge now. "Investigating?"

"We're merely helping Lord Liverpool," Adrian
said. "We don't mean to keep you, Mrs. Jenkinson.
We shall call on you soon."

"Of course." She opened her mouth then closed it
again. "Good day."

Adrian offered Sophia his arm, and they continued
along Piccadilly toward St. James Street. Something told
him to look back. Millie Jenkinson was still standing
there, watching them and ignoring the apple seller, who
was holding out his choicest wares for her to inspect.
Damn him if Sophia's talk of intuition wasn't getting
to him, because he couldn't help but think Millie
Jenkinson knew something she wasn't telling them.

❧

When they turned onto St. James Street, Sophia noticed
the crowds thinned and the clamor all but ceased. A
very few bucks were up and about this morning, and
no dandies or fops that she could see. St. James was all
but deserted. The dark windows of the gaming hells and
clubs gave them a sleepy, half-lidded appearance.

She wished Adrian were not with her. Not because
he wouldn't be an asset when she questioned Linden.
The fact the two were old school chums would make

the encounter that much smoother. She wished she were alone because Adrian distracted her.

She wanted to push him into one of the dark doorways and kiss him. She wanted to shove her hands underneath his starched linen shirt and run her nails over the muscles of his chest. She wanted him to push her against a wall, wrap her arms around him, and...

She shivered.

"Are you cold?" Adrian asked.

She cleared her throat. "No." Far from it. Why couldn't the man see she wanted him as much as he wanted her? But she couldn't risk it. Yes, she knew she was a failure as a wife. She hadn't produced an heir, and she wouldn't be able to produce an heir. And now Adrian said he wanted a family. After what she'd learned about his family last night, about his feelings toward his traitorous father, she understood why he wanted children of his own. She knew what he needed to prove.

She wanted a family with him, too. Her heart ached when she thought about how she couldn't give him, either of them, the children they both desired. She thought about all the Christmases before them. She could not remember a Christmas they had spent together. Perhaps because there was no reason for them to spend it together. The holiday and excitement of opening brightly wrapped packages and gifts was for children. She'd seen Cordelia's little ones' eyes grow big when presented with a gift. Sophia knew she would never watch her own child's eyes light up in the same way.

She would never hold a sleeping baby in her arms,

never watch him attempt those wobbly first steps, never hear her laugh with innocent abandon.

A small part of her wanted Adrian to be right. Maybe if they tried again…

But how many times did she need to fail before she admitted she was not capable of producing a child? The third time had convinced her.

"Do you remember the direction?" Adrian was asking.

"His flat is on King—" Her nose itched. She rubbed it with her hand. "I believe it's number twenty-seven." Her nose itched again. "I…"

Her nose itched!

Without another word, she reached in her boot and drew her dagger. She felt Adrian tense, go on alert. He sensed something as well. They were passing a small side street housing mews. Sophia saw the flash of movement, but Adrian pushed her to the ground before she could warn him.

She heard the ball as it flew over them.

"Bloody hell." Adrian was up and dashing into the alley. Sophia had to untangle her skirts before she could go after him. She drew her pistol and, using a bit more caution, stepped into the gloomy street.

As her eyes adjusted to the murky light, Adrian hissed from her right, "Straight ahead."

There was an abandoned cart ahead of them, the perfect place for an assailant to hide.

"I'll flank him," she said. That gave Adrian the more dangerous task of approaching the cart directly, from the front. She didn't like the thought of putting him at risk, but she could more easily keep to the shadows and surprise their attacker from behind.

"Go," Adrian said and began to move forward.

She shifted into the shadows, thankful she had not chosen to wear a light color this morning. The burnished red would conceal her nicely. She knew the attacker had a pistol, so she dug her pistol from her reticule and tucked her dagger into her boot. Little good the dagger would do against a pistol, but she might need it later. In fact, she hoped she needed it later. She was a miserable shot.

She crept forward, seeing Adrian do the same from her peripheral vision. It was her own fault she was a bad markswoman. She didn't practice nearly as much as she should. She supposed that was because she disliked the impersonal nature of the pistol. If she were going to be killed, she'd much rather look into her killer's eyes as he or she plunged the knife in. She didn't want to be taken by surprise with a shot in the back.

She was even with the rear of the cart now, and crouched down, making herself small. Adrian was almost at the front of the conveyance, and their attacker had made no further move. She tilted her head, peered under the cart, and saw nothing.

Either the man was gone or he was hiding behind one of the wheels. Which one?

She angled for the cart, making a wide sweep so she'd approach it from behind. She moved silently, trailing her skirts in the dirt and muck of the side street. Another gown ruined.

She was still a good five feet from the cart when she saw him move. He popped up and pointed a pistol in Adrian's direction. "Down!" she called as she lifted her own pistol and aimed it. She cocked it, pulled the hammer back, and fired.

Damn it! The shot went wild. But now the man had turned toward her, and she had to dive to avoid the lead ball he fired. Her knee protested with a sharp scream of pain, but she ignored it and was up again, charging the man. Now was her chance, before he reloaded. She had her dagger in her hand but no intention of using it except to wound him. She wanted information. Someone obviously wanted them dead, and she suspected that someone was the person responsible for George Jenkinson's murder.

Another pistol shot rang out, echoing through the gloom. She ducked but heard a soft cry. Adrian?

Her heart thumped wildly against her chest, and panic welled inside her. Not since the Paris fiasco had she felt such panic on a mission. "Adrian?" she cried. "Adrian?"

It seemed an eternity before he finally answered. "I'm fine. That was my pistol."

Damn it. He'd hit their attacker. Sophia rushed to the cart and saw the man's form slumped over the box. She slowed, palmed her dagger, and approached cautiously. He wasn't moving, but that didn't mean this wasn't a trick.

Adrian was moving in carefully from the other direction, but she reached the man first. She poked his shoulder with her dagger and received no response. She pushed him with her hand, and he began to slide. She caught him, turned him, and watched as he fell hard onto the ground. Even in the gloom, she could see his eyes were open and staring.

Dead.

Fourteen

"Bloody hell." Adrian stared at the dead man. He hadn't meant to kill him. The man would have been far more useful to them alive.

Sophia huffed out a sigh. "Well, that's unfortunate. I would have liked to question him, find out who he was and why he wants us dead."

"It must have something to do with the Jenkinson case."

"Probably, but we can't assume that. We both have enemies."

Adrian knelt down and checked the man's pulse, just to be certain. Nothing. He began going through the man's pockets, hoping to find a clue as to his identity. "Agent Wolf has enemies, but they don't know where to find me. Rarely have I been assaulted on English soil."

"Anything?" Sophia asked. He handed her the man's cheap pocket watch and a pound note found in the man's pockets.

"That's all."

"Not very enlightening." She sighed. "If only you hadn't killed him."

Adrian rose. "I was trying to save you, madam."

It was the wrong thing to say, and he knew it immediately, even before she put her hands on her hips and glared at him. "I don't need to be saved."

He didn't want to argue with her, but he couldn't allow this to pass. "Your shot was wild. You weren't even close to hitting him. He would have fired on you next."

"It would have taken him a moment to load another ball and gunpowder. I had my dagger. And I was trying to save *you*. He almost hit you."

"The point is," Adrian said, starting for the mouth of the side street and not really caring if she followed or not, "if you had wounded him, I wouldn't have needed to shoot to kill." He said the last over his shoulder and heard her stomping after him.

"Oh, I see. You had to kill him because I'm a poor shot."

Adrian kept walking. "I didn't mean to kill him. I was going to wound him." But instinct had taken over. For a second, he had feared for Sophia's safety, her life. In that moment, he hadn't cared about who the assailant was or what information he might hold. Adrian just wanted Sophia safe.

"So you're such a good marksman, you killed him accidentally."

He scowled and rounded on her. "Sophia—"

A dagger flew past his head and landed in the wall behind him. Too late, Adrian blinked, but he was able to control the instinctual flinch.

Sophia stood staring at him, her arm outthrust. "I'm not so bad with a dagger, am I, my lord?"

Adrian took a deep breath, turned to study the dagger protruding from the wooden wall behind him. If he backed up, he had no doubt the dagger would be a hair from his face. "Perhaps in the future you should avoid pistols."

"Perhaps I will." She retrieved the dagger and tucked it in her boot.

He offered his arm, and with a small smile, she took it. "What should we do with him?" She gestured to the dead man.

"I'll send a note to Melbourne, have one of the agents pick him up. Perhaps someone knows who he is—was."

"If the attack was related to the Jenkinson case," Sophia began as they turned toward King Street and Randall Linden's flat, "then this is bigger than we first thought."

She was right. It meant Jenkinson's death was no act of anger or revenge. It was planned, and planned by someone with the resources to hire assassins like the one they'd just encountered.

Adrian wanted answers. Now. Unfortunately, he didn't think Randall Linden would have them.

Sophia remembered the address—she did seem to have an uncanny ability to remember numbers—and he knocked on the freshly painted yellow door of the ground-floor flat.

"A bit garish," she whispered.

"I'm sure it's *dernier cri*," Adrian said. "Linden is nothing if not fashionable."

"Perhaps we should have our unfashionable black door painted yellow."

Adrian winced. "I leave those decisions to you, madam."

Adrian knocked again, and they stood a good five minutes before the door was opened by a young manservant with his hair flying in several directions. "May I be of assistance?" he croaked, obviously just out of bed.

"Lord and Lady Smythe to see Mr. Linden," Adrian said, pushing the door open and moving past the servant to enter the drawing room.

"Mr. Linden is not at home," the manservant said stiffly, and Adrian, whose patience had worn thin a quarter of an hour and two bullets ago, grabbed the man by his wrinkled tailcoat and slammed him against the drawing room's wall. Sophia stepped demurely out of the way and pretended to study a vase.

"Listen…?"

The servant swallowed. "Jarvis," he squeaked.

"Listen, Jarvis. You have a choice. You can either go rouse your master from his inebriated slumber, or I will do it for you."

"I'll wake him."

"Do that." Adrian released the man, who started for the closed door at the other end of the room. "And Jarvis? Be quick about it."

The manservant hurried across the room, quietly opened the door, then closed it behind him.

Sophia wandered the room, studying the shabby furniture, dirty plates and bowls strewn about the room, and the overturned glasses. The room reeked of brandy and stale smoke. She lifted a man's coat from a chair, draped it over a side table, and sat. "We might as well make ourselves comfortable," she said. "It will likely be a few minutes."

Adrian grunted and paced. He was going over the attack in his mind. How was it tied to the Jenkinson murder? Who would want them dead?

The barely grieving widow? Adrian didn't think so. Or had it been coincidence she'd met them on Piccadilly this morning?

The business partner? But did he have the funds to hire an assassin? The man who had attacked them had given little warning that he'd been following them. He'd been a good shot, too, and smart enough not to carry any identification on him. He wouldn't have come cheap.

That eliminated all of the Jenkinson servants— not that Adrian had suspected any of them in the first place.

Their last two suspects were Randall Linden— Adrian shook his head at the very idea the man had hired an assassin; though he had to admit, as the heir to a barony, Linden had access to the funds—and Callows, the Jenkinson valet. Would a valet have the money to hire a professional assassin? He wouldn't earn enough, but what if he'd been stealing from the Jenkinsons?

Adrian shook his head. The Jenkinsons were in debt. They were unlikely to leave monies lying about.

"Adrian," Sophia said. "Come sit down. You're making me nervous with all that pacing."

He moved toward her just as Linden's bedroom door opened and Linden, looking surprisingly clear-eyed and tailored, emerged. He was in shirtsleeves and trousers, but his boots were shined and his linen was starched. He hadn't had time for a cravat, and from the way he touched his neck, Adrian surmised the lack thereof bothered him. His brown hair curled over his brow in the Roman style, and he was freshly shaved.

Adrian clenched his fist. He'd told the butler to hurry, not to dress Linden in his best. If he saw Jarvis again, the butler was going to regret it.

"Lord Smythe, old chap," Linden said with a puzzled smile. "To what do I owe this honor?"

Sophia stood, and Linden's brows rose considerably.

With exaggerated movements, he bowed, sweeping one hand so wide it almost felled a lamp. "My lady." He glanced at Adrian. "Lady Smythe, I presume?"

Adrian scowled and nodded.

"I had no idea you were married to a diamond of the first water."

"Neither did I," Adrian grumbled.

Sophia held out a gloved hand, and Linden took it, bending to kiss it. He held her hand longer than Adrian thought was necessary, looked into her eyes, and said, "I'm charmed."

Sophia smiled. Why the bloody hell was she smiling at the man's nonsense? "No, Mr. Linden, *I'm* charmed. I apologize for waking you and for appearing in this state." She indicated the mud on the hem of her dress.

"It's quite all right. I assure you I'm awake on all suits."

"Good." She took her seat on the chair again. "Do you have a few moments to answer our questions?"

Adrian noted his smile faltered slightly, but Linden said, "For you, madam, I have all day." He looked about, appearing a bit at a loss. "Shall I have my manservant fetch us tea?"

"No," Adrian said quickly. He had a pretty good idea why Jarvis was keeping his distance. He took the armchair next to Sophia and gestured for Linden to take the sofa across from them. He had intended to allow Sophia to handle the interrogation. After all, it was she who wanted to speak with this idiot. But he couldn't stand to watch the man flirt with her. "What do you know about George Jenkinson's murder?" he began.

Sophia frowned at him.

Linden, however, sighed. Dramatically. "That's a fine kettle of fish. Put me in a tight corner, if I do say so myself."

"Because of your relationship with Mrs. Jenkinson?" Sophia asked.

Linden blinked innocently. "A gentleman never kisses and tells, my lady."

Sophia smiled, and Adrian leaned forward. "The lady in question has already told us everything we need to know. Where were you the night Jenkinson was murdered?"

"What concern is it of yours?" Linden feigned offense, but Adrian wasn't fooled. The man enjoyed the attention, even this early morning call. It relieved his ennui, affected or otherwise.

"Lord Liverpool asked us to look into the matter."

Linden's eyes went wide. "Liverpool, eh? Why you two—"

"Linden," Adrian snapped. "Answer the bloody question."

Linden opened his mouth then closed it again. Adrian clenched his jaw in frustration, while Sophia said patiently, "The night of the Jenkinson murder?"

"Oh." Linden straightened, touched the spot where his cravat should have been, and frowned. "If you've spoken with Mrs. Jenkinson, I think you know the answer to that question."

"Answer it anyway," Adrian ordered.

Linden glanced at Sophia. "I don't like to speak of such things in the presence of a lady."

"I assure you it's nothing I haven't heard before," Sophia said. She withdrew her dagger from her boot, making Linden's eyes go wide. She twirled it expertly with one hand. "I'm not the delicate sort."

"I can see that. Bang-up prime trick, my lady. Can you show me—?"

"No, she can't," Adrian interrupted. "Just answer the question."

"You always were the impatient sort, Smythe," Linden said. "I remember you at school, rushing here and there. No time for the pleasures of life."

"If by pleasures you mean seducing servant girls and getting foxed on gin, you're exactly right. No time."

Linden looked at Sophia with undisguised sympathy. "Yes, I was with Mrs. Jenkinson the night of her husband's murder. We were here all night." He leaned closer. "In bed."

"How did you hear of the murder?" Sophia asked matter-of-factly, not giving Linden the appalled reaction he'd been expecting.

Linden tapped a finger on his cheek. "Mrs. Jenkinson came to see me the next day. She was understandably distraught. I tried to offer her some comfort."

"I'm sure you did," Adrian drawled. "How do you feel about the child the widow is carrying?"

Linden's eyebrows shot up. "She was pleased; so I was pleased."

"You knew it was your child," Sophia said. Adrian glanced at her. She had taken his exact words.

"She said it was. I had no reason to doubt her."

"And yet, the child would carry the Jenkinson name," Adrian added.

"Of course. Jenkinson was no nodcock. He knew the child wasn't his, but that didn't mean he wanted to admit it was another man's by-blow. I've known men born on the wrong side of the blanket. It's a difficult life, not one I'd want for my own child."

"But now your child will grow up without a father," Sophia pointed out. "Do you intend to marry Millie?"

Linden's eyes widened. "Jump into the parson's mousetrap? Willingly? Madam, I'm no pudding-heart, but I see no reason to go to extremes."

Adrian looked at Sophia. "Translation?"

She pressed her lips together, hiding a smile. "He's not going to marry her." She looked at Linden. "She's in love with you, you know."

He smiled. "Of course she is." He grinned, and before he even spoke, Adrian wanted to punch him. "I could make you fall in love with me as well."

Sophia raised her brows and twirled the dagger again. "Do you really think so?"

"A dangerous woman. I—"

"Linden," Adrian cut in. "If you're done wooing my wife, I have a few more questions."

Linden sighed heavily. "I don't know anything about the murder. I don't care about it except that it upset Millie. Jenkinson was in queer territory. Perhaps his creditors grew tired of waiting for their brass."

"And who were his debtors?" Sophia said, again taking the words from his mouth. They were working surprisingly well together today, unlike their interview with Hardwicke.

"Well, he was a knight of the elbow." Linden leaned back, yawned. Adrian could see the novelty of the interview was wearing off.

"Where did he gamble?"

"At our club. Your club too, if I recall. Skilled ivory turner. Still, he lost more than he won."

Adrian sighed. Practically every gentleman of the *ton* was in the same situation. It didn't usually result in the man's murder. It would be easy enough to find out who Jenkinson owed. Adrian was rising when Sophia cleared her throat.

"Did you often see George Jenkinson at your club?"

"On occasion. Under the circumstances, we weren't exactly chums. But we'd nod at one another politely."

"When was the last time you saw him at your club? Who was he with?" Sophia probed. Adrian glanced at Linden and saw something flicker in the man's eyes.

He pounced. "What is it?"

Linden looked at him, his eyes unfocused. "Pardon?"

"You thought of something. What was it?"

"I'm sure it's nothing…"

"We'll decide that, Mr. Linden," Sophia said.

"What exactly is your association with Lord Liverpool?" Linden crossed his arms. "Does he know you're here?"

"He's a friend," Sophia said. "What did you think of?"

"Millie—Mrs. Jenkinson—and I arranged our rendezvous when we met at soirees and the like, but occasionally one of us would send the other a letter. It was difficult for her to come here, so when Jenkinson was away, she'd send me a note to come to her." He looked a little abashed, revealing this, and Adrian understood why. If he ever found another man with Sophia, under his own roof, he'd skin the man alive. Linden disgusted him.

"Was there something in one of the notes she sent?" Sophia asked, appearing unperturbed.

"Over time, she sent several notes, saying Jenkinson was at his club. I'd instructed Jarvis to bring any correspondence from Mrs. Jenkinson to me right away, so on occasion I received these notes at my club. Not once was Jenkinson there, nor did he appear."

"Perhaps he arrived after your departure."

Linden shook his head. "I'm no henpecked gaby. If I'm flush in the pocket, I don't leave the table, no matter what wench is waiting to toss up her skirts."

"How very romantic," Sophia drawled.

"I might make an exception for you."

Adrian stood.

"Don't plant me a facer!" Linden held up his hands. "You have no sense of humor, Smythe."

"The point is," Sophia interrupted, standing and

shaking out her skirts, "Jenkinson told his wife he was going to his club and did not."

"Exactly." Linden had risen when she did. She held out her hand, and he took it, bowed.

"Thank you for answering our questions, especially at this early hour."

Linden looked like he wanted to say something flirtatious but closed his mouth when Adrian stepped toward his wife.

"And? Have I solved the mystery? Do you know who killed Jenkinson?"

Sophia only smiled and angled for the door. "Good day, Mr. Linden."

Adrian followed her, and Linden followed him. "Perhaps I'll see you at Lord Dewhurst's ball," Linden said.

Adrian opened the door for Sophia, and she glided through.

"Save me a da—"

He slammed the door on Linden's words.

"You're right. This was a waste of time," she said, adjusting her cap as they stood on the other side of the yellow door. "I'm sorry I—"

Adrian grabbed her, pushed her back against that garish yellow door, and claimed her mouth in a fierce, possessive kiss.

❧

Sophia's breath whooshed out, and the heat from Adrian's body and persuasive mouth whooshed in. Her legs went suddenly weak, and she had to grab onto him to keep from sliding into a puddle over Linden's boot scraper.

It would have been embarrassing if she'd had time to think before Adrian's hand caught her around the waist and pulled her against his hard erection. His lips grazed her ear, and she clutched him tighter.

"I want you."

"Here?" she managed. The idea excited her, and in the state she was in, she might even go along with it.

"No. Let's take a cab home. I don't want to wait."

He pulled her off the stoop and along King Street, searching for a hansom cab. She had a moment to collect her thoughts. "Shouldn't we see Melbourne? We need to tell him about the…" She gestured to the side street where, presumably, the dead assailant still lay.

"I'll take care of it later." He flagged a cab, and the jarvey called, "Whoa!" Adrian pulled her toward the conveyance, helping her into it then settling beside her. He gave the jarvey the direction then closed the curtains and kissed her again. This time his hand brushed her calf and traveled seductively up her thigh.

"Shouldn't we discuss the interview?" she said, voice breathless.

"Later." He bit her neck, and she had to fight not to arch it for him.

"It's better to discuss it while it's still fresh."

He pulled back, looked at her with narrowed eyes. "You'd rather work than endure my caresses?"

"Endure? Your caresses are hardly something I have to endure. I just thought—"

He pulled away, sat straight on the threadbare squabs. "Perhaps you'd prefer Linden."

Sophia shook her head. Was that was all of this was about? He was jealous of Randall Linden? "I'm not interested in Linden. He's amusing, I grant you, but—"

"Oh, and you like amusing men. I'm not amusing."

"Ah." She licked her lips. "You're Agent Wolf. I don't expect you to be amusing."

He glanced at her.

"I don't want you to be amusing. I do think we should discuss the interview and call on Lord Melbourne—"

"I told you I would take care of it."

Now she frowned and gave him a narrow look. "Why don't you want me involved? Is there something I'm missing?"

He gave her an annoyed glance, and she felt her own annoyance break through the last haze of arousal. "Linden's comment. He said Jenkinson lied about going to his club. You think there's more to that?"

"Yes, but—"

"He has—had—a lover? He was meeting with the killer?" Dread was welling inside her. If Adrian knew something she didn't, if he solved this murder, she would lose that position in the Barbican group. For a few hours, she'd almost forgotten they were adversaries, almost began to trust him.

Her mistake.

"I don't know," he was saying.

"Don't know or don't want to tell me?"

He moved across from her and parted the curtains slightly, probably to see her better. "Why are you so suspicious? Why don't you trust me?"

How dare he put this back on her! "Why should I trust you?" she countered. "You've done nothing but attempt to use my affections to gain the upper hand and win the Barbican position back."

The dark look on his face told her she'd gone too far. Well, so be it. She wasn't afraid of him—Adrian Galloway or Agent Wolf.

"Is that what you think is going on? I made love to you only so I could lure you into complacency and then betray you later?"

"It wouldn't be the first time," she shot back without thinking. But that was unfair. Damn it!

"What does that mean?" Adrian all but yelled it. "I've never betrayed you. I thought I made it clear last night, I never will."

She clamped her mouth shut, annoyed at herself. She should never speak when she was angry. She said things impulsively, revealed secrets.

"Bloody hell, Sophia. When are you going to let me in? When are you going to trust me?"

"I don't know!" she yelled back. "Maybe never. I want to trust you. I want to let you in, but then I think about Henry and—"

Adrian held his hands out. "Henry? Your brother? What the hell does he have to do with this? With us?"

Sophia swallowed. "Henry didn't die in a carriage accident."

Adrian fell back against the squabs so hard they creaked in protest. "Good God. Here we go again. Is anything about you what I thought?"

"I couldn't tell you before I knew you were Agent Wolf."

"So you lied to me."

She gave him a searing look. "As though you never

lied to me? How was I supposed to tell you Henry was an agent for the Crown?"

Adrian sat forward and attempted to look patient. He didn't succeed, but the way he clasped his hands and set his mouth told her he was at least trying. "Is there anyone in your family *not* a spy?"

"My mother isn't."

"Now that we have that out of the way, tell me what happened to Henry, and pray try to explain what his death, which apparently was not by carriage accident, has to do with us."

"Henry was betrayed by a double agent, a woman he considered a friend, a woman he had asked to be his wife."

"Wait a moment." Adrian held up his hands. "Are you telling me your brother was engaged to a female agent? I assumed you were the only one."

She glowered at him. "Why? Haven't I proven I'm every bit as good an agent as you are?"

"Yes, but—"

"Don't say it, Adrian. You'll only vex me further. In any case, as far as I know"—she have him a pointed look—"and obviously I don't know as much as I thought, I am the only female operative. Rosemary and Henry were engaged when I was but ten. I don't know how she became an agent for the Crown. I only know she and Henry began working together. She probably arranged that in some way. He fell in love with her, and she used his higher status to steal secrets."

"What kind of secrets?" A dark look crossed Adrian's face.

"The names of spies—code names, real names, personal information. Men died because their identities were compromised. Others had their wives or children threatened or taken hostage. Henry didn't want to believe Rosemary was behind what was happening, but finally my father forced him to look at the truth. Henry confronted her, and she killed him."

"How?"

"Poison. He died in agony, and she fled back to France. We later learned she had been working for the French government all along. Her code name was Épine Rouge."

"Red Thorn. I've heard of her."

The cab slowed, and the jarvey jumped down and opened the carriage door. "'Ere you are, gov."

Adrian assisted Sophia, and she walked straight into the town house. The fight with the assailant, Linden's interviews, and her memories of Henry had made her weary. She simply wanted to lie down and rest. In her room, she dismissed her maid, took off her hat and gloves, then sat to remove her boots. When she looked up, Adrian stood in the doorway.

The midday sun beaming through her open curtains flashed on his polished Wellington boots. He stepped forward. "Now tell me what Henry has to do with us. You can't possibly believe I'm a double agent."

She looked away from him, removed one boot, and started on the next. "I don't trust anyone, don't believe anyone, and it's saved my life many times." She removed the second boot, and when she looked up again, Adrian was before her. He pulled her up and into his arms.

"It's a good philosophy, one I subscribe to as well. But you don't need it with me, Sophia. I won't betray you."

She shook her head. "How can I believe that? We both want this position in the Barbican group. You have more reason than most to betray me."

"I don't need to resort to deception to win this position, not any more than you do. We're working together, and Liverpool will choose the best man… or woman."

She let out a small laugh. The fact that he acknowledged a woman could attain the position was progress.

"But let's talk about the real issue."

Sophia raised her brows, feeling prickles along the back of her neck. Whatever he was going to say, she knew she didn't want to hear it. She tried to step away, but he held her shoulders, kept her close enough to feel his heat, smell the clean scent of his soap.

"The real issue is you're afraid."

Sophia huffed. "Afraid? Don't be ridiculous. I've taken more risks—"

"With your life," he said. "Not with your emotions, Sophia. Not with your heart."

She stepped away, breaking free of his hold. "I told you, I don't want to discuss this anymore. There's nothing else to say." She turned away from him, moved toward her dresser—for what she knew not.

"Oh there's a hell of a lot to say. This pertains to me as well, and I want to discuss it."

She rounded on him, saw the surprise on his face. "You want a child. You've made that abundantly clear. Then go ahead and divorce me," she spat. "You have reason. Marry someone who can give you what you want."

"I want you."

"You want something I can't give you."

He came for her, and despite the hand she threw up, he grabbed her around the waist and held her close. He touched his nose to hers, but she continued to squirm. "You can. You're afraid to try again, and I understand why. I wasn't there for you last time. We went through our pain separately."

Now she stilled. He had never spoken of his feelings about the losses before.

"I grieved too, Sophia. I know I didn't show it. I'm sure I didn't feel the losses like you did, but I grieved. And I felt so helpless." He released her now, raked a hand through his dark blond hair. "I wanted to *do* something, to make it right for you, and I couldn't. I didn't know how to comfort you. Instead, I let you shut me out."

She couldn't breathe. Just the simple admission that he'd grieved for their lost children made the tears she struggled to keep in check well up. He'd loved their babies too. "You don't know how much I've needed to hear that," she whispered. She put a hand to her eyes to dash the tears she so hated.

He crossed to her, caught her hand, and kissed the wetness on her cheeks. "Give me another chance. Let me be the husband I should have been."

She wanted to, but inside everything felt tight and strained. She couldn't risk another loss...

"I want only to be your husband, Sophia. I'm not going to force you to try and conceive. We can go on as we have. But I need your trust."

"And the Barbican group?" she asked.

"We're on the same side. I vow I won't betray you."

He was a man who kept his vows. She sighed, relief flooding through her. She didn't know what would happen when it truly mattered, but she knew he would not intentionally deceive her. "I trust you," she answered.

He raised his brows. "Do you?"

She frowned. She could never tell what he was thinking from one moment to the next.

"Yes." For the moment.

He crossed his arms over his chest. "Good. Then prove it."

Fifteen

She didn't like Adrian's expression. It made her think of a wolf on the hunt. It took no amount of imagination to figure out where his code name had come from. She knew she would regret asking, but she did it anyway. "How can I prove it?"

"Take off your clothes." He didn't blink.

Neither did she. It was the perfect challenge. She'd never been naked before him in full daylight. To stand before him, exposed, left her defenseless. "Are you going to take your clothing off, too?"

"Not even my coat." He'd given their butler his hat and gloves upon arrival, but otherwise he was fully dressed.

"And what's to happen when I'm undressed?"

His smiled. "Undress, and we'll find out."

"Very well." She walked toward the window, intent upon shutting the drapes on the window facing Charles Street.

"Leave them."

She stilled, her back to him. "That's rather daring."

"Hardly. No one on the street can see this high, and

the nearest neighbor with a view is across the street. But let's make it daring."

She glanced at him over her shoulder. Now what did he have planned?

"Stand in front of the window." His voice held a note of challenge, and his eyebrow lifted to echo the sentiment. He expected her to decline. She could see it in the way his lips curved.

But she wasn't going to refuse, and she suspected he knew the risks of discovery excited her. "Very well. I need you to help me with these buttons."

His grin widened. She went to the window and placed her hands on either side of the casement. On the street below, a carriage sped past and a servant from one of the nearby houses hurried along with a parcel under his arm. No one looked up. She did not think they would.

She felt his hands on her back. He started at the base of her spine and trailed them up the line of small, prim buttons. She shivered, picturing his long fingers opening the first of the small buttons just beneath her hair. Indeed, his hand brushed the back of her neck, and she closed her eyes. Perhaps if she focused on sensation—his fingers grazed her skin as he loosed the next button—she would not feel embarrassed.

Sophia was not easily embarrassed—there went another button. As Agent Saint, she had acted in a play on the Venice stage, masqueraded as a sparsely dressed dancing girl in Gibraltar, and pretended to be an opera virtuoso in Vienna—a ruse that didn't last once she had to sing.

Adrian loosed two buttons quickly, and Sophia felt her bodice begin to give.

She wasn't overly modest. She'd been naked in front of seamstresses and ladies' maids on more occasions than she could count. She'd been almost naked in Cordelia's garden last night. But last night it had been dark, and she doubted a seamstress cared one whit what she looked like without her clothing.

But Adrian cared. Adrian would be looking—closely—at every inch of her.

He opened another button, and she realized he was almost finished. Her underclothing would take a few moments to discard once he loosened her stays, but not nearly long enough to still her nerves.

Her body was far from perfect. Her hips were too wide, her waist not small enough, her legs a little on the stubby side. She'd always wanted to be tall and willowy, but no one in her family had much height, and she was no exception. In clothing, she could disguise her imperfections. The high-waisted fashions concealed waists, hips, and legs while revealing shoulders and breasts.

But even there she had help. Her stays gave her just enough lift. Now Adrian would see all of her flaws. What would he think? Her pulse kicked with both trepidation and arousal.

And wasn't that exactly the reason he was making her do this? So she could prove she trusted him to want her no matter what? She wished she could trust that he loved her, but spies didn't fall in love. Neither of them could afford to engage their feelings that deeply. But there could be passion, respect, lust...

"Done." Adrian's breath tickled her ear, and a tremor shot through her. She reached for her hair, watching a hansom cab roll past on the street. His hand on hers stopped her. "Leave it up. For now."

"Very well." Still facing the window, she unfastened pins and tapes, then slid the gown off, tossing it on a nearby chair. Now she stood in petticoat, stays, chemise, and stockings. The petticoat she removed easily, but she couldn't manage the stays by herself. Adrian knew this, of course, and his fingers went to work on the ties. "Do you want me to turn around?" she asked now that she had only the thin chemise and her stockings left.

"Not yet." His voice sounded slightly hoarse, and she smiled.

Below, a man and woman, followed by a chaperone, passed. The woman's parasol blocked her face from view, but the man looked up to admire the buildings. Sophia held her breath, but he didn't look at her window.

She bent, undid her garters, and rolled her stockings down. They, too, were tossed on the chair, and then she had only her chemise. Not that it hid much. The sunlight penetrated the thin fabric, revealing everything. She stood undecided for a moment. Should she lower it over her breasts or lift the hem and take it over her head?

She'd lower it—hide her hips and legs as long as possible.

She glanced at him over her shoulder and allowed one strap to fall down her arm. Adrian's gray eyes were almost blue as he watched the slide of the strap down her skin. She could feel the heat of his gaze on her flesh. Then without warning, he leaned forward and kissed the spot where the strap had been. Sophia closed her eyes and sighed. Perhaps if she could distract him with kissing, he wouldn't look at her so closely.

But even as she reached for him, he moved away. "Keep going," he said, his voice dark as midnight.

She slid the other strap off, allowed the silk chemise to skim down her back, revealing inch by inch by inch. Finally the material was at her waist, and she closed her eyes and allowed the rest to fall in a puddle on the floor. Unsure what to do with her hands, she braced them on the casement again. She didn't want to see Adrian's face, so she opened her eyes and stared down at the street below. Two carriages passed, but the coachmen didn't look up. She imagined she'd see the look of surprise on their faces if they had.

Suddenly she felt Adrian's hand on her waist. Was he noting how it wasn't small enough?

"Turn around," he whispered. His voice sounded almost…

She turned, chanced a look at him. His eyes were on her face, his expression nothing less than reverent. "You're exquisite." He traced a hand down her shoulder, along her breast, against her waist, and over her hip.

"I'm not." She shook her head but didn't say more. She was no fool. She wasn't going to point out her flaws if he didn't see them.

"I want to touch every inch of you."

She arched a brow. "Every inch?"

"Twice." He pushed her gently back against the

window. It was warm from the sunlight, and she could imagine the view from below. But at least anyone passing wouldn't see her face.

She thought he would kiss her, but he didn't. He took one finger and began at her forehead. His hand trailed over her face, and when he reached her lips, she nipped one of his fingers, drew it into her mouth.

"You're distracting me."

"Why don't you take your clothes off?" she said, suddenly wishing to see him in the daylight as well. She could picture him undressed, but not clearly. Too much darkness and shadows. She knew him by touch. Now she wanted to know him by sight.

"Not yet," he said, leaving his finger in her mouth and allowing his other hand to roam down her neck to her shoulder and then instinctively to her breast. His finger brushed her hard nipple, and she let out a little gasp.

His finger free, he withdrew it from her mouth and put that hand on her other breast. Just the mere brush of his fingers against those taut nipples made her sigh. And when he cupped her breasts, rubbed them lightly, she couldn't stop the small moan.

"Your mouth," she said. "Put your mouth on me."

"Is that an order?"

Her eyes flew open—she hadn't even realized they were closed. "I didn't mean—"

He leaned forward and kissed her mouth. "I like it. Tell me what you want me to do."

"Kiss me."

"Be specific. Tell me where, how."

She hadn't thought he'd like receiving orders from

her, but if that was what he wanted… "Put your mouth on my breast. Yes, that one."

"Where?" he asked, kneading her.

"On the side. Yes. Now run your tongue along it until you reach the nipple." When he licked her nipple, she jumped at the jolt of arousal. She allowed her head to fall back. "Take it in your mouth." She moaned. "Suck—gently."

She didn't need to tell him what to do. He knew what she liked. Even without her telling him, he began to suck harder. She moaned again, pushed her hips toward him.

"Tell me what else to do," he growled.

"Rough," she moaned. "You know I like it rough."

He gripped her about the waist, savaged her other breast with his mouth, his tongue, his teeth. She was practically panting. His hands caught her hips, pulled them hard against him. She could feel the wool of his trousers against the bare skin of her thighs. He teased her stomach with tongue and teeth while his hands molded her bottom then slid forward and between her legs.

"There," she commanded. "Touch me there." She was already wet for him. She could feel the moisture as he slid his fingers over her small nub. She wanted him to stop right there, but he stroked her, inserting one finger then pulling out.

"Stop teasing me," she ordered.

"Open your legs," he ordered right back. She spread them farther, and he slid his finger in again, slid it out, and rubbed it slowly over that perfect spot.

"Again," she demanded. "Harder."

He complied, his gaze locked on hers. His eyes were dark, and she could see he was almost as aroused as she.

"Faster." She was breathless now, her body bucking, yearning, seeking, groping for the pleasure he was offering. "Oh, yes... more."

He stroked her again, and she exploded. She had to clutch his shoulders to stay on her feet, and bite her lip to keep from screaming out and alerting the entire household. And still her cry of pleasure echoed in the room.

For a full minute, she couldn't move, couldn't speak, couldn't catch her breath. And then she opened her eyes, and Adrian was smiling at her. "I've never seen your face when that happened before. I want to see it again." He stroked her, and she convulsed.

"No more. Not yet," she begged. "You take off your clothes. Let me see you."

"I suppose fair is... bloody hell!"

"What?"

He wasn't looking at her, though. He was looking past her, out the window. "Another agent is approaching the house."

She jumped back and behind the curtains then peered down. Agent Blue was staring directly at her window. He waved. Curtain firmly in place, she waved back.

"You know Agent Blue?" Adrian asked.

She slammed the drapes closed. "Yes. Do you?"

"We worked together in Brussels last year."

She went to her clothespress, futilely hoping Adrian wasn't watching her every move, and withdrew a voluminous robe. "This isn't exactly proper," she said, slipping it on, "but I don't have time to dress."

"How do you know he's come to see you?" Adrian asked.

"He's come to see me here before." She finished knotting the sash and turned to him. "Do you think he knows you and I—?"

"No. But he'll know now."

"Not if you stay abovestairs." She started for the door, but Adrian followed.

"If he has something to tell you, I want to hear it."

"You can't possibly be worried about Blue seeing me in *déshabillé*. I don't think I interest him… in that way."

"No." Adrian opened her door and motioned her out into the hallway. "But if he has news from Melbourne, I want to know. I sent a note before I came up, telling Melbourne about our little skirmish this morning. Blue might be bringing his reply."

Sophia nodded. "In that case, he might be coming to see you."

They reached the first floor just as Wallace appeared on the landing. "My lord, there is a man here to see Lady Smythe. I told him she was not home, but—"

"That's all right, Wallace. Show him into the drawing room."

Wallace flicked his gaze at Sophia in her dressing gown then, without showing so much as a flicker of surprise, turned to fetch Blue.

❧

Adrian watched Blue's piercing eyes quickly take in the scene in the drawing room. The man was a scene in itself, dressed in a persimmon coat and lemon waistcoat. Blue greeted Sophia formally then nodded to Adrian. "You must be Lord Smythe."

For a moment, even Adrian couldn't be sure if Blue remembered him from the job in Brussels. The spy's face was a perfect mask of polite aloofness. Adrian nodded back. "I think you know me better as Agent Wolf."

One of Blue's eyebrows lifted ever so slightly.

"It's all right, Blue," Sophia said, motioning him to a place on the couch. "He knows I'm Agent Saint. You don't have to pretend you don't know us."

"I'm not pretending," Blue said, sitting carefully on the richly upholstered green-and-cream cushions. "I had no idea you were"—he gestured futilely—"who you are."

Adrian could well believe it. He had no idea who the other man was when he wasn't Agent Blue. He wondered how much Sophia knew. She obviously knew Blue better than he. She'd had no qualms about wearing her dressing gown in his presence. Not that it wasn't every bit as formal as many of her gowns and a good deal less revealing than some. She looked small and delicate in the apple green satin with small pink stripes.

"You didn't know we were married?" Adrian asked Blue. He'd had moments where he'd wondered if everyone knew he and Sophia were married but he and Sophia. Perhaps the entire Barbican group was in on the secret.

"I had my suspicions, but she didn't recognize you when you stole Ducos from under her nose, and that threw me."

"I didn't steal Ducos," Adrian began, protesting.

"Yes, our identities were a surprise to us as well," Sophia said. Blue's lips turned down slightly. "Shall I call for tea?" she offered.

"No, my lady."

She shook her head. A few tendrils of her hair, loose from their earlier lovemaking, tumbled down about her neck. "Call me Saint."

Blue nodded at her then Adrian, who joined Sophia on the matching couch opposite Blue. "Why are you here? Did Melbourne send you?"

"No. Why would he?" The question was phrased carefully.

"We're on a special case, and I sent Melbourne a missive, asked him to take a look at…" He glanced at Sophia, wondering at the best way to describe a dead assailant.

"A piece of evidence," she supplied.

"I see. He hasn't asked me to look at it." Blue withdrew a slip of paper from his coat. "Yet. I bring this from Lord Liverpool."

Adrian waited for Sophia to take the paper, but she gestured to him. He took it and slipped it open, angling it so she could see as well. It was a request for them to meet him at eleven the following evening at Lord Dewhurst's ball. The phrasing was such as to leave no doubt Liverpool expected answers. Adrian glanced at Sophia. She was watching him. Clearly, neither of them had answers. Adrian thought of the dead assailant and the valet they would interview on the morrow. He hoped one of them possessed a clue to Jenkinson's murder. At this point, he was no closer than Bow Street to ascertaining the identity of the killer.

Adrian looked at Blue. "Anything I can do to be of service?" Blue asked.

Adrian began to shake his head, but Sophia said, "Can you meet us at Lord Melbourne's office in two hours? There's something we'd like you to look at."

Adrian cocked a brow at her. He wasn't so certain they should bring Blue in without consulting Melbourne first.

"Of course," Blue said, rising. "I'd be happy to assist."

Adrian rose, showing Blue to the door. "We'll see you shortly," Adrian said.

"Looking forward to it. Agent Saint?"

Sophia was a few steps behind Adrian. She raised an expectant brow.

"You might want to have your draperies replaced."

Adrian was still watching Sophia, and he saw the color flood her cheeks.

"I'm afraid they don't obscure much from the street."

"O-of course," she stammered. Blue tipped his hat and exited with a flourish.

Adrian took Sophia's hand. "I do believe this is the first time I've seen you blush, and it's definitely the first time you've stammered in front of me."

She glared at him. "It's your fault. What were we thinking earlier?"

"I know what I was thinking." Adrian allowed his gaze to slide over her. He could picture her naked quite easily now he'd seen her with sunlight streaming over her lovely body. He wouldn't mind doing more than picturing her. "Perhaps you can find a way to pay me back."

She looked thoughtful. "Perhaps. But right now we ought to discuss the case."

She was right, and yet his body still burned for her. He gritted his teeth and tried to focus. He went to the small writing desk, sat, and set a sheaf of paper and a pen on the polished wood. "If we're to proceed in the most logical fashion, we should make notes about the knowledge we have and the questions still outstanding."

Sophia gave him a vague look. "I don't know about the benefit of notes, but my nose itches every time I think of Millie's valet. I have a feeling he knows something important." She paced behind him. "And our assailant. There's something we're missing there. That's why I asked Blue to take a look at him. Blue knows everyone and everything. If this man is an agent, Blue will know him."

"I trust your judgment in the matter."

She stopped pacing and stared at him.

Adrian raised a brow. "Is that so difficult to believe?"

"Yes, actually." She caught a lock of her hair and attempted to secure it in one of her many hairpins. "You've spent the past few days questioning my every method."

Adrian shuffled the papers before him. "I still don't agree with your methods."

"And I don't agree with yours, but I respect your results. If we're going to work together, let's discuss what we know so far."

Adrian dipped his pen in ink. "First, Millie Jenkinson. The most pertinent piece of information she gave us is that her husband had secret meetings, possibly with foreigners."

Sophia glanced over his shoulder as he wrote. "And I got the feeling this morning she knows something she's not telling us."

Adrian's hand stilled. He'd had the same feeling, but he wasn't bloody well going to admit he put any credence in *feelings* to Sophia. Not yet, anyway. He wrote *knows more* and leaned back. "Jenkinson owed Hardwicke money and was suddenly able to pay it back."

"Hardwicke also mentioned foreigners."

Adrian frowned, made a note, then said, "Only after you did. Linden didn't mention foreigners."

"No, but he did say Jenkinson was lying to Millie about where he was going."

Adrian waved a hand. "Men lie to their wives all the time. It doesn't mean anything."

"Well, perhaps Jenkinson was a spy, like you." She rubbed her nose. "That would give him reason to lie to his wife."

Adrian sighed. "Be serious. He could have been going to see his mistress or Hardwicke…"

"Or some of those foreigners." She flopped on the couch. "We're not getting anywhere. Who would want Jenkinson dead, and why?"

Adrian made several more notes then said, "And are we so close that the murderer felt the need to protect himself—"

"Or herself."

"—today?"

They stared at one another, and Adrian could almost feel how close they were.

Sophia stood. "I'm going to dress. Perhaps Blue or Melbourne will enlighten us."

When she was gone, Adrian studied his notes, added details. He put his pen next to Millie Jenkinson's name, then an *X*. He did the same with Randall Linden. He paused at Hardwicke's name, thought about the assassin this morning. Hardwicke hadn't hired the man. Hardwicke didn't have the funds or the connections. Adrian put an *X* next to Jenkinson's partner.

The valet was the key—both he and Sophia agreed on that much. He rubbed his eyes and thought about that first night, meeting Liverpool in the East End. Adrian had been so distracted by Sophia—her beauty, her fighting skills, the revelation she'd been a member of the Barbican group—he'd hardly taken in Liverpool's comments.

He thought back to them now. The prime minister had been visibly shaken by the state of his brother's body. He'd called it *shocking* and *gruesome*. What had he meant? Adrian had seen men die from stabbing. Was the prime minister upset by the blood? The violation of the body?

Or was it something more?

He paced, looked at his notes again, stared at his bookshelf, running his fingers over the volumes. He paused when he touched Shakespeare's *Julius Caesar* and thought of Marc Antony bemoaning Caesar's wounds, calling them "poor, dumb mouths." Adrian would speak for Jenkinson's poor, dumb mouths. And if he wanted his position in the Barbican group back, he would find his Brutus.

Sixteen

SOPHIA STOOD OVER THE DEAD BODY OF THEIR ATTACKER from this morning and tried not to breathe. She desperately wanted to put a handkerchief over her mouth and nose, but none of the men had done so, and if they could handle the smell of death, so could she. The man hadn't been dead long, and she'd smelled far worse. Still, her stomach wanted to rebel, and even though she firmly forbade it to do so, it churned and threatened. A year or so ago, she'd been trapped in a closet with a ripe corpse for two hours, and she still shivered when she thought of its yellow fingernails scraping the flesh on her arm.

Blue peered at the man again and frowned. Melbourne walked around him, apparently studying him from several angles. Sophia wanted to scream for them to hurry up, but instead she clutched her hands behind her back and tried to look bored. She'd thought she was relatively successful until Adrian gave her a look of concern. Perhaps she'd been looking grim rather than bored.

"He's not one of ours," Melbourne finally said.

Sophia blinked, exceedingly grateful for the interruption. She'd never actually met Lord Melbourne,
leader of the Barbican group. She'd received dozens
upon dozens of missives and directives from him over
the years, but this was the first time they'd met face-
to-face. He was no less impressive in person than the
stories of him had led her to believe. He was an older
man, midfifties, with hair graying at the temples. He
had an athletic build, broad shoulders under his finely
tailored coat, and long, muscular legs, highlighted by
fitted breeches and stockings.

When they'd arrived, he hadn't seemed the least
surprised to see her with Adrian and had treated her as
though they'd been acquainted for years—which she
supposed in a way they had been. Adrian had greeted
his mentor rather coolly, she thought, but perhaps she
had misunderstood their relationship.

"What do you think, Blue?" Melbourne looked at
the agent beside him.

"I concur." Blue stepped away from the body and
wrinkled his nose delicately. Thank God someone
besides her was bothered by the odor! "I've never seen
him before, which makes it unlikely he's an agent at
all. I know most of the French, Spanish, American,
and Italian agents."

This was news to Sophia, but she didn't ask for
details, not that they'd be given to her anyway. She
supposed she'd run into a fair number of foreign
agents herself.

"Then who is he?" Adrian asked. Sophia would
have liked the answer to that question as well, but
was this room really the place to hold the discussion?

At the moment, Melbourne's office was infinitely more appealing.

"When you find Jenkinson's murderer, Agent Wolf, you'll have the answer to that question."

"Then you think the attack was related to the Jenkinson case as well?" Adrian asked.

"I do."

The men were standing over the dead body, arms crossed, casually discussing the case. Was she the only one who couldn't wait to be out of here?

"Might we discuss this in your office?" Adrian said. Sophia flicked her gaze to him, saw he was watching her, and gave him a grateful smile. She didn't care if he saw her need to leave as weakness. She didn't care if he realized she had a vulnerability. All she could think was Adrian was taking care of her—not that she needed him to, but it was lovely all the same.

She could handle herself. She could stand in this awful room with its rank smell all day if she had to. And she would have, if that was what it took to prove herself. But she no longer felt she needed to prove herself—not to Adrian, at least.

They removed to Melbourne's office, Blue crying off as he claimed to have other duties. When it was just the three of them, and Adrian had gone over the work they'd done on the case thus far, Melbourne sat back. "I knew I was right in recommending you to Liverpool. It may not feel like it, but you're close."

"I agree," Adrian said. "The attack proves that much."

Melbourne turned his green eyes on her. "What's your opinion, Agent Saint?"

She straightened. "Someone wants to protect his or

her identity. We've stumbled on something, even if we don't know what it is yet, that could compromise our killer."

Melbourne steepled his fingers, looked from Adrian to Sophia and back again. "You're working well together. I didn't foresee that."

Adrian shifted, and Sophia could almost feel the waves of anger radiating off him. "So then you knew, all along, who she was. Her identity wasn't a secret."

"Not to me." If Melbourne was at all disturbed by Adrian's poorly disguised annoyance, he didn't show it. "I knew who she was long before you ever set eyes upon her." He leaned forward. "What I didn't expect was for the two of you not to realize who the other was. No other agent, with perhaps the exception of Blue, could have kept the secrets you two did."

"I appreciate the compliment," Adrian growled. "But I would have preferred you, of all people, to have been honest with me."

"Oh, I see." Melbourne's eyes softened. "You see this as another betrayal."

Sophia thought of Adrian's father and wondered how much Melbourne knew.

"I don't see it that way," Adrian countered.

"Don't you? Did you ever think perhaps I was doing you a favor by keeping your identities secret from one another?"

"How so?" Sophia asked.

"I was giving you some semblance of a normal life. That's something most agents never have."

A normal life. That was all she'd ever wanted, until she couldn't have it. But what was her definition of *normal* now? Now that she and Adrian knew the truth about one another, she couldn't imagine not working together. "If we're as good as you claim," she said to Melbourne, "why not reinstate us into the Barbican group now?"

Melbourne laughed. "That's why I like you, Saint. You're bold. If it were my decision, I'd reinstate you both today, but it's Liverpool's call. He made the determination we needed to cut agents. There are others with skills more necessary than those you two possess."

Adrian was on his feet. "What skills? I can—"

Sophia touched his arm, and he stalked away. He hated not having control. It frustrated her as well, but she'd had more experience with loss of control than he. Melbourne spoke to her but kept his gaze on Adrian, now standing with his back to the Barbican's leader. "Have you considered that you might enjoy retirement?"

"What's to enjoy?" Adrian barked behind her.

"We both miss being in the field," she said.

"Why? What precisely do you miss? The long days away from home? The uncomfortable travel? The hours of surveillance? That's not life." He lifted a file on his desk, turned it over. "But perhaps I've misjudged. Perhaps you don't want to have a life together."

Sophia opened her mouth then closed it again. She was afraid to look at Adrian, because Melbourne was right. The Barbican group would only take her away from Adrian, just as she was beginning to want to be with him. But one of them would be reinstated. One of them would leave the other. If she'd had a child, she could have borne Adrian's absences. She could have doted on her son or daughter and not counted every hour, every minute Adrian was away.

But she had nothing but a big empty house without him. Better she leave it than walk its echoing halls alone.

She rose, feeling unsteady. "It's late, and we have several engagements tomorrow."

Adrian was immediately at her side. "One of us will see you again soon."

Sophia nodded absently. He seemed to want this position so badly. Did he still care about a life with her? What about his promises to support her if she conceived again? Where would those promises stand when he was given an urgent mission?

Melbourne stood. "I'll be on pins and needles until one of you walks through that door again."

She followed Adrian into the corridor then out of the nondescript building. The Mall was dark but far from quiet. Groups of men dressed in tailcoats and breeches hustled by, giving Sophia appreciative looks. Carriages clopped past, and Sophia caught quick glimpses of white-gloved arms and jewel-laden necks. The *ton* was out and celebrating tonight, but Sophia didn't feel a part of it. What would her life have been like if she were a typical viscountess? Would she live for routs and balls, think of nothing more strenuous than what she should wear and with whom she should dance?

She glanced at Adrian, but his features were dark and unreadable. He'd signaled to their coachman, but it would take a moment for their man to steer the conveyance through the throng. Sophia put her arm on Adrian's elbow. "I didn't realize you were so close to Melbourne."

"He taught me everything I know."

Her father had taught her, and, she supposed, in a way, so had Adrian's.

"He couldn't tell you I was Agent Saint," she said, "any more than he could reveal your identity to me. You know the rules."

"I know the rules," he said. "I'm tired of the rules."

So was she. But did Adrian mean it? "They're for our protection," she said weakly.

He looked at her, his intent gaze making her heart leap a little. "Did I need protection from you? My own wife?"

Sophia thought of Henry. He'd needed protection from the woman he almost made his wife.

"But I know the motto," Adrian said darkly.

So did Sophia. *The mission is everything.*

Sophia had always agreed wholeheartedly. Henry's death had taught her not to trust. Her own losses had given her position with the Barbican group even greater importance. But now she wondered if missions were all there was to life. Was Adrian having second thoughts as well?

The carriage stopped before them, and their footmen jumped down. "Let's go home," Adrian said as he assisted her into the conveyance. "I want to go over everything one last time."

Sophia settled on the squabs. It was going to be a long, and not particularly enjoyable, night.

꩜

Adrian woke early, warm and violently aroused. He was also violently uncomfortable. He slit his eyes open and realized the reason for both the arousal and the discomfort. He and Sophia had fallen asleep in his library. She was curled in his arms, and the couch was too small for one person, let alone two.

The room was dark, the fire in the hearth low, but Sophia was facing it, and he could make out her features in the soft light. She looked so young when she slept. When she was awake, she inevitably narrowed her eyes, tightened her mouth, and notched her chin high. But in sleep, her mouth looked soft and relaxed, her long, dark eyelashes swept across her eyes, and her chin was tucked against his chest. Her hair had come loose, and he could feel the silky curls against the skin of his forearms, where he'd rolled up his sleeves the night before.

He didn't know how late they'd argued, debated, and pulled apart every facet of the Jenkinson case. He only knew he'd lain on the couch, thinking to close his eyes for a mere moment. At some point, Sophia must have joined him.

The buttons on the bodice of her lavender gown were open, and Adrian admired the slim column of her neck. He leaned close and inhaled the scent of oranges. He could stay here all day—well, perhaps not here, but he could hold her in his arms for hours. He liked the feel of her body against his. He liked the soft sound of her breathing.

Once again, he found himself questioning his need for the Barbican group. He'd loved the adventure and the excitement of it, but more than that, he'd liked that he could do something noble. He liked proving, if only to himself, he was nothing like his father.

But now, looking at Sophia sleeping so peacefully in his arms, he wondered what else he needed to prove. For years, he'd wanted nothing more than to serve his country. Now, it seemed more important to serve his wife, his future children.

He didn't believe Sophia couldn't carry a child. She could do anything. They'd had bad luck. True, they might fail again, but there were orphanages, children in need. Why had they never discussed that option?

Because he needed an heir to inherit the title. But Adrian could live without an heir. He wasn't so sure he could live without Sophia.

"What are you thinking about?" she said without ever stirring or opening her eyes. He hadn't even known she was awake.

"How beautiful you look."

Her brown eyes opened, and she smiled. Why had he never noticed what a sultry smile she had? He liked the way her lips turned up at the corners just so.

"Is that all?"

"I'd like to stay here all day with you."

She put her arms around his neck, drew him down. "That sounds heavenly." She pressed those still-smiling lips to his mouth, and he drank her in. Kissing Sophia was unlike kissing any other woman. He'd kissed his fair share—perhaps more than his fair share—before they'd married.

He'd always enjoyed it, but more than the act of kissing, he'd liked the other acts it led to. But he could have been content—almost content—to kiss Sophia all day. She never kissed him the same way twice. She kissed him shyly; she kissed him boldly; she kissed him lightly and deeply.

Now she kissed him sweetly. Warmth, slow as honey, flooded his veins.

"I see every part of you is awake this morning," she murmured and stroked a hand along the hard length of him. He didn't know how she managed the feat in their cramped position, but he didn't care enough to try and figure the logistics. He dipped his mouth to her neck and kissed the bare skin.

"You have too many clothes on," he said when he reached the material covering her breasts.

"I think we can rectify that. But first, you." She tugged on the waistband of his trousers, freeing his shirt. Her hand stroked his chest as she raised the material.

"Oh!" a female voice squeaked from the doorway. The door slammed shut just as Adrian raised his head. "What the hell was that?"

Sophia kissed his chest, flicking her tongue out and distracting him. "Parlor maid. She was probably planning to clean in here. We're supposed to be in our beds."

"Splendid idea." He rose and pulled her to her feet. She looked wonderfully disheveled. He had to resist the urge to pull her clothes off right there. "Your bedroom or mine?"

"Mine is closer," she breathed.

He grabbed her hand and tugged. In the vestibule, he paused to kiss her again before the stairs. A passing footman carrying a silver tray stopped midstride, turned, and went back the way he'd come.

Wallace was not so obliging. "My lord. My lady." His voice was sober. Adrian glanced at him, saw his eyes were on the ceiling. He held out a silver tray. "This was just delivered."

Reluctantly, Adrian released Sophia and lifted the stiff, white, folded note. He was about to open it then saw it was addressed to *The Right Honorable Viscountess Smythe*. He handed it to Sophia, who raised her eyebrows but took it. She broke the seal, scanned it, then handed it to him. "It looks like we'll not have as much leisure time as anticipated," she said.

The note was from Millie Jenkinson. George Jenkinson's valet had arrived home late the night before and was packing to leave her employ. She begged them to come immediately, despite the early hour, if they wished to speak with the man before he departed.

Adrian glanced at the tall case clock in the vestibule. It was barely seven. "The valet seems in quite a hurry," he said.

"My thoughts exactly." Sophia started up the stairs, glanced back at the butler. "Send my maid immediately, Wallace. I'll need to dress quickly."

"Yes, my lady."

"And call for Jackson and the carriage," Adrian told him as he started after her. He knew his valet would be ready and waiting.

At quarter to eight, Adrian listened to the horses' bells jingle as the carriage made its way through deserted Mayfair. The day was warm and sunny, and he found he enjoyed being awake early enough to benefit from the solitude. They passed a nanny pushing a baby carriage, and he saw Sophia look quickly away. He wondered if she dreaded seeing the expectant Millie Jenkinson. No one would ever suspect how much she suffered the loss of their children. Even he hadn't known her anguish. He had supposed she moved past the grief as he did, but now he wondered if she ever could, ever would.

"Sophia? Would you rather not see Mrs. Jenkinson today? I can handle the valet interview."

She looked at him for a long time, her expression a war between mistrust and gratitude. Finally, she said, "Thank you. I'll be fine."

The carriage slowed, and he parted the drapes, revealing the Jenkinson town house. Before they'd even alighted, the butler opened the door. "My Lord and Lady Smythe." He gave a stiff bow. "If you would follow me to the parlor, Callows is waiting."

It seemed to Adrian, upon entering the parlor, Callows was being held prisoner. The valet was a small, thin man with dark, thinning hair, a sharp, pointed nose, and as was expected, perfectly tailored clothing. Two footmen stood at the parlor door and Callows glared at them with red-rimmed eyes. He turned his glare on Adrian when he entered.

"Well, this should be easy," Sophia quipped as she strode into the room.

"I demand to be released!" The valet jumped to his feet, the Chippendale armchair he'd been occupying tumbling over. "I've done nothing wrong. You can't hold me against my will."

"Sit down," Adrian ordered.

"I will not. I demand—"

Sophia strolled up to the valet and looked the rather

petite man in the eye. "Lord Smythe asked you to be seated. It wasn't a request."

The valet stared at her, the footmen stared at her, and the Jenkinson butler stared at her. Hell, Adrian couldn't keep from staring at her. He had the urge to sit after listening to the tone of her voice.

Slowly, the valet righted the chair he'd spilled and sat stiffly on the edge. Sophia smiled, all sweetness. "Thank you, Callows."

The butler moved aside, and Millie Jenkinson rushed in. She was still dressed in mourning, and the dark smudges under her eyes gave her a haunted appearance. Why wasn't she sleeping? A late rendezvous with Linden? Grief? Or something else? The widow crossed directly to Sophia and took both of her hands. Adrian saw his wife hesitate just for an instant before she gave in.

"Thank you so much for coming, Lady Smythe." She glanced at him. "Lord Smythe. I asked Callows to remain for a few hours so you might question him, but he seemed intent on leaving right away." She gave the valet a sheepish look. "I didn't want to restrain him, but…"

"You did the right thing, Millie," Sophia reassured her. "And this interview will take only a few moments." She glanced at the valet. "Assuming Callows is cooperative, he can be on his way directly."

"Very well. Do you mind if I stay and listen?"

Adrian opened his mouth to protest, but Sophia was already shaking her head. She steered Millie to the door, saying quietly, "I've found the staff often doesn't like to speak freely in front of employers, even former employers. If it's not too much inconvenience, we'd like to speak to him privately." She glanced at the footmen and the butler.

"Of course. Please let me know if there's anything you require." And with a wave of Mrs. Jenkinson's arm, the butler, the footmen, and the widow departed. Adrian looked at the seated valet and the all-but-empty parlor. How had Sophia accomplished all of that in, he glanced at the clock on the mantel, three minutes?

Sophia sat in a Chippendale armchair matching the valet's and smiled up at Adrian. At that moment, he wanted nothing more than to kiss her. Soundly.

"My lord, you may begin when ready."

He blinked, cleared his throat. "Mr. Callows, when was the last time you saw George Jenkinson?"

He rolled his eyes. "The night I found him dead." His tone indicated this should be patently obvious. Adrian gritted his teeth and resisted the urge to punch the valet.

"Walk us through that night," Sophia said, sounding far calmer than he felt.

The valet sighed. "Is this really necessary?"

Sophia examined her glove then smoothed her cream skirts. "Take your time, Mr. Callows. We have no pressing engagements."

"You can't keep me here against my will." The man's pale face flooded with color. "I demand to see the constable."

"Of course." Sophia smiled. "After you answer our questions." She glanced at Adrian. "Should we call for tea, my lord? I fear we may need refreshment."

"Fine. I'll tell you what I saw." The valet visibly

shuddered, and Adrian flicked his eyes to Sophia. She'd noticed as well.

"Start at the beginning," Adrian ordered. He was prepared to give the valet one last chance to cooperate. If the man still resisted, he was going to ask Sophia to step out of the room and employ Plan B.

Callows rolled his eyes, and Adrian almost hoped he had to ask Sophia to give him a moment alone with the valet.

"Mr. Jenkinson arrived home at close to midnight."

"From?" Adrian asked.

The valet glared at him. "I did not inquire. I'm only the valet, *my lord*." Adrian started for him, not caring if Sophia was still present, but she rose and swiftly stepped in front of him.

"Did Mr. Jenkinson retire?"

"Yes." The valet's gaze never left Adrian's. "He dismissed me and went to bed, so far as I know."

"What did you do?" Adrian said through clenched teeth.

The valet looked like he had another quip ready, but he hesitated for a moment then said, "I also retired. At about three, I thought I heard a noise. I rose and went to check on Mr. Jenkinson."

Adrian frowned. He rarely summoned his own valet after the man had been dismissed for the night. "Did Mr. Jenkinson often require your services in the middle of the night?"

"No."

Sophia was still standing beside him, but she lowered her hand from his arm. "Then why did you go to him?" she asked. "Did he call out or ring for you?"

The anger and annoyance on the valet's face ebbed away, and he shook his head. "No. I—this might sound strange." He looked at Sophia now, clasped his hands in his lap, and unclasped them. "But I had a feeling something was wrong."

Sophia sank into the chair beside the valet. "That doesn't sound strange at all. You sensed something was amiss."

The valet nodded. "Exactly."

Adrian wanted to tear his hair out. He didn't believe in *feelings* and *sensing*. He believed in concrete, tangible things. "Mr. Callows, I'm not as… intuitive as my wife. Think back. Did you hear a sound or see a light? What woke you?"

The valet shook his head. "Nothing. I sensed something was amiss. When I woke, there was naught amiss or disordered. I almost went back to sleep, but I had a—" He looked at Sophia. "A feeling. I acted upon it, dressed, and entered Mr. Jenkinson's room."

"What did you see?" Sophia asked.

The valet shook his head. "Madam, it's not a fit topic for a lady such as you."

Adrian couldn't agree more, but he knew Sophia would rather stick her hand in a roaring fire than be excluded from the interview because of her gender.

"Mr. Callows," she said, "I stood over the body of a dead man for three-quarters of an hour yesterday. It wasn't the first time I've done so. Whatever you saw, I can guarantee you, it won't shock or surprise me."

"Very well." The valet's mouth was thin and hard again, Adrian noted. The man did not want to speak of this. "I walked into Mr. Jenkinson's chamber and found him displayed on the floor."

Adrian stopped him. "What do you mean, *displayed*? That's an unusual choice of words."

The valet sighed impatiently. "If you'd seen the body, you'd understand. It was, for all intents and purposes, on display."

"Describe it," Sophia ordered.

The valet's lip curled in disgust. He shut his eyes. "Mr. Jenkinson was unclothed. This was not his state when I left him. I helped him dress in his nightshirt and cap."

"Did you see it when you entered the room?" Adrian asked.

"Not immediately. But I spotted the nightshirt later. It was cleanly cut in two and tossed on the bed. The nightcap had been used as a—" He cleared his throat, shut his eyes again. "A gag."

Adrian nodded. So Jenkinson's attacker needed to prevent the victim from crying out or alerting the staff. Still, the valet had awakened, and despite what Callows claimed about his *feelings*, Adrian believed Jenkinson had been able to make some sound of distress.

"The body was..." He wiped a hand over his eyes. "The state of the body..."

Sophia gripped the valet's hand, her action surprising Adrian. "If you say it quickly," she said, her voice reassuring, "it's sometimes easier."

The valet took a breath, nodded. Adrian wondered how he had ever conducted interviews without Sophia. It seemed she flirted or coaxed the information from every one of their suspects. Intimidation had always worked for him, and he grew impatient with Sophia's slower methods, but he had to admit that they worked.

"He'd been sliced," the valet said rather quickly. He swallowed. "All over. Deep cuts from his neck to his toes, dozens of them."

"The wounds were horizontal?" Adrian asked.

The valet nodded.

"Was there any pattern?" Sophia asked. "Anything unusual?"

The valet stared at her. "Besides the fact that he'd been all but sliced open?"

She pressed her lips together. "Yes."

"Good God, but you two are a cold pair. I've just told you the man was sliced a dozen or more times. He lay in a pool of his own blood so deep and thick, some leaked through the ceiling of the floor beneath. And you want to know about patterns?"

"I know this must be difficult," Sophia said.

The valet stood. "You have no idea. But since you ask, yes, there was something unusual. Amidst the cuts, the letter *M* had been carved into Mr. Jenkinson's chest."

Seventeen

SOPHIA HADN'T THOUGHT ANYTHING CALLOWS TOLD her would shock her, but the idea of someone carving a letter—an initial?—on a man's chest did shock and sicken her. Had Jenkinson been alive when the initial had been carved? Had the initial stab wounds killed him?

They'd questioned Callows for another hour about the details of the body—the amount of blood, whether it had been spattered, the type of knife he thought had been used. They'd gone to Jenkinson's room and examined it. The room had been cleaned and the carpet removed, but Sophia had no trouble picturing the scene as Callows had described. It made her stomach revolt.

Now she and Adrian stepped into the bright midday sunshine, and she squinted. It seemed they had been inside the dark Jenkinson town house for days, not mere hours. And while inside, all was gloom and death, outside, the world was sunny. Birds sang, flowers bloomed, a phaeton carrying a dandy and a laughing woman in a fashionable hat streamed past.

"I'll have a footman call for the carriage," Adrian said, turning back to the dark house.

Sophia put her hand on his arm. "Let's walk. I could use the fresh air."

"Very well. I'll instruct Jackson to drive home, then." He left to give the orders, and she watched his back. Admired the graceful way he moved, like a cat prowling. His dark blond hair was mussed, as he'd run his hand through it half a dozen times. She liked it disordered. He was so serious, so regimented. Sometimes she had the urge to grab his cravat and pull it askew. And yet, if he'd been more spontaneous, as she was, she wouldn't have liked him as much.

She wouldn't have felt safe with him, wouldn't have trusted him. And was it just her imagination, or had he softened slightly? He no longer argued with her methods; he no longer insisted she not pursue the case or avoid jumping into dangerous situations. She could tell he didn't like it. Yesterday when they'd been attacked outside Linden's residence, she had known he was angry she was put in a vulnerable situation. But she liked to think she'd earned his respect.

And she liked that she could be vulnerable and still keep his respect. He seemed to understand her need to walk in the sunshine today, to shake off some of the darkness and cold of death. He didn't ask her why, didn't complain that the walk was long and the coach was readily available. Adrian just took care of her, gave her what she needed.

It was an amazing feat, considering at times she didn't even know what she needed. But now she knew what she wanted. She wanted a life with him—whether that was traveling around the world, working for the Barbican group, or staying home and raising their children.

She felt her stomach tighten and had to swallow the lump threatening to rise in her throat. She clenched her fists. Why could she not get past those losses? Why must they torment her so she thought of them whether she wanted to or not? Why must she blame herself?

Perhaps because everyone but Adrian faulted her for their childlessness. If a couple were unable to reproduce, it was always the woman's fault. Sophia almost wished she were barren. At least she might never have had the hope, might never have known it was her own body that failed her.

After the first miscarriage, she'd been so careful. When she even thought there might have been a chance she'd conceived, she'd refused all missions, all social engagements, and stayed in bed. She'd hoped that by resting, the little baby would thrive and grow. But she'd awoken one night, her body wracked with pain and blood staining her sheets. The doctor had come, and the look on his face when he shook his head had rent her heart.

She'd felt so helpless as the little life in her drained away. She'd wanted that child so badly, imagined a little girl with Adrian's blond hair and gray eyes or a little boy with her dark coloring. She'd been left with nothing.

After time and healing, she and Adrian had tried again. They'd never spoken of the miscarriages, and she'd never told him she wanted to try again. She just made it clear, in subtle ways, he was once again welcome in her bedroom. And again, as soon as she thought she might have conceived, she took every single precaution. When she'd known for certain she was pregnant, she'd even forgone going up and down the stairs. That child had lived longer than any other. But in the end, she'd lost it as well.

Why? She screamed at the doctor with the sad face. *What is wrong with me?*

He hadn't been able to answer her and recommended rest and trying again.

These things happen, he'd said.

It was better than what previous doctors told her. She'd caused the miscarriage with a foul mood. Another told her she worried too much, and that caused her miscarriages.

But this doctor had shrugged. *These things happen.* Sophia had repeated the words to herself over and over and over.

It was cold comfort.

After the final miscarriage, she'd taken every mission, asking for the most dangerous. She'd wanted to feel strong and in control. She didn't want to feel helpless anymore. Perhaps that was why the loss of Ducos to the agent she now knew was Adrian had cut her so. Once again, she'd felt helpless, out of control.

Now as she stood on Millie Jenkinson's walkway, she realized she didn't feel helpless anymore. She didn't feel she needed to be in control all the time. She could give some of that control to Adrian. She saw he was worthy of her trust. She was not Henry. She could trust Adrian to take care of her, and she would take care of him.

Sophia had never been in love before. She'd loved her parents and her brother. She'd loved those little unborn babies. But she'd never loved a man. She'd wanted to love Adrian, had certainly lusted after him, but she'd never been able to give all of herself. Had that changed now? Now he knew who she was, who she *really* was. And she could trust him with that knowledge. She knew he would stand beside her no matter what.

Was that the beginning of love?

Not lust—they had once again found their passion, that frenzied heat of attraction. But did it go deeper? Did Adrian feel more than mere passion for her now?

"Sophia?"

She jumped, startled by the sound of his voice. She hadn't heard him approach, and that was telling in itself.

He was frowning at her. "I said your name three times."

"I was thinking." She smiled, tried to reassure him.

"Of what?" He started down the steps and offered her his arm.

She looked into his eyes. Eyes that had once looked on her with nothing but cold, gray disinterest now looked warm as molten steel. "Passion," she said.

His brows shot up, then he narrowed his eyes. No fool, that Agent Wolf. "Are you certain you feel well enough to walk? I can still summon the carriage."

She squeezed his arm. "I feel fine. And we can discuss the interview with Callows as we walk. I know how you like to dissect each and every detail."

He didn't argue, not that she'd expected him to. "What are your initial impressions?" he asked as he led her along the street.

"He's scared."

Adrian looked at her sharply. "Why do you say that?"

"It's obvious. The murder horrified him, and he's afraid whoever did it will come back for him. That's why he was so uncooperative. He wants to run and hide."

"Whoever did this isn't after him." Adrian stepped aside to allow a woman leading three small, yapping dogs to pass.

"I don't suppose he's willing to take chances. What did you think of the way he described the body? Have you ever seen anything like that before?"

They crossed Regent Street and headed back toward the heart of Mayfair. Sophia's nose itched, and she glanced behind her.

"Never." Adrian answered. "You?

"Hmm?" She turned to look at him. "Oh, no." But something didn't feel right. She looked over her shoulder again.

"Still, there's something familiar. When we reach home, I'll show you something in… What are you doing?"

She'd stopped and bent to check her half boot. Without looking up, she said, "There's someone following us. Just now, when I paused and bent, he ducked into that butcher shop."

"Are you certain?"

She didn't dignify the question with an answer.

Adrian frowned. "Fine. What does he look like?"

She rose, pretended to shake out her skirts, and then extracted the glass from her reticule. "He's wearing dark blue trousers and a green coat. Light-colored waistcoat and brown hat." She transferred the small glass into one hand and took Adrian's arm with the other. "I can't see the hair, but he has dark-colored eyes and a scar on his left cheek."

"You got a good look at him."

She shook her head. "Only a glimpse, but he's been tailing us since we left the Jenkinson residence." She lifted the glass, pretended to fix her hat as they strolled along Conduit. "He's behind us again."

"Are you watching him in the glass?" Adrian asked. She nodded.

"Clever girl. I say we have a little fun and catch this one."

She tipped her hat to him. "I'll follow your lead."

They strolled amiably for another block or so. Sophia watched their shadow in her glass, and then without even warning her, Adrian cut down an unfamiliar side street. As soon as they were out of sight of the main street, he took off at a jog. He kept hold of her hand, and with her free hand, she lifted her skirts and followed. She understood his strategy immediately. He was going to double back and surprise their shadow.

At the end of the street, Adrian turned left. The smell of horse manure and the shuffling sounds of the beasts alerted her to the mews before they reached them. A few of the gates were open, but most were closed, as the horses had been fed and tended in the morning and were now out and about, pulling the carriages of the wealthy and titled.

"Damn it!" Adrian slowed. "I thought there was a break right here." He gestured to a wall of mews up ahead.

Sophia put a hand to her waist, caught her breath.

Running in stays, a shift, a petticoat, skirts, and a spencer was exhausting. No wonder most spies were men. "If we don't cut back, we're going to lose him."

"Bloody hell."

Sophia scanned the alleyway. Up ahead, right before the mews began, she spotted a low wall. It was probably the back of a shop on Conduit, perhaps a storage area of some sort. "There!" She pointed, and Adrian frowned at it then at her.

"Do you think you can scale that?"

She blinked at him. "Is that a challenge, Agent Wolf?"

"Why not? First one to catch our shadow wins." He started for the wall, and she was right behind him.

"Wins what?"

He had the advantage of height, and he had only to jump to catch the top of the wall with his hands. She watched as he used strength alone to lever himself up. Was it wrong of her to wish he was shirtless? She could imagine the way the muscles on his arms and back rippled and bunched, but she wouldn't have minded seeing it. She was still watching him when he grinned down at her. "The prize is to be determined by the winner." He raised his brows. "At this point, it looks like that will be me." And he jumped down.

"That's what you think," she muttered to herself and took three steps back. She was going to have to run at the wall, jump, and hope she made it high enough to reach the top. Then she could pull her feet up and vault over. She'd done it before, but never in skirts.

But hell would freeze over before she allowed Adrian to win.

She angled her head, took another step back, judging the distance. Hiking her skirts, she took a deep breath just as the doors to the mews beside her opened and a groom led a prancing white horse harnessed to a white-and-gold phaeton into the alleyway.

Sophia stamped her foot in frustration. Now she was going to have to wait until the groom led the conveyance away, and Adrian would surely have their man by then. The spirited white horse danced toward her, and Sophia glanced at the animal again.

Oh, she really shouldn't.

But she could already imagine the look on Adrian's face as she dashed past him, driving the beautiful white phaeton and the strutting horse. She looked at the groom. He was watching her with a sideways glance. After all, a noblewoman was a bit out of place here. But Agent Saint wasn't.

"Excuse me." She walked up to the groom, took the horse's reins from his hands, and leapt into the phaeton's box. The groom stared at her, too surprised to move for a long moment, and then when she snapped the reins and the horse jumped into action, he held up his hands and made a mad grab for the animal's bridle.

"Madam, what are you doing?"

Sophia snapped the reins again, and the horse reared. He was anxious for a run, and she was more than willing to allow him to stretch his legs. "Get out of my way," she called to the groom. "I need to borrow this carriage for a few moments."

"Absolutely not!" But he'd lost his grip on the horse's bridle, and Sophia urged the beast down the alleyway. If she hurried, she could still catch Adrian before he caught their man.

The groom made a last attempt to thwart her, jumping in front of the phaeton. Idiot! Did he want to be trampled? It was probably better than losing his position when his employer found out he'd lost the carriage.

Sophia yanked on the reins, and the horse cut to the side, barely missing the groom.

"I'll have it returned to you!" Sophia called to the groom as she left him behind. He shook his fist and yelled something she assumed was not complimentary, and then she was directing the horse to take the opening on her left. But they were traveling too quickly, and the phaeton took the turn on only one of its two wheels. Sophia hung on, jouncing horribly when the airborne wheel hit the ground again. Up ahead was Conduit and her man. The street was rather crowded, far too crowded for her to emerge at this speed, but she'd rather take her chances than lose the shadow… or lose to Adrian.

The magnificent animal jumped onto Conduit, narrowly missing a cart full of charcoal. Sophia prayed both wheels would stay on the ground as she negotiated yet another sharp turn. She was standing in the box, her legs braced apart, searching the wide-eyed, slack-jawed pedestrians for the man in the brown hat and green coat. She sped past Lady Ramsgate, chairwoman of the society for something or other, and Sophia gave her a jaunty wave. No doubt Lady Ramsgate would be removing Lady Smythe from their membership roster after this incident.

No wonder she preferred working abroad. Far fewer complications.

Up ahead, Sophia spotted a man running and slapped the reins. He'd lost his hat, and she frowned when she saw the dark blond hair. Why was Adrian running? Damn it! Had he caught their man already?

Adrian reached for the closed back of a gig cutting through traffic, and Sophia immediately understood. Their man had realized their plan and was trying to escape. She slapped the reins again, called a warning to a man about to cross in front of her, swerved, narrowly avoiding him but jostling a cart and spilling potatoes in her wake.

"Sorry!" She gave an apologetic wave to the cursing farmer then turned back just as she came alongside Adrian. He'd missed the gig and had fallen behind. "Jump on!" she called.

For a moment, he stared at her as though he didn't know her—that was a good sign, perhaps Lady Ramsgate hadn't recognized her either—and then angled for her. She slowed just enough for him to grasp hold of the box and lever himself beside her.

"Where the bloody hell did this come from?" he asked.

"Providence. Is that our man up ahead?" She nodded to the gig swerving through carts and horses.

"That's him. Spotted me and stole it after a short tussle with the coachman."

"I like him already." Sophia slapped the reins, and the phaeton gained on the gig.

"We'll never catch him," Adrian said, hanging on to the seat to keep from bouncing out. "You might be faster, but he's carrying one, and we're—Good God! Watch out for the—"

But she'd already seen the maid carrying three hatboxes and swerved around her. The maid was unscathed, but the hatboxes went flying, spilling their frilly contents in the middle of the street. Too bad. The one with the lavender ribbons looked most fetching.

"We'll catch him," she assured Adrian. "I know how to drive."

"That's debatable."

She glanced at him. "You're welcome to try running again."

"Keep your eyes on the street! Sophia!"

But her horse had a feel for her now, and he swerved around the slow carriage without her direction. With Adrian balancing the phaeton out, both wheels remained on the ground. They were gaining. Soon she'd be level with the gig lamps. Then it would just be a small matter of transferring the reins to Adrian, jumping to the gig, and restraining their man.

The hard part would be deciding what to claim from Adrian as a prize for her victory. She could think of so many delicious rewards...

Her beautiful white horse was now level with the gig's hood, and she spurred the animal onward. The road before her was blissfully open, and she curled her fingers around the reins. "Twenty seconds," she murmured. "Nineteen. Come on, come on..."

Beside her, Adrian sat forward, and she could tell he was anticipating her victory as much as she. "A little closer," he called.

She swallowed her fear and steered her horse a fraction closer to the gig. In a moment the wheels would be almost touching. Fifteen seconds. "Come on."

She was watching the gig and didn't see the cart right away. Adrian grabbed her hand, and when she looked up, she swore loudly and yanked the reins so hard she thought her muscles would pop. Adrian had her about the waist, to steady her, and the horse screamed. In front of them, a large cart, laden with furniture, backed slowly onto Conduit, the driver unaware of the chase heading directly for him.

"We're not going to make it!" Adrian predicted the same moment Sophia realized the same. She had no choice but to swerve onto the sidewalk or collide head-on with the lumbering cart. She closed her eyes and yanked the reins, praying anyone in their path would jump to safety. They bounced over the curb, hit something and rolled over it, then came to a clattering stop.

Sophia opened her eyes again and looked about her. The horse was staring at a woman pinned against the wall of a bakery, while around them, flowers were strewn in piles and bunches. Sophia peeked behind her and saw they'd run over the flower girl's basket. She, poor, thin thing, was staring at them, her blue eyes huge. Slowly, she bent to gather the flowers she could salvage.

With a sigh, Sophia turned to the street and watched the gig dart through traffic and race out of sight. She sat with a thud and surveyed the damage around her.

She glanced at Adrian. He had a daisy stuck in his

hair and a carnation caught on his coat. He looked at her, clenched his jaw, and said, "Next time, I drive."

Sophia could barely suppress a grin.

❦

Lord Dewhurst's ball was the last major event of the Season, or so Adrian had been assured by his valet. Why that warranted having his cravat tied, untied, and discarded three times, he had no idea. The man had wanted to give it another go, but Adrian had put his foot down. Marksby had looked as though he would pout the rest of the evening, and probably most of the next day, so Adrian had relented and allowed the man to fuss with his hair. When Marksby was finished, Adrian thought it looked exactly the same, but he complimented the man's efforts anyway. He had enough to deal with without a peevish valet.

Adrian paced the vestibule, aware Wallace was standing in the shadows, watching him. Not for the first time, Adrian wondered how much the butler knew of his and Sophia's lives. Certainly he must suspect they were up to more than merely making morning calls when they returned with bits of flowers clinging to them and driving a phaeton that did not belong to them. But Wallace had merely nodded when Sophia instructed him to have their coachman return the conveyance with their apologies for the mistake in taking it.

As though anyone with half a mind would mistake the elegant, one-of-a-kind horse and carriage for their own.

They should have caught the man trailing them. Adrian had thought he had the shadow. He'd emerged over the wall, cut through the shop, and fell in step directly behind the man. But he must have given himself away or the man had been expecting him, because the next thing he knew, the man was in the gig and Adrian was running after him.

He thought he'd lost him for sure, knew Sophia had absolutely no chance, until he'd heard the hooves of hell clopping behind him, turned, and saw his wife bearing down on him.

God, she was beautiful. If Helios had a daughter, it would have been Sophia. She might not have set the earth on fire, but she'd certainly singed it a bit. Still, to see her in that one instant, it was worth the inconvenience of paying the flower girl for her lost wares, apologizing to the Duchess of Trembly—who they'd trapped between the horse and bakery glass—and dealing with the multitude of others who'd descended to complain about Sophia's driving.

She'd been standing, hair whipping in the wind like a hundred chocolate ribbons, cheeks flushed pink, eyes positively lit with excitement. Her cream-colored skirts flew around her legs like frothy clouds. In that moment, he'd wanted to shout to everyone she was his. And then she'd spotted him, and her mouth curved into the smile she reserved for him, and he'd felt his heart clench in a way it never had before.

He could have taken her right there, right in the center of Conduit Street. If only he could have caught her.

And when she slowed for him, he could do little

but stare in amazement as she took every risk, every daring chance and then some. If he'd ever had a doubt she was Agent Saint, he didn't now. It was bad luck they hadn't caught the shadow. Bloody furniture cart. They'd get him next time. They could have been closing in on him and Jenkinson's killer right now if it wasn't for the bloody Dewhurst ball.

When they'd returned, Adrian had arrowed for his library, but Marksby had intercepted him, just as Sophia's lady's maid had intercepted her, and they'd been whisked away to prepare for the evening.

So work had to bow to social obligations for the night. Normally, Adrian would have told Marksby he could eat that starched cravat, but Liverpool had specifically told them to meet him at the ball. A good agent knew that work sometimes had to be interrupted to report to one's superiors.

Besides, he was interested in Liverpool's opinions on…

A flash of crimson caught his eye, and he stopped pacing, whirled, and stared at the steps leading to the upper floors. The chandelier above him blazed bright, reflecting off the rubies sparkling at Sophia's pale throat. The gems matched her gown, a deep red in glossy silk. Her hair was equally glossy, coiled and woven in an artful style with just enough tendrils escaping to fire a man's imagination.

Adrian decided then and there he was firing Sophia's maid. She was too good at her job.

Sophia smiled at him and took a step down. Still speechless, he watched her move, watched her skirts swish, watched the play of light on the rubies. The waist of her gown was impossibly high, the neckline impossibly low, and he had an enviable view of her ample breasts cushioning the rubies. He remembered them now. They'd been a present—three weeks late—for their first anniversary. When he'd given them to Sophia, she'd smiled vaguely, said they were pretty, and he'd never seen them again.

Of course, she'd still been dressing in high-necked sacks at that point. Perhaps he'd thought they might encourage her to dress in something more alluring. Perhaps he thought she'd think them pretty. Perhaps he hadn't been thinking at all. But if he'd known then she could look as she did now, he might have bought her a shawl or a cape or a robe with a collar to her chin instead.

She stopped before him, cleared her throat. "You look handsome, my lord. I see you decided on a new style for your cravat this evening."

He frowned. Had he? He'd forgotten even to look at Marksby's work.

"And your hair." She nodded. "The style suits you."

It looked no different than it had this afternoon, except it was free of daisy petals.

He continued to stare at her; there were small rubies in her ears—those he hadn't given her. He wanted to reach out and stroke her ear. She had such small, delicate ears. "Where did you get these?" he asked, giving in to touching her and using the excuse of the earrings to do so. If Wallace and several footmen hadn't been standing by, he would have done much more than put one finger to her earlobe.

"Prague." Her brows arched. "Is that all you have to say? I thought you more charming."

"I could be charming," he admitted. "But the flesh on display makes it difficult for me to think."

She laughed and nodded to Wallace, who brought forth her pelisse. Thank God she'd be covered for a few moments. "I'll take that as a compliment," she said and tucked her hand in the crook of his arm.

Wallace opened the door, and they stepped out into the cool night. A breeze swept past him, and he caught the scent of citrus. Her scent. He led her down the walkway, staring at their coach, knowing in a moment he'd be inside with her. Alone. Curtains drawn. He hoped the Dewhursts lived very, very far away. Derbyshire would suit him.

He handed her into the coach and took the seat opposite her, but as soon as the footman closed the door, he was beside her, his hand cupping her neck, his mouth on hers.

He hadn't realized he was tightly coiled, ready to snap. As soon as his lips touched hers, everything loosened and relaxed. She moaned slightly, her hands clutching his shoulders. "I've missed you," she murmured against his lips.

He'd missed her too. They'd been apart—what? Three hours? Four? It had felt like days. "I feel like I'm nineteen again," he said, bending to press his lips to her neck. And there were those escaped tendrils of hair brushing his lips with their fragrant softness.

"I didn't know you at nineteen," she said. "What were you like?"

He grinned up at her, not certain she could see in the dark. "Impatient."

"Ah." Her fingers stroked down his arm. "I know the feeling."

He reached up, loosened her pelisse, and watched it fall open, revealing that swell of skin. Reverently, he ran the back of his fingers over her. She sighed and shivered. Unable to resist, he bent his mouth to the soft flesh, felt it give enticingly as he pressed lips to breast.

"I want to climb on top of you right now," she murmured, voice husky. "I want to pull the bodice of this gown down, hike my skirts up, and let you take me as we ride through London."

He'd been hard before, but now he was painfully so.

"But you know we have work to do."

He did know. He knew it all too well. Always work. He placed a finger under her chin, tilted her face up to his. "We work now, but later…"

She nodded. "Later." It sounded more like a threat than a promise.

"Lord Dewhurst's residence!" the coachman called.

Adrian sighed and shifted back to his seat. "Let's find Liverpool and get out of here quickly."

"Agreed," she said, adjusting her pelisse.

The coach stopped, the doors opened, and the glittering lights blinded him for a moment. Then he stepped out, reached back for Sophia, and led her into the lights, music, and crush of perfumed guests.

Apparently, Marksby hadn't exaggerated when he'd predicted the Dewhurst's ball would be the event of the Season. The baron's town house was modest in size, similar in proportion to Adrian's own, but it was bursting with the powdered and plumed. Adrian didn't know Lord Dewhurst. The man was a celebrated dandy, if an overfondness for coats and gloves and snuffboxes could be celebrated.

"The Dewhursts only just returned from America," Sophia said, smiling at one lady after another as they made their way through the crowds and into the actual vestibule. "So you might inquire about their voyage."

Adrian was grateful for the information. He never knew what to say at these gatherings and usually remained silent. It gave him a rather unsociable reputation, but he didn't really care about his reputation.

"They have a daughter." Sophia never stopped smiling and nodding, even as she shed her pelisse and handed it to a waiting footman. They were announced, and Adrian saw the Dewhursts up ahead, receiving their guests. He was blond and far too pretty. She was a redhead, and in green silk, almost as stunning as Sophia.

"Don't ask about the daughter's name," Sophia was saying.

Adrian frowned down at her. "How do you know so much about these people? You can't have much more time than I to follow the scandal sheets."

"Dewhurst used to work for the Foreign Office," Sophia said, still smiling and nodding. "I worked with him before…" She trailed off, apparently not wanting to speak of the Barbican group where there was any possibility they'd be overheard.

"Well, I say, old chap!" Dewhurst, a tall blond man in a complicated cravat and tight coat, bowed with a flourish then smiled broadly. "It's about time I met you. Known Soph there for years."

Adrian raised a brow. Soph?

The aforementioned Soph stepped in. "Good to see you again, Freddie." She offered her hand, and he raised it to his lips, kissing it with great ceremony. Adrian wondered if there was anything the man didn't do with ceremony.

"You've met Charlotte, haven't you?" Dewhurst put a hand on his wife's arm, and she turned from a conversation with a beautiful blond—Lady something or other—to smile at them.

"Why, Lady Smythe!"

Adrian noted she pronounced it *Smith*.

"How good to see you again. I declare, it's been ages."

"And this is Lord Smythe," Dewhurst said. Adrian bowed, and Lady Dewhurst executed a very formal curtsy.

He caught Sophia giving him a meaningful look and realized it was his turn to say something. He'd been taken off guard by the woman's American accent. "Sophia tells me you've recently visited America. I hope your voyage was uneventful."

"It was lovely," she said in that Southern American drawl. "Alvanley had the time of her life in Charleston."

"Alvanley?" Had they taken the dandy with a famous fondness for apricot tarts with them?

"Our daughter," Dewhurst explained. "Don't ask about the name," he hissed.

Lady Dewhurst rolled her eyes. "No need to worry. I've quite forgiven you for that horrible wager. Oh, but your dress is beautiful, Sophia."

Dewhurst nodded. "I quite approve."

"High praise indeed," Sophia said. "But we're holding up your receiving line. Has Lord Liverpool arrived yet?"

Dewhurst's brows rose slightly, but Adrian would

not have noted the man's surprise if he hadn't been looking. "Not yet. I'll let him know you're in attendance when he does so."

"Thank you."

Lady Dewhurst smiled at him as they made their way into the ball. "Do have some champagne, Lord Smythe. Freddie ordered it all the way from France."

Sophia was on Adrian's arm again, but he wasn't leading her. She was pulling him away from the ballroom. "Let's find somewhere less crowded, so we can breathe for a moment." They stepped into a parlor, tastefully decorated in muted tones, where several young women lounged, obviously intent on escaping the crowds as well. It would still be an hour or more before the dancing began, and no one wanted their gowns wrinkled before they were put on display.

Adrian leaned against a wall, and Sophia stood beside him, fanning herself. "How do you know Dewhurst again?" he asked.

Sophia smiled. "You heard me the first time. And, yes, I know it's difficult to believe, but he really was quite good at what he did."

"Well, no one would suspect him."

Sophia nodded. "That's exactly the point."

Adrian was tempted to check his pocket watch, but he knew seeing the time would only disappoint him.

"You really hate these affairs, don't you?" Sophia asked.

"Don't you?"

"No. These days I find them more amusing than the theater. You see, everyone here has something to hide. Something they don't want others to know. It's fascinating trying to discover what it is."

"All right. What's the brunette over there hiding?"

Sophia glanced at the young girl in a white dress with pink flowers. She was shifting from foot to foot and fumbling with her fan. "That's too easy. She's nervous about the ball. This is her first Season, and she's yet to make a match."

Adrian didn't argue. It didn't take a trained observer to see the woman's nervousness and her exaggerated laughter and smiles to cover it up.

"You're right. Too easy. What's Lady Dewhurst hiding?"

"She's expecting again."

"You can't know that."

Sophia shrugged. "When we entered, she was talking to her good friend Lady Selbourne, and touching her belly. She's expecting."

Adrian had seen only the redhead and the blond conversing. He hadn't looked for more. He crossed his arms. "What am I hiding?"

She laughed. "Nothing. You're making it quite clear to everyone that you find this extremely tedious."

"Fine. What are you hiding?"

She looked at him for a long time, so long he thought she might not answer. Then she said, "I envy Lady Dewhurst."

He felt his gut spasm as though a knife had plunged into it. He could hear the pain in her voice. "Sophia—"

The parlor door opened again, and a footman nodded at them. "Lord and Lady Smythe, could you come with me, please?"

Adrian gave Sophia a look then offered his elbow. They stepped back into the throngs, following the footman past the seemingly endless receiving line. Lord Dewhurst caught Adrian's eye and gave him a mock salute just as the footman turned into a dark corridor. The din of the crowds faded as they left the ball behind. At the end of a short corridor, the footman paused and opened a door. He gestured into the darkness.

Sophia moved ahead, but Adrian held her back. After the events of the last few days, he was on alert. He pushed her behind him, an action he expected her to protest. But she sighed and allowed it, waiting as he stepped into the dark library alone.

Eighteen

SOPHIA WAITED UNTIL ADRIAN HAD STEPPED INSIDE the library then looked at the footman. "Is it Lord Liverpool?" She appreciated Adrian's caution, but sometimes it was more expedient to simply ask the servants.

"Yes, my lady. He didn't wish to draw attention by making an appearance in the ballroom."

"Thank you." She stepped inside the library and waited for her eyes to adjust to the dimness. The first thing she noted was the sumptuous decor. Freddie never faltered in that regard. Her slippers sank into a rug in blue-and-green tones. She was no judge of rugs, but she was pretty certain this was an Aubusson. As the current style was all things Greek and Roman, she wasn't surprised to see paintings and busts in that style all about the house. But none lurked here. Everything in the library spoke of seriousness and masculinity. The furnishings were leather, the color palette dark; even the desk, which was so large it took up half of one wall, was a dark mahogany.

She smiled when she saw a yellow-haired doll lying forgotten on one of the large couches. Freddie might appear the fop on the outside, but here, when he was alone, he was obviously a different person altogether. The same could be said for Adrian, only she had never looked past his Greek and Roman busts to see the real man—not that Adrian had any Greek or Roman busts. He wasn't that fashionable...

"Lady Smythe," the prime minister said, rising from one of the couches. Adrian stood before the fire, and she moved to join him so they faced Lord Liverpool as one. Liverpool watched, and the effect was not lost on him. "Quite a difference from your behavior several days ago. Then I was given to believe you actively disliked one another."

"I can't imagine why." Sophia took Adrian's hand and squeezed it. It felt wonderful to stand beside him tonight. To know she had a partner in all things. He squeezed her hand back, reassuring her.

Liverpool gestured to the couch opposite him. "Please take a seat."

"I'd prefer to stand," Adrian said. Sophia nodded.

Liverpool spread his hands. "Very well. Go ahead with your report. Lord Smythe, would you begin?"

He released her hand, and she felt him take a deep breath. "My lord, we've interviewed all of the suspects—Mrs. Jenkinson, the Jenkinson servants, Mr. Hardwicke, Mr. Linden, and the valet Callows."

"And?"

"None of them are responsible for your brother's death," Sophia said. She glanced at Adrian, knowing he harbored doubts about Hardwicke. "Although some are still under suspicion."

"No, you were right the first time," Adrian told her. Sophia raised her brows, surprised at this admission, especially with the prime minister listening. "Hardwicke had nothing to do with this."

Liverpool crossed his legs. "Then who did?"

"We don't know yet."

Sophia could hear the hesitation in Adrian's voice. She knew, first hand, the feeling of failure one experienced when giving a report not full of successes. Behind them, the low fire crackled. The room felt suddenly too warm.

"But we're closing in," she added. "Recently we've had several encounters leading us to believe that whoever killed your brother knows we're after him and doesn't want us to succeed."

"You've been threatened?"

"In a manner of speaking," Adrian said. "And when we uncover the man trying to kill us, we'll have your brother's murderer."

Liverpool pressed his lips together. "I didn't intend to put you in any danger."

"We're not," Sophia assured him. "We can handle ourselves, but we do have a few questions for you, my lord." She felt a trickle of perspiration run from her neck down her back and moved slightly forward, away from the hearth.

Liverpool's brows rose. "Am I a suspect?"

She smiled. "Not yet, sir. Several of our suspects mentioned Mr. Jenkinson's association with foreigners." She tried to keep her tone light. "Do you know anything about your brother's personal or business dealings with foreigners?"

"Foreigners? Whom do you mean? The Americans? The Dutch?"

"I was thinking the French," Adrian said. Sophia glanced at him in surprise, but his face revealed nothing. In fact, he looked as cool and composed as ever. The heat of the fire did not seem to be bothering him. And was it just her imagination, or had he moved away from her, separating them?

"I highly doubt my brother had any dealings with the French. Until very recently, they were our enemy."

Adrian remained silent as the implication sank in. Sophia bit the inside of her cheek. Slowly, Lord Liverpool rose. "What, exactly, are you saying, Lord Smythe? Are you accusing my brother of associating with the enemy?"

"No," Adrian said, his tone carefully neutral. Sophia's heart was pounding now. She wasn't certain where this was going, but she knew they should tread carefully.

"The manner in which your brother was murdered..."

"Ghastly," Liverpool said with a shudder.

"I've heard of something similar before."

"You have?" Sophia asked. Adrian flicked a glance at her, as though to indicate she should leave it for later. But that wasn't going to happen. She faced him, stepped closer, into the gap he'd created. "Why didn't you mention this before?"

"I did. I told you it seemed familiar when we were walking back from the Jenkinson residence, but we were interrupted."

"Am I to understand this is a new development?" Liverpool asked.

"I haven't had time to discuss my suspicions with Lady Smythe." He looked at her, raised a hand slightly as though he would touch her, but he didn't. "I haven't even had time to confirm them."

She couldn't argue. But it still bothered her. Was he intentionally keeping this information to himself, or was he telling the truth? Damn it! She clenched her fists and stepped back from him, hating that she still doubted him, hating that Henry was the first thought to cross her mind. A moment before, she'd felt so certain of her partnership with Adrian, and now she felt as though she were all on her own again. And she'd be alone much more if Adrian was given the Barbican position and she was left behind in London.

"Share your suspicions now, Lord Smythe," Liverpool said.

"Yes, Lord Smythe, do share." She gifted him with a bitter smile.

"I don't have anything tangible. As I said, I haven't had time to research anything." He gave her a look as though to indicate she should know this well. "But when Callows described the body, it triggered a memory of something I'd heard before."

"Which is?" Liverpool demanded.

Adrian crossed his arms, and Sophia knew the wall had gone up. She sighed.

"I'd rather not say until I have more concrete information. But to return to my original inquiry, my lord—did your brother have any ties to the French?"

Liverpool gave him a cool look. "No. He did not, and I am trying very hard not to take offense at the mere suggestion."

"Thank you, my lord. If I might ask another, potentially offensive question…?"

"You're a brave bastard, aren't you?"

Adrian raised a brow. "That's why I'm called Agent Wolf."

Liverpool looked at Sophia. "Why are you called Saint?"

"Because my work is perfect." But she didn't think Adrian was called Wolf for his bravery. He was called Wolf because he was a hunter, a predator. Once he had his prey's scent, he never relented. She wondered if his prey ever just capitulated in the end, tired of fighting him, knowing failure was inevitable. Wasn't that how she felt in the carriage earlier tonight with his hands and mouth driving her mad? She would yield to him. He'd made sure she had little choice.

"And yet, you haven't uncovered my brother's murderer," Liverpool noted.

"Yet," she said. "And I think the indelicate question Agent Wolf wants to ask is about your brother's financial records."

Adrian nodded.

"What of them?" Liverpool frowned, showing no sign of guilt. "I sent you all I had."

"They're incomplete," Adrian said.

"That can't be. Millie and I went through George's desk together. She gave me all there were."

"Did she?" Adrian gave Sophia a look she was

beginning to know well. She had a feeling they would be calling on Millie Jenkinson again.

"Yes, she did." Liverpool clasped his hands behind his back and paced. "I must say this report is entirely unsatisfactory. I expected you to have some answers. I was told you were two of the best. But if you can't solve this crime—"

"We can and will solve it," Sophia said. "We need more time."

"Time we're wasting running about London attending frivolous balls."

Liverpool stopped in midstride and turned slowly. Sophia took in a slow breath, knowing Adrian had pushed too far.

"Is meeting with me an inconvenience to you, Lord Smythe?"

"Honestly, sir, yes. It is."

Sophia closed her eyes. Even though she agreed with Adrian, she hadn't been prepared to say so. But she couldn't exactly leave her husband hanging from the noose he'd hung, no matter how tempting. "My lord, meeting with you is never an inconvenience, but we might serve you better if we used our time to work on the case."

Liverpool raised his brows at her now. "I see. So I should come to you next time."

"That would be—"

Sophia dug her nails into Adrian's arm, silencing him. In the quiet, she heard Dewhurst's clock ticking on the mantel, and Lord Liverpool's angry breathing. "I'm afraid I'm going to inconvenience you once again, my lord."

Adrian nodded, obviously a man accustomed to taking orders, although he liked it little more than she. "How so?"

"I'm going to ask you to dance with your wife."

"What?" Sophia sputtered. She released Adrian's arm. She hadn't danced in years.

"You've made an appearance here. Together. And that's something you haven't done in some time. If you leave without being seen enjoying the ball, there will be speculation, and I think we can all agree that the last thing you two need right now is more attention. I heard something about a runaway carriage this afternoon?"

Sophia looked away, and Adrian cleared his throat.

"I think a dance would be the easiest way to satisfy everyone's curiosity. I assume you don't object. You looked rather friendly when you entered."

And she'd felt friendlier when they entered, before she'd realized Adrian withheld information from her. But if she had to dance with him, so be it.

"Fine," Adrian said, sounding as enthusiastic as she felt. "Anything else, my lord?"

Liverpool stood before Dewhurst's desk, one hand on the polished surface. "Find my brother's killer," he said, stabbing his finger at the desk for emphasis. "And do so before I decide you're both worthless and exile you to Wales or some other miserable locale."

"Yes, my lord," Sophia said before Adrian could speak. If the tightness in Adrian's jaw was any indication, she didn't want Liverpool to hear it.

"The first one who comes to me with information about the killer will be given the place in the Barbican group," Liverpool said. He adjusted his coat and strode toward the door, opening it and pausing. "Right now, I doubt either of you deserve it."

The door closed with a thud behind him, and Sophia sighed. "That went well."

"Sophia." Adrian reached for her, but she moved.

"Don't." She didn't want his apologies.

"I don't know anything you don't. I have some suspicions I want to look into. I want *us* to look into. I told you that earlier."

She shook her head. "Why are we still trying to work together? You heard him." She gestured to the door. "Only one of us can take the position. Perhaps it's time we went back to acting alone."

"No." It was a command, and she bristled at the tone.

"You can't order me to cooperate with you. It doesn't work that way."

"Then how does it work? I thought things were going well."

She wasn't certain if he meant with the investigation or with their marriage. "They were."

"Then why are you stepping back?" He stepped closer, and damn it if she didn't have to resist the urge to retreat. "What are you afraid of?"

"Nothing." But that was a lie.

"I don't believe you. How many times do I have to prove I'm not going to betray you?" He brushed her cheek with one finger, and she curled her toes to keep from shivering.

How many times *did* he have to prove it? "Perhaps I'm afraid of losing that position in the Barbican group." And that was a lie as well. She was afraid of losing *him* to the Barbican group.

"If you do, it will be lost fairly. That I swear." He brushed his thumb over her lips. "Dance with me."

She gave him a curt nod. "Fine. Let's go."

He grasped her elbow and drew her back. "No, *dance* with me, Sophia. Stop doubting me. Stop questioning."

"I'm not—"

"Shh." He put a finger on her lips. "I want to dance with you, Sophia. I want no suspicions between us."

She stared at him, lost in his gray eyes, wanting to kiss him and afraid of where that would lead. If she crossed the point of no return, what would she do if she lost him? The clock on the mantel chimed half-past eleven, and she blinked. "I suppose we had better dance, then." She started for the door, glad for a momentary respite from his closeness. "But I must warn you, Dewhurst favors the waltz."

"That doesn't scare me," he said from behind her, his breath tickling her ear.

It didn't scare her, either. Much.

∽⌒∾

Sophia allowed Adrian to shoulder his way through the crush of silk and diamonds until they reached the ballroom. It was stunningly arrayed, which, knowing Dewhurst's impeccable taste, was no surprise. On one side, an orchestra played on a raised dais. On the other side of the long room, a table of refreshments bowed beneath the overflowing bounty. Even without perusing the table's contents, she knew every delicacy in England and half the Continent would be offered. Flowers, from the simple lily to the rarest orchid, graced Ming and Sèvres vases. The chandeliers sparkled, the champagne glasses tinkled, and a light breeze blew in from the French doors opening on the exquisitely manicured lawns. On the windows, gauzy curtains blew about like dancing specters. Their heavier blue-velvet counterparts, seeming chaperones, stood formal and dignified beside them.

The flowers, the lights, the enchanting music wafting over her made Sophia smile. She was glad her work for the evening was done—for the moment, anyway. She rarely if ever attended any social function for pleasure. Now, she was allowed a few moments' pleasure, and this ball was the perfect venue.

Adrian found them a spot next to the dance floor, and she watched the couples glide by, executing the steps flawlessly and gracefully. Dukes and duchesses, knights and their ladies, even a foreign prince and his princess danced under the glittering chandelier crystals. They were dancing a quadrille, four couples in a square formation, and Sophia hoped the next dance would be another quadrille or a contredanse. She had no hope Dewhurst would allow a minuet. It was far too staid and old-fashioned for his taste, and if he had allowed it, it would have opened the ball.

She glanced at Adrian, wondering what he made of the ballroom. She expected to see him frowning, but he looked about with interest. Perhaps he didn't detest these social affairs as much as he claimed. He hadn't caught her watching him, so she didn't look away. She studied the hard set of his square jaw. It was a strong jaw, but now she noted it had a small, jagged scar near the chin. She'd never seen it before.

Knowing they were being watched and feeling as

though she should give the *ton* at least something to talk about over breakfast, she reached up and traced the scar with her gloved hand. Adrian didn't react overtly, but she felt his body stiffen. "Let me guess," she said, loudly enough for his ears but not with enough volume to carry any farther. "Knife fight?"

He glanced at her, his eyes warm. "Nothing so interesting, I'm afraid."

"Broken bottle in a tavern brawl?"

The music was slowing and the dance ending. She took a deep breath, preparing for their dance together. When was the last time they'd danced together? She was certain it was before their wedding.

Adrian took her hand and led her onto the dance floor. She noticed several couples moved out of their way, and several others rushed to join them. She heard the first strains of the waltz and almost groaned. Of course.

Adrian turned her to face him, took her in his arms, and said, "Not a tavern brawl. A kitten."

She shook her head. She'd lost the trail of the conversation somewhere. "What did you say?"

"The scar. A kitten scratched me." He turned her, expertly, and swept her across the floor. Sophia's head was reeling from the dance.

"How did a kitten scratch you?"

"Oh, it was the proverbial cat caught in a tree. I climbed up and fetched it for a little girl."

She narrowed her eyes. "I don't believe you."

"It makes a better story than a shaving mishap."

He turned her again, and Sophia was glad she hadn't partaken of the champagne. Her head was swimming.

It was a heady enough feeling, being in Adrian's arms, but having him hold her closely and twirl her about the dance floor took her breath away.

She'd never danced a waltz before. Oh, she'd learned it because, as Agent Saint, she never knew when such knowledge would be required. But when she and Adrian had been engaged, the waltz was not acceptable. It was barely acceptable now. Indeed, most of the girls making their first come-outs were not dancing. Sophia recalled Adrian and she had only ever danced together a handful of times. She thought if they ever had danced the waltz, she probably would have fallen in love with him right then.

She was in love with him now.

The knowledge did not surprise her, but her admission of her feelings was not exactly welcome. She didn't want to love Adrian. Loving him made everything so much more complicated.

And their relationship was complicated enough.

She was Agent Saint, and he was Agent Wolf, but she was also Sophia and he, Adrian. Where did one identity stop and the other begin? When she'd worked for the Barbican group, she was almost always Agent Saint. Even between missions, she held on to the one part of herself she could be certain of. Now all of that was changing. She felt more like Sophia Galloway and less like Agent Saint. How could she go back to life as a spy? How could she ever reconcile the two parts of herself?

And yet, how could she *not* go back? If she lost the position to Adrian, she feared she would wither away and die of loneliness and boredom. She would grow to resent him as well—Agent Wolf, who left her for weeks, embarking on untold adventures.

And wouldn't he feel the same if she were to win the Barbican position?

But one of them had to win, and the other would lose.

He turned her again, and when she gasped, he smiled at her. He didn't smile much, and she felt herself melt with pleasure at his genuine happiness. What was she doing, analyzing and thinking so much she forgot to enjoy the moment? That was Adrian's style, not hers.

Yes, she loved him. She loved Adrian Galloway and Agent Wolf and Lord Smythe. She loved every part of him, every facet. She loved her husband. She should love her husband. There was nothing wrong in that.

She saw her vulnerability and quickly popped the bubble of fear accompanying it. When was she just going to give in to this attraction, this love, and stop trying to shield herself? She took a deep breath. Everything in her—her instincts—told her now was the time. Adrian was right. She needed to stop questioning everything, take Adrian at his word, close her eyes, and just dance. No more thinking. No more second-guessing. She would let the music, let their new life carry her where it would.

Adrian leaned down and whispered in her ear, "You look beautiful. Have I told you that tonight?"

"No, but you certainly showed me your approval in the carriage."

He touched the rubies at her ear, the brush of his fingertips making her shiver. "But I haven't given you the words. You're beautiful, Sophia. The most beautiful woman in the room."

"Thank—"

He put a finger over her lips and lingered just long enough for heat to infuse her belly. "I'm not finished. You're not only beautiful, you're intelligent, daring, bewitching…" His fingers traced the rubies at her neck. Rubies he'd once given her but she'd never worn. His gaze met hers. "You're the best operative I've ever worked with, *will* ever work with. I'm not saying that because you're my wife. I'm saying it because it's the truth."

She blinked at him. This was her fantasy—Agent Wolf telling her she was beautiful, that she was a skilled operative. Only this was ten times better, because in her fantasy, Agent Wolf would clearly want her, but she'd have to refuse him because she was married. Tonight, she didn't have to refuse Agent Wolf at all. She could have him. She could do every delicious thing she'd dreamed about doing with him and not feel one ounce of guilt, because Agent Wolf was her Adrian.

She became aware of Adrian's hand on her back, dipping toward her waist. She felt the heavy, solid pressure of it, the way he used it to effortlessly guide her. She felt his other hand, cool and strong, holding hers, and she couldn't help but glance at their joined hands.

Adrian followed her gaze, and she smelled his scent. She would have recognized it anywhere, but now she took a moment to decipher it—leather and boot polish, she thought. He smelled masculine, just as Agent Wolf should.

And he looked so handsome tonight with his stylish

cravat and his carefully tousled hair. She wanted to loosen that cravat, run her fingers through that hair, and so much more.

As though sensing her thoughts, Adrian pulled her closer, so her breasts grazed his chest. Her nipples were instantly hard, pushing achingly against the fabric dividing her skin from his.

"What are you thinking?" he murmured.

"We're dancing far too close for propriety," she said, studying his eyes. The gray looked almost blue tonight.

"Liverpool said to give the *ton* something to talk about."

"We're doing that."

He swept her around again. "What are you really thinking?"

She thought for a moment then decided, why not tell him? "This is my favorite fantasy."

He furrowed his brows. "Dancing with me at Dewhurst's ball? I'm sure we could have accomplished that long before."

"No. I used to fantasize about Agent Wolf."

His eyebrows shot up in a cocky expression. "Oh?"

She shook her head. She might come to regret this. "I'd heard so much about him, and I admired him. I dreamed about meeting him one day."

"And what would he say to you?"

"He'd say he'd heard of me, and I was the best agent he knew of. Of course, I'd tell him he was better, and then he'd tell me I was beautiful…"

"I don't think I like where this is going." He turned her, this time a bit more roughly.

"It wouldn't have gone anywhere. I would have

walked away because I was married and loyal to my husband. But tonight I don't have to walk away. I can go home with Agent Wolf." She tightened her grip on his hand. "I can go to bed with Agent Wolf. I want to. I want to go to bed with my husband. I want you to make love to me, Adrian."

He didn't speak for a long time. His steps never faltered, and his gaze never left hers as they glided across the ballroom. Sophia was aware of others watching them. She was aware of a blur of faces and a hum of voices, but only Adrian was in focus for her. Only Adrian mattered.

He brought her hand to his lips. "What does that mean?"

She smiled. Adrian, ever cautious.

What did she mean, exactly? Was she truly ready? Was she willing to risk the hurt, the pain, the chance of loss again? Adrian pulled her tighter, and she knew she was. She wanted to be his wife again. She wanted a chance at a family with him, children. And if that chance never came, then she didn't want to regret not trying.

And if she did conceive again, this time she wouldn't be afraid. This time she wouldn't hide in her room and fret over every movement or jostle. She would walk in the sun and fresh air. She would continue living her life and trust that everything would be all right—no matter how a pregnancy turned out. She would trust in her love for Adrian and the new marriage they were building together.

She took a deep breath, trying to ignore the way her chest hitched. "It means exactly what you think it means." His eyes darkened and emboldened her. "Shall I spell it out for you, Lord Smythe?"

He grinned over her knuckles. "Will I be able to keep dancing without making a spectacle of myself?"

"Probably not, but you like a challenge."

"Tell me, then."

"I don't want you to touch me in the carriage. I want to wait until we're home, in my bedroom, and then I want you to undress me, slowly, kissing every inch of me as you do so."

He inhaled. "Sophia…"

She ignored him. "And I mean every inch, Adrian. Do it softly, delicately. Kiss my neck—you know where I like your mouth—kiss my ear, my shoulder, my breast, my navel, the back of my knee, the arch of my foot. I want it so slowly and so sweetly that it drives me to madness, and then I want you to take me. Hard. Rough."

"Yes." He was nodding, his eyes so dark now they were unreadable.

"Make me come with your mouth, and then I want you inside me."

He almost stumbled. She felt the slight hesitation, but she knew no one else would have noticed.

She nodded. "I want you, Adrian. All of you. I want us to be husband and wife again. In truth."

"Then what are we waiting for? Let's go."

And before she could protest, he had her hand in his and was dragging her out of the ballroom. He didn't do as she'd told him, but then had she really expected him to? Did she really want him to?

No.

So when the carriage set off, the lights from Dewhurst's ball fading, and Adrian pulled her into his lap, she only smiled and turned to straddle him. His arms came around her waist, his hands pressing into her back. She could feel his muscled thighs under her legs, and she ran her hands over his hard chest. She wanted to rip his coat off, loosen his cravat with her teeth, and tear open his shirt.

She could only imagine the looks from the servants if they arrived home in that state, so she settled on touching her lips to his. She meant it to be a light kiss, something to hold them over until they reached the privacy of her bedroom, but as soon as her mouth met his, everything she'd held so tightly inside broke apart. A flood of passion washed over her, and she couldn't seem to get enough of his lips. She wanted to devour them. She wanted to somehow link her mouth to his for all eternity. How had she survived without his lips on hers these past few hours?

Adrian's reaction to her kiss was just as frenzied. He bit her lower lip, opened her mouth, and invaded. There was no other word for what he did to her. His mouth, his tongue, his teeth overwhelmed her. She could hardly catch her breath, and she didn't want to. She never wanted him to stop.

Their tongues twined, fought, sought each other out even as she dug into his chest with her nails and he pressed her body close to his. She was pressed against him so his heat infused her, his scent became part of her. Oh, how she wished they were naked. Her clothes suddenly felt too cumbersome and heavy. The thin silk was like a brick wall, guarding her body from his.

"Damn these clothes," she murmured into his mouth. "I can't wait to get you naked and beneath me."

She pulled back. "Who said you could be on top?"

He grinned then bit her neck gently. "I do."

"You don't always get your way," she said, arching to give him better access. His hands slid down and cupped her bottom.

"Oh, yes, I do."

She felt his hand on her calf before she knew what he was doing. And then when she realized he was tracing a hot trail up her inner thigh, she considered stopping him. After all, he was trying to prove he always got his way. But when his finger stroked the top of her inner thigh, she decided she didn't care if he always got his way. She *liked* his way.

His hand finally reached her center, and he cupped her lightly. "You're so wet," he said in her ear. "Let me see if I can make you wetter."

His fingers stroked her, teased her, made her rock against him. He put his mouth to her breast, bit her nipple lightly. Even through all the layers of clothing, she could feel the warmth of his mouth, the scrape of his teeth. "Adrian…" she moaned.

"Is there something you want? Tell me."

"You."

He found the small nub aching for his touch, and she almost jumped at the surge of pleasure she felt. He tapped it, tantalizing her but giving her no relief.

"You have me, my love, my Saint."

Infuriating man! He knew what she wanted. She opened her eyes and looked into his. "I want you inside me. Put your finger inside me."

He slid effortlessly inside her, his thumb still stroking that small, sensitive nub. His finger slid in and out, and she wanted to scream in anticipation of the release she knew was coming.

"Shall I continue?"

With great effort, she managed to groan, "If you stop, I swear I will kill you."

"Then come for me, Saint," he said against her ear. "I want to feel you squeeze me like a glove. I want to hear you scream your release."

"Adrian... Wolf..." She was rocking against him, her hips moving in rhythm to his fingers. And then he made one small adjustment with his thumb, circled her slowly, and she burst apart like an exploding star. She shuddered against him, the hand cradling her back catching her else she would have fallen backward.

Lethargy and sweetness trickled through her like a fine glass of wine, warming her, easing all the strain of the day. Finally, she collapsed against him. She could feel his heart beating. It thundered against her ear even as his hand came up to stroke her hair as one might comfort a child.

This was where she wanted to be, she thought. In his arms, listening to his heart, forever. She wanted it to be like this forever.

No, she wanted even more. She wanted to know she had all of him, and for the first time in her life, she wanted to give someone all of her.

Her heart tightened with fear even as her body sang in anticipation.

The carriage had slowed, and she looked up at him.

"Make me your wife again, Adrian," she said as the carriage halted before their town house. "Make love to me."

Nineteen

ADRIAN GATHERED HER IN HIS ARMS AND CARRIED HER out of the carriage and up the front walk of the town house. Sophia laughed. "What are you doing?"

"Old tradition. Certainly you're familiar with the groom carrying the bride over the threshold."

She smiled, and he saw moisture in her eyes. Bloody hell, if she cried now, he was going to lose it completely. He knew why she was emotional. They were starting over tonight. This was a new beginning for both of them. He didn't know what tomorrow would hold, but tonight was for the two of them.

Wallace opened the door. "Good evening, my lord. My lady." He didn't even blink to see his master carrying his mistress.

"Good evening, Wallace." Sophia gave a short wave as Adrian started up the stairs. Then he paused and turned back. Wallace stood, hands behind his back, at the ready.

"Wallace," Adrian said, "why doesn't anything Lady Smythe or I do seem to surprise you?"

Wallace's blank expression remained unchanged.

"You are part of the aristocracy, my lord. I've worked for the nobility for forty years. There is nothing I have not seen."

Adrian shrugged. "I see." He turned to continue up the stairs.

"That and you and Lady Smythe work for the Foreign Office. I've always found spies rather unpredictable."

Adrian felt Sophia's quick intake of breath, and her gaze flew to his. They shared a moment of surprise, and then Adrian allowed his mask to fall back in place. He glanced over his shoulder, but the butler wore the same bland expression. "Carry on then, Wallace."

"Thank you, my lord."

They reached the landing, and Adrian started down the corridor to Sophia's bedroom. The wall sconces flickered as he passed, illuminating old portraits and priceless art, much of it bad, passed down from generations.

"How do you think he knew?" Sophia asked finally.

"I think the better question," Adrian said, kicking her door open, "is how didn't we—the spies—know he knew?" He kicked the door shut behind him and started for the bed.

"Do you think we can trust him?"

"I think we can trust him implicitly. Now, what was it you were saying in the ballroom?"

She smiled wickedly, and he set her on her feet. "I said you should undress me slowly."

"Yes, well…" Adrian snatched off her cloak. "I'm not very good at following orders. I want you naked. Now." His hands were on the fastenings of her gown, opening the bodice, pushing the skirt down. He wished he'd lit a candle, as the light from the low fire in the hearth didn't allow him to see her as he'd like, but soon he had her petticoats and stays off, and she stood in only her chemise. The fire was behind her, and it outlined her body in all its splendor.

Slowly, he bent and grasped the hem of the gauzy chemise. Allowing his fingers to trail over her stockings, he lifted the garment inch by exquisite inch. When his fingertips grazed the bare skin of her thighs above her lacy garters, she shivered. He caressed her hips, followed the dent of her waist, then flared out again at her breasts, finally pulling the chemise over her head.

She stood naked before him except for her stockings and her rubies. She reached for them, but he stilled her hand with his. "Leave them."

She raised a brow and lowered her hand.

"But take your hair down," he said, stepping back to admire her. "Slowly."

She nodded and reached up, pulling one pin from the coil of thick chestnut hair. A curl sprang free, cascading down her shoulder to graze the round fullness of one breast. Adrian clenched his hands. "Keep going."

"Yes, my lord." She freed another pin, and piece by piece, tendril by tendril, the elaborate coiffure came down, covering her in chocolate ribbons. And yet her hair was the perfect length. It ended just above her rosy nipples. They were hard, waiting for his mouth, his teeth, his fingers…

He looked at her face and thought how young she appeared with her hair down about her, how vulnerable. She wanted him to be rough, but he would not start that way. He wanted this to be perfect.

"Now you, my lord." She stepped forward, and he could smell the faint scent of citrus on her skin. She twined her fingers in his cravat, yanked, and freed his neck. Next she put her hands on his shoulders and dragged the tailcoat over them. She dropped the garment on the floor and grasped his shirt. She unfastened it at the throat and wrists then pulled the tails out, and running her hands over his chest, plucked the shirt over his head.

She reached for his breeches but not before she moved closer, rubbing her breasts against his bare chest. He gazed down at her. He didn't think she had done so mistakenly. She smiled innocently then dipped her fingers into his breeches. She released the fall, and he sprang into her hand.

"What has you so excited, my lord?" she asked, voice deceptively innocent.

"What doesn't have me excited?" he growled and pulled her against him. He did it gently, but he was quickly losing his restraint. He wanted to ravage her mouth, but instead, he took it tenderly, tasting her first with the tip of his tongue. Gently, she opened for him, and he entered her tentatively, searching for her tongue, stroking it languidly as though he were not ready to come in her hand.

She didn't encourage his restraint. Her hot mouth moved over his hungrily, and her hand stroked him, making him want to drive into her. Bloody hell, she was naked before him. He could toss her on the bed—the floor even—and bury himself inside her in mere seconds.

But he didn't.

He teased her mouth until she was sighing and moaning. He ran his fingers over her shoulders, her ribs—barely grazing the sides of her breasts—then stroking the curve of her hip and the roundness of her bottom.

"Adrian…" She allowed her head to fall back, and he kissed the curve of her throat, gradually making his way to the hollow just beneath her ear. When he reached it, she shuddered and grasped his buttocks. "Take these breeches off," she demanded.

He kicked off his shoes then sat on the bed to deal with stockings and the breeches themselves. She did him the favor of standing before him, and when he was naked, he grasped her small waist and pulled her between his legs. He reached out with one finger and flicked her nipple. It responded by swelling slightly, and he leaned forward, kissing it with the barest caress of his lips.

"Adrian." She tried to arch back, but he clamped his legs on her thighs, keeping her trapped. He lifted his hands and brushed them over the soft skin of her shoulders, inching down until his fingertips skidded over the swell of her breasts. He cupped them, testing their weight and fullness. Then he leaned forward and touched his tongue to her hard nipple.

She grasped his hair and pulled him hard against her. "You're driving me mad," she whispered. "Take me."

He wanted nothing more, but he was in no hurry. He rolled the nipple with his tongue then sucked it lightly into his mouth. Her fingers dug into his shoulders, and he scraped his teeth along the hard pebble.

"Adrian!" She was breathing heavily, and her breath

hitched as he slid one finger down her abdomen, pausing at her navel. He toyed with her nipple as she writhed against him, then he allowed his hand to dip into the curls between her legs. "Yes," she murmured when he stroked her.

And then suddenly he was flat on his back, and she was over him. He wasn't certain how it had happened. One second he'd been in control, and now she was looking down at him. She gave him a slow, sensuous smile before slanting her mouth over his. He hadn't moved his hand, and he stroked her, feeling her reaction as she kissed him deeper and harder. Finally she wrapped a warm hand around his erection, and straddling him, brought it to her core.

He wanted to plunge into her. Knew she wanted it too.

But there would be time for sweet savagery later. Now he wanted tenderness. He tried to flip her, but she clamped her legs down.

Bloody hell. He bit her lips gently to distract her. She was going to get tenderness whether she wanted it or not.

She drew back. "What are you doing? You can be on top later."

"*You* can be on top later." He tried flipping her again, but she countered his move and held her position. He reached for her hand, intending to trap it and take some of her balance, but she grabbed his wrist and held it on the bed.

"Two can play at this game, Wolf."

"This isn't the time to fight me, Sophia. Roll over."

"No."

The look in her eyes and the determined set of her lips was making him want her even more. What other woman would argue with him in bed, fight him?

What other woman had even a chance at winning? Not that she was going to win.

He stroked her again, his finger sliding through her wetness and rubbing that sensitive area. She raised her gaze to his. "You're not playing fair."

"I never do." He delved inside her again, and she tightened around him.

"Adrian…"

It was all the distraction he needed. He flipped her over and caught her wrists with his hands. She arched upward, not in pleasure but in fury. "You bastard." He smiled even as he held her wrists down. That wasn't for show. She would have hit him given half a chance.

"You won't be cursing me in a moment."

"Yes, I…"

He brought his mouth to her breast, took her nipple in his mouth, and scraped his teeth over it. Now she bucked again, but this time she moaned his name. All right, so he wasn't going to be quite as tender as he'd wanted. He laved her with his tongue then dipped to her abdomen, kissing her belly and her navel. He loosened his grip slightly, but she didn't protest. Her eyes were closed as he pressed her legs open. He kissed her there, tasting her, loving the way she moved with him.

Her breath came short and fast, but instead of surrendering, she grabbed his hair. "I want you. Inside me," she panted.

He studied her for a long moment. "Are you certain?"

"Yes."

"Sophia, if you're not ready…"

She grasped his shoulder, pulled him up to meet his gaze directly. "I'm ready. I want to be your wife again. Completely."

"And the risks?"

"Are you willing to take them with me?" she asked.

"Yes. But if we never have a child, I can live with that. I can't live with losing you."

"You won't lose me. Not ever." She wrapped her arms around his shoulders and kissed him. It was tender but passionate. She wrapped her legs around his hips and opened her eyes. He'd never seen her look so vulnerable. So scared.

He would replace that fear with pleasure.

Slowly, he guided his erection into her, feeling her tremble. "Shh." He stroked her hair, soothing her, and she closed her eyes. "Let me make love to you, Sophia. Let me be part of you."

"Yes." She brushed a hand over his hair, and he felt her body relax. He pushed again and was fully inside her. "Oh, yes. I remember this now," she whispered.

He kissed her and moved. He hadn't forgotten what it felt like to move inside her, only the reality was far more vivid than his memories. She moved with him, taking him deeper, bringing him to the brink of pleasure and then pulling away again.

He wasn't certain who was making love to whom.

He looked down at her and met her gaze. Before it had always been too dark to see her, or she'd had her eyes closed or focused elsewhere. Now she watched him and allowed him to see her, truly see her. Every reaction was plain on her face. She hid nothing from him, bowing her body so she could join with him completely and not seeming to mind the erotic view it gave him.

"Now, you're driving me mad," he growled, nipping her breast.

"Don't stop," she moaned. "Don't stop."

His body was telling him to go faster and harder, but he resisted the urge, moving slowly instead. He was rewarded when her eyes widened and he saw the first glimmer of hot pleasure in her gaze. He slid in and out again, and her breath hitched. Her cheeks were flushed pink now, her nipples hard and rosy. She moved against him with a sort of desperation, but he never faltered, never wavered in his slow, steady movements.

"Adrian, I can't hold on."

"Come for me," he murmured. "I want to feel you. See you." He held his breath for a moment. They'd made love a dozen times and never been so intimate. Faces always turned away. Cries stifled. Climaxing politely.

There was none of that now. She allowed him to see the rapture steal over her face as her body sought his one last time. She opened her mouth, closed her eyes, and grasped him as though she couldn't get enough. And then she shuddered, tightening around him, clamping her legs hard about him so he was forced to drive into her. It started his own climax, and before he could stop it, pleasure was rushing through him.

He'd intended to pull out at the last moment. She

might say she was ready for a child, but he did not want to push her. But she sensed what he was doing and held on to him. Instinct told him to bury himself deep, and he couldn't fight both of them. With a cry, he sank into her, emptied himself.

He burrowed his face into her citrus-scented skin, and when, several moments later, he could raise his head again, he did so tentatively.

She smiled. "I like you on top. But now it's my turn."

He groaned. "You can't possibly be serious."

She laughed and rolled over him, pinning him with her arms on either side of his head. "I suppose I can give you a few moments to recover. Not to mention, I'm starved."

"Then let's go downstairs and pilfer the kitchen. I have something I want to show you in my library, anyway."

She raised a brow. "Tell me it's not a dungeon with whips and chains for her ladyship's pleasure."

He frowned. Exactly what missions had she been assigned to? "It's not a dungeon. I think you'll find this intriguing."

He took her hand, pulled her up, then drew on his breeches and shirt while she donned a light dressing gown. "I don't see why we can't ring for a servant and stay in bed."

"You won't regret this. Come on." He took her hand and pulled her from the room.

❧

This was about the Jenkinson case. She knew it. Only Adrian would be thinking about work after so thoroughly bedding her.

On occasion, Sophia had spent time in conversation with other wives, and over tea the ladies sometimes confided in her. She didn't know why they should do so. None of them knew her well, but part of her job as an agent was to elicit trust. Perhaps she elicited it whether she wanted to or not. On a few of these occasions, a woman had confided to her that after her husband did his marital duty, he fell right asleep and snored so loudly he kept her awake half the night.

Not Sophia's husband. He was energized to work. She would have preferred he ravage her again. Or, rather, she ravage him. Instead, they traipsed downstairs and entered his library. He lit a lamp and stoked the fire then sat at his desk.

She plopped on the couch across from him. "Do you really want to talk about the Jenkinson case at"— she glanced at the clock in the corner—"quarter of two in the morning? I can think of more pleasant ways to spend the night."

He was rummaging through a drawer but glanced up at her with a raised brow. "Is getting me into bed all you think about, madam?"

She gritted her teeth. "No. Sometimes I think about shooting you."

"I'm fortunate you are a poor shot. Ah, here it is." He held up a large key. "Almost couldn't find it myself."

"The key to the dungeon?" she asked, but she sat forward. He was right. She was intrigued now.

He rose and crossed to the wall with the tall case clock. He shoved the clock aside and ran his hand along the wall. Just as she was about to conclude he was daft, he gave the wall a push, and it popped open.

"A secret door?"

He grinned at her over his shoulder then lifted the key and inserted it into a door just inside the opening in the wall. Sophia was on her feet now and peering over Adrian's shoulder. The key turned silently, and the door swung open, slowly revealing a small antechamber. Adrian reached around her, grasping the lamp on his desk, and stepped inside. Sophia followed without being asked. Inside the walls were lined with drawers stacked upon drawers. A small, bare table had been placed in the center of the room, and Adrian placed the lamp on top. He crossed to a section of drawers and pulled open the top one. Thumbing through the contents—papers and files, Sophia surmised—he pulled out a file and flipped through it.

"What are you looking for?" she asked.

"I keep thinking about the way Jenkinson was murdered. I told you it was familiar, but I can't remember what I saw or read."

And they were back to that again. True to his word, Adrian was including her in his investigation. Why had she ever doubted him?

"And you believe you have the answer to your suspicions here?" She gestured to the rows of drawers. How many files did he have in here? Thousands? Thousands upon thousands? Here she was, living with Agent Wolf and his... spy library right under her nose, and she never even knew. If only she'd been more curious about Adrian, she would have realized his true identity years before.

But what spy kept a library? She destroyed everything tying her to a mission.

Of course, she didn't have a hidden spy chamber.

"No, this isn't it." Adrian replaced the file, shut the drawer, and opened another.

"May I help?" She was eager to peruse these files. Were they all missions Adrian had been a part of? She touched one of the drawers and gingerly pulled on the handle. The files stared up at her in perfect alphabetical order: *Waterloo, Wellington, Wigs, Wood (Types)*.

Sophia shook her head. Why would he need a file on types of wood? She reached for the file, but Adrian called out, "This is it!"

"This is what?"

He placed the file on the table and stared down at it. "The Maîtriser group."

"I haven't heard of them." She stood across from him and studied the file. It was sparse, only two pages. One page gave information about the Maîtriser group. They were French in origin and operated mainly on the Continent.

"Nothing familiar?" Adrian asked.

"No."

"This file is information I collected incidentally. I've never run across them, either."

She looked down at the top page. "This says the group was involved mainly in blackmail and extortion. A little smuggling. They pay their people quite well, so obviously their ventures are lucrative. What does this have to do with Jenkinson?"

"Look at the next page." Adrian pulled it out and placed it before her. She read quickly, inhaling sharply when she saw the note at the bottom.

"Known for carving words and signs on the bodies

of those they consider traitors," she read. She glanced up at Adrian. "It might be a coincidence."

"I don't really believe in coincidence."

"Neither do I." She glanced around the room full of drawers and information. "Do you have anything else on the Maîtriser group? Who is their leader? Do they have any bases here in England?"

"We can search, but I believe our best option is to go to Melbourne in the morning and see what he knows."

"But I already know what you're thinking. You quizzed Liverpool about it last night."

He rubbed a hand over his jaw, now beginning to darken with stubble. "Jenkinson needed money, and he acquired money from sources unknown."

"What if one of those sources was the Maîtriser group?"

"Exactly."

She turned and paced. "They are French, and both Millie and Hardwicke mentioned his involvement with foreigners. But what could Jenkinson have that this group might want?"

"We need to ask Millie Jenkinson for the answer to that question. She knows more than she's telling us."

"Then let's pay a call on Millie." Sophia was suddenly impatient to move forward. She could understand why Adrian couldn't wait to get his hands on these files. The answer they sought had been waiting here all along.

"You forget it's the middle of the night. If she's home, she won't see us. We could push our way in, but that's not the best way to solicit information."

Sophia stopped pacing. "Very well. We wait until morning. I suppose we'd better get some sleep." But she knew she wouldn't be able to sleep. Her thoughts were rushing too fast.

"I'll lock the file room before we retire."

She followed Adrian back into his library proper and watched as he locked and concealed the file room again. With the clock back in place, Sophia could detect no alteration in the wall. She stood and studied it for several seconds, but the seam was cleverly concealed. She wanted to believe she would have spotted it if only she'd spent more time in Adrian's library, but truthfully, she knew she would never have even looked.

She glanced at the clock's face. It was two thirty. Still hours and hours before they could make anything remotely resembling a respectable call. Adrian came up behind her and wrapped his arms about her. He kissed her ear. "Let's go back to bed."

She shook her head. "I'll never be able to sleep now. I have too many ideas floating about in my mind. Too many possibilities."

His lips made a slow trail from her ear to her neck. "I might be able to find a way to distract you."

Yes, he very well might. She shivered as he kissed her neck delicately. She still wanted him. That was not in dispute. She'd forgotten how it had been between them. She'd forgotten how good it could feel when she wasn't focused on trying to conceive a child or worried about losing another. And yet taking that step with him tonight had not been easy.

She'd been terrified.

She hadn't thought she'd be afraid. She hadn't thought she'd tremble with fear and worry. And she'd never thought her husband would be so understanding and so tender. His words had melted her fear away. *If we never have a child, I can live with that. I can't live with losing you.*

She couldn't live with losing him, either. Their lovemaking earlier might result in a pregnancy. She wanted it and feared it, but she no longer felt as though she had to deal with it alone. Adrian would be beside her, no matter what.

She turned into his arms, and he lifted his mouth to meet hers. She wanted him inside her again. She wanted to be one with him to know he was hers as he would never be anyone else's.

"Let's go upstairs," he murmured in her ear.

"I don't think I can wait that long." She stepped back, loosened her robe, and allowed it to fall open. Adrian's eyes darkened as the robe shrugged off her shoulders and pooled on the floor. Naked, she placed her hand on his chest and gave him a small push. He stepped back, and she pushed again. Finally his legs met the couch, and he sat. She straddled him, sighing as he took her nipple into his mouth. She leaned her head back, closed her eyes… and then her nose itched.

In frustration, she lifted her hand to rub it then went rigid. Adrian must have felt the change in her immediately. "What is it?" he murmured against her skin.

"Don't stop." She kept her voice low and breathy, but slowly she opened her eyes and peered lazily about the room.

Even looking, she didn't see him right away. He made no sound as he slipped in one of the French doors across the room. Even as she watched, he stepped behind a curtain, concealing himself. He was a slim man dressed in black from head to toe. His black beaver hat concealed his features, but she managed to catch a glimpse of a mustache and dark shaggy hair brushing his collar. She had not seen him before, but she would have given fifty pounds he was part of the Maîtriser group.

He was certainly no friend, if the pistol he held in his hand was any indication.

If only she had a weapon… or clothes…

Her eyes darted to Adrian's desk. A candlestick was little use against a pistol.

"What is it?" Adrian asked.

Sophia hurriedly kissed him, moaning for effect. He kissed her back, but she sensed his confusion. She nibbled her way to his ear and whispered, "A man is hiding behind the curtains near the French doors."

She felt him tense, but he made no other indication he'd heard.

"He has a pistol," she whispered.

Adrian rose, taking her with him. "I want you on my desk," he said, voice husky, but she could detect the underlying concern.

"Yes," she said, wrapping her legs about his waist and risking a peek at the curtains. The man hadn't moved. He was waiting for his moment.

He wasn't going to get it.

Adrian swept a hand over the top of his desk, sending the contents scattering on the floor. Sophia winced for him, knowing how he prized order. But the effect was perfect. The intruder would think they were swept away with passion and had no idea he was present. When Adrian set her down on the cold, wooden surface, she felt something hard—a pen perhaps—jab her bare bottom. Adrian leaned over her, pushing her down and kissing her, but also reaching over her to fumble with the drawer. She moaned louder, hoping to cover the noise as he slid it open. It seemed to her hours passed as he blindly searched the drawer. She could not see the intruder. Adrian's body blocked hers, but the last thing she wanted was to hear the sound of the pistol firing and feel Adrian slump over her.

Her heart was racing, and she clenched her hands on Adrian's back, hoping it looked like an act of passion.

Finally, she felt Adrian jerk and knew he'd found what he sought. His hands were in her hair as he leaned down and murmured, "Entwine your fingers with mine."

She released his back and clasped his hand, feeling the cold metal of the pistol.

"It's primed and ready," he said against her throat. "I'll move out of the way, and you shoot."

Oh, damn it. He knew she was a miserable shot. But he also knew she'd seen the location of the intruder, and she was in a better position to aim and fire.

She took a shallow breath for courage. "Take off your clothing," she said, loud enough for the intruder to hear. Adrian stood, and she moved the pistol between their bodies to conceal it.

Her gaze met Adrian's, and he began to remove his shirt. As he did so, he shifted to the left, and she glimpsed the intruder stepping out from amidst the curtains.

Adrian was pulling the shirttails over his abdomen,

and she gave him a slight nod. Fast as lightning, he moved and ducked. She raised the pistol and fired at the intruder. She'd aimed for his shoulder, because she wanted him alive. What good was a dead man to them now?

Amazingly, she hit his arm—not so far off from where she'd aimed—and he dropped his pistol with a cry of pain. But it took only a second for him to drop and roll, reaching for his lost pistol with his good arm.

This was no amateur.

Sophia flew off the desk, vaulted over the couch, and kicked the man's pistol out of reach. She issued a swift, hard kick to the man's ribs, and he rolled into a ball and groaned. His hat fell off, revealing unkempt brown hair falling over his forehead and collar.

"Who are you?" she demanded.

He opened one eye, stared up at her, and smiled—why was he smiling when she'd just kicked him? Then she remembered she was naked.

"Put your robe on." Adrian bent beside her and lifted the man roughly to his feet. Sophia caught a glimpse of the sleeve of his coat, saw it was only torn, and deduced the bullet had just grazed the man.

"Don't get dressed on my account," the intruder wheezed, his accent perfectly English and educated but with a trace of something else, indicating he had acquired his accent rather than been born with it. He wheezed again, and Sophia had the satisfaction of knowing her kick had some effect. Sophia found her robe and shrugged it on, but before she could tie the sash, Adrian held out a hand.

"Give me the sash. I'll bind his hands."

Sophia handed the sash over and hugged the robe closed. Adrian marched the intruder to a Sheraton chair, forced him to sit, and pulling his arms back, tied him securely with the purple silk sash. Then he bent so he was eye to eye with the man. "Look at my wife again, and I'll kill you."

The man sneered. "I—"

Adrian's fist plowed into his face, and Sophia winced as blood spurted in a fine arc. How were they going to explain that mess to the servants?

The intruder kicked with his feet, but Adrian stood and moved out of range. "What's your name?" he demanded.

"I dink you broke ny mose!" the intruder yelled. Sophia wanted to shush him. She didn't need a footman coming to investigate.

Instead, she walked to the back of the chair, leaned over the man's shoulder, and murmured in his ear, "Tell us your name, or you'll have more than a broken nose. My husband has a rather nasty propensity for violence." She inhaled and allowed her breath to feather over the man's neck. "I confess I'm rather aroused by it. The blood, the crunch of bones breaking, the howls of anguish…"

The man turned his head sharply, his eyes wild. "You're mad—"

"*Don't* look at my wife." Adrian took a step closer. "I asked you a question, sir."

The man's head whipped forward again. "I can't tell you."

"You mean you won't," Sophia corrected. "Poor decision." She glanced at Adrian, and he flashed a smile at her. It felt, quite suddenly, as though they'd been working together for years. They'd found a rhythm, and she didn't want to think too hard about it lest she interrupt it.

Adrian drew his fist back.

"Wait! You don't have to—oof!"

Adrian's fist plowed into the man's abdomen, and the intruder slumped over. Sophia bit her lip. She wasn't going to allow this to go on long, nor did she think Adrian would beat the man unmercifully. But they had to scare him a little... or a lot.

Adrian stepped beside her, grabbed a handful of the man's hair, and yanked it up. "What is your name?"

The man's mouth moved, but no sound came. Adrian waited about thirty seconds then repeated the question.

"Twombley," the man wheezed. "That's all I can say."

"Oh, no it's not." Adrian yanked hard on the intruder's hair, unbalancing the chair so it fell over. The man landed on his back with a groan. Adrian put a foot on his chest. "You come into my house. You look at my wife. You point a gun at me. You have a lot more to say."

But the man shook his head. "Go ahead and shoot me. Cut me up. He'll do worse if he finds I've talked to you."

Sophia knelt beside Twombley. "Who will do worse, Mr. Twombley?"

He didn't look at her, kept his gaze on Adrian. "I've already said too much."

"We know you're part of the Maîtriser group," she told him. "We know you killed Jenkinson."

"I didn't kill him. *He* did. He'll do worse to me if I betray him."

Sophia looked at Adrian. She couldn't imagine what might be worse than having an *M* carved into your body. She stood and walked behind the desk. Adrian followed. "I can keep working on him."

"You might get information," she admitted, "but he'll probably lie to appease you. He's scared of the man who killed Jenkinson. Who wouldn't be?"

"We need the leader's name and location."

"And this man could send us on a fruitless chase all over England or the Continent."

Adrian frowned and ran a hand through his disordered hair. He had blood on his knuckles, she saw now, and scarlet dots spattering his white linen shirt. "Let's take him to Melbourne. If nothing else, we leave him in Barbican custody for the time being. We bloody well can't leave him here."

Sophia was nodding. "We see what Melbourne knows then pay Millie Jenkinson a morning call." She scratched her nose again. "We're definitely closing in."

But Adrian was watching her. "How did you happen to see him enter? I thought I had you pretty well distracted."

She smiled. "You did. Fortunately for us, my intuition can resist even your allure." She tapped his nose. "I'm going to get dressed."

"You might as well rouse the house. I'll need to call for the coach and change before we take him to Melbourne." He looked at the man on the floor, and Sophia followed his gaze to the blood on the wall and the carpet. "How are we going to explain all this?"

She shrugged. "I say we let Wallace do it."

"I agree, and Sophia…"

"I know." She opened the library door and stepped out. "Give him a raise."

Twenty

ADRIAN DIDN'T KNOW WHAT SOPHIA TOLD WALLACE or the rest of the staff, but no one looked twice when he hauled the hooded intruder to their coach and four an hour later. She looked as though she'd just awakened after a long, restful slumber. She wore a white walking dress with lace ruffles about her neck. The sleeves were loose and wide, and on her feet were pretty white slippers. Her hair was tucked under a simple round cap with satin and lace on the edges and a white rose in front.

She looked fresh and innocent.

"Interesting choice of attire for three in the morning." He pushed Twombley onto the floor of the coach and crawled over him to take a seat. Sophia did the same, sitting opposite.

"It's a morning dress. Besides, by the time we deal with him, it will be morning and then we'll call on Millie. I don't want to appear unfashionable."

"God forbid."

"Where are you taking me?" Twombley grumbled, his voice muffled under the hood.

"The cemetery," Adrian said. "We're going to bury you alive."

Twombley issued a small whimper, and Sophia scowled at Adrian. He shrugged. He didn't feel the need to be nice to men who tried to kill them. Not that she'd been particularly nice earlier. Adrian didn't think he'd ever forget the image of Sophia, stark naked, jumping over his couch and landing like some sort of jungle cat beside Twombley. No wonder the man had trouble taking his eyes off her. She was magnificent—clothed or not.

They slowed, and Adrian peered out the curtains then called, "Here, Jackson." He'd wanted to avoid the gazes of those heading home from the theater or a ball, so he'd instructed the coachman to leave them in a side alley. He'd haul Twombley into the Barbican offices through the back.

Sophia had sent a message to Lord Melbourne, and Adrian hoped his superior was waiting. The Barbican offices were always busy—any time day or night—but Adrian preferred to get this over with quickly rather than standing about enduring the curious glances of the discreet Barbican staff.

He yanked Twombley out of the carriage and helped Sophia descend. Before they even reached the Barbican's secret back door, Blue stepped out of the shadows. "Looks as though you've had a busy night." He peered closely at Twombley. "Is that blood seeping through his coat?"

"Flesh wound," Sophia said. "It probably needs to be bandaged."

She was trying to coddle the prisoner again. Before

she offered him tea and scones, Adrian asked, "Where is Melbourne?"

"On his way." Blue gestured for them to follow him, but to Adrian's surprise, he headed away from the Barbican's offices. "He dispatched me to take charge of your package."

"Where are we going?" Sophia asked, and Adrian remembered why he liked having her around.

"Private offices." Blue extracted a key from his yellow coat—bloody hell, the man had the worst taste in fashion—and slipped it into a nondescript door just down from the Barbican's secret door. The first door opened into a small passageway with several additional doors. Blue took a second key and unlocked the door farthest from them. He gestured them inside then followed.

They stood in a dark corridor, but Blue lifted a lamp, lit it, and Adrian studied the bare white walls and closed white doors. Using yet a third key, Blue opened another door. A fire already burned in the hearth of what appeared to be a library.

"Wait here," Blue ordered. "I'll take care of…"

"Mr. Twombley," Sophia offered.

She stepped into the library, and Adrian followed reluctantly. He wanted to see what Blue was doing with their man. Blue shut the door behind them, and Sophia made a circuit of the room. It held shelves of books, the cheery fireplace, and a small desk. The desk was clear, and Adrian didn't note any personal effects whatsoever.

"I've never been here," Sophia said.

"Neither have I."

Her eyebrows rose. "Really? I thought you knew everything about the Barbican group. I only just met Melbourne the other day. He usually sent my assignments via Blue or an encrypted document."

"Encrypted? You break codes?"

"Of course," she said as though everyone did.

Blue opened the door and entered alone.

"Where's Twombley?"

"Secure," Blue said. "You can have him back when you want him." Blue crossed to the desk and opened a drawer. He set three wine glasses and a bottle on the desk.

"How is Twombley's arm?" Sophia asked.

"Flesh wound, as you said. Wine?"

"A little. We need to call on Millie Jenkinson in a few hours."

Adrian nodded when Blue offered him a glass. "What do you know about the Maîtriser group?"

Blue sipped his wine. "I know of the group. Is Twombley a member?"

"We believe so, but it's going to take a bit of effort to get any information out of him."

"You can break both of his legs, but he won't talk." Blue took a seat on a cream-colored chair. It was the only furnishing that didn't clash with his yellow coat and green breeches. "He'd rather die than talk."

Footsteps echoed in the hall, and Adrian tensed. He saw Sophia draw in a breath and tighten her grip on her reticule. Who knew what weapons she had secreted inside?

The library door opened, and Melbourne stood

in the opening. He was dressed impeccably, but the shadow of a beard indicated it had been a long day for him as well. Adrian ran a hand over his own stubble.

"This had better be worth it," Melbourne growled. "My wife is not pleased, and when she's not pleased, *I'm* not pleased."

"A man broke into my library tonight," Adrian said. "Agent Saint and I caught him."

"So?" Melbourne marched forward, and Blue, who had risen and returned to the desk upon Melbourne's arrival, handed him a glass of wine. Melbourne drank it in one swallow. "I don't wake you every time someone breaks into my home."

"Does that happen often?" Sophia asked.

Melbourne gave her a dark look.

"We have reason to believe this man"—Adrian interrupted—"he says his name is Twombley, is part of the Maîtriser group."

Melbourne gave him a hard look and sat behind the desk. "Go on."

"I need information about the group, where it's headquartered, who leads it."

The silence in the room stretched. The fire crackled, and somewhere a horse and carriage clopped by.

"I thought you were working on the Liverpool assignment."

"We are."

Melbourne closed his eyes. Then quite suddenly he rose, slammed his fist down, and cursed. "How can the Maîtriser group be involved?"

"That's what we're trying to find out, sir," Sophia ventured.

"Liverpool is going to have my head," Melbourne muttered, taking the wine Blue poured for him. "You know what this means, don't you?" He glared at Adrian.

"Yes. Jenkinson was selling them something, probably information, but we need the proof before we go to Liverpool."

"Oh, you need more than proof," Melbourne said. "You need to be damn sure—more sure than you've ever been in your life—before you accuse the prime minister's brother of being a traitor."

"Then we need to find this Maîtriser group," Sophia said, moving to stand beside Adrian. He resisted putting an arm about her waist, because he knew she wouldn't like it, but he couldn't help feeling protective of her. He didn't want her involved in this. He wanted her safe at home, and he knew if she was the kind of woman who stayed safely at home, he wouldn't be in love with her.

"And you think I know where they are?" Melbourne asked, voice defiant. "If I knew that, Foncé and his thugs would be dead."

"Foncé is the leader?" Adrian asked.

"That's our most recent information, but it's over a year old," Blue informed them. "The agent watching the Maîtriser group was found dead in Nice right after his report was filed. His throat had been slashed, and his body had been marked."

"With an *M*?" Adrian asked. "The same way Jenkinson's was marked."

"What?" Melbourne shook his head. "I have no record of that."

"Liverpool didn't want to discuss the details. We had to coax it from the valet, who, by the way, was so scared he's probably long gone by now."

"Smart man," Blue said. "The Maîtriser group is dangerous. Over the years, we've assigned half a dozen operatives to them. All have ended up dead or missing."

Adrian definitely wanted Sophia home now.

"You don't have to continue," Melbourne said. "You can tell Liverpool your efforts were unsuccessful. I'll support you."

"And give up the position in the Barbican group?" Sophia shook her head. "I don't think so."

"I've never failed at a mission yet," Adrian pointed out. "I'm not going to quit."

"That's an admirable record, Agent Wolf." Melbourne toasted him with the glass of wine. "But this isn't worth dying over."

"And how many more agents will die if we give up now?" Sophia asked. "Is it worth it to bring some justice to the dead? We can't allow the Maîtriser group to go on unpunished."

No one spoke for a long moment. Adrian saw Blue and Melbourne exchange a look. Finally, Melbourne said, "All right. Here's what you're going to do."

∽

"Mrs. Jenkinson is not at home," the butler told them before Sophia could even speak her request. It was obvious he'd dressed quickly. His cravat was askew and his shirt still untucked under his coat.

"Is she with Linden?" Adrian demanded.

The butler's brows flew up. "My lord. It is not even seven in the morning. If you would deign to call later at a decent hour, I assure you—"

Adrian pushed the door open, and though the butler tried to stand his ground, he moved back when Adrian towered over him. Sophia almost felt sorry for the servant who was only doing as he ought.

But then Adrian and his brute ways saved her quite a bit of time. If she had been alone, she would have had to talk her way in. Besides, watching Adrian flex his muscles made her heart beat just a little harder. "I'm afraid Lord Smythe will not be deterred from his purpose this morning," she told the butler. "Is Mrs. Jenkinson in her bed? If so, I will go ahead and make sure she is presentable."

The butler didn't speak, and Adrian shoved him aside, starting for the steps.

"Sir! You can't go up there!"

Adrian ignored him, and Sophia followed. She patted the man's shoulder as she passed him. "You made a valiant effort."

"Which door?" Adrian asked when they'd reached the second floor.

"I think it might be that one." Sophia pointed. "The one Mr. Linden just came out of, brandishing his walking stick."

"What the hell is going on here?" Linden, dressed only in a woman's robe, waved the stick and barreled down the corridor.

Adrian gave her a look. "Do you want to handle this, or should I?"

While sparring with Linden might be a good deal

of fun, her gown was new, and she didn't want to risk dirtying it. "You take him. I'll find her."

Adrian nodded and started forward. Linden swung at him, and Adrian caught the stick, using the momentum to force Linden against the wall.

"Thank you!" Sophia squeezed by, leaving thumps and the sound of a painting crashing to the floor behind her. She entered Millie's bedroom, and following her instinct, ducked and rolled. The vase Millie had been holding crashed against the dresser beside her.

"Oh!"

Sophia looked up and saw Millie had her hands to her mouth.

"Lady Smythe! I thought you were an attacker."

Sophia rose to her feet. "Reasonable assumption. Lord Smythe is just disarming Mr. Linden. He'll be here shortly, if you want to take a moment to dress." She was clutching the sheet to her bare body. Behind her the large bed looked rumpled and well used.

"Yes." Millie looked about, appearing confused.

"I think Mr. Linden borrowed your dressing gown. Do you have another?"

"I—ah—"

Sophia went to the dressing room, opened the clothespress, and pulled out a mantle. "Here." She handed it to Millie. "Put this on."

Keeping the sheet about her, Millie donned the mantle as Adrian walked into the room. "Where's Randall?"

Adrian raised his brows. "You don't really want to speak of this in front of him, do you?"

Millie swallowed. "No."

"May I?" Adrian gestured to a dainty chair before a dressing table, and without waiting for permission, turned it backward and sat. It would have looked ridiculous—such a large man straddling such a small, delicate chair—if it had been anyone but Adrian. Instead, he looked formidable and more than a little enticing.

Sophia swallowed her lust and turned to the objective at hand. "Millie, we need to ask you—"

"She knows why we're here," Adrian said. "Are you going to make Lady Smythe go through a charade, or are you going to tell us what we want to know?"

"Lord Liverpool went through all of George's papers. I gave him full access to the library." She clutched the mantle to her throat.

"But that wasn't all of your husband's papers, was it, Mrs. Jenkinson?"

"N-no. There were others hidden in his bedroom. I thought about giving them to Robert, but I was scared. Callows was scared. He said we should destroy them."

"Tell me you didn't destroy them," Sophia said.

Millie's face fell, and tears welled in her eyes. "What else was I to do? Callows was afraid. I was afraid. I didn't want them to come back and hurt me or the baby."

"Who?" Adrian asked. "What did the papers say?"

Millie closed her eyes, pressed her fingertips to them. "There were numbers."

"Don't play with me, Millie."

Millie cast an appealing glance at Sophia, who gave her no sympathy.

"All right. They were amounts owed. George was collecting money from someone. He'd made a list of the amounts owed and when each was paid."

"Who was paying him?"

Millie shook her head. "The only name I saw was Foncé. I don't even know if that's a name or a place."

Sophia felt her heart thump against her ribs. They'd been right. Dear God, they'd been right. What would have happened to Millie had she turned those papers over?

"Last question," Adrian said. "What was your husband collecting money for?"

Millie shook her head. "I don't know. I don't want to know."

"Perhaps it's better if you don't," Sophia agreed. "Lord Smythe, if I'm not mistaken, we have another appointment."

He rose, tipped his hat.

They stepped into the corridor, and Sophia raised her eyebrows at the pink lump on the floor. "What did you do to him?"

"He bumped his head with his walking stick."

"Of course. Happens all the time." As they passed Linden, she tried to bend to check on him, but Adrian grabbed her arm and ushered her forward. Just as well, she thought. It was almost eight, and Mr. Twombley was scheduled to escape at half past.

❧

Adrian hated waiting. He'd conducted his share of surveillance—done his apprenticeship, as he liked to think of it. When he'd been Agent Wolf, lesser operatives conducted surveillance for him. Now, he was right back where he started. He glanced at Sophia.

Maybe not right back.

Sophia, still wearing her white muslin morning dress, crouched beside him in what amounted to a heap of rotting vegetables. The cart had been strategically placed outside the back alley of the Barbican group's offices to give Adrian and Sophia a view of the exit when Twombley made his daring escape.

"Do you think he'll realize what we're doing?" she asked, pushing a cabbage aside to better her view.

"Blue promised he'd put up a good struggle."

Sophia sighed into a tower of parsnips. "I hope he goes directly to this Foncé. I don't relish following Twombley about for days on end."

Neither did Adrian, but if Twombley was smart—and he was—he'd take a circuitous route to the Maîtriser group's headquarters. But eventually he'd lead them to Foncé, and Adrian couldn't wait to get his hands on the man. What he'd done to Jenkinson was bad enough. No man should have to die that way. Jenkinson deserved justice. But this Foncé had also killed British operatives—men who risked their lives for the Crown. For that, Adrian wanted vengeance.

Sophia grabbed his arm and hissed, "Did you hear that?"

"There's no need to whisp—"

"Shh! There it is again."

Adrian heard it this time. A thump and the sound of something breaking. Blue might have been making this look too good. For a moment, Adrian wondered if he should go to the operative's assistance, then the door of the building across from their cart burst open and Twombley appeared. He'd lost his hat, and his clothes were in disarray. Hair standing on end, he looked wildly about.

As one, Adrian and Sophia ducked. Their gazes met among the rotting potatoes, and Adrian slowly raised his head to peer over the produce. Twombley was running at a good clip, hugging the sides of the alley. He peered over his shoulder several times and then ran full out.

"Let's go."

Sophia was already jumping off the cart and starting after Twombley. Adrian joined her, moving quickly but unhurriedly. There was no need to risk Twombley seeing them. Operatives had been stationed along all the likely escape routes and would direct Wolf and Saint toward their man, allowing them to keep their distance lest Twombley recognize them. Once Twombley thought he was safely away, Adrian and Sophia could move in.

As expected, Twombley headed toward the most populated area of London nearby—Piccadilly and Bond. The first operative, a man in the garb of a candle seller, pointed them toward an arcade swarming with early shoppers. Adrian took Sophia's hand in his and, weaving through the clusters of people, followed the trail. They received several curious glances, as their clothing still had pieces of rotten produce hanging on it, but Sophia kept her head high, and Adrian thought she could make even rotten potatoes seem like the latest fashion.

"Smart of him to attempt to lose himself among the

crowds," she said, stepping hastily aside as a small boy
chasing a ball almost ran her down.

"He'll tire of running soon enough." Adrian
spotted Twombley at the far side of the arcade,
walking quickly and with his head down, and pulled
Sophia beside a stall offering shawls and other wraps.
While Adrian pretended to admire the shawls and
chatted with the vendor, his body blocking Sophia's
from view, she peered around him and kept watch on
Twombley. It took effort for Adrian to keep his attention on the vendor, to smile and converse, to pretend
he had nothing else to do. Every instinct in him urged
him to turn his head, to scan the area for Twombley.
His brain screamed warnings. If they lost Twombley
now, they'd lose everything.

Adrian looked at Sophia. He had never trusted
another operative with so much when everything
was at stake. Adrian liked to be the one who made
all the decisions. Now he relied on Sophia to keep
Twombley in sight. He waited for her to give the
signal to move ahead.

And then just when he was certain she had lost
track of him—why else in bloody hell was she waiting
so long?—she took his hand and yanked. "He's
leaving. Let's go."

Abruptly, Adrian turned away from the vendor,
leaving her squawking in indignation, and locked
his sights on Twombley. Sophia's timing had been
perfect. Twombley was on his way out of the
arcade, and he was walking at a much more relaxed,
leisurely pace.

Adrian and Sophia emerged on the other side of the

arcade and looked right then left. A groom brushing a horse pointed north. "'E's 'eaded that way. Stepped out and changed 'is coat. Wearin' a blue coat now instead o' the black."

"Much obliged," Adrian said and sprinted north toward Regent Street.

"Do you think he was one of ours?" Sophia ran beside Adrian, surprising him by keeping up even in a gown and slippers.

"Yes, and I think that's the last. We're on our own. There he is." He veered left and yanked Sophia with him, into the doorway of an abandoned shop. "Let's keep our distance."

"Good idea." She bent and caught her breath. "I forget how much I hate this kind of work. Sneaking about, hiding in alcoves." She gestured to the doorway. "Give me a good fight any day."

Adrian grinned then leaned down and kissed her soundly. She frowned at him and raised her brows. "What was that for?"

"Because I couldn't agree with you more."

"Oh, well… good."

He'd flustered her, which made him smile again.

"But now I've lost track of Twombley."

"I haven't," Adrian said. He watched Twombley circle back after passing a tavern, and with a last quick look over his shoulder, open the door and disappear inside. He pointed to the tavern. "He's in there."

Sophia sighed. "He could be in there for hours, eating breakfast and drinking tea."

"Or he might be looking for a way to sneak out the back."

"That's what I was afraid of." She pursed her lips. "We split up. I cover the back, and you stay here?"

"It means one of us follows him to what is most likely the Maîtriser group's headquarters." And, though he didn't say it, it meant that person would probably receive credit for solving the murder. And perhaps it was best to allow Fate to decide which of them would win back the position in the Barbican group.

Sophia nodded. A quick glance at her dark eyes, and Adrian knew she'd come to the same conclusion as he.

"The Maîtriser group is dangerous," Sophia said slowly. "Perhaps neither of us should attempt to confront them without assistance."

Adrian cocked his head as though considering. "Good point." It was a good point, but the truth of the matter was neither of them was the least bit concerned about the Maîtriser group. He knew she thought she could take them down by herself, just as he did. He didn't want her in there alone, but he trusted her abilities like he trusted his own. And now he would have to trust her again—they would have to trust one another. "In that case, whoever follows Twombley meets the other back home. We can ask Melbourne to send some of his operatives with us and return tonight under cover of darkness."

"Agreed. See you tonight." She stepped away, already heading for the tavern's rear exit, then paused and ducked into the doorway again. She touched a gloved finger to his cheek and smiled at him. "It's nice to have a partner, isn't it?"

He studied her. The skepticism and distrust of him

were still there. She didn't know if he would keep his word any more than he could be sure she would. But in her gaze he saw something that hadn't been there before—hope.

Adrian bent and kissed her, this time tender and filled with promise. "I'll see you at home."

With a quick bob of her head, she was away again. "Be careful!" she called over her shoulder, but it was too late for that. He jammed a shoulder against the casement and stared at the tavern. It was far too late for caution. He was in love with her now.

Ridiculously unfashionable to be in love with one's wife, but Adrian had never cared for fashion. And truth be told, he thought he'd been in love with her for years now. If he hadn't loved her, it would have been so much easier to go to her, to try to make amends earlier in their marriage.

But he'd feared making a mistake and losing whatever he had left of her. That in itself had been the mistake. To think of all the days, the months, the years they wasted apart, when they could have been in one another's arms.

The shadows began to fade as the sun rose higher in the sky, and still Twombley did not make an appearance. When afternoon fell and Adrian's mood with it—he was hungry, thirsty, and tired—he decided a bit of reconnaissance was needed. He grabbed a boy selling charcoal, his cry of "Charcoal! Get yer charcoal!" grating on Adrian's nerves, gave the boy Twombley's description, and offered him a pound to go into the tavern and look for the man. He wouldn't have offered so much, but he didn't have anything less.

The boy, a lad of no more than twelve, gaped at him. "An 'ole quid, sar? Just fer lookin' for a man?" He had a grimy face—some of it soot from the charcoal he was so intent to sell—and a wiry body. He looked like he could use a good meal.

"That's right." Adrian drew out the pound note and waved it. "I'll be here, and be quick about it."

"Yes, sar!"

The lad was quick. Five minutes later he returned with a full report. "No man like you described be in there, sar." Holding up his fingers, he ticked off the tavern's occupants, none of which remotely resembled Twombley.

Adrian held the pound note out, and the boy's hand snatched at it, but Adrian didn't release it. "Does the tavern rent rooms?"

The boy shook his head. "No, sar. Least I don't think so."

Adrian released the note, and it disappeared into the boy's coat faster than a slithering snake. "On your way, then."

When the boy was gone, Adrian sauntered across the road, skirted the tavern, and went around back. He hadn't expected to see her, but the barren yard behind the tavern made him sigh nevertheless. Crates and broken bottles, rotting vegetables and a few stray cats littered the yard, but Sophia was not there. Nor was there any sign she ever had been.

Shoving his hands in his pockets, Adrian started for home.

Twenty-one

SOPHIA STEPPED QUIETLY INTO THE LIBRARY AND closed the door behind her. Adrian was facing away, his boots propped on the bookshelf behind his large desk. The desk was clear. She knew he worked all the time, but he never left files or books or papers lying about. She admired that quality in him, as it was something with which she struggled.

"You can leave the tray on the table," he said absently, not turning to look at her.

"I'm not the housekeeper," she said, "and I don't think there's time for tea."

He didn't turn to look at her, but somehow she knew he was smiling. "I find I'm not as thirsty as I thought." He did turn now, and his gray eyes were shadowed with... suspicion. "You had the luck today."

"If you mean Twombley slipped out the back of that rank tavern and I followed him to the Maîtriser group's buildings, then you are correct. I had the luck." She stepped forward, rounding the desk so she was before him. "But *we* will have the luck tonight. We must leave now."

"Have you seen Melbourne?"

She shook her head. "No, and there's no time. In the time it took for me to do light surveillance of the perimeter, Foncé was already preparing to leave. Men were scrambling to load carts and carriages."

"And yet you took the time to come back here."

"Yes."

She watched the suspicion in his eyes flicker, and knew he was debating whether or not to trust her. She could give him a moment—no more—to sort it out. After all, she would have felt much the same had their positions been reversed. And she wouldn't lie and say she had not been tempted to slip inside the buildings and take this Foncé herself.

Two things stopped her.

One, she was no fool. She knew her skills were unsurpassed by any other agent save perhaps the one seated before her. But all of the Barbican group's agents were superior. Foncé had managed to take out more than one Barbican agent in the past. Sophia couldn't afford to allow herself to become arrogant and careless. She needed help.

Two, she wanted that help to come from Adrian. She wanted to close this matter together. She wanted to see their partnership through. She would not be the one to betray the fragile trust between them—not for pride, not for a position in the Barbican group… not for anything.

He dropped his boots on the floor, and she stepped between his legs. He had changed into clean clothing, while her once-white gown was now dirty and rumpled.

"What's your plan?" Adrian asked.

Sophia almost smiled. She could not imagine Adrian asking such a question five days ago when this mission began. And she could not imagine the answer she was about to give. "I thought we could discuss that in the carriage after I've changed. There really is no time to lose."

For the mission she was about to undertake, she needed more practical garb. Allowing herself five minutes, she donned black trousers, a man's black shirt, and a black coat. She twisted her hair in a knot and tucked it under a cap.

Ignoring the servants' surprised stares, she ran through the house and met Adrian, similarly dressed in dark clothing, in the carriage.

His brows rose when he saw her, but he said nothing.

"Let's go," she said, and with a rap of his knuckles, they were off.

As the carriage rambled through Mayfair, she outlined the headquarters buildings for him, helping him to visualize the house and the guards she'd seen. "If anything is working in our favor, it's that he's sent most of his men away."

"How do we know he hasn't gone with them?"

She shrugged. "We'll find out soon enough. I know the plan of attack I think best, but I'm certain you'll prefer to reserve judgment until you see everything for yourself."

"Of course. What are you wearing?"

She knew he'd been staring at her since she'd climbed into the carriage, but she pretended to just now notice her male attire. "Something a bit more practical."

"Let me take a look."

She held her arms out. "As you see." It was dark in the vehicle with the curtains drawn. They hadn't bothered to light the lamps, not wanting to attract attention. Still, she saw the glint of something raw and aroused in his eyes.

"No, a closer look." He took hold of one of her arms and had her in his lap before she could sputter a protest—not that she had any intention of doing so. It would take another half hour at least to reach the Maîtriser group's headquarters, and she was always a bundle of nervous energy before a strike like this one.

She could think of worse ways to use some of that energy than in Adrian's lap. She slid her hands down his chest.

"I feel rather wicked with you dressed as such." But he was already wrapping his arms around her waist, pulling her mouth to his.

"I assure you I am all female under these clothes," she promised.

"I'll need to test that." He nipped her lips. "I like proof."

"As do I." She pressed her mouth to his and felt the charge immediately. It was like touching fire to oil. She was suddenly warm and bright and alive. His mouth slanted over hers, claiming her completely. She liked being taken, liked that she could allow herself to be taken and not feel as though she was giving up power. Adrian restored her rather than depleted her.

She eased her legs on either side of him so she was straddling him on the squabs, and still his mouth continued to plunder her. He kissed her roughly. His tongue didn't so much twine with hers as thrust and parry. His lips didn't brush hers as much as they locked on and stole her very last breath. When Adrian kissed her, she could think of nothing else, do nothing else, be nothing else. She was his.

His hands gripped her bottom, and he pulled her hard against his erection. His mouth broke free of hers, and she moaned with the sudden yearning to have it back. "I missed you," he growled in her ear, his teeth playing havoc with the delicate skin of her neck.

"Apparently. I thought we were making a plan to do away with the Maîtriser group—or at least their leader."

His hands tore at her collar, revealing her collarbone to his wicked mouth. Meanwhile, his hands pulled the shirttails from the trousers and eased the coat off her shoulders. "We'll have time for that in a moment."

"It will be at least another twenty minutes until we reach the house. What shall we do with twenty minutes?" Her hands stroked him through his trousers, and with a groan, he yanked the shirt over her head. She heard material rip and felt something pop, but then his mouth was on her breasts, and she was aching to feel him inside her. This time she wasn't afraid. This time there was only need and desire and love.

She thought how perfect it would be if they conceived a child now—on their way to do what they were both born to do. And she knew if they were to conceive a child, she wanted it to be something born out of love. She wanted fear to play no part.

Adrian was fumbling with her trousers. They were too big for her anyway, and he easily pushed them over her hips. She rose, keeping one hand on his shoulder for balance in the rocking vehicle, then slipped them off. Wearing only her half boots, she climbed back on his lap.

He sighed, and she could feel the slight tremor from the effort it took for him to restrain himself.

With a smile, she released the fall of his trousers, freeing him. She took him in her hand and stroked his hard, velvet length. His head fell back, revealing the strong column of his throat, and Sophia forgot about her own needs. She could have touched him, pleasured him, all evening. She loved watching him.

And then his eyes opened, and his molten gray gaze met hers. "How did I survive all these years without you?" His hands on her hips tightened. "*You*—the real you."

"Miserably, I suppose." She stroked him again, and he shuddered.

"Yes. And I was miserable tonight, waiting for you."

"That's because you didn't trust me." She allowed one finger to tease him, and he teased her right back with tongue and teeth on her nipple.

When they were both breathless and aching for more, he said, "I admit, I had my doubts. But you're here now. Bloody hell, are you here." He put his mouth on her again, and she didn't comprehend his next words. If he wasn't inside her soon, she thought she would begin screaming in frustration.

"But you're here now," she heard him saying when she could concentrate again. "And everything is… you."

She knew just what he meant. Everything was brighter and darker and louder and softer when they were together. There was something that held them—even when they were estranged for all those years—that bound them and could never be severed. She supposed that was why neither of them had ever strayed. She'd had opportunity, and one look at him told her he'd had opportunity as well.

But they were bound. Now. Forever.

She lifted her hips and angled them over him, stroking the tip of his erection with her core. His gaze, hot and dark and full of desire, locked on hers. His lips moved, as though he struggled to speak. Finally, "Are you sure this is what you want?" His voice was low and husky, filled with effort.

She nodded. "More than anything." Slowly, torturously, she took him inside her. She felt every inch of him slide against her, filling her, warming her, making them one. And when he was embedded to the hilt, she rocked back, causing him to groan, and then forward again so he gripped her hips. But she didn't want him taking control. She waited until his grip relaxed, and rocked again, setting her own pace and rhythm. She wanted slow and steady, like the rocking of the coach. She wanted to prolong the pleasure, the torture, until they were both gasping with it. But when she felt him swell inside her, she could hold back no longer. She let go and rode him hard and fast. The climax slammed into her like a runaway carriage, and she could only hold on and see it to the end.

But just when she thought she could stand no more pleasure, Adrian reached between them, touching her, and she soared again. Adrian thrust inside her, making a guttural sound, and then he was with her—flying, soaring, falling, and slamming into the most profound ecstasy she had ever experienced.

They were lying half on the seats and half off. Sophia had no recollection of how they'd come to be there, but she opened her eyes, and Adrian was on top of her. Her back was on the squabs, but one shoulder was jammed against the door. Adrian rolled off her, slamming his knee on the seat opposite them in the process. He winced, found his balance, and raked his fingers through his hair. "That was—"

She looked at him, waited. When he couldn't find the words, she laughed. "Yes, exactly." She tried to sit, faltered, and he pulled her up. She attempted to find her clothing, but it was too dark. Adrian held up something that looked like a shirt... or a coat.

"I think there was something we were discussing before..." Adrian gestured vaguely. Sophia noted his cravat was still tied perfectly and wondered how they'd managed that. "Something important."

"The Maîtriser group," she said. "We have to infiltrate their headquarters, capture their leader, and force him to confess to Jenkinson's murder."

"Is that all?" He glanced at his pocket watch, still miraculously in place. "I suppose we'd better get started."

❧

Ten minutes later, they sat on a dark residential street a few houses down from the one Sophia had seen Twombley enter earlier that day. Adrian was supposed to be watching the house, but he couldn't keep himself from watching Sophia as well.

When she'd climbed into the carriage that night, he'd almost ordered the lad out of his coach before he realized the small boy in black was his wife. And then he gaped. Her hair was tucked under a cap, and he could have sworn she moved differently. Gone was the sway of her hips. In its place was a cocky swagger. Adrian couldn't have said which was worse. The sway had been arousing, but knowing what he knew about the legs and hips and bottom hidden in those trousers, the swagger all but undid him.

She glanced away from the house and met his gaze. "My lord, are you observing?" she asked.

"No. I'm a bit… distracted." He indicated her attire. She smiled. Why did he have the feeling she found this amusing?

"This is easier for me to maneuver in. We're going to have to scale a wall—possibly more than one. I couldn't get a good look at the other side of the garden. And there are guards. I counted half a dozen, and that was after the mass exodus. I imagine there are at least that many still on the premises."

As she continued to speak, Adrian closed his eyes and tried to see the picture she painted—the layout of the complex, the number of men, the possible entrances and exits. And every time he thought he succeeded, he'd picture her bottom in those trousers and lose focus.

But he was a bloody professional, and he would bloody hell be damned if he was going to allow a woman's curves—even his own wife's curves—to distract him from something so important.

With sheer force of willpower, he looked past the trousers and coat—why did he have to know she wore nothing under that shirt?—and concentrated on forming a plan. A few moments later he instructed their coachman to drive on and leave them several blocks from the Maîtriser group's complex. The coach rolled to a stop, and Adrian's mind was sharp and focused on the main objective. He could pull that cap off her head and watch her curls tumble down later...

The night was warm with the faintest scent of hollyhocks on the breeze when he stepped out of the coach. Though the summer weather persisted into mid-August, Adrian thought he could detect the crisp smell of fall under that fragrant sweetness. He glanced up, noted the clouds obscured the moon tonight, and hoped for continued good fortune.

Sophia walked slightly ahead of him, keeping to the shadows, although in this residential area of London, it seemed no one was about. The tree-lined street was quiet, and the houses, with their flower boxes and warm, glowing windows, were their only observers. When she cut down a narrow path between two houses, Adrian looked behind him to ensure they were not observed, then followed. She paused after leading him a few yards, crouching beside a tall stone wall.

"Twombley went to the front of the house," she said, keeping her voice low. "This is the garden wall I told you about."

"We scale it and enter through the back of the house."

"We could, but it's not my first choice."

"What's your first choice?"

"We knock on the front door."

Adrian blinked. "I don't understand."

"We could scale this wall, creep through the garden, dispatch the guards, and end up tired and bloody before we ever find Foncé."

"And?" What else did she expect? That was the job.

She sighed. "Or we knock on the front door and avoid all of that."

"Why do you think Foncé will agree to see us? This is late for a social call."

"Because he's expecting us. Twombley will have told him everything by now. If not, he wouldn't have started preparations to leave."

She had a point. But as they'd seen no movement in the house after watching a quarter hour, Adrian surmised that the final departure had either already taken place or been postponed. The question was until when? If morning, they had time to go back and get another operative or two to assist. If the plan was to leave later tonight, they had to move now.

He looked at the wall before them. "We still have to scale it. I need to get an image of the back in case we need to escape that way."

"Of course. Watch out for the guards."

Adrian pulled a pistol from each pocket and readied them. "I'm prepared."

"So am I."

He watched as she withdrew a long, sharp knife from her boot and tucked it up her sleeve. He could only send prayers of thanks she'd elected to forgo her pistol tonight. Otherwise, he'd have had to look out for more than the guards.

He was about to tell her he'd scale the wall first and cover her descent, but she already had a handhold and was climbing nimbly up the stone. She was quick and fast like a monkey, and Adrian was almost glad she had gone first. He doubted he would be as graceful.

When she reached the top of the wall, she peered over cautiously, then gave him a nod and jumped over. He heard the soft thud of her landing before he scrambled over.

He landed beside her and ducked under the shadow of a hedge.

"There." She pointed toward the main house, some distance away, and he watched as a dark shape moved across a lighted door. "And there." She pointed to another guard.

"Well, they haven't evacuated yet." But he noted two of the guards were busy moving several crates from a storage building to the main house. The departure preparations were still under way.

They couldn't afford to delay.

Adrian turned calculating eyes on the structures. The house was large but not overly so. It boasted several smaller buildings—what looked to be a greenhouse, a kitchen, and some sort of storage building. Adrian doubted any were what they seemed, but from the outside all looked innocuous enough. The house itself was brick and stone, nothing special. The gardens were large, but no gardener lived here. They were filled with shrubs and trees—no flowers or any of the other plants those interested in botany always seemed to be discussing. But the gardens were well kept. No overgrowth to hide his approach.

Sophia and Adrian sat and watched for a quarter of an hour, not speaking, and in that time, Adrian counted six guards. All but the two moving items— guns? money?—were on patrol, and all looked alert and aware. Adrian assumed all were armed as well.

They'd probably been told to shoot first and ask questions later.

"Have you changed your mind?" Sophia whispered. "Do you want to go in this way?"

It was what he knew, what he was used to. He'd fought his way into places more heavily guarded than this. But if an operative couldn't be flexible, then it was time he found a new line of work. He took her hand. "Let's go."

She raised her brows. "In through the front door?"

"Why not? I like to live dangerously."

❦

Adrian gave her a last dark look before he rapped on the plain gold knocker. Sophia noted much had changed since the afternoon. No guards stood at the front of the house now, and it was no longer a hive of activity. The house was quiet and appeared at rest. Foncé had better be inside. If they had missed him…

Sophia bit her lip and tried to stop fidgeting. She stood behind Adrian, her long hair falling over her shoulders. She'd lost her cap on the way back over the wall and hadn't bothered to retrieve it. No need anyway—they weren't pretending to be anything other than who they were now.

She bounced on the balls of her feet, feeling the weight of her knife tucked in her sleeve, ready to slip into her hand. She didn't know who would open the door—or even if it would open.

They stood there, her heart pounding ten, eleven, twelve times, and no sound came from the house. Adrian scowled at her. "Try again," she said.

He knocked louder, the sound seeming to echo down the quiet street. Finally, she heard the clicking of shoes on a hard surface. The door opened, and a quiet, unassuming little man stood before them. "May I help you?" he asked pleasantly.

Sophia almost apologized for the interruption before she realized this was all part of the ruse. Adrian never even hesitated. He handed the man a card. "Lord and Lady Smythe to see Monsieur Foncé."

The butler took the card, his brow furrowing delicately and his mustache twitching. "Who? There's no Monsieur Foncé at this address."

"Then we'd like to speak with Mr. Twombley," Sophia said, "or any representative of the Maîtriser group on the premises."

"The what group?"

But she'd seen the flicker of fear in his face, and before he could back up and slam the door, Adrian moved to wedge his foot in the opening. "Do you mind if we take a look around?"

"Why, yes! Please remove your foot at once!"

But Adrian wedged his shoulder against the door and shoved it open. Once again, Sophia appreciated the benefits of having Adrian with her. He went in first, and she followed, sliding her knife in her hand as she did so. Immediately, a large man with a jagged scar on his cheek stepped into the vestibule. He went for Adrian, who pulled one of his pistols. The guard stopped and grunted.

"Go get Foncé."

"No need, monsieur. I'm right here."

Sophia whirled at the sound of the cultured voice

with the heavy French accent. Standing behind them, in the doorway of what appeared to be a small parlor, was a tall, broad-shouldered man with long black hair, a generous mouth, and piercing blue eyes. She didn't think she'd ever seen eyes that blue before. She felt his gaze on her, and when he curved those lips into a seductive smile, she warmed unwillingly.

"I see we have guests. From the Barbican group, I presume?"

The butler handed Foncé their card as the handsome man stepped into the vestibule. "Lord and Lady Smythe, sir."

"Ah." Foncé made a show of looking at their card, while another guard sidled into the vestibule. Sophia gave Adrian a look.

"It's becoming a little crowded for my liking," Adrian said. "I'd like to chat in private."

Foncé raised his brows. "What makes you think I have anything to chat with you about, monsieur? Madame?"

"The least you could do is offer us some refreshment." Sophia smiled and extended her hand. She counted on Foncé reaching for it. Foncé knew she was an operative, but it was instinct to take a lady's hand. Even as he realized his mistake, Sophia had his arm behind his back and her knife pressed to his throat.

The butler let out a small screech, the two— no, now three—guards moved forward, and Adrian stepped so his back was to the wall, his pistol aimed at the guard nearest Sophia.

Foncé was tall, and Sophia was on tiptoes to hold her knife in place. It meant the point dug into his neck and kept him very still. "Monsieur Foncé," she murmured in his ear. He smelled clean and woodsy, like evergreen or pine. "I think you know I won't hesitate to use this knife."

"Yes, but where will that get you?"

"It would rid the world of a bastard like you. However, if you would be amenable to a brief conversation—a private conversation—I might be persuaded to allow you to remain in this worldly realm a little longer."

Foncé didn't move. She couldn't feel his pulse pounding, which meant he wasn't terrified. He was considering. She had no idea what his answer would be, and she sent Adrian a warning look. *Be ready.* They might yet need to fight their way out of this.

"Vincent," Foncé said, voice level and with a touch of ennui, "step outside with your men. I'll call for you if I need you."

The guard with the jagged scar frowned but signaled the other guards without argument. "*Oui, monsieur.*"

The guards and the small butler withdrew, leaving Adrian and Sophia alone with Foncé. Not that Sophia was relieved. The guards would return, and neither she nor Adrian would know when to expect the attack. Adrian kept his pistol trained on Foncé, but Sophia withdrew the knife from his throat. He adjusted his cravat then gestured to the parlor behind him. "Why don't we speak in here?" His voice was pleasant, and his smile appeared genuine, but Sophia knew not all snakes gave a warning before striking.

Sophia entered the small parlor and quickly scanned the room—small sofa, two chairs, a fireplace with fire, and a lady's antique escritoire. One of the chairs had a book laid over the arm. Apparently, Foncé had been reading. The room was papered with a pattern resembling green ivy, and the rug on the floor matched. Sophia could only assume the house had come furnished, as she did not imagine this was Foncé's taste. No, he would favor heavy furnishings and dark, masculine colors.

"Where is Twombley?" Adrian asked.

Foncé walked to the chair with the book and sat gracefully, crossing his legs. "Monsieur Twombley is in the cellar."

Adrian scowled. He'd moved to Foncé's right, and she was on his left. "Send for him. I'd like to speak with him."

Foncé gave him a patient smile. "Oh, he is in no condition to speak with you, monsieur."

Sophia swallowed. She had no doubt, were they to visit the cellar, they'd find Twombley dead. She could only hope Foncé hadn't hacked into the poor man.

"We're investigating the murder of George Jenkinson," Sophia said. "We have reason to believe the Maîtriser group killed him."

Foncé lifted his book, thumbed through it idly. "Investigating a murder. I didn't realize the Barbican group concerned itself with such matters."

"We're not with the Barbican group." Adrian sounded pained to say it.

"Oh?" Foncé's brows shot up. "That lessens your prestige considerably."

"Even so," Sophia said, "we're taking you into custody for the murder of George Jenkinson."

"Go ahead." Foncé set his book on the arm of his

chair. "You'll never prove it, of course." He reached into his coat. "Unless you have copies of these."

Adrian's eyes narrowed, and Sophia could see his fingers twitch. He wanted those documents. "What are those?"

"Records of payments made to George Jenkinson." He turned the papers in his hand as though seeing them for the first time. "With the information obtained for each payment."

"He was selling confidential information about England's war efforts," Sophia said.

Foncé shrugged. "*Naturellement*. But here is the problem." He wagged the documents. "It's such a scandal. The brother of the prime minister selling England's secrets? *Oh là là!* Your Liverpool will allow me to go rather than involve himself in such a scandal."

Unfortunately, he was correct, Sophia thought. Liverpool would not want to sully his name. But Melbourne could see Foncé was dealt with, if not for Jenkinson's murder, then for his other crimes. But she needed those documents. They needed to know how many of England's secrets had been compromised by Jenkinson.

"Give me the documents." Adrian cocked the pistol and pointed it at Foncé.

"Let me go," Foncé said.

"We can't do that." Sophia held out her hand. "Give them to me."

Foncé held the documents toward her then jerked his hand and tossed them in the fire. Sophia inhaled quickly, and too late saw Foncé reach into his coat.

"Down!" she ordered, but the pistol shot screamed through the air even as Adrian dove for the fire.

Twenty-two

"BLOODY HELL!" WHITE-HOT PAIN SHOT THROUGH Adrian's leg. He'd made a leap for the fire and the documents, and his leg had obviously collided with some furnishing.

Except this hurt more than a simple bump. This felt like…

He tried to get his bearings, lifted his head, and looked into the fire. The documents had landed on the edge of the hearth. They were still intact, but the fire licked at them, clawing closer.

"Adrian!" Sophia was across the room, looking down at him. Was he on the floor? How the bloody hell had he ended up on the floor. "Adrian!"

And then Foncé was behind her. Before Adrian could warn her, the man had his arm about her waist. She immediately jabbed her elbow into his abdomen, but the man gripped her hair, yanked her head back, and put a knife to her throat.

Sophia's knife.

She stilled, her gaze meeting Adrian's. He could see the plea for him to stay put, not to intervene.

She wasn't afraid, not for herself. She was afraid for him.

Foncé dragged her across the parlor, through the door, and out of sight.

The hell he was going to stay put. He would... But when he tried to rise, his leg buckled. He tried again. And failed. Levering himself to a sitting position, he glimpsed his leg. "Bloody hell."

No wonder his thigh was throbbing. He had a gaping hole in it, blood pouring from his leg and onto the ugly green-and-white carpet.

He stared at the door Sophia had disappeared through, then looked at the fireplace. The flames had singed one corner of the documents, and the parchment was smoking now.

And he was lying on the floor like a bloody invalid.

He heard the sound of something shatter, and grinding his teeth, reached for the chair leg nearest him. Black spots danced before his eyes as he struggled to hold on.

❧

Sophia stumbled into the vestibule, feeling the cold metal of her knife—*her own knife!*—at her throat. Foncé's arm was warm and solid about her waist, and it hadn't escaped her notice that he held her closer than was necessary.

"Unhand me," she demanded.

"Tired of my embraces already, Lady Smythe? Or should I call you Agent Saint?"

She stiffened involuntarily, and he laughed, low and husky, near her ear. She was able to control the shiver.

"That's right," he whispered, his lips grazing her ear. She closed her eyes, trying to block the sensation. "I know exactly who you are, and I must say, you are far more beautiful than I was led to believe."

"I'm far more dangerous as well. Unhand me."

"I don't doubt you have a nasty bite, and that is precisely why I will not unhand you." The knife he held dug into her neck, and she felt the prick of the sharp blade. A blade she'd sharpened herself. "Unlike your esteemed colleague, I'm going to give you a chance to live. One chance, madame."

She swallowed, knowing the best strategy here was to play along. "What chance is that?"

"Join me."

She almost laughed. She couldn't believe he was serious, and then he whirled her to face him, and she saw how deadly serious he was. She tipped a table, causing a vase to shatter, but the knife was still in his hand. She hadn't thrown him off balance. He gripped her neck and bent it back, but he was tall enough to lock his gaze with hers. "I think we could make a good team. We already have the most important component—passion."

She shook her head. "I don't—"

"Try and deny it, but I can see you want me."

She couldn't deny he was attractive, but then she imagined the devil himself could appear handsome when he so chose. Obviously, Foncé found her appealing, and that she could use to her advantage.

"Want you?" Sophia gave him a sultry smile. "I know I shouldn't, but…"

Foncé's lips descended on hers, and she dug her nails into the palm of her hand to keep from retching.

Adrian dragged himself to his knees and rested his forehead on the chair. The fire poker was at arm's length, but it required him to put pressure on his bad leg. If he could grasp it, he could use it to fish the documents from the flames, and as a crutch, to make it across the room. With an oath, he reached for it. His leg screeched in agony, and his forehead poured with sweat, but he closed his slick fingers around the poker. His leg buckled, and as he fell, he made a desperate swipe at the fire.

Sophia kissed Foncé back. It was her only chance. This wasn't the first time she had had to feign passion to survive, and she knew how to make a man lower his guard. She kissed him hard and with fervor, and when he lowered the knife and pressed her to his arousal, she struck out. She bit his roving tongue, and drove her knee into that arousal. Then, when he attempted to slash her with the knife, she sidestepped, causing him to lose his balance. She kneed him in the face, and he went down, the knife clattering into a far corner.

Sophia left it and raced for the parlor, Foncé's shouts of "Guards!" echoing in her ears.

Adrian groaned, but something was pulling him out of the darkness. Sophia's face swam before his, and he shook his head, tried to close his eyes again. She clasped his face in her hands.

"Foncé," Adrian croaked. "The documents."

"You have the documents right here." She lifted them and tucked them into her shirt. "Foncé is still a concern. We need to move."

He nodded. "Let's go." But he couldn't find the strength to rise.

Sophia's face disappeared for a moment, and he felt something probe at his leg. Then she was looking down at him again. "You've been shot," she said unnecessarily.

"That's four for me," he groaned and tried again to stand, eliciting a string of curses he probably shouldn't utter in front of his wife. "We're even."

"You're competing with me? At a time like this?"

His head felt fuzzy, but there was no mistaking the worry in her voice. Foncé was probably collecting his troops even as they spoke. In a moment, the guards would burst through the door, and then Foncé would be carving letters on Sophia's perfect porcelain skin in the cellar. "Get out of here."

"I'm not leaving without you." She looked over her shoulder at the door. "Can you walk?"

He scowled at her. "Madam, have you seen my leg?"

She scowled right back. "I'm *not* leaving you." She bent beside him, and he thought she would help him to his feet, but she reached in his pocket and withdrew his pistol. Tucking it in her coat pocket, she lifted the other from where it had fallen on the floor and put it in his pocket.

"God help us now. You're armed."

"Stubble it." She bent, got her arms hooked around him, and said, "Stand."

He knew enough to do it quickly, so putting all his

weight on his good leg, he levered himself up. "Give me the poker."

She did, and he leaned some of his weight on it.

"Lean the rest on me." She adjusted position so she was beside him, supporting him. "Let's go."

"We'll never make it out. Go without me."

"You're wasting time."

She began to move toward the door, and he tried to follow. The first shuffling step went well, and then he put the smallest hint of pressure on his injured leg, and black dots swam before his eyes. He prided himself on not whimpering when his leg screamed in protest, but he thought he might have screamed a bit in sympathy. "Have mercy," he panted. "Leave me."

"No." She pulled him forward, and he found the next step as excruciating as the last, but this time he was prepared. She opened the parlor door, leaned him against the doorjamb, and peered out.

Foncé's butler was standing in the vestibule, wringing his hands. He squealed when he saw them. Sophia pointed the pistol at him, and since the man didn't know she couldn't have hit him had he been standing at the barrel's end, he lifted his arms. "I surrender!"

"Go call for your master's coach."

"B-but, my lady, it's already out front. Monsieur Foncé called for it just now."

"And where is he?" Adrian asked.

The butler shook his head, and Adrian thought he would not answer. "He went to fetch his *tools*," the man whispered, fear in his voice.

Sophia glanced at Adrian. "That doesn't sound promising. Let's go."

"And if we go, Foncé won't be here when we return."

"And if we don't go, you and I will end up in the cellar beside Twombley. I know when to cut my losses, Wolf. We've got the documents. We'll get Foncé later."

She pulled him into the vestibule, and he clenched his jaw and followed. Behind them, he heard the rumble of men running and the sound of voices.

"Open the door!" Sophia screamed at the butler. He flapped his hands then ran to do her bidding. The butler moved away from the door, and the man with the jagged scar stood in the opening, grinning.

❧

Sophia raised her pistol and fired. She was aware of Adrian's weight on her side and tried to compensate with her aim, but really, she couldn't fail to miss at such close range.

And she didn't. The man fell backward, clutching his abdomen.

"You hit him."

She scowled at Adrian. "Don't sound so surprised." She handed him the pistol so he could prime it, and yanked him out the door, wincing when he made a sound of pain as they descended the steps. Behind them, she saw Foncé's men swarming into the vestibule. "Shoot!" she ordered.

"Shoot what?" he asked.

"Anything!"

He turned and fired, forcing the men converging on them to duck and take cover. She dragged Adrian toward the carriage. The coachman was running away—not that she blamed him—so she would have to secure Adrian inside and drive the vehicle herself. The distance to the coach seemed interminable. Her instinct was to run, but she tamped it down and supported Adrian. She hadn't underestimated his strength. He must have been in enormous pain, but he was moving quickly.

She leaned him against the door of the coach, and he prepared his pistol to fire again. Just as she swung the coach door open, shots rang out from the house. "Damn it!" she yelled, ducking.

Adrian returned fire before she pushed him inside the carriage then ran around the far side to avoid being hit. Lights came on in the house across the street, and she could only imagine what the neighbors must think. Sophia wasn't frightened now. She wasn't even thinking. At this point, she simply acted.

Shots rang out again as she reached for the footboard. The horses were spooked and jostled the carriage, causing her to lose her grip. But finally she was in the box and reaching for the reins. The horses needed no urging; they danced into motion. One of the faster guards reached the carriage and grabbed the lead horse. Sophia grabbed for her knife, realized she'd lost it in the struggle with Foncé, and grasped a horseshoe on the floor of the box instead. She hefted it at the guard, hitting him in the forehead.

With an oath, he fell back. Another approached, but Adrian, somehow he was still conscious and fighting, shot at him from the carriage window.

And then she had the animals under control, and they were speeding away. She gave one look back, saw the guards streaming into the street, saw Foncé standing on his front stoop, holding a dark valise.

"This isn't over," she called.

He gave her a salute and stepped back inside.

♺

"These aren't completely useless," Melbourne said, smoothing Foncé's charred documents on his desk deep in the Barbican's headquarters. "The little information I can still read is fairly damning." He glanced at Liverpool, who was pacing behind the chair where Sophia was seated.

It was two weeks after The Fiasco—as Adrian liked to think of it—and Adrian's leg still hurt like hell, though Farrar, the Barbican surgeon Sophia had insisted he see, told him he was lucky the bullet had missed the major blood vessels.

He didn't feel lucky, but he wasn't going to take any more of the mind-numbing medicine Farrar had offered him, so he propped his stitched and bandaged leg on the couch and clenched his jaw whenever he accidentally moved it. Sophia cast him another of her worried looks. She didn't think he should be out of bed, and she was probably right. But he wouldn't have missed this meeting for anything.

Liverpool stopped pacing and clasped his hands behind his back. "We can't allow word of this… this treachery"—he swallowed—"to become public."

"Of course not," Sophia agreed. She was seated near Adrian in an old leather chair. "But at least now we know what information the French were given. We're lucky we know what codes were compromised, and have the names of several English traitors working with the French."

"They'll be arrested," Liverpool said. "I can't abide a traitor." He began pacing again, and Adrian thought he heard him mutter, "My own brother."

Adrian could understand the prime minister's feelings. Once he had struggled with his own father's duplicity. Now, given the chance, he would have told Liverpool that the sins of the father did not reflect upon the son. Liverpool wasn't responsible for his brother's betrayal any more than Adrian needed to atone for his father's.

"It's a shame Foncé was allowed to get away," Melbourne said with a glance at Adrian. Sophia had gone back to the house with other members of the Barbican group, but there was no sign of the Maîtriser group. No sign they had ever been in residence.

Melbourne was still angry Adrian hadn't sent for assistance, even though Adrian had explained there had not been time. But after a failed mission, it was natural to ask what if and to wonder what could have been.

Adrian had been over everything so often he dreamed about it. "We'll find him. It's personal now."

Liverpool ceased pacing. "I suppose I owe the two of you thanks for discovering this treachery, and I did make you a promise—a position in the Barbican group. And that position goes to—"

"Lord Liverpool," Adrian said. "Wait."

From her chair nearby, Sophia glanced at him. "What are you doing?"

"I'm telling Lord Liverpool I think you should be given the position."

Liverpool raised his brows and gave Sophia a side-long glance. "I see."

"Adrian, no…"

"She's the better agent by far," Adrian said. "She's clever, daring, and her intuition is unsurpassed. I'll never have that sort of sense about things. Agent Saint deserves the position in the Barbican group."

Sophia rose and went to him. She took his hands. "Oh, Adrian."

"I want you to take it," he told her. "I'll probably die an early death from worrying about you, but I want you to take it." He didn't need the Barbican group anymore. He had what he wanted—Sophia and the possibility of children with her. She was his family, and nothing could matter to him more than giving her all she desired.

"This is quite a different tune from the one you were singing a mere week and a half ago," Liverpool said. "I believe then your attitude was, may the best *man* win."

Adrian remembered quite clearly his words the night he'd discovered Sophia was Agent Saint. He hadn't thought a woman capable of what she'd done. What she *could* do. "I was misinformed," he said stiffly. He glanced at Sophia and saw the sheen of tears in her eyes. "Oh, bloody hell. If you start crying on me, I take it all back."

She laughed and dashed them away.

"Well, this presents quite a dilemma," Melbourne said.

"What dilemma?"

"Agent Saint spoke to me privately before we began this meeting," Liverpool said, "She argued *you* should be given the position in the Barbican group."

Adrian stared at her. "Why?"

"You're Agent Wolf," she told him as if that said it all. "You're the best." Now she looked at Liverpool. "He's smart and strategizes like no other agent I've ever met. Not to mention he's a crack shot with a pistol and excels at interrogation."

Adrian shook his head. "You've a much more subtle way with interrogation—"

"But you're a better bully, and some men respond to that."

"Yes, but—"

"This is all well and good," Melbourne interrupted, "but I have an urgent mission in Prague, and I need an agent tonight. Who is it going to be?"

Adrian looked at Sophia, and she squeezed his hand then entwined her fingers with his. Adrian stared at their joined hands and understood what Sophia was telling him—they were two parts of the whole, stronger together than apart. Maybe that was why he'd never found what he needed in the Barbican group. Sophia raised her brows at him, not speaking but trusting him to make the right decision.

"Neither of us," he answered with a glance at Melbourne. Adrian looked back at Sophia.

"We'll come back only if we can work together," she added. "We're partners now."

"Until you have two spots, we're retired." Adrian reached for his walking stick and levered himself to his feet. He hated having to rely on it, but until his leg was healed, it was a necessary evil.

"You're retired?" Melbourne said with a laugh.

"The day you retire is the day the prince regent finds some sense," Liverpool added. "I don't believe it."

Ten days ago, Adrian wouldn't have believed it either. He wouldn't have believed his wife was Agent Saint or that he could love her—even all her ramblings about *intuition*—so completely. He wouldn't have believed he would walk away from the Barbican group, but that was exactly what he was doing.

And he'd never been happier.

Sophia was smiling too, her face lit up with the same happiness he felt. "Good day," Sophia said to Melbourne and Liverpool as she and Adrian reached the door. Adrian followed her into the hallway. They nodded at other agents and staff moving purposefully about, and then they were stepping out of the dark building and into the afternoon sunshine of Pall Mall. Adrian signaled for the carriage. He'd stood in this same spot three weeks ago, feeling alone and defeated.

He looked down and saw his hand was still entwined with Sophia's. Neither of them was alone anymore. And together...

Together, what couldn't they do?

∽∾

Sophia pulled her rust-colored spencer close about her as the breeze whipped the skirts of her gold gown. Fall was coming, and she was glad. It had been a long summer. She looked at Adrian.

"Are we really retired?" he asked.

"It appears that way."

"What a fortunate day for Prinny, then. A sensible man at last."

"Yes."

She saw the hint of a smile on his lips. "Of course, there is still the matter of Foncé."

There was that. She'd done some research—quite a bit of questioning and probing actually. "I have it on good authority Foncé is on his way to Lisbon."

"Lisbon." Adrian nodded, considering. She watched the way his jaw clenched, knew he wanted another chance with Foncé. She did as well. They had unfinished business.

"I've always liked Lisbon in the autumn," she said.

"Who doesn't?"

She laughed. He was so perfect for her. Right there, in the middle of the Mall, she put her hands on his shoulders and kissed him. An older woman with her lady's maid gasped and hurried by, but Sophia didn't care. "Have I ever told you I love you?"

Adrian blinked at her. "No, but I surmised as much when you wouldn't leave me to Foncé's devices."

"Did you?" She laughed again. Really, what had she expected him to say?

She was about to release him, but he curled a hand around her waist. "Have I told you I love you?"

She had to force herself to breathe and hope her heart began to beat again. She hadn't realized how much she needed those words from him. "No, but I surmised as much when you…" Oh, she was never any good at surmising… or deducing and hypothesizing, for that matter! "Oh, *everything* you do tells me you love me, Adrian."

He took her mouth with his, and she thought she would never catch her breath again. Someone hooted, and a child cried, "Mommy, look over there!"

"I think we're making a scene," she said.

"Wouldn't be the first time."

They pulled apart, but he held onto her hand. They stood in silence for a moment, and then he cleared his throat, searching for a topic of conversation, she supposed. It was either that or tear one another's clothes off.

"So is Lisbon next?" he asked. The carriage was slowing before them. "Or shall we embark on some other adventure first?"

"Hmm." She watched the footman open the carriage door and lower the steps, and on impulse said, "Lisbon might be next. Or, we could always try parenthood."

The look on his face was worth a hundred opportunities with Foncé. She had been debating whether or not to say anything. The familiar signs were present, but it was still too soon to be certain she was with child and far too soon to know if the pregnancy would be successful. But she felt different about this pregnancy.

Hopeful.

Adrian was still staring at her, openmouthed. She laughed and climbed into the carriage, her laugh abruptly dying when she spotted Agent Blue seated on the squabs.

"What is that supposed to mean?" Adrian climbed into the carriage after her. "Are you saying—?"

"We have company, Agent Wolf." Sophia sat across from Blue and pulled Adrian down beside her.

"How the hell did you get in here?" Adrian asked.

Blue studied his gloves. "I dare say you would like to know, wouldn't you?"

"Yes, as a matter of fact."

"I heard you have retired from the Barbican group," Blue said.

"How could you have possibly heard that?" Sophia asked. "We just decided it ourselves."

Blue gave her a look.

"Never mind. Of course you know. The last time we met in a carriage like this, you told me I no longer had a position. This time I've retired on my own."

"Quite so, but I also gave you another opportunity." He reached into his citron coat—Lord, it was awful—and produced a heavy cream card. Sophia took it, glanced at the address and the hand-printed *midnight*. She handed it to Adrian.

"Another midnight rendezvous?" he asked, but Blue was already climbing out of the carriage.

"What do you think?" she asked. "Should we go?"

Adrian put the card in his coat, but she didn't think she mistook the look of interest in his eyes. She knew she didn't misinterpret the quickening in her own pulse.

He tapped his walking stick on the roof, and the carriage lurched forward. "Let's decide later. We might have more important tasks to attend to at midnight."

"There are still several hours before midnight," she pointed out. "Plenty of time for whatever you have in mind."

He arched a brow. "You don't know everything I have in mind."

"Then perhaps we should begin right away."

He pulled her into his arms. "Madam, for once, you and I are in agreement." Lowering his mouth to hers, he kissed her.

Acknowledgments

Every time I write a book, my acknowledgments page grows longer. I may sit alone, lost in my own thoughts, tapping away on my computer, but I feel like I have a dozen people standing behind me, supporting me and encouraging me (and after you read this, you may wish I'd stopped at a dozen).

First of all, I'd like to thank Sourcebooks. This will sound cliché, but they really are more like a family than a publishing house. I'm so lucky to be able to work with Deb Werksman, a fabulous editor and wonderful lady. I'm fortunate to work with Dominique Raccah, who makes me feel like I'm the most important author she has. And then there's Danielle Jackson, Susie Benton, Cat Clyne, and Skye Agnew. You ladies rock! Thank you for all you do for me. I'm sure there are others whose names I don't know, and I want to thank you as well for all your hard work on my behalf.

I think I have the best agents in the world. Danielle Egan-Miller and Joanna MacKenzie have believed in me from the beginning. Your advice on writing, parenting, and everything in-between is invaluable.

Thank you for fighting for me, steering me in the right direction, and dropping everything to work for me (including interrupting family vacations). Thanks also to Lauren Olson. I have a feeling you do way more than we authors know about.

This is a novel I've wanted to write for a long time. It's a book of the heart, as we writers say. Several people have answered my questions and been willing to read my sketchy initial drafts and offer insight and critiques. Thank you to Linda Andrus, who read an early version and helped me make major changes. Thank you to my critique partners, Christina Hergenrader and Tera Lynn Childs for reading closely and suggesting improvements. And thanks to everyone who supports me and cheers me on—the members of West Houston RWA, especially Sharie Kohler and Vicky Dreiling; the Sisterhood of the Jaunty Quills, especially Robyn DeHart, Kristan Higgins, Margo Maguire, and Emily McKay; and the Casababes. I also want to thank my longtime web designer, maddee at xuni.com. I love working with you, maddee!

Finally, I wouldn't be able to write without the support of my husband, Mathew. 143.